# THE
# DEVIL
## AND THE DEEP
# DEEP

## Also Edited by Ellen Datlow

# THE
# DEVIL
## AND THE
# DEEP

## HORROR STORIES OF THE SEA

EDITED BY Ellen Datlow

**NIGHT SHADE BOOKS**

**NEW YORK**

Night Shade books may be purchased in bulk at special discounts for sales promotion, corporate gifts, fund-raising, or educational purposes. Special editions can also be created to specifications. For details, contact the Special Sales Department, Night Shade Books, 307 West 36th Street, 11th Floor, New York, NY 10018 or info@skyhorsepublishing.com.

Night Shade Books™ is a trademark of Skyhorse Publishing, Inc. ®, a Delaware corporation.

Visit our website at www.nightshadebooks.com.

10 9 8 7 6 5 4 3 2 1

Library of Congress Cataloging-in-Publication Data is available on file.

Cover artwork by Kevin Peterson
Cover design by Claudia Noble

Print ISBN: 978-1-59780-907-8
Ebook ISBN: 978-1-59780-908-5

Printed in the United States of America

Thanks to Stefan Dziemianowicz and to my editor, Jason Katzman.

# TABLE OF CONTENTS

# INTRODUCTION

I grew up loving the ocean. My family went to New York's Rockaway Beach for many summers when I was a child and through my teenage years. I loved the beach, lying on the sand, baking in the sun (pre-cancer scares) with my friends, the smell of the tar in the parking lots—and of the ocean—and body surfing in the waves. I also went fishing with my dad (in lakes and ponds), and even went on a deep-sea fishing trip with a friend in my early twenties (we caught nothing).

But in 1975, something happened. I went to see *Jaws*. It scared me so badly that I had a difficult time going into the ocean after that. For a (very) brief time, I was even fearful of lakes and swimming pools. Then, in 1977, *The Last Wave* was released, about the end of the world heralded by a tsunami on a coast of Australia. Those two movies made me realize that the sea and the simple act of swimming in it could be frightening, even terrifying.

We, like all other forms of life, come from the sea, and yet we're intimidated by it. Why? One reason could be that the seas are more vast on our planet than the land we live on, and 95 percent of the sea is still unexplored. It's a natural human tendency to fear the unknown, and our relative ignorance about the sea fosters superstitions, myths, and legends about it and what might inhabit it (sirens, sea monsters, forms of organic life that we can't even begin to comprehend because the conditions in which they flourish are inimical to human life). H. P. Lovecraft populated the spaces between universes with extra-dimensional monsters, but he also populated the sea with them in *The Shadow Over Innsmouth*, a story that serves as a touchstone for a lot of horror fiction written since. Lovecraft, like numerous other writers

(William Hope Hodgson in particular), saw in the vastness and alienness of the sea the same potential for horror that has persuaded writers since the dawn of the tale of horror to infest the dark with monsters and boogeymen. The sea is a watery terra incognita, a huge blank canvas that invites writers to imagine horrors onto it.

But, come on. In reality it's only water, so why should we fear large bodies of it? Well, those sharks, especially the Great White—a predator's dream, a swimmer or surfer's nightmare. Also, those mysteries in the deep blue sea—awful mysteries like eons-old fish that shouldn't exist today but apparently do. Then there are fish like the dragonfish, with its big teeth and hideous face and the black seadevil, with sharp teeth, both found in the deeps of the Mariana Trench.

Another aspect of what makes the sea so horrifying: it seems hostile to us (although, really, it's as indifferent to human existence as Lovecraft's monsters are). We're of it, but we can't live in it. One can drown in a minimal amount of water, but it's more likely that a riptide will drag unwary swimmers out to sea, or you might just develop a cramp, preventing you from getting back to shore with no lifeguard to save you.

We build ships to sail upon the ocean, deluding ourselves that we can master it, but shipwrecks prove that some of our sturdiest inventions are at the mercy of the sea. People (and sometimes vessels) lost at sea are often never found: the sea is like a vast ravening maw that can swallow us in one bite.

Remaining on shore is no guarantee of safety, either. If we stray too near the sea, it can pull us from our safe haven on land (sort of like the monster under the bed reaching up to grab us). And we've all witnessed the damage tsunamis can wreak on shorelines around the world, killing thousands. There's a lot of talk about global warming these days, and the consequence: rising sea levels. As the sea encroaches on the world that we've built for ourselves, it has the potential to sweep away everything that human progress and civilization have created—everything that our species stands for. The sea coughed us up, but some day it's going to reclaim us, and there's precious little that we can do about it. *We* are puny. *It* is monstrously vast and overwhelming. It makes us realize that, on our planet, we are only temporary, while the sea is permanent.

The stories in *The Devil and the Deep* cover a range of aspects of the sea and the shores around it, from obvious monsters to the mysterious; there are tales of shipwrecks, haunts, monsters—human and inhuman—one story even taking place on what was once an inland sea, long gone. All these tales have been conjured up from the imaginations of the fifteen contributors. Each is basically about people, and how they deal with the mysterious entity surrounding us.

# DEADWATER

## SIMON BESTWICK

Above the sea, the railway ran; a hundred yards inland a 4x4 stood empty on a dirt track, keys still in the ignition. There was no one inside, no sign of a struggle, and no witnesses. That whole part of the coast is hills and empty fields, with the odd farmhouse hidden in bristling crops of pine.

A rainy sky, and the tide was in, the dull grey sea gnashing at the edge of the shingle beach.

The 4x4 belonged to one Robin Gaunt. Police Constable Lewis popped into the Harbour Café that morning to ask if I knew him. The Harbour's the most popular café here—both locals and tourists love it. I've part-timed at half the other places in town, too—work here tends to be seasonal, so you take whatever's going—which means there isn't much I don't hear about. Clive makes me his first port of call whenever he wants to know something. Fringe benefit of being his girlfriend, I suppose.

Around here people are like the tide: some flow in, some flow out. Ten, fifteen years ago there'd been an influx of New Age types, all coming to commune with Nature; Robin had been one of them. Now they were being displaced in their turn, by urban professionals buying second homes. Frankly, I was missing the hippies already.

I told Clive most of what I knew. Robin popped into the Harbour once or twice a week for a Full English or a sandwich, but didn't have much motivation beyond getting high and saying "wow, man" at the scenery a lot. The scenery around here *is* pretty "wow"—we're on a nice stretch of coast, with mountains all around—but after a while, you hardly notice it. Unless you're like Robin.

We'd meet some evenings, when Clive was on nights. Look, I'm young and I get lonely. Around here, you find some company or you climb the walls. We smoked some weed—usually out in his car—and slept together twice. The first time we were stoned, and I was going through a bad patch with Clive. The second time was a mistake, and I told Robin it wouldn't happen again. He accepted that, and my statement that I still wanted to be friends. *Go with the flow* was his philosophy: that was how he'd ended up here. And why I liked his company. He was easy-going, didn't make demands. I told Clive none of this, of course. As a small-town copper, he tends to see things in black and white.

Clive had been to Robin's rented cottage, but no one had answered the door. No, he hadn't broken it down—this wasn't the big city and all he had so far was an empty car. Robin had probably smoked too much draw and walked back into town instead of driving along the narrow, winding, ill-lit coastal roads. He was either at a friend's house or so comatose he hadn't heard Clive knock.

That didn't sound right to me, even then. No matter how caned he was, some weird homing instinct always got Robin home at the end of a night. I didn't know what it was—some sort of OCD, something that had happened to him—but he never felt safe under someone else's roof, or in a strange bed. Similarly, anything like a knock on the door would snap him instantly awake, no matter what. But explaining how I knew that to Clive would have been awkward.

In the end, it made no difference. A few hours later, the tide went out, exposing the shingle beach. There's an outfall pipe there, emptying fifty feet from the shore. Robin lay next to it, face-down, seaweed in his hair, arms outstretched towards one of the rusted iron struts holding the pipe in place. A pair of handcuffs were looped around it, fastened on his wrists. The pathologist said he'd still been alive when the tide came in.

◄o►

"Must have been bloody horrible," said Clive.

I stroked his hands. We were sitting at a table in a corner of the café. Technically I was at work, but it was a quiet day and Jeanette—the owner—likes being on good terms with the police.

"There'd be no one around to hear," he said, "not that time of night—if he'd changed his mind, I mean. Even a train going by wouldn't have seen him."

This time of year, the tide takes about an hour to come in. An hour can seem very short or very long; I could guess which it would have been for Robin. Then I registered what Clive had said.

"Changed his mind?" I said. "You're not saying he did that to himself?"

"Looks that way. Doesn't seem to have had any enemies round here."

"But he was handcuffed . . ."

Clive glanced round to ensure we weren't overheard. "Just between us, Emily, okay?"

"Okay."

"Gaunt was a known druggy. History of mental health problems. He'd tried topping himself two, three times before he came here. And you should have seen his forearms—Christ alive. Looked as if someone had been playing tic-tac-toe with a razorblade."

I *had* seen them, but didn't tell him. Robin had worn long-sleeved shirts, even in summer. He'd only taken them off in bed.

"Looks like he wanted to do himself in but kept bottling out. So he found a way to make sure. Cuff himself to the outfall, let the sea do the work. Like I said"—Clive took another sip of tea—"I hope he didn't change his mind."

◄o►

Clive was working the night shift. Once I'd finished wiping down tables and serving customers, I went for a walk along the seafront.

The beach here is beautiful, but I prefer the far end of the promenade, where the yellow sand gives way to shingle and rock broken up by tall wooden groynes. It isn't as pretty to look at or as nice to walk on, so there aren't as many people. Not that there were many today in any case; it was raining—lightly, but enough to keep away the day trippers. That was why the Harbour Café had been so quiet that afternoon.

Normally, an evening like this, with no Clive to snuggle up with in front of the TV, I would have gone over to Robin's for a coffee, maybe gone out with him for a spliff. But of course I couldn't do that now.

It's the absences that get you, with any death. The gaps, the depths, the holes people leave behind: they're what we mean by ghosts.

I got to the end of the sea wall and looked up the rocky beach that stretched away beyond it. The small, shallow cove where Robin had died was about two miles to the north.

A druggy, a self-harmer, a mental case. That was the pigeon-hole Clive had put Robin in. He really had no idea, but that was my fault. There was a lot he didn't know about me. I'd cut more carefully than Robin had, back in the day. My cuts had either healed without scarring, or the scars were where Clive hadn't yet found them. And he wondered why he'd never made CID.

Not that they were any better. They'd put Robin in the same box. A suicide, because that's the way the damaged and the broken are meant to go, if they've any decency. Take their mess and awkwardness out of everyone else's life. And of course, we often do. Maybe I would one day, if the dark ever welled up in me again and I found no way to drain it off. Maybe Robin had.

But I didn't think so. I might be wrong, of course; there were any number of reasons why I wouldn't want to think it. All I had, really, was a feeling, and I couldn't share the little I had to back it up with the one copper who might listen. More absences. More holes, more ghosts, more deeps.

There's a little café at the end of the sea wall. It's nowhere near as pretty or popular as the Harbour, but they get by. A quiet, friendly Kurdish guy called Hish runs it. He makes good coffee, so I went in.

"Emily. You're well?" He took a closer look at me. "Ah. I see. No."

"Did you know Robin?"

"Robin?"

I described him. Hish nodded, sighed. "Yes. Was he the one who drowned?" I nodded. "A friend of yours?"

"Yeah."

I didn't say anything else. Hish looked down. "You want some hummus?" he said. He's not the most expressive guy. His first response to any situation is to do something practical, usually food related. That's okay, though. He's a good cook.

"Thanks," I said.

The hummus came with a plate of toasted pita strips. I ate slowly, sipping coffee and watching as it got dark. It wouldn't be hard to ask around, maybe see if I could dig something up, enough that Clive might take a closer look at Robin's death. The worry was, as always, what else might get stirred up in the process.

I'm good at compartmentalising; I like to keep things well ordered. Things, and information: about me, in particular. There was plenty Clive didn't know, and his uncovering one thing might quickly bring others to light. And what then?

I wasn't that different from Robin, really. People break in different ways and places, and have different ways of coping. Robin's and mine had been much the same: find a place to hide, and hide there.

My time here had been a good one: I'd hidden enough of me away to pass for normal. If the hidden stuff came out, I couldn't live here anymore. I'd have to go. Find another hiding place, try and root myself there. I supposed I could do it, but I didn't want to. I was tired of running.

Robin and I had been enough alike that he'd have understood that. But still, the idea he'd be dismissed as a suicide when he wasn't bothered me more and more. I told myself we fucked-up ones had to stick together, but most likely I was thinking of myself. People usually do. My own death—my own murder—might as easily be passed off the same way.

I shivered, and drank more coffee to chase the chill and the black dog's shadow away.

When you pass over them, the deeps are cold.

◄◦►

"Inquest's next week," said Clive in the morning, when he got in, "but by the look it'll be open and shut. Like I said, with his history . . ." He shrugged and carried on undressing.

He slept, but I couldn't. I got out of bed, drank some coffee and watched the sun come up over the estuary. I'd already more or less made up my mind, but that clinched it. If I could find anything that might make Clive look again—without revealing anything about myself I didn't want him to know—I'd do it.

Frankly, it wasn't as hard as it might sound. Most information came my way as gossip sooner or later. The trick here was to get hold of something specific, ideally without making it too obvious I was digging.

With Clive still sleeping, I slipped out for a long walk—I do that, sometimes, when I can't sleep. I walked up and down the prom, letting the sea calm me, till it was time to go to work.

◦

After the lunchtime rush, when I finally got a half-hour break. I slipped to the ice-cream parlour further along the quayside. "Daniela around?" I asked Krisztof, the owner.

"Out back, having a smoke."

"Thanks."

I found Daniela in the yard behind the parlour. "Emily." She hugged me. "I heard about Robin. Are you okay?"

I shrugged. "I'm still here."

She led me to the bench in the corner of the yard, gave me one of her Marlboros. "What are you thinking?" she said.

The face of a *Vogue* centrefold, the eyes of an interrogator. Daniela's my best friend in the town. I'd never told her about Robin and me—compartmentalising, again—but I think she guessed at least some of it. Just as she doesn't know what my secrets are, but knows damn well I have them. She's smart like that: make a better copper than Clive ever would. But she's not a copper, and she's smart enough not to ask about anything I haven't volunteered. She has her secrets, too, I know—most likely about how she got here from Prague. She's a little broken, same as Robin and me—not as much, but enough. That, or she hides the cracks better.

"They're saying he killed himself," I said.

"I heard. But you don't think so?"

"I don't *want* to."

"That doesn't mean anything."

"I know." I dragged on the Marlboro. "Did you see him? I mean that night, before he—"

"Yeah," she said. "It was quite late—gone midnight, I think. I was walking back from the Lion."

Daniela does the odd night shift at the Lion on Church Street. I don't know where she finds the energy, but she seems to manage.

"I was going up the coast road," she said. Home for Daniela is the caravan park just out of town, along the coast road leading north. "He was on a bench there. Looked pretty wiped out. I was going to see if he was okay, but a guy came along, started talking to him. He woke up then, anyway."

"Did you know the guy?"

She shook her head. "No, but I've seen him around."

"Tourist? Local?"

"Tourist," she said. "He brought his boat into the harbour a couple of days ago. It's still there." Daniela grinned. "It's named after you."

⟷

It was a nice boat, too—a white motor yacht with EMILY emblazoned across the stern. The man on its deck wasn't quite as good-looking, but not bad. He was about ten years older than me, late thirties or so. Around Robin's age, within a couple of years.

When the café closed, I slipped home and got changed. A quick shower, then some careful make-up and an outfit that ought to catch the eye: a red T-shirt with a white skull, black-and-white-striped tights, boots and a short black skirt. I put my black bobbed hair into bunches and skipped back down to the quay.

"Nice boat," I called down to him. He looked up and smiled. He obviously liked what he saw, even though he was as conservatively dressed as you could be on a boat.

"Thanks," he said. "You work in the café, right?"

"Yeah."

"Want to come aboard?"

I hesitated. Too easy for word to get back to Clive; too many questions I wouldn't want to answer that way. But how else was I going to talk to him? If I sat on the edge of the quay, I'd be even more visible to prying eyes. "Okay, then," I said, and climbed down.

"Coffee?" he said, motioning belowdecks. "I was just making some."

"Okay."

He passed me a mug. "Ed York."

"Eh?" I realised that was his name. "I'm Emily," I said, and grinned. "Like your boat."

"No way." He smiled. "Named it after my Mum."

"Ooh." I pulled a face. "Oops."

"Why 'oops'?" He filled his own mug. "Same name, that's all."

There was something familiar about this, tickling the back of my brain, but I wasn't sure what it was. "True. Like I said, anyway, it's a nice boat."

"Hm." He wasn't particularly tall, but there was something imposing about him. He was well groomed and tanned, in shorts and a T-shirt that were probably a lot more expensive than they looked. Wavy brown hair, greying at the temples, crow's feet at the corners of his eyes. Good-looking, though, with or without the money. Not movie-star handsome, but the kind of face you'd want your dad to have: warm, kind. My dad hadn't been either.

That thought took me by surprise, and not pleasantly. I don't like remembering my dad, what he did to me or what I did to him in the end. Luckily Ed claimed my attention back by moving closer to me—no prizes for guessing what he thought I was here for. "I'm a good cook, too," he said. "If you want to stick around."

"Okay, then," I said.

◄o►

I was a little uncomfortable when he steered the *Emily* down the estuary inland, but on balance I decided eating on the deck in the middle of the river was better than doing so at the quay, where anyone might spot us.

Ed had caught a couple of bass earlier on, and grilled them on a barbecue on the deck, serving them with a squirt of lemon and not much else. We ate with the river lapping gently at the yacht's hull, the hills rising either side.

"This your first visit here?" I said.

Ed nodded, sipping from a bottle of beer. "Always meant to come to this part of the world," he said, "but I never did. Pressure of work, as much as anything else. Funny, really."

"Funny?"

"Well—now I'm in charge I've got a lot more free time. You'd think it'd be the other way round, but now I get to delegate. Before, I was the one it got delegated to."

"Rank hath its privileges," I said. Clive had come out with that more than once.

"That's the one. What about you? You lived here long?"

"Five years."

"You happy here?"

"Yeah, course." I gestured round. "Who wouldn't be?"

"Yes, but—you must want more than this?"

"Why? I'm happy, I have a home. And I'm here. What else would I want?"

"Money? A career? A family?"

"I'm happy with what I have."

"You seeing anyone?"

"Are you?"

He shook his head. "Divorced. Now what about you?"

"A boyfriend," I said. I saw Clive's face for a moment, but pushed it away. Back into its box. Its compartment.

"You're so happy with what you've got," Ed said, "that you're out on a boat having dinner with a stranger?"

"I'm happy with what I have," I said, "and I take what I can get."

"That's more like it." He smiled. "So what about your family?"

"What about them?" I wasn't able to keep an edge out of my voice.

"They don't live around here?"

I shook my head. "I don't have a family." I looked at him long and level, willing him to get the hint that this wasn't a topic for discussion. When I saw him open his mouth to speak again I knew he hadn't, so I spoke first. "What about you?"

"Me?" His smile turned crooked and a little sour, as if he'd suddenly developed a gut pain. "I'm the same, actually."

"Yeah?"

"Yes. No family. Not anymore. Another beer?"

"Okay." I'd tipped judicious amounts of mine over the side when Ed hadn't been looking, as I wanted a clear head. "So what about yours?"

"Oh, it'd just been me and Dad for years, ever since Mum died. It's the family business, you see. That I work for. That I *run*, now."

"That's why you don't have to delegate anymore," I said.

"Right."

"So it's just you now? No brothers or sisters?"

Again his smile went funny. Again that look, as though something had turned sour in his belly. "No," he said. "I had a brother, but . . . he's gone."

"Oh, I'm sorry."

And that was when I realised what had seemed familiar before. I took another swig of beer to make sure he didn't see anything in my face. I didn't think he would have, anyway. I'm good at that.

"So." Ed got up and moved towards me, crouching beside my deckchair. "What next?"

I could have played hard to get, I suppose. But I wasn't sure of him, and I might need to keep on his good side. More to the point, he was used to getting what he wanted.

So I put my beer down and I let him kiss me. Not long after that he took me belowdecks again, and I let him fuck me. I sucked him off, too. I'm good at that. No, I didn't feel dirty. It was—necessary. To be safe. To maintain control. I'd had a lot of practice with that. You go away, step back from it. It's just your body; it isn't all of you. It's a good way of coping with things you don't want to be there for. Things you don't want to remember afterward. The kinds of things that live in the deeps, that you have to keep at bay with pills, or by cutting yourself, or whatever other ways you can find. Dad taught me a lot, without meaning to. In the end, he wished he hadn't.

In a distant way I registered that Ed wasn't a bad lover. Quite sensitive, in fact. I had a good time, or would have if Robin hadn't been hanging over me. Clive? Well, Clive was never going to know what I'd had to do. Compartmentalising again.

Afterward, while Ed was in the toilet, I slipped his wallet out of his shorts and checked inside. There was a business card for a company called Yorkguard: *E. York, Managing Director and Chairman.* I put the card back in the wallet and the wallet back in his shorts before he came back.

"Tide's turning," he said. "Best get back now."

"Okay," I said.

I dressed and went up on deck. Ed was in the wheelhouse, guiding us back up the estuary. He didn't turn around, but I saw a red flush creeping up his neck.

"Will I see you again?" he said at last.

"Sure," I said. "Tomorrow?" Clive was working nights the rest of the week.

"Okay."

I slipped off the *Emily*, hoping I'd gone unnoticed, and made my way home, where I showered to get every trace of Ed York off and out of me. After that I made a strong cup of coffee, lit a cigarette, and sat by the window of my flat in a thick bathrobe, a towel around my hair, watching my laptop power up.

I checked out Yorkguard's website first. They were a security firm, based in Kent, and the Managing Director and Chairman, Edmund York, was indeed the man I'd just slept with. A quick shufti at the Company History section of the site gave me the details of his father—Sir Richard York, no less, who'd died six months ago. No mention of another York brother, though, past or present.

I googled Sir Richard next: he'd been a big enough name to have garnered three obituaries on major newspaper sites. I scrolled through them, skipping the details of York's career and achievements, looking for information about his family.

And then I had what I needed.

—◦—

Clive woke me up in the early hours by crawling into bed with me. By the time I was awake, though, he was asleep, so I just lay there for a while, watching him. He looks about twelve when he's sleeping.

I couldn't sleep, so I got up and went for another walk. To clear my head, and be ready for what was coming.

—◦—

I went to the Harbour for another day's work, taking orders and wiping down tables as fast as they were vacated. Even from inside the café I could see the *Emily*, moored at the quay. While I was cleaning the tables out front, Ed came out on deck. He waved at me and smiled. I smiled back, but didn't wave.

"So," said Daniela at lunchtime, "I hear someone went on a little boat trip yesterday."

"They don't miss much around here," I said. "Do they?"

"Does Clive know?"

"I don't know," I said. "Does he?"

"Well, he won't from me, you know that."

I smiled. "True."

Daniela tapped ash from her cigarette. "Emily, I know it's not my business, but . . ."

"Nothing happened," I said. "Nothing like that, anyway." And in a funny way, it was true. Yesterday's fuck had been no realer than any other act I put on to keep things separate.

"As long as you know what you're doing," said Daniela.

"I think I do," I told her. "But in case I don't . . ." I gave her an envelope. "Can you hold onto that for me? And promise not to open it?"

Daniela studied me, then nodded. "Okay," she said. She didn't understand everything, but she didn't have to. She understood enough.

"Thanks," I said. "Can I steal one of your Marlboros? I've run out."

◄◦►

As the end of my shift approached my stomach became a knot, and it only tightened as I walked home to get changed.

Clive had left a note for me. Nothing much, just that we had to have dinner once he was off nights. He'd booked a table at the Nook. I had to smile; the Nook's the best fish restaurant in town, and he knows I love seafood. Even though he hates it, and they only have about two meat dishes. That's Clive. He's not the sharpest, but he's sweet.

Love? I don't really know what that is, but he's mine. So I look after him.

I went into the wardrobe and took out a small box hidden at the back. There were things in it I hadn't used in a long time. Pieces of old lives. I took what I needed, and went down to the quay.

"Hi there." Ed smiled up from the deck of his boat.

"Yo," I said. "Permission to come aboard, Cap'n?"

He laughed. "Board away."

I climbed down the ladder to the deck, knowing he'd be watching my arse. Good. Let him. He looked at my body and thought it was me, while the real me was in a control room, working levers and gears and watching everything unfold.

"So," I said, "where to now?"

"Another trip along the estuary?" he suggested.

"Maybe," I said, "or . . ."

"Or what?"

I nodded out towards the bay.

"Yeah?" he said. "We could do a trip along the coast. There and back. Weather's supposed to be good, so we could just drop anchor and . . ." He ran a finger down my arm.

I kept the smile on my face and managed not to draw back. "Sure. Why not?"

"Okay, then. Let's get underway."

⟶

The sky was grey and dull, but the sea was flat enough. The town and the harbour shrank away from us, merging into the low dark ridge of the coast. I couldn't pinpoint the exact spot where Robin had been found, but it wouldn't have been far from here.

"Okay!" said Ed. "Left at the first star and straight on till morning." He put his hands around my waist and pulled me against him. He was already getting hard. "Shall we go below? Or do you fancy doing it on deck?"

"In our life jackets?" I said. At his insistence, we'd both donned them.

"It'd be different, anyway," he mused.

"Maybe," I said, slipping out of his grasp and sashaying back towards the rail with a come-hither look. He grinned and followed me. "Actually," I said, "I just wanted to ask you something first."

"Yeah?"

"Yeah."

He spread his hands. "Well, then. Ask away."

"Okay," I said. "Why did you kill your brother?"

There was a moment that he blinked, still grinning, thinking it was a joke. Then his smile changed, became the crooked, soured thing it had been yesterday, and he went very still. The way a conger or a moray eel will, lying in its hole and waiting to strike. "What?" he said.

"Robin," I said. "Robin York. Or Robin Gaunt, as he called himself around here."

Ed licked his lips and his gaze strayed off to the side. I didn't look, but I guessed there was something he thought he could use as a weapon. His eyes were uneasy, but there was a predator's coldness in them. "How did you know?"

"His mum was called Emily, too," I said. "He told me once." It had been after the first time I'd slept with Robin; I'd forgotten about it until yesterday. "Twenty minutes on Google took care of the rest. Your brother vanished, didn't he?"

"More than ten years ago," Ed agreed, very still now, except for the slow tensing of his arms and legs. He was readying himself to leap; a moment's inattention and he'd go for me.

"I found an old picture," I said. "I had to look hard to see the resemblance—he didn't have the long hair or beard in it. But that'd have been the point, right? He didn't want to be recognised."

Ed shook his head. "He always was difficult. Wrong."

"Wrong? He's not the one who killed someone."

"He was a misfit," said Ed. "He had so many advantages in life—advantages other men would have killed for. Dad never had them—he had to fight for everything he had. And what did Robin do? He threw it all back in Dad's face. And then he ran away and vanished."

"So why come and find him?" I said. "Why murder him?"

"I hadn't heard from him in years," said Ed. "Christ, we all thought he was dead. Dad had him *declared* dead, a couple of years ago. But then he wrote to me. Out of the blue."

"What did he want?" I said. "Money?" Robin had never seemed particularly bothered about that, beyond the odds and ends he could pick up with odd jobs around town.

"Money? Oh, no. He had no interest in that, he said. Why would he? But he wanted to talk, Emily. He wanted *to talk about the abuse.*"

"What abuse?" But it was all falling into place. Robin had never said much about what had happened to him. There'd been stories of exploits and escapades with friends—equally wasted, of course—but nothing about his family, about wherever he and his wounds had come from.

"There *was* no abuse," Ed shouted. "That's the whole point. Dad was a good father. Stern, yes. He believed in discipline. That was all. Christ, you clip some little shit around the ear these days and it's child abuse. He was just trying to bring us up right. To be men."

But his eyes were full of pain, and I saw too much there. What had their childhoods held? What had Sir Richard York thought fit means to discipline his sons? Whatever it had been, it had left Robin afraid of anywhere that wasn't his own four walls, left him starting awake at every sound in the middle of the night. And his brother? Everyone breaks in different ways, and finds different ways to deal with it. Robin's had been to run and hide in another life. Ed had become the damage and called it normality.

That's one of the things that lies in the deeps, never far enough from the surface; the only real difference between the broken ones and everyone else is that the broken ones know there isn't one.

"But here was Robin—weak, he'd always been weak, and decadent, with his drugs and his sponging—here he was, putting our father—*my* father—in the same category as some bloody child molester. I wouldn't have it. I wouldn't let that degenerate blacken his name."

"But he didn't want money?" I said. The wind had started rising.

"No!" snapped Ed. "I told you. No, he just wanted to *talk* about it."

"To who? The press?"

"To me, that's what he said. But it wouldn't have ended there. He'd have kept going, till it all came out. And I couldn't have that. I wouldn't allow it."

"So you came here," I said. "And you found him—on the coast road, right?"

"Crashed out on a bench," said Ed. "Barely knew where he was, or *who* he was."

"And you got him back into town, and then on here." I nodded at the *Emily*'s deck. "How did you get him to the beach? A dinghy?"

"He was out of it." Ed had sidled towards me, a little. "Vegged out as soon as I got him on the boat. He only came round at the end."

He'd gone pale, with a greasy sheen of sweat. His eyes didn't quite seem to see me. He didn't look warm anymore, or kind. There are places in your head that have no room for those things. "I was going to hit him with something. Stab him, then put him over the side. But I couldn't. Too . . . final. But I couldn't let him go on. He'd . . ." Ed focused on me, and his eyes were almost pleading. "Dad dying, you see, it had brought everything back to him. That's why he'd started talking about it, and if he wasn't made to shut up he'd have told someone else, and it would have got out, and . . ." He gestured helplessly. "I couldn't have that."

And I *did* understand. You do whatever it takes to cope with the damage. And if anything threatens your coping mechanism, your safety, your sanctuary, you do whatever it takes to protect it.

"So you got him on the beach and cuffed him to the pipe." Clive had been half right, then. Robin's death had been the work of someone without the resolve to commit the act themselves, so they'd snapped on the cuffs and let the tide do the work. He'd only been wrong about who.

"He was unconscious," said Ed. He was shaking. A single tear ran down his cheek. "He didn't wake up. I didn't hear anything. *I didn't hear anything.*"

He said it again, and then again. I wondered how many times he thought he'd have to before he believed it.

I thought at first that that was it: something else had finally broken, and he had nothing left to say or do. I'd wondered at first why he'd stuck around—why not leave once the job was done?—but it wasn't hard to understand. If anyone had ever worked out who Robin really was, his long-lost brother spending a few days on this beautiful bit of the coast would probably rouse less suspicion than if he'd popped in and out of the harbour on the day of Robin's death.

I unzipped the pocket on my denim skirt, but as I did Ed moved, lunging for me. I kicked him under the knee and he fell with a scream that echoed across the whitecaps on the bay. I make a point of always ordering boots with steel toecaps. They're more weight to drag around, but if you ever need to defend yourself they're a big help.

Before he could get up, I took the cuffs out of my pocket. They'd belonged to an old—and slightly kinky—boyfriend, but they were police issue. I snapped one around Ed's left wrist, looped the chain around one of the iron railings on the deck and snapped the other bracelet shut around his right.

"What the fuck?" he shouted. He leapt up, or tried to, and I stepped back as he jerked and yanked at the chain. When I was sure the rail wasn't going to give, I walked back along the deck, to a small box at the base of the railings. I guessed that was where he'd been looking towards before. Inside were a flare pistol and a couple of distress flares. I loaded the pistol, pocketed the spare, then went into the *Emily*'s wheelhouse and pointed her prow out to sea, before pushing the engines to full power.

"What the hell are you doing?" screamed Ed.

I ignored him and his frantic yanking at the chain, then went belowdecks and opened the seacocks. As water started flooding into the yacht, I went back up top, the flare gun cocked and ready just in case he'd got loose.

He hadn't. He was slumped on his knees, red-faced and exhausted. "What are you doing?" he said. "What?"

The boat was already wallowing. Water splashed over the decks. "Justice," I said, then pointed the flare gun skyward and fired. The distress flare streaked up. I reloaded and fired the other one, too, then climbed over the rail. "Oh, and by the way," I said, "your brother was a better shag."

He started screaming when I went over the side. I struck away from the *Emily*, watching as she surged forward and went under, her own screws driving her down. Into the deeps. Ed seemed to scream for quite some time before he choked and gargled into silence.

Reluctantly, because I hated to lose them and replacements would be hard to come by around here, I kicked off my boots, feeling lighter as they sank. Out towards the coast, a flare burst in the sky. The lifeboat was on its way.

I'd need to find Daniela as soon as I could, get the letter back and burn it. Meanwhile, as my teeth started chattering from the cold, I rehearsed what I'd tell Clive. Most of it would be true, but I'd leave out certain things—and, of course, Edmund York would be the one who'd opened the seacocks and chained himself to the railings, in a fit of remorse. But only after firing the flares from the gun he'd been aiming at me to stop me interfering.

As some old comedian used to say, all the right notes, but not necessarily in the right order. Robin's death was paid for, Clive wouldn't know anything he didn't need to, everything would stay in its proper compartment, and life would go on.

I told you: you do whatever it takes to protect the safety you've found.

The grey sea heaved, capped with foam. I looked a little longer towards the place where the *Emily* had been, then turned and struck out towards the shore.

# FODDER'S JIG

## LEE THOMAS

Leaving my office on a cool autumn evening, I nearly collided with a woman dancing on the sidewalk. She wore a navy blue skirt-suit designed too narrowly for her plus-sized frame, and she moved in spasms as if in the throes of a standing seizure. Her hands flew into the air and then thrust toward the ground, pulling her shoulders with them until she bowed as low as her ample midriff would allow. Remaining bent at the waist, she launched her arms back and upward as if mimicking wings, all the while stomping her feet—*left, right, left, left, right*—against the sidewalk. She whipped into an upright position and glared at me. Though I considered the possibility the woman had missed a text changing the time or place of whatever flash mob she'd intended to join, I came to the more likely conclusion that the dancer was just plain crazy. Dilated pupils, black portals into a demented nothingness, noted neither me nor the real world I inhabited. After a beat of absolute motionless, the woman grunted a series of nonsensical phrases, directing them my way and sending me back several steps as the blunt syllables wormed into my head. She restarted her frantic, tribal dance while a meager crowd gathered around. Several members of the ad hoc audience had their phones out, but they were using the devices to record the performance. Admittedly, the spectacle was entrancing in its ferocity and unlikeliness, but the woman needed help, and no one seemed willing to offer it. I took out my phone and dialed for emergency, but the moment the operator came on the line, the woman's dance ended.

When her limbs ceased their bizarre choreography, she looked around with clear eyes, seeming genuinely confused. A skinny kid with a scraggly beard that reached the military beret atop the image of Che Guevara on his T-shirt fell into a fit of laughter and clapped his hands viciously. Others in the crowd picked up the applause. The woman appeared terrified and rushed into the building.

Within a week, the dancers were all over the news. Most of the reports came from cities along the Gulf Coast, but a few trickled in from landlocked towns. Message boards and wiki pages filled with information about the afflicted and offered uninformed, often ridiculous speculation regarding the cause of what was being called "Boogie Fever." One callous jokester set the video of an elderly man thrusting and stomping and contorting his emaciated form in the middle of a road to the *Benny Hill* theme song. The clip went viral: over a million hits in three days.

For many of the afflicted, dancing was the first symptom.

◄o►

Three months later, I stood in the living room of the condominium I'd shared for a bit less than a year with a man named George Caldwell. George called the apartment his "divorce shack." In reality, the place was a spacious and beautiful condo with a view overlooking Galveston Bay, and though it may have fallen short of the manse he'd spent thirty years of his life paying off, most people wouldn't have complained.

The morning had all but vanished as I packed a few remaining mementoes and the items of clothing I considered necessary. My suitcase and two small boxes waited by the door. I procrastinated, checked drawers and cupboards, sifted through the closets one last time. I wouldn't be coming back to this place.

Memories of George filled the apartment like the morning light, suffusing the rooms, pinging with painful glare from shiny surfaces. Before the dancing and the seizures, before the horrifying news reports, and the night he'd walked in a trance to meet thirty-six others on the sandy shore of Galveston Bay, I'd shared this home with a handsome, gruff, good-natured man, who would never again walk across its polished oak floors.

A remembrance of scotch set my tongue to tingling. The scent of his cologne momentarily filled my nose.

A marble-and-glass table ran across the center of the floor-to-ceiling window opening onto the patio and overlooking the bay. At the table, I placed a set of keys, George's set, on a brochure for the trip he and I would never take. I reminded myself to contact the cruise line to inform them we would not be sailing from Amsterdam to Budapest on their luxury liner, and then I wondered if it was even necessary.

None of the cruise lines would stay in business. Civilians were avoiding the water these days.

The brochure held my attention. Covered in dust, it was like a funeral program, memorializing a future that was never going to happen. I'd looked forward to traveling with George. I'd looked forward to everything with him.

We met online through a hook-up app two years before the Emergence. George's profile was typical for a "discreet" married man. No pictures of his face. No real information save for his sexual endowment and the things he liked to do with it. Our first meeting tracked a predictable course: an awkward "Hello," followed by frenzied groping and undressing. After sex, we both rinsed off and engaged in a little more conversation-sans eye contact. Then, George presented me with a hurried "Let's do this again," before he fled my house, stumbling over the threshold as he dashed for the Mercedes he'd parked around the corner.

I chanced a look outside and saw the bay. The surface glittered under the early morning sun. The twinkling touch of sunlight on the surface would have been beautiful under different circumstances. But I could only see glimmering blades, metal shards. Teeth.

After that first visit, I didn't expect to hear from George Caldwell again, but he surprised me. Sort of. The next couple of months, he visited sporadically. Our encounters were mostly physical. He was a married man of standing in the community, and I was a drive thru: convenient, quick, fundamentally satisfying, but a pleasure he felt embarrassed for indulging.

Three months in, he began staying longer. Brief chats evolved into actual conversations. I found out about the man and his life, which revolved around a perpetually dissatisfied wife, a spoiled son who had grown into an unbearable adult, and an obvious, if muted, depression. He admired me. He envied me. He asked me to spend a weekend with him in Austin.

I said no.

At that point in my life, I wasn't looking to train a sixty-three-year-old closet case. I'd come out in the late 70s, survived the 80s, and had spent the next twenty years with a quiet, though pleasant, alcoholic named Calvin, whose liver finally disintegrated the year after we'd retired to Galveston.

The other issue, which I found to be the more significant reason to avoid a weekend retreat with George, was the fact that ever since our first meeting, I'd spent far too much time thinking about him. In the days between George's visits, I swung from whimsical notions of how we would spend our next meeting to outright fury every time he had to cancel. At the center of these fluctuating emotions was sadness. Or maybe melancholy was a better word. I understood the cliché, even as I lived it: hopelessly pining for a married man. I'd started loving him too quickly, and that was not a thing to be encouraged, considering our situation.

Closing my eyes against another view of the disconcerting bay, I turned from the window and stepped to the center of the room. When the doorbell rang, I flinched.

I couldn't imagine who would be at the door. Maybe it was the real estate agent, though I doubted it. She'd agreed to swing by, "If I can." Her disinterest was understandable.

No one wanted to live near the water now.

⟨o⟩

"It's happening all along the coast," I call to George.

On the evening news a video clip of a little girl with a purple butterfly barrette in her blonde hair fills the screen. The child is dancing the same tribal dance I had witnessed only a few days before. The video comes from Holly Beach, Louisiana. An anchorwoman with silky black hair appears following the clip, and she says that more than a dozen incidents have been witnessed in the past week. She smiles and expresses her certainty that "Boogie Fever" is just the latest cultural meme, no different from Planking or the Mannequin Challenge.

George walks through the room with a glass of scotch, the flavor of which I'd never enjoyed until I tasted it on his tongue. He is naked, as is usually the case when he is home. A devotion to nudity is one of the many lifestyle changes George has adopted since leaving his wife. His body is burly and well shaped, having far more to do with genetics than any devotion to exercise. We go to the gym three days a week, and while I earn sweat on the treadmill and weights, George frequently chooses to lounge in the steam room until I am finished.

"*What's* happening along the gulf?" he asks, taking a moment to pause in front of the window to gaze over the nighttime bay.

"This dancing thing," I say. "Like that woman outside my office."

"People will do anything for attention," he says. "Why is something like that even on the news? The economy is going to shit again; protests and riots are springing up every other day; and two nights ago, about thirty people walked to a beach in Bermuda and vanished. Any one of those things strikes me as considerably more relevant than a bunch of idiots wiggling their asses for a camera."

"Wait, Bermuda?"

He sips his scotch. "These people—police think it's around twenty or thirty of them—just got up in the middle of the night, walked out of their homes, and disappeared. Loved ones reported a bunch of missing persons, and the authorities tracked several of them to a cove. They found footprints and some personal items, but no people. Bermuda isn't a big island. I went there on business a few times. You can't really hide there."

"They could have chartered a boat."

"Not likely," George says. "The missing persons weren't part of a social club. In fact, two of them were just visiting the island. They had no connections to anyone there."

I don't have a response to that.

"Anyway," he says, "I'm going to bed. I have to meet the lawyers in the morning. Time to see what else Eugie thinks she's entitled to for having me pay her bills for thirty years."

George doesn't sound bitter. He sounds exhausted. The divorce proceedings have dragged on far longer than he'd expected. He'd made it clear he wasn't going to put up much of a fight. He accepts the divorce as his fault, his problem, despite years of unhappiness on both sides of that bed. He just wants out, but Eugie's lawyers are gouging deep, too deep.

"You go on in," I say. "It's still early."

"I don't think so," George says, crossing to the sofa where I sit. "You are vital to my reason for going to bed early."

He bends over, carefully balancing his glass so his whisky doesn't slosh, and he kisses me hard.

◄◦►

I opened the door of the apartment to find a middle-aged man standing in the hallway. My throat grew tight and my breath lodged in the constriction. A chill blossomed on my neck and then rapidly vanished as I reconciled the man before me with the man I'd momentarily imagined him to be.

Barry Caldwell resembled his father so much that if the younger man were to slap a gray wig on his head, the two could have passed for twins, as long as you didn't look below the neck. Whereas George's physique had remained well proportioned and firm, Barry's didn't stand a chance against his indulgences and his sloth. I found it a shame that such a handsome face should rest on a body that might have been sketched by Dr. Seuss.

According to George's description of the man, they were in all other ways quite different. Our awkward meeting at the reading of George's will did nothing but support this notion.

"You're here," Barry said. His voice projected annoyance and indignation, as if I were the one intruding in *his* home. "We need to talk about my dad."

◄◦►

My shoe sinks in the sand, sending me off balance and into George's thick shoulder. He laughs and wraps an arm around me for support. He gently knocks the side of his head into mine, a display of affection I always found strange.

"After they found that whatever-it-is down here, I got curious," he says. "Weird fucking things."

"You mean the carcass that washed up last week?"

"Globsters," George says. "They call them globsters on the news. I don't think you can call them carcasses. No one's sure they're actually animals, at least not whole animals. They're like giant tongues or something. No eyes or mouths, just large chunks of smooth meat."

"What did it look like up close?" I ask, feeling a twinge of jealousy that he's found adventure on his own. We'd waited a long time to be together, really together; I want to share important moments. Every one of them.

"Like I said, just a wad of pale blue meat, about the size of a dolphin. Gulls swarmed the thing. Apparently, they find globster extremely tasty. I watched for a bit, but then this group of people in blue polo shirts showed up with tackle boxes. I guess they were with Fish and Wildlife or something. They put on surgical masks and did their best to shoo away the gulls so they could get a better look at the thing."

George's phone buzzes in his pocket. A cold, salty gust pushes in off the gulf as he draws the phone from his jacket. He sneers at what he finds on the screen.

"Eugie has started calling again."

"I thought she insisted all communications go through your lawyers?"

"Apparently, that only applies to me." George knocks his head against mine again. "She's getting nearly everything. I can't imagine what she wants now. But we're going to be living on peanut butter sandwiches if this keeps up."

"We discussed this," I say.

"I know, sweetheart. It's just going to take some adjustment."

"We'll be fine," I say.

He slides around in front of me and kisses me hard on the mouth. "I know that."

We continue along the beach, and George barks out a startling laugh. "God, I almost forgot the smell."

"Eugie's smell?" I ask.

"No, though I could tell you stories."

"Please don't."

"No, I mean the globster. Jesus, I've never encountered anything so rank in my life. It was like someone made a gas out of fish rot and seaweed and bombed the entire beach with it. I had to have been twenty yards away from the thing, and the shit got in my throat. I gagged half the afternoon."

I released a grumble of distaste.

"Didn't bother the mosquitoes any. The little bastards were everywhere."

George likes to swear. Eugie had forbidden it. For thirty-two years, "darn" and "gosh" were the expletives Eugie allowed her husband. Now, he showers the world in vulgarities: another freedom of which he takes full advantage.

◄◦►

Without invitation, George's son entered the apartment. He tromped through the living room like it was a hotel lobby. His presence struck me as wholly wrong. He didn't belong among George's things, among *our* things. This place was a sanctuary, and Barry was a marauding force.

He'd been calling for a week, ever since the reading of his father's will. I had no interest in speaking with him. George had told me enough about his son, about the privileged boy who could never quite make life work for himself, to know we'd clash. I'd endured his sneers in the lawyer's office, along with the glares of disgust from his mother. A chasm of status and finance had separated me from this aggressive tribe, but even gone, George remained a bridge, spanning the gap.

"Why are you here?" I asked.

"I told you, we need to talk about my dad."

"What's left to say?" I asked.

He knew what had happened to George. Everyone knew.

Barry walked to the table by the window and lifted the set of keys.

"Are you going to sell the place?" he asked.

"Who'd buy it? The Gulf Coast is a ghost town. People have been evacuating since . . . that night. I've alerted the bank that George is deceased. They'll take it over and claim a loss with the government."

"Where are you going to live?"

"Far from here."

Barry crossed to the bedroom and pushed open the door. He stepped over the threshold and then stepped back.

"What do you think you're doing?" I asked, outraged.

"Just wanted to see the place," he said. "Dad never had me over. Not once. That's not right. A family all split up like that. It's a nasty thing. Bad business, all of it. I've stopped by a few times this week. You were never here, or you weren't answering the door. Whatever. Just wanted to see it. It's not bad."

"The bank would probably give you a good deal on it."

He chuckled. "Nah. My wife and I moved in with Mom. Beautiful house. Incredible house. My boyhood home. Of course, Mom's under a lot of stress right now. Real bad. Dad's will was a shock to her. To everyone, really."

George had left substantial assets to me. One evening after we'd first moved in together, he'd set me on the sofa and performed a presentation, regarding the contents of his will, as if he were attempting to sell the proposal to a board of directors. The numbers shocked me, as they represented a financial security I'd never imagined, but even before George delivered the caveat-"The divorce is going to change all of these numbers dramatically."-I recognized his bequest, while sweet, was fundamentally symbolic. He wanted to show me how important I was to his life.

Even so, he'd been a responsible man. A good man. He hadn't been neglectful of his family.

"He accounted for both of you in his will. In fact, he was extremely generous."

"I'd expect you to see it that way. Of course you would." Barry's tone was critical. It was harsh, and more than ever, I wanted him out of George's home.

◄◦►

I wake in the early morning hours, startled and terrified to find George bent over my side of the bed. His face hovers a few inches from mine, and from his throat, a guttural and explosive chant emerges as if he is denouncing me in a violent foreign language. I roll away to George's side of the bed. The sheets press too hot against my skin. His attention follows. Blank eyes. Hardened expression. Growling and grinding words that have no place in civilized language. I say his name. Shout it. Beg him to snap out of whatever nightmare he is attempting to vocalize, but the chant continues for another full minute.

Then, his posture changes, and he is standing tall and rigid. His arms rise above his head as if he's celebrating a touchdown and his feet stamp–left, right, left, left, right.

By the time his eyes clear and his face slackens, I am in tears. I don't know if this is a stroke or dementia or some mental instability that stress has ignited, but it scares the hell out of me.

His eyes grow focused. His features soften. He stands upright and scratches the back of his head and says, "Hey, that's my side of the bed."

◄◦►

I didn't want to talk about George's estate, not with his son. George had made his last wishes clear. Even his lawyer, who was not above editorial-izing–making his own displeasure with George's late-in-life behavior known through head shakes, shrugs, and shaded provisos–admitted that the will was a binding document. Though he did comfort Barry Caldwell and his mother with the word "Contest," on more than one occasion.

"When did Dad get sick?" Barry asked.

"About a month before . . . before the beach," I said.

"So, he spent a month just dancing around this place?"

"That's not how the virus works," I said, wishing I could think of a chore to accomplish, so that I could busy myself rather than stand before Barry's arrogant gaze. But I'd already packed everything of value, at least everything I valued. Despite a compulsion to throw the man out on his ass, I didn't. He'd been tracking me with a purpose, and until I knew what it was and how to address that purpose, I'd endure him. "It was sporadic. I only saw George in seizure a couple of times."

Barry retraced his steps to the bedroom and then paused by the fireplace. He looked at the pattern of wrought iron vines on the screen and the mesh wires joining them. Then his head cocked to the side so he could peer at the bedroom door. "And you're not worried?" he asked.

"Worried? What more could happen?"

"I'd be worried. I'd be shitting myself. You could have caught it."

"It's not a cold, Barry."

"Yeah, but they're saying it can be sexually transmitted, right? A bunch of reports. Lots of 'em. They're coming out all the time."

For a moment, the lie achieved its goal. Steel shards of panic jabbed my neck and abdomen. But the deceit held only a transient power. I'd been thorough in my research.

"And it's not like you'd know you were sick unless someone told you," he continued. "The victims never remember their seizures."

He eyed me with a blatant fabrication of concern and stepped closer to the fireplace. I allowed him a moment to enjoy his petty jab, seeing the remarks for what they were. A tormentor's lies. A fiction he hoped would infect and linger and sting. It was the shitty move of a bested bully.

When he turned to face me, he was smirking. Perhaps he was attempting a sympathetic smile. Perhaps not. Wolves often looked as if they were grinning as they circled prey.

"Thank you for your concern," I said. "But your father and I fucked a lot, Barry. I didn't catch anything."

Barry's taunting smile disappeared. His eyes clouded as his mind attempted to process information I imagine it had struggled to deny, or at least disregard as an irrelevant abstraction. Unfortunately, his befuddlement and my satisfaction were both momentary.

"It's funny, right?" Barry asked, the grim smile returned to his lips. "How they were all synched up?"

"Excuse me?"

"The way they all danced at the exact same time, even though they were spread out all over the city? Hell, all along the Gulf, as far as anyone knows. It's like someone pushed a button and *bang*, all these people dropped what they were doing and got their grooves on. You have to admit, it's kind of funny."

No, I didn't have to admit that. There was nothing funny in the primal choreography, not even when it was set to the *Benny Hill* theme song.

"You know, one guy went missing. Disappeared. Everyone thought he was dead but he showed up a couple days later," Barry continued. "He wanted attention. He was a lonely old guy. Real lonely. Pathetic. And he figured he could climb on the bandwagon and suck some sympathy out of his family. Cruel thing to do. Nasty thing."

"George didn't need anyone's sympathy."

"No," Barry admitted, "but maybe he needed something else."

"I'm not sure what you're implying, but if you have doubts, you can speak to the police. I provided all of the information on George's behavior and his recent medical history to them."

"Yeah, his medical history," Barry says. "Well that's a funny thing. I spoke to his doctor. He hadn't seen Dad in months."

◄O►

The window is open, allowing a salt-scented breeze to wash over our bodies. I'm on the bed, and my heart still races from exertion. George's head rests on my belly, facing away from me. He gets his hair cut once a week and the horizon of silver drawing along the deeply tanned neck fascinates me with its precision. His stubble pokes agreeably on my skin as he turns his head to kiss my stomach.

He draws a finger from my navel to my cock. "You're sticky," he says. This makes him chuckle.

"Don't forget the neurologist tomorrow."

"You're making a big deal out of nothing," he says. "I was sleepwalking."

"You were doing more than walking. And stop that."

"No," George mutters, now drawing patterns in the semen on my belly. "I'm playing."

"You're a strange man, George Caldwell."

"Probably."

"This is serious."

"Maybe."

"You could be sick."

"I'm not." He stops tracing circles in the fluid on my skin.

"Look, I know it's frightening. No one knows exactly what this illness does long term, but you have to accept this. We need to explore treatments. You can't hide behind denial."

"This isn't denial," George whispers. "This is fucking survival."

"You think you have a better chance without medical attention?"

"Sweetheart, if Eugie finds out about this, it's over," George says. "This isn't some crap like West Nile. This affects the mind. It affects my *behavior*. I'm not actually divorced yet, which makes Eugie my next of kin. She would be able to have me declared incompetent and then take over my life. And even if I lucked out and found a judge who took the divorce into account, Eugie would just recruit my kid. The doctors don't know enough right now. Yes, maybe it started with those things on the beach, but if there's any doubt, they could attribute all of my actions for the past year or *years* to this."

"The courts would never . . ."

"One judge, sweetheart," George says emphatically. "All it would take is one bible-clutching judge to make the decision, and believe me, this town is swimming in them. They could take everything. They could take *me*, and I am not going to spend the last years of my life playing with crayons in an institution. I want to be with you. I want *our* life."

"I had no idea."

"You've been spared the barbarity of the privileged. Why do you think I asked to see your doctor and not mine?"

"I didn't think about it."

"My doctor is part of Eugie's circle. My lawyer is part of her circle. These people play dirty, and nothing brings them together faster than the opportunity to destroy a life. So, I am not sick. I do not have the Gibbet Virus. I'm of perfectly sound body and mind."

◄◦►

"George asked to see my doctor."

"Interesting," Barry said, as if he were a detective whose suspicions were being realized.

"He had it," I told Barry. "After his first seizure, I insisted he see a doctor. He asked to see mine. I have the paperwork. I had to file it with the police. This was before the CDC even had a webpage about it, though by this time, they had a less ridiculous name for the sickness: Gibbet Virus."

"Because of that island."

"Yes. But no one knew anything. They don't know much now."

"They've connected the virus to the unidentified masses that have been washing up along the coast," Barry said. "Mosquitoes are feeding on the things and spreading the disease like they do with West Nile and Zika."

I didn't correct him, not even his mispronunciation of Zika. Barry's information was old.

In the weeks following George's first seizure, I'd used research as a shelter from concern and ultimately grief. I had pages and pages of information about the virus, the globsters, and the Emergence in manila folders packed into my suitcase. Video clips and online articles choked my laptop's hard drive.

The CDC had tracked the virus's path from the globsters to the gulls that fed on them. The virus was metabolized by the gulls, where it incubated in their blood streams. Then mosquitoes entered the vector, transmitting the virus from birds to human beings. But while they could trace the virus's path, they had no idea how it worked.

What kind of infection created spontaneous spasms that looked more like tribal choreography than epileptic fit? What kind of disease caused the afflicted to chant an ugly and indecipherable language at the top of their lungs? What sickness summoned thirty-seven people to the water's edge, where they waited to die?

◄◦►

The earliest visual evidence of the Gibbet Virus I can find precedes the Bermuda incident by a month. I sit at the dining room table, gathering information, staring at the screen of my laptop.

The video clip was shot in Cuba. Two men sit on the hood of a vintage '62 Plymouth, smoking cigarettes and smiling. One looks into the sky and says something in Spanish. The other breaks up laughing and slaps him on the shoulder. In the background and far to the left of these men, a woman in a pale blue dress stomps the concrete of a recessed doorway. Shadow engulfs her, washing out the specifics of her face, but the familiar, violent jig is apparent through the gloom.

I follow links and fill my search engine with key words. I gather data as if it were the ingredients for a cure. I don't even notice George when he enters the room.

"We could get out of town," he says, sipping from his drink.

"Should you be drinking?" I ask. "Until we know more about this, you need to be careful."

"Bullshit," George says.

"But your immune system might be compromised, or the virus could affect the liver."

"Don't care," George says. "I spent my whole life following rules, and I'm still fucked. Now, what do you think about getting out of town?"

"I suppose I could get time off work."

"No," George says. "I'm not talking about a vacation. I'm talking about moving. If I'm here, then someone could see me . . . acting up. Maybe we could sell our places, head north. I just keep thinking my family is going to find out. It scares the shit out of me. I can't even function."

"I can't retire," I say. "Not for another couple of years at least."

"We'll find jobs."

"At our ages?"

"Well, I don't know!" George shouts and throws his arms wide, sloshing whisky over the lip of his glass. "Am I supposed to just hide in here all day, waiting to see what new atrocity is lurking around the corner?" He sits on the arm of the sofa, staring at the splash of liquid pooling on the floor. "I suppose I could go by myself."

The suggestion creates a painful vibration in my ribs. He doesn't mean to be cruel. I know it.

"Don't say that."

"This fucking world," George says. "I'm finally happy and then *this*. I thought Eugie would be my downfall, maybe Barry, but a fucking mosquito?"

"If you want to move, really want to do it, we'll find a way. We can go anywhere you want."

"I don't care where," George says.

"Then let's leave," I say. "Let's get in the car and drive. We'll head north until we find a place."

"If you're serious, I'll need time to make arrangements," George says. His mood is not bright, but the darkest edges are off of it. "I can't just vanish or Eugie will release a squad of investigators to find me so the divorce proceedings aren't inconvenienced."

"Tell me when, and I'll be ready."

"A couple of days? I have an old friend who owns a B&B in Colorado. We'll be okay there until we have a plan."

⋙

Barry crossed to the dining table, a table George and I rarely used for anything as we tended to eat on the sofa in front of the television. He grasped the back of a chair upholstered in fawn-colored suede and shook his head.

"He shouldn't have kept this from us. We're his family. Family is everything."

"He was embarrassed," I said. "Once they had identified the virus, and we knew his seizure wasn't a one-time event, he didn't want to leave the apartment. Then after the people vanished at Holly Beach, George started to panic. Families of the missing came forward. They talked about the dancing and the chanting. It was the first connection between the Gibbet Virus and the disappearances. It hit him extremely hard."

"We should have been told," Barry said, rocking his belly against the back of the dining chair as if attempting to discreetly hump the piece of furniture. "*We* would have gotten him the help he needed. We'd have gotten him great doctors. The best doctors. He wouldn't have just been walking around waiting for that *thing* to come along. He'd be alive right now, and my mother wouldn't have to worry about her future."

George had been right about his family. They *would* have declared him unstable and likely would have institutionalized him. He was their golden goose, and he'd gotten out of the pen. The sickening unease I'd felt since Barry's arrival intensified. Hot and cold static avalanched from my face to my stomach and a tremor ran through my muscles. He was accusing me of negligence, incompetence, but this wasn't the grief of a mourning child, it was the disgust of a disappointed heir.

This privileged brat couldn't imagine what I'd lost with George. Why should he? To him, his father was an old piece of furniture, something to stick away in a basement or attic until it could be sold at auction. He didn't understand the losses of aging. He couldn't be bothered to see how amazing it was to actually gain something so late in life, something so important.

Everything I knew about growing old told me I would lose and lose, and then I would die. My body had changed. My cells refused to repair themselves; they became bungling and languid. My senses changed, became less than they were. The world looked different. It sounded different. It felt different. Everything was harder and colder to the touch. I accepted these losses as natural, as part of my flawed human existence.

But to gain something, to find someone at this stage of my life?

It was unexpected, because nothing I'd witnessed had prepared me for it. How could I expect the bloated trust-funder to understand exactly how precious George had been to me?

I couldn't, and I knew I couldn't, and I knew I shouldn't have to.

"I've told you what you need to know," I said.

Barry continued to hump the back of the chair. "You haven't told me anything. Nothing that can be proven."

"You are welcome to speak with the authorities, but right now, I'm mourning the man I loved, and I find it completely fucked up for you to come into my home and accuse me of . . . What exactly do you think I did?"

He shrugged and looked away. "You let him die," Barry said.

His tone was so dismissive, so much like a teenager's response of "Whatever," that I wanted to punch him in the face. He gave up on the chair and turned back to the window.

"Is this where it happened?" he asked, gesturing to the beach beyond the glass.

◄○►

The enthralled crowd ambles in a line over the gulf, appearing like saviors walking on water beneath a radiant moon. Amid the perfume of salted air, a deeper, fouler odor rises: the rot of fish; the pulsing stink of seaweed. Straining my vision, I note a glow drawing a path into the gulf, like a mesh of pale white wires. This mesh provides a bridge, over which the throng slowly march.

◄◦►

I shook my head. Sudden misery clotted in my throat, and I squeezed my lips tightly to keep from making a sound. Tears coated my eyes. Pointing to the south, I managed to say, "About half a mile."

"But you have no proof he was there. He could be in the Bahamas."

"He was there," I said. A plea began to chant in my mind: don't make me say this, don't make me.

"None of the witnesses could definitively identify my father as one of the victims. Not one. I've asked them."

"That's not true," I said. "I can."

The information startled Barry. "What?"

"I saw him on the beach. I saw that thing in the water. I watched George die."

◄◦►

My panic as I search the apartment is venom, stinging and spreading through my system as I shout George's name. He never came to bed. He was planning our escape from Galveston and was making a list of people he needed to contact and a set of talking points to keep his story straight. He tells me to get some rest, but I can't sleep. After thirty minutes, I get up and join him at the dining room table, where I notice he is still dressed. He's so consumed with his plans that he's forgotten to indulge his nudity. We chat until he shoos me off so he can concentrate.

An hour later, I again climb out of bed. But George isn't at the table. He isn't anywhere in the apartment.

I throw on clothes and run into the hall, but it is empty and quiet. My mind babbles in static bursts, like a radio picking up desperate cries. We had talked about this. This was a possibility we'd considered.

In the grip of the Gibbet Virus, George could enter a trance and wander off. I'd found material about Bermuda and Holly Beach, suggesting the Gibbet Virus could be connected to the vanishing crowds. It struck me as unlikely when he'd suggested it, but I'd learned to take George's paranoia seriously, if only to keep him grounded.

His cell phone. I call and get voice mail. I call again and again. The device is useless.

Except it isn't.

At George's insistence, we'd linked his phone to mine with a tracking application. If he has the phone, if it is receiving a signal, I can find him.

I run down the beach, the distance between the small blue dot on my cell's screen and another green dot slowly diminishing. In the distance, I see people. They trudge through the sand, smudges in the night. At first I count only three, but as I draw closer to the light swath of sand, I make out so many more.

They converge from the west and north and south. They walk in unison, like robots programmed to a lazy march. Left. Right. Left. Right. Already a large group has gathered at the water's edge. Their chant pummels the air. The violent syllables share no pitch, but the cadence is matched precisely. It is a tone-deaf chorus, casting their voices at the waves.

And I see George at the water's edge. He has not reached the entranced throng. He is still thirty yards away from the growing crowd.

I catch up and move in front of him to block his path but he marches into me. His eyes are blank. His throat rumbles with the indecipherable mantra. I struggle with him, but he continues toward the gathering at the water's edge.

With tears turning cold against my eyes, I punch him in the jaw, and then I tackle him, wrestle him to the sand. George grunts beneath me, voicing the primal chant. Wet, pasty sand grinds into my elbows and forearms.

As I attempt to soothe him, assuring him everything will be okay, the gulf itself rises up.

An enormous blister forms on the water. It forces waves to crash with greater force against the shore on either side of the entranced brigade. The blister keeps growing, but I can't see what creates it. Maybe I see movement under the water; I can't be sure. Violent waves crash over George and me, and as I splutter and blow the stinging salt water from my nose, the thing breaches the surface of the gulf.

Far down the beach on the other side of the entranced crowd, another witness screams. More shouts, only a handful really, climb into the air.

It rises, long and flat like the crushed fuselage of an airplane surfacing after years below the waves. The thing is transparent, as if its skin is cellophane encasing the enormous white organs throbbing inside it. My first thought is that it is a species of whale, but I'm quickly convinced it is something different. Something new or extremely old. Spines and lumps cover its back. Triangular fins like those of a giant manta ray lay out like sandbars eighty feet to either side of the bulbous, distorted body. Long black slits run near the center of the face. I see no eyes anywhere on it.

And there are lesser creatures, like crabs with beaked heads, scurrying over the clear, wet tissue. Their pointed legs jab into the meat of the thing for purchase as they panic in the chill night air. One of them skitters down the clear face of the monstrosity and plucks a vaguely glowing gelatinous wad, maybe a jellyfish, from between the black trenches, before racing back over the crown to vanish amid the protuberances and bristles.

As the water settles, the entranced begin to walk into the water, but they don't submerge. They tread near the surface on a bizarre, glowing mesh, walking toward the monstrous creature as if being summoned. Their chant continues.

Maybe I have caught the virus from George, and this is the kind of horrifying thing he sees when he falls into his trances. Perhaps what plays out before me is not an example of mysterious nature, but rather an amalgam of sickening pieces, cobbled together by my infected mind.

Except it's not, and I know it's not.

◄०►

Barry's eyes grew wide as I described the Emergence. Certainly he'd seen the video clip one witness had captured that night, but the clip would be a pale, flat fiction compared to an eyewitness account.

"Then, George went crazy. He punched me and kneed my body and convulsed like he was attached to a live wire. I couldn't hold him down. I tried so hard to keep him with me, but I failed. During the struggle he managed to kick my knee. I didn't even notice the pain until I tried to stand. I fell on my face and started to crawl after him but I wasn't fast enough.

"George made it to the bridge just before it broke the surf. The mesh rose into the air, but remained level. Beneath the rising bridge, the water again swelled as the creature notched its head back, like a ship in the final stages of sinking. Its lower jaw emerged from the waves then. Scooped like a canoe, only ten times the size, the creature's mouth became apparent, and with this came the realization that the marchers who shared George's affliction walked steadily over this nightmare's tongue.

"I screamed. I think everyone who wasn't infected screamed. I'm not sure. I was so focused on George.

"The glowing mesh bridge began to fray at the end and curl skyward behind your father. Filaments pulled away and whipped violently against the purple-black horizon. The crab-like creatures moved in a wave over the bulbous back to swarm the top of the creature's head, driving their appendages into the face for purchase.

"Then the end of the bridge, the part that lingered near the beach, came fully apart. It unwove, or unraveled. Something. I don't know. The ends began to snap through the night like a collection of glowing lashes. The bridge bucked upward, sending everyone flying, and the cords creating it came apart completely.

"As the victims fell toward the waiting jaw, the wiry filaments of tongue lashed them. But these strands didn't just wound. They severed, slicing off limbs and opening torsos. I tried to keep my eyes on him, but George . . . h-he . . . remained whole for only a second. Half of his head vanished in a spray of blood, and then he came apart completely. The mechanical hiss of the whipping cords filled the night, but the creature's food made no sound. Before the first piece of meat hit the thing's mouth, the people that had marched over the gulf had been reduced to insignificant shreds.

"Standing on the mound of the creature's face, the lesser crab-like creatures scurried about for bits of meat and drops of fluid cast off by the whipping threads.

"The tongue rewove itself and then retracted quickly into the mouth. Inside the mouth, a long, pale blue wad of tissue streaked through with purple veins rode the interior of the cheek like a blister. It was one of the globsters George had seen."

During the story's telling, I'd wandered the room. When it was complete, I found myself near the front door. I stepped to the wall and leaned against if for support as I struggled with the weight that had settled in my chest.

"Did you tell the police?"

"Yes," I said. My voice cracked, breaking the syllable in two. "I told them."

"No," Barry said, shaking his head. "I've read every article about that night. You were never quoted."

"I was one of six witnesses. I didn't *want* to talk about what happened, and the other five did. The media didn't need me."

"It's a shame," Barry said. "You could have banked a fortune if you'd have filmed the Emergence with your phone," He sounded disappointed, yet smug, as if under the same circumstances he would have succeeded in making a bankable clip from the atrocity. "The only other video is garbage. The guy caught about three seconds of the monster before he started screaming and running off. Can't see much of anything except the water swelling up and flooding the beach. Stupid fuck."

"Yeah," I said. "Stupid."

We'd witnessed the emergence, or perhaps reemergence, of a life form that could produce spores containing a commutable virus, a virus that appeared to act as some kind of link between its monstrous source and the people it infected. Through this link, the creature could manipulate human behavior, summoning hordes of men and women to its waiting mouth. And this idiot could only think of photo opps and bank accounts.

And it occurred to me in that moment, that while I didn't know exactly what Barry wanted, the man might not know either. The erratic path he'd taken through the conversation and the non-sequiturs suggested flailing and grasping, a struggle to remain in control. But he had no control here.

When he finally got to his point, it came as no surprise.

"We're going to fight you on the will," Barry said.

"I figured you would," I replied. "You'll be happy to know I don't intend to fight back. Make a reasonable counter offer, something that shows even a modicum of respect for your father's wishes, and I'll sign off on it."

"Really?" Barry asked. "Just like that?"

"Yes," I said. "Your father and I had a lot in common, including the desire to have you and your mother out of our lives forever."

⬦

After a bout of pointless outrage, Barry finally left. I said goodbye to George's divorce shack and carried the suitcase and boxes to my car. Driving across town, my temper settled and the rage heating my face lessened. I'd never sold my house, though I hadn't spent more than the occasional minute there since moving in with George. After the Emergence, I was grateful to have a place at the center of the island, away from the water. With the sound of Barry Caldwell's voice still infecting my ears, I couldn't wait to be back among my things.

I trudged to the door and inserted the key. The door opened onto gloom. Gray light and black shadows filled the room like heaped corpses reduced to char and ash. The shapes in the room made no sense. Tears smeared the chiaroscuro and I pressed back against the closed door, exhaling deeply as if the air in my lungs was the weight that held me back and not grief.

Reliving that night ruined me. Picturing George on the tongue of that unfathomable creature, blankly marching toward its gullet, played in a loop behind my eyes. The *Benny Hill* theme accompanied it, only the tune had been slowed to a moaning dirge, every beat in time with George's footsteps, and those of the other fodder, crossing the beast's tongue.

At the bedroom door, I wiped my eyes and took several deep breaths.

Some lies are told to protect the ones we love. Others are told to protect ourselves. The lie I'd told Barry Caldwell was both.

Pushing the door open, I forced a smile to my lips and stepped inside.

On the bed, George turned his head to me. He'd never reached the creature's tongue the night of the Emergence. He'd walked to the beach. He'd struggled. Those things were true, but he'd never gotten away from me. I'd never have let him.

The leather cuffs at his wrists and ankles had held. His gag remained firmly in place. Eyes squinted against the meager, though unexpected light. Then they grew wide.

I sat on the edge of the bed and ran the back of my hand down the side of George's cheek. Leaning over, I knocked my head lightly against his.

"They won't come looking for you," I said. "They'll offer me a fraction of your estate when they contest the will, and I'll take it."

He squeezed his eyes closed and tears spilled down his cheek to pool against my thumbs. Gently, I removed the gag, and he sobbed softly.

"Thank you for this," he said. "Can we go now?"

"The movers will meet us in Denver. Then we'll go into the mountains. We'll disappear."

The deception had been his idea. In death, his family could no longer hope to control him. His family would get the bulk of his estate, and that's the only closure they required. With all the disbelief and chaos surrounding the Emergence, and with no conflicting testimony from witnesses, the authorities had accepted my story with little more than a nod.

Now, we could disappear. We could build something new without the accumulation of his life littering our happiness. We'd decided to move far away from the Gulf, from all connected masses of water.

The Emergences were becoming more frequent, and those afflicted with Gibbet's remained at risk. The victims still blacked out. They still wandered, requiring constant observation or restraint. They still danced.

"So, we're okay?" George asked.

His hopeful eyes lost their life and turned hard. The grunting chant bubbled low in his throat, and I managed to get the gag in place before the violent syllables bellowed forth. I pulled away from him, but kept one hand on his cheek as he ranted into the muffling fabric.

"We're okay," I told him. "We're just fine."

# THE CURIOUS ALLURE OF THE SEA

## CHRISTOPHER GOLDEN

So stunning was the view from the deck of her new house that Jenny thought it might be worth the loneliness. Late afternoon sunlight made monstrous shadows of the pine trees on either side of the property, but straight back from the deck where the ground dropped away toward the rocks, she had the perfect vista—nothing but the indigo sweep of the Atlantic Ocean, the cold wind off the water, the white froth of the chop around the island, the circling gulls, and the occasional seal basking on the rocks. The romance of it plucked at her heart. She stood on the deck, tugged her thick wool sweater more tightly around her, and thought there might not be a more beautiful place on Earth. The house was hers. The deck was hers. But she couldn't share it with anyone.

Not ever.

◄◦►

It started months earlier, on the rainy autumn morning when they found her father's boat. Tom Leary had gone missing two days earlier after a lifetime at sea. Jenny had spent the time praying for him to radio in, praying the Coast

Guard would find some trace of his fishing boat, the *Black Rose*. Praying for it, and dreading it as well.

Matt Finn knocked on her door at just past seven that morning. She opened the door of her rented cottage in pajama pants and a threadbare Patriots shirt, an arm placed self-consciously across her chest, eyes narrowed because she was too sleepy to open them all the way just yet. Officer Finn normally cut a fine figure in his uniform—Matt had been proud of his badge since his first day on the job, back when they'd still been dating—but that morning he just stood in the rain looking tired and sad, blues soaked almost black, and Jenny took one glance at him and knew.

He hesitated as he tried to muster up the words.

Jenny just shook her head. "I'll get some clothes on and be right out."

She shut the door and let him stand out there in the cold September rain. It never occurred to her until much later that she should have let him in. By then, she'd wish that she had. If she'd known how things would turn out, she'd have savored every moment of contact she could get. But wisdom always came too late.

In the car, Matt shut off the crackling voices on the radio. She was pretty sure he wasn't supposed to do that, but the silence helped.

"They found the *Rose*?" she asked.

Hands tight on the wheel, Matt nodded. The wipers swished the rain off the glass and the engine hummed, and it took him a moment or two before he spoke.

"He wasn't on it."

"No sign of him at all?"

In answer, Matt reached out and took her hand, holding it there on the seat between them as the police car carried her out to the dock. When they'd parked and gotten out and were walking the rest of the way, and she saw the dark figures milling about in the gray storm light, and the Coast Guard ship, and the *Black Rose* bobbing against the dock beyond it, she wished Matt could take her hand again, almost reached for him but thought better of it. He was married now, and didn't belong to her anymore.

Cops murmured words she barely heard. Three strutting seagulls had landed on the boat's bow railing and were squawking at each other in some kind of territorial dispute. When a fourth tried to land, they banded together to chase it off.

A Coastie put a hand on Jenny's shoulder, trying to prevent her from boarding the *Rose*, but a cop intervened and the hand vanished. Her heart broke with the force of her gratitude. She had to see for herself. Her father had always known the sea would take his life, but he'd always said it gave him life, too, so that would only be fair.

It didn't feel fair.

The boat creaked under foot as she stepped down onto the deck. She glanced around, saw an abandoned life vest and some long black Guinness cans, empty of course. This was the debris of her daddy's idea of fishing. His catch would be in the coolers, no doubt, though one would have several more of those black cans. The life vest made her brow furrow, though. Why had he dragged that out from its usual resting place? There hadn't even been a storm.

A couple of the gulls hopped to the deck and started making their way back toward her, angry at her intrusion. Lost in the worst of dreams, Jenny noticed the oddness of their behavior, but only barely. Ignoring the birds, she stepped into the wheelhouse.

It felt haunted, but it took a moment for her to realize it was the silence that gave it that ghostly atmosphere. The boat was too dark. Too quiet.

A creak behind her caused her to turn, but it was only Matt and another cop.

"The engine?" she asked.

"Dead."

"How does that happen?"

The cops shifted uncomfortably. "It's being investigated."

"He still had his cell phone, Matt. Radio or not, he could've called. And he would have, unless he thought he didn't need to. Could he have flagged down another boat? Maybe someone . . ."

She didn't want to think about it. About violence toward her father.

"Anything's possible," the other cop said. "The weird thing is there's no damn fish."

Jenny frowned, glanced past the cops toward the deck. "He drank at least three beers, which meant he was out for a while before . . . whatever happened. No way did he spend that kind of time and not catch anything. This is Tom Leary we're talking about."

Matt shot a dark look at the other officer, then shrugged. "No fish. No sign he'd even been fishing. Equipment all put away, nice and neat."

Her frown deepened. She hung her head, pondering what her father had been up to on that morning two days past. The emptiness of the wheelhouse began to feel suffocating, the air too close despite the side windows being open. She took a deep breath and felt a tingle at her back, as if someone might be in there with them, watching from a shadowed corner. Jenny turned, but saw no one. Instead, she felt her gaze drawn to the hook to the right of the throttle, where her dad had often hung his hat. In its place was a grimy silver necklace upon which dangled a flat rectangular stone about two inches in height.

Jenny bent to study that stone, reached out to lift it into her palm, chain still looped around the hook. The stone had been carved with three spirals, all connected at the center so they seemed to flow one toward the other in a never-ending circle.

*Waves*, she thought. *They look like—*

"Hey, Jen, don't do that," Matt said, taking a step toward her. "You know you're not supposed to touch anything."

Jenny let the stone talisman slip from her fingers and it swung for a moment below that hook. She took out her cell phone, opened the camera, made sure the flash was on and snapped a shot. Her fingers felt warm where she'd touched the stone and the urge to reach out for it again grew powerful. An unfamiliar regret ignited inside her, and for just a moment the loss of that stone, the wish to return it to her grasp, seemed more important than the mystery of what had happened to her father.

"Looks pretty old," the other cop said, crouching to peer at the stone. Jenny fought the urge to keep it from him.

"Your father's?" Matt asked.

Jenny pulled herself away, skin crawling with unease at the way the presence of that stone tugged at her insides. "I guess it might've been. I don't remember seeing it before."

Matt bagged it for evidence while she stood out on the deck in the rain. Jenny felt the eyes on her as she waited for him to drive her home, knew they were wondering just as she was what happened to Tom Leary, whether he'd gotten drunk and fallen overboard or if there'd been some kind of foul play, or if—as happened from time to time with those men who spent most of their lives alone out on the water—he had just given himself over to the sea.

"The Coast Guard'll keep looking," Matt promised later, as he was driving her home, the shush of the windshield wipers and the drum of the rain on the cruiser's roof making her sleepy. The words sounded hollow coming out of his mouth. Jenny barely heard them and certainly didn't believe them. "We'll find him."

But of course they didn't.

Someone stole the spiral-carved stone out of evidence on that first night. Jenny couldn't stop thinking about it, couldn't stop looking at the photo she'd taken with her phone.

The morning after the Coast Guard called off the search, she had that ocean symbol tattooed on the inside of her right forearm. Three days later, she went back to the same shop and had the friendly, bearded artist tattoo her father's name in the same spot on the opposite arm. She mourned, of course. Grief cut into her in moments quiet and loud, sometimes out of nowhere. Sorrow welled up like blood in a wound, spilling over and staining whatever it touched. And yet there were good moments as well, and anytime she looked at the tattoo, the ocean rolling on forever in that circle of waves, the infinite sea, a kind of peace filled her. Healed her. Though she'd never been much for fishing, Jenny had inherited her father's love for the sea, felt its allure just as he always had. With that tattoo, it felt like the sea remained with her wherever she went.

And her father, of course. Tom was with her as well.

As much as it hurt to lose him, she felt as if somehow they were still together, out on the water, sharing that serenity. But it was the skin on the inside of her right arm that drew her gaze most often. Sometimes she would trace the three spirals with her fingertip. It relaxed her completely, made her feel as if she might float away. The thought did not trouble her at all.

All would be well. She felt sure of it.

◄o►

On the third day after her second tattoo, she noticed the behavior of the gulls. In the aftermath of her father's death, Jenny had put off her real estate clients the best she could and spent her time cleaning up after him. The funeral had brought with it a maelstrom of emotions. She'd listened to a hundred stories about her dad, some of them new to her and others comfortingly familiar. There'd been tears and laughter, and the unwelcome presence of her Aunt Eleanor, who'd spent the wake and funeral with her lips in a constant twist of disapproval. She'd come with her son Forrest, this woman who'd never understood the way the sea had called to her brother and always believed it had been laziness that caused him not to make "more" of himself, as if a man who earned his living out on the water could ever be conceived of as lazy.

Jenny had wanted to be polite but only barely stopped herself from telling Aunt Eleanor and her tax attorney son to go fuck themselves. Maybe down the line, when Jenny could clear her head, she'd realize she ought to dig through her father's things and mail some keepsake or other to Eleanor, but as she began to go through the old man's belongings, she found nothing her aunt deserved. Not that there was much to choose from. The boat still had a loan and would need to be sold. The house, though—she'd grown up in it, and so had her father. The taxes were nothing to sneeze at, but it had no mortgage, and she was grateful for that. Over the years he'd gone through very lean times, but Tom Leary had never given in to the temptation to take the money out of the house. There'd be an official reading of his will and it would have to go through probate, but she knew what was in it. Whatever he'd had would come to her.

All of these things were swirling in her mind as she parked her car outside the Whale's Tale, a pub that looked over the harbor. As she climbed out, her shoes crunching in the gravel, the tattoo on her right arm felt strangely cold, as if it were winter instead of early fall. She slammed the car door and shivered despite the sweater she wore. She turned her wrist to stare at the tattoo on the inside of her forearm. It looked just as it had before and she felt foolish, wondering what she had expected.

Jenny took the walkway next to the restaurant—the main entrance opened onto a wooden boardwalk facing the harbor. She scanned the handful of people seated on the outside deck in spite of the chill and wondered if her lunch date would have opted for inside. It was comfortable for September, but the sky hung low and the clouds promised rain. She wished Matt had been her lunch date—he'd been so kind and attentive since her father's death that she wondered if they might start over—but instead she was meeting with Rudy Harbard, who'd been one of her dad's competitors and wanted to buy the *Black Rose*. They'd never liked each other much, Dad and Rudy, but Tom Leary had always respected the man.

As she stepped onto the boardwalk, Jenny inhaled deeply. The smell of the ocean, the sound of it, filled her heart. She glanced out at the water, at the boats bobbing out there, at the men working on their decks, and she longed to be with them. For a moment the idea of selling the fishing boat felt so wrong that she couldn't take another step. She had always loved the sea, but now she felt a yearning so deep her bones sang with it. If she sold the boat—

A flash of white and gray whipped past her face. The gull cried out as it struck her right arm. She felt its claws but its momentum carried it past her and she twisted away from it. The bird alighted on the boardwalk, sending several people scurrying out of its path. Jenny glanced down at her arm, saw the small trickle of blood there, and then stared at the bird.

"You little shit," she said. "You're in for a kicking."

She marched toward the bird, expecting it to hop backward or fly away, but instead it came toward her. A shiver went through her. Jenny heard another cry and looked up to see other gulls alighting on the little fence outside the restaurant's porch and on top of a trashcan on the boardwalk.

A man touched her back. Startled, she jerked away from him, feeling as if she were under attack. The gull hopped closer.

"Let me help you," he said, so calmly that he almost seemed to be sleepwalking. Maybe fifty years old, handsome and tan but leathery from a lifetime in the sun, he stared at Jenny as if he'd never seen another human being before, studying her as if to decipher some puzzle she represented to him.

"If you want to help—" she started.

The first gull cawed and took flight, right toward her. The leathery man dragged Jenny into a protective embrace. The bird might have struck him, she wasn't sure, but then he turned and shooed it away. A toddler carrying an ice cream cone shrieked as the bird zipped over her head. Two other gulls jumped down to the boardwalk, and the leathery man shooed them away as well.

Over a dozen passersby had paused to become spectators, not including the people on the deck of the Whale's Tale who were observing the show. Several of them, Jenny saw, were focused on her instead of the weirdness going down. One woman had her head tilted, her mouth slightly open, as if she'd taken the world's best drugs. Jenny felt her skin crawling with the attention.

The man with the toddler—her father, she assumed—abandoned his child and walked toward her, scrutinizing her in a way that reminded her of a hundred showing-up-naked-at-school nightmares.

"Hey," he said softly as he approached. "You. I need . . . I want . . ." He blinked and crinkled his brow like a flicker of common sense had tried to push into his forebrain. Then he shook his head. "What *are* you? Why do I want to—"

Leathery guy grabbed him from behind and slung him away. The quiet man almost tripped over his own toddler, startling the girl into letting her ice cream drop from the cone. She stared down at the strawberry glob on the boardwalk and her lip trembled, and then she started to cry.

The little girl's sobs drew everyone's attention. Even those who'd seemed somehow mesmerized were distracted long enough for Jenny to rush to the hostess stand. The fiftyish brunette had been watching the whole thing unfold and she frowned with maternal worry as she escorted Jenny straight to the restaurant's entrance.

"Come inside, honey," the brunette said. "We can call the cops—"

The tattoo on her right forearm prickled with the cold, as if the ink had turned to ice on her skin, and Jenny rubbed at it to try to drive that chill away.

"It's okay. I don't need . . . it was just—"

"Fuckin' peculiar is what it was," the hostess said with a glance over her shoulder. She dragged open the door, put her free hand on the small of Jenny's back, and gently guided her inside. "Have yourself a drink, at least. Take a breath. I'll let you know when those guys are gone."

"I'm supposed to meet someone," Jenny started to say, as the door swung closed behind them.

The crack of impact made her cry out as she and the hostess grabbed hold of one another. Jenny spun, backing away, staring at the spider-web pattern splintered into the door and the smear of blood streaking the glass. Through the clear, unbroken glass toward the bottom of the door, they could see the seagull that had just killed itself trying to reach her.

"What the hell?" the hostess whispered.

She glanced at Jenny and for the first time that maternal concern vanished. Instead, the woman took a step away, as if to move out of the line of fire, in case of whatever came next. Resentment kindled in Jenny's chest, mingling with anger and wonder and a kind of helplessness she'd never felt before. She stared at the hostess, infuriated by the idea that the woman was afraid to come near her.

Later, she would remember that moment and wish that she could make everyone as hesitant to approach her as the hostess had been.

⤖

Over the following days, it escalated quickly. Everywhere she went there were men and women who looked at her too long, watched her too closely. Not everyone—whatever the allure, it wasn't universal—but enough to make her increasingly uncomfortable. Even small children rushed to invade her personal space. Out for a morning run, Jenny encountered Emma Brill, a friend from high school, who'd been walking her infant son in one of those fancy jogger-strollers. The moment the boy saw Jenny, he'd begun to cry, stretching his arms toward her as if desperate to be held. As if Jenny were his mother instead of Emma. For a few minutes, Jenny complied, just so she and Emma could continue their conversation—though it consisted of the same beats as most of her recent conversations, full of condolences and shared memories.

When she'd given the baby back, the infant had loosed a piercing wail, shrieking as he tried to hold on, his face turning purplish-red. Emma apologized, trying to soothe the baby. Jenny whispered her own apology, promised to talk to Emma soon, and started off again on her run, sneakers crunching on the sand and grit in the road. The baby shrieked on, inconsolable, and even when Jenny had outrun the sound, the wind would gust and carry it to her in small, lonely snatches, as if the baby would scream forever.

Gulls cawed and circled in the sky. As she ran along a narrow path just a few hundred yards from the ocean, small crabs scuttled out from the high grass and scrub. At first she ran over them, careful not to step on and crush them, but after half a minute she noticed they all seemed to be moving in the same direction—toward her—and she paused to look back the way she'd come. There were dozens of the little things, and more emerging from the grass. All of them were moving in her direction. The ones she'd passed had changed course to follow her.

A tremor of fear went through her. Jenny sneered at the emotion, angry with herself, and she started running again, part of her convinced she could still hear Emma Brill's baby screaming for the loss of her. Her heart pounded and the tattoo on her right forearm went colder than ever before, as if the ice had slid deeper inside her, right along the tracks of her veins. She put a hand on it as she ran, taking peace from the contact, drawing comfort from the symbol there. For a little while it seemed like her thoughts became softer, and her feet carried her forward in a sort of trance.

The path branched to the right, toward the street that led to her neighborhood. A dozen steps toward home, gulls cawing above, twenty of them circling now, she staggered to a halt.

Three people waited along the path, the high sea grass waving on either side of them. One she didn't know, but the other two were fisherman. Men who'd spent their lives at sea, who felt the call of it in their hearts the same way Tom Leary did.

Jenny backed away. At the split in the path, she took the other fork, picking up her pace. A gull darted past her head close enough that she had to duck, but she only ran faster, kept running without really thinking about where she might go, although in the back of her mind she'd known all along. She fled to the place she'd always run to when she was in trouble.

Home.

The cottage she'd been renting was only a few miles from the old Federal Colonial where she'd grown up, and now her run brought her onto a path that emerged two houses down from her childhood home. All the houses along Dunphy Road sat on a bluff, facing the ocean, with nothing but the street and a pile of enormous rocks separating them from the steep drop off the bluff into the water. Jenny sprinted along the road toward the front steps, heart already lightening.

A car rolled up beside her, slowing to match her speed, and then the tires skidded to a halt. Jenny turned, startled, to see Matt climbing out in that familiar uniform. She saw the pain and regret on his face as he walked up to her and her only thought was of her father.

"Did they . . . did they find his body?" she asked.

Tears welled in Matt's eyes. One slid down his left cheek, and others followed.

"I'm sorry," he said.

Seagulls fluttered down to alight on his police car and on the front porch of her house. Across the street, a woman had been photographing the ocean. A professional, with a camera strapped around her neck that looked as if it cost more than Jenny made in the average home sale commission. Now the photographer turned and gazed at her like Dorothy at the gates of the Emerald City.

"Where did you find him?" Jenny asked. Horror swept through her as she imagined having to identify her dad after his body had been in the water for weeks.

Matt grabbed her by the arms, held her tightly, and leaned in to breathe in the scent of her hair. "I'm sorry," he said again.

She started to protest and he nuzzled her throat, pressed his cheek against hers, kissed her forehead lightly.

"I can't . . ." Matt said. "I can't keep away. I just needed to come to you. Get lost in you."

The words might have been romantic if not for his grip on her arms. If not for the hopeless look in his eyes and the fearful, desperate tone of his voice.

"Matt, no." She tried to extricate herself from his grip. Took a step back, drawing him with her instead.

She saw the expectant look in his eyes, as if he felt certain she would understand. And the truth was that she did. Jenny said his name, looked down in frustration at the grip he had on her arms and saw that his hand covered half of the triple-spiral tattoo.

"No!"

She twisted her arms down and outward, breaking his grip, then stepped in and shoved him with both hands. Matt staggered backward, arms pinwheeling, and fell on his ass at the edge of the road. The gulls on his car took flight, darting toward her. Jenny spun and raced for the porch, took the stairs two at a time, lifted her arms to protect her face as the gulls there flapped up from the railing and came at her. She batted at them, heart pounding, fighting the scream that had been building inside of her.

Tom Leary's wicker chair sat on the porch. Jenny picked it up with both hands and used it to shield herself, keeping it aloft with one hand while she plucked the spare key from on top of the lantern to the right of the door. Gulls cawed and pecked at the wicker.

Matt cried out her name and the plaintive tone in his voice made her own tears begin to fall.

The key scratched around the lock and she wanted to scream, but then it slipped in. She turned it, then grabbed the knob and gave it a twist. The door swung inward but the wicker chair caught on the frame and she released it.

The gulls scrabbled away from the chair as it fell, just long enough for her to spin around and slam the door, locking it from the inside.

Trying to catch her breath, she glanced at the tattoo inside her left forearm, taking comfort from her father's name inked there. But she felt her gaze pulled toward that other tattoo, and only when she let her eyes shift to it did she find real peace.

A sound broke through her reverie, gulls clawing at the door. She looked up at the peeling paint, and the door shook in its frame.

"Jenny, please!" Matt called.

"Go away!"

"I can't. God help me, I can't."

She turned and bolted up the stairs to the second story, then all the way to the third. At the front of the house, a bay window looked out at the sea, but Jenny had more interest in the yard below. With her left hand, she covered the spiral tattoo, soothing herself. From the vantage point at the window she couldn't see the front porch, where Matt still pounded on the wood and gulls still roosted.

But she could see the road. She could see the cars and pickups that had pulled up there, and the men and women who had begun to gather, gazing up at her home with the sad eyes and heartfelt longing of people who knew the thing that so fascinated them would be forever out of their reach, that the thing they most loved could never love them back. Fishermen and tourists, the photographer and several small children who seemed to belong to no one, who seemed to have wandered away from their parents to follow the allure of something they would never understand, whether as children or as adults . . . they all wore that same look.

Jenny had her hand on the tattoo, knew she could take that peace with her wherever she went, but there would always be those who felt the same allure. She wondered about the talisman, where her father had acquired it, how deeply it had affected him. If it had killed him.

Though she knew the answer. Of course she knew.

She could remove the tattoo, of course, but she felt it just as others did. It called to her, soothed her, satisfied a yearning in her, and Jenny couldn't surrender that. Not for anyone or anything.

Yet even as she understood that, she also understood they would never stop being drawn to her. She had to get out of there, could make it down the steps and out the back of the house. Her father's old Harley was there, in the shed he'd used as a workshop forever. She knew where he hung the keys. She'd go. She'd do it right now, leave all these people behind, escape whatever drew them to her.

But she knew what drew them. Knew she'd never leave it behind, even if it weren't inked into her skin.

Still, she couldn't stay here.

She bolted. The Harley waited for her.

Beyond that, she didn't know. Not at first.

◄◦►

The current of her life swept her out to sea.

Jenny had given up her rented house, put a For Sale sign in front of her childhood home, and entered a lease-to-own agreement on this starkly isolated spot on Comeau Island. There were twenty-seven other year-round residences on the island, but the nearest was half a mile through the piney woods from Jenny's place. They weren't the drop-by-for-a-welcome sort of neighbors. Nobody came to borrow a cup of sugar. People didn't live on a remote island off the coast of Maine because they felt like being neighborly. The best she could hope for would be that someone would come to check on her if they saw smoke rising from her property that couldn't just be the chimney.

These were the only neighbors she could allow herself.

Questions lingered. How long could she last out here? How long would the proceeds from the sale of the family home allow her to live without a real job? The money would be substantial, at least four times what this island cottage would cost to purchase, but it wouldn't last forever. To many people she'd known, it would be paradise—nothing to do but read, watch movies, and gaze at one of the most beautiful views imaginable. But even heaven could become hell if you were a prisoner there.

The questions haunted her, but not as much as they might have. The tattoo on her right arm would turn cold as ice and she would cover it with her left hand and be suffused with that sense of peace for which she'd yearned her entire life. It soothed her, made the questions withdraw into the recesses of her mind. In those moments, her doubts and regrets seemed small and unimportant. When the gulls landed on the railing of her deck or came too close and she had to chase them off, even fight them off, even kill them when it came to that . . . she found solace in the infinite ocean inked on her arm.

Four days into her exile, Jenny stood on the deck again in a thick blue sweater she'd owned for years, the sleeves pushed up, her hair tied back in a ponytail. Coffee steamed from the same mug she'd used the previous three days and she cupped her hands around it, enjoying the warmth on that chilly morning. She glanced warily at the sky, watching for the gulls. By now she was familiar with their patterns, the way they would begin to diverge from their natural flight, circling closer and closer until they descended. She had fifteen or twenty minutes to enjoy the deck and the breeze, so she took a deep breath, sipped her coffee, and reminded herself how many people would trade anything to wake to this view every day.

The triple spiral on her arm sent the chill down to her bones and she smiled. Somehow that icy cold made the rest of her warmer.

Her view through the pines had a golden, early-morning glow. She'd walked down to the water on her first two days here, but yesterday she had not ventured out. It wasn't worth the trouble to bring the baseball bat to deal with the gulls, and the crabs had proliferated between the first and second days. Several sharks had begun to patrol the end of her creaky little dock, and though she knew they could not come after her, still it gave her a shudder to see them gathering like that.

Jenny breathed in the aroma of her coffee, let it fill her head a moment before she took another sip. Gulls circled out over the dock, but there were more of them now, and several looped nearer to the house.

Another sip of coffee. Another pulse of ice from the ink on her arm.

She pressed her eyes closed and inhaled the smell of the ocean. When she opened them, she noticed something moving down by the dock. The rocks and sand seemed to be shifting, but it was too far away to see in detail. Jenny placed her coffee mug on the railing and slid her phone out of the band of her sweatpants, opened the camera function, and zoomed the picture.

The tiniest of sounds escaped her lips. Her hand shook and she almost dropped the phone, but she managed to steady her right arm—left hand over that tattoo, calming her.

The rocks and sand were moving, all right. Shifting and scuttling, covered with crabs large and small. Even horseshoe crabs. There were a few lobsters, dying on the rocks. A small octopus slithered across the sand toward the path, moving almost without moving, as if it glided in her direction by will alone. Down at the water's edge, fish flopped in the surf like they had tried to come ashore.

Staring through the zoomed camera image, breath caught in her throat, Jenny scanned the path and the water's edge again, but something at the upper edge of the image drew her attention and she tilted the camera up to see pale hands gripping the weathered boards, and then a dead woman hauled herself up onto the dock.

Jenny cried out. Dropped the phone. Heard it crack but reached for it anyway. Bumped it with her fingers so it skittered out of her reach and she had to follow it and pick it up, opening the camera again. Zooming again.

The woman on the dock wasn't alone. A bald man in sodden, salt-bleached tatters crawled and rolled in the surf, managed to get onto his knees, and then stood. He turned and looked through the opening in the pines, straight up at Jenny's house. Or he would have, if he'd had eyes. At this distance, even with the zoom on the phone, it was hard to tell, but they looked like nothing but black pits to her.

Out in the water, something moved. Not a shark fin this time. The top of a head, another man, walking toward shore, his white hair and beard tangled with seaweed.

Three so far, moving in like the crabs. Moving in like the gulls. People who'd been called by the sea and whose lives had ended in its depths, one way or another. Pale things, drawn back by an allure they'd never understood while alive.

Strangely calm, Jenny placed her cracked phone on the railing beside her coffee mug. She closed her eyes, breathing deeply. She traced her fingers over the triple-spiral tattoo, that infinite wave, then clamped her hand down over it. The ink turned so cold it felt like teeth biting deep.

◄◊►

Tears welled in her eyes as that familiar floating calm lifted her and she took several breaths. If only she could have kept her eyes closed and floated in that peace forever.

Instead, she opened them. The gulls had begun to circle closer. The blanket of crabs scuttled up the path between the pines. The small octopus would be down there, gliding along with them, although she couldn't make it out.

The people, though . . . she didn't need the camera zoom to see those figures stumbling in the shadows of the pines.

She wanted to give herself over to the ink. To the infinite sea. But she had been a fool to think that she could stay in one place and not have the lure intensify.

Jenny turned in a slow circle, looking past the pine trees and her new house, imagining what lay beyond it all, trying to think of someplace, anyplace, she might run. A flutter of wings made her spin around and she stared at the single gull that alighted on the railing between her coffee mug and her cracked phone. It stared at her, black eyes yearning.

She left the gull there on the deck, left her coffee and her phone and went inside, drawing the sliding glass door closed behind her. The house breathed, quiet except for the crackling in the fireplace. The wood smoke gave the whole place the scent of autumn, reminding her of better days.

The metal screen curtain on the fireplace slid back easily. Jenny took the little iron ash shovel that hung with the tongs and poker, and she rested it on top of the burning logs. Crouched there, she waited while the iron grew hot, waited as her knees began to ache. When the first gull hit the slider, she didn't flinch. It happened many times a day and she'd learned to ignore the sound. Her gaze shifted to her left forearm. Her sweater sleeve had slid down to cover the tattoo there and she slid it back up so that she could look at her father's name and wonder how it had come to this. Had he been searching for the talisman or had he brought it up from the sea bottom with his net or a hook? Had he cut open a fish and found it inside?

It didn't matter now, but still Jenny wondered.

The little hairs on her arm stood up and she shivered. Despite her nearness to the fire, or perhaps because of it, the ink on her right forearm felt icier than ever. The cold seemed almost to cut her, but she didn't look at that triple spiral now, refused to glance at that symbol of the infinite sea despite the yearning in her.

Long minutes passed.

Another thump against the glass. Something scratched against it but she didn't look. Jenny told herself it was just a gull, or maybe the first of the crabs to arrive.

She took the iron shovel from the fire with her left hand, stretched out her right and placed the flame-heated metal against the spiral tattoo. Hissing through her teeth, shuddering, she squeezed her eyes shut and kept the metal pressed there, as tightly as she could. The smell of searing flesh nearly made her retch and she went down on both knees, weeping silently as she fought the urge to take the shovel away.

At last she slumped to her side and let it fall from her hand. Breathing fast, almost hyperventilating, Jenny forced herself to look at the ruined skin. The tattoo had been cracked and blistered and reddened, but the ink showed through.

The cool solace of the sea slid up her arm, soothing the burn.

Jenny sat up and reached her left hand into the fireplace. She screamed as she grabbed the top log, cried out in agony as she dragged it out and pressed it to the spiral tattoo. Body rigid, she held it until her vision went dark and she slumped again to the floor.

The heat on her face brought her around. Her eyelids fluttered and she found herself staring at the still-burning log, bright embers glowing in the wood. It had landed on the tile between her body and the fireplace, and she knew the whole house could have gone up in flames. The idea did not terrify her the way it should have.

Her left hand sang with pain. Her right forearm screamed with it. Awkwardly, she shifted into a sitting position, cradling that left hand in her lap and the right arm across her knee. Full of dread, she braced herself to look down at the tattoo she'd worked so hard to destroy.

Even before she saw the wreckage there, saw the hideous, blackened, oozing flesh that would bear the scars of this day forever, she shuddered with relief. That peace she'd found had left her. The symbol had been burned away. No cool solace touched her skin.

Slumping, crying softly out of pain and gratitude, she found herself staring at the other tattoo. The one on the inside of her left arm. The one with her father's name and the dates of his birth and death.

A terrible thought occurred to her.

The most terrible thought.

"No," she whispered, launching shakily to her feet. "Oh, no."

In agony from her burns, Jenny stumbled to the sliding glass door. With her good hand she dragged it open, then ran out onto the deck and down the stairs, ignoring her cracked phone and her coffee mug, noticing only that the gulls were gone.

"No," she whispered as she turned at the bottom of the steps and ran down along the path between the pines.

If only she'd waited.

Heart thundering, left hand still cradled against her, she picked up speed, stumbled and nearly fell but managed to catch herself as she ran in the shadows of those trees. There were still crabs there, dozens of them, but they scurried away from her as she ran past them, disturbed by her presence. Searching for some comfort she could no longer provide.

At the dock, she paused a moment, staring out at the waves. Her burns throbbed, the pain only growing, and she felt as if they were still on fire.

Jenny strode out onto the dock, scanning the water for any sign.

"Daddy?" she called, quietly at first. Then again, louder, almost screaming.

She fell to her knees on the warped and weathered boards and stared out at the open sea.

It gave her no peace.

# THE TRYAL ATTRACT

## TERRY DOWLING

"A skull watches everyone in the room."

—Anonymous

The sole condition Will Stevens set for letting me spend the night in the room with the skull was telling him everything it said.

My elderly neighbour was insistent about that. "Just be honest with me, Dave. I've lived with this for nearly three-quarters of my life. I need it put to rest."

"I swear it. I need this put to rest too."

Will stood in the doorway, a tall, weathered figure with a narrow face, pale eyes, strands of white hair combed in close against his own skull, wearing tan slacks, a cardigan over a white shirt. He was holding Solly, his big Persian cat, stroking it as he watched me settle in. "Well, I hope you're comfortable," he said. "I had Maggie set it up when she was here. My daughter comes by every day. Stays over on weekends when she can. She'd like closure about this too."

"It looks great."

A collapsible bed had been set up along the eastern wall of the small square tower room, with a side table with lamp, a digital clock, a decanter of water and a glass, a torch in case one was needed by a stranger in a strange house, even eye-shades since there were no curtains at the windows this high up. And, quaintest touch of all, there was a chamber pot.

"You know where the toilet is, Dave, but it's a bit of a hike if you're half asleep. You might prefer this."

"Thanks, Will."

"And, Dave, about the skull. I've slept here with it many times, all the good it did. Just don't let it upset you. The whispering, I mean. I'll believe whatever you tell me."

"I'll log it all in the notebook like I promised."

"Thanks. And don't mind if Solly joins you in the night. He sleeps wherever he wants. Goodnight."

"Goodnight."

And that was it. Will had closed the door and headed for the staircase at the end of the landing that opened into both the modest square tower and the old Victorian mansion's upper floor. I heard the stairlift whirring as it took him to his own digs at ground level.

I changed for bed as if I were in my own bedroom seven doors further along Abelard Street, eased between the covers as if it were my own bed, then checked the time.

It was 10:07 p.m. Same street. Pretty much the same night sounds through the half-open windows on all four sides: the same chirruping of insects; the occasional tock-tock of a frog in the front-yard pond; the sound of late traffic on Ryde Road; a plane on late approach to the airport on the other side of the city, way across these late-spring suburbs.

The rush of wind in the trees was closer, of course, this high up amid their foliage. But it was a good sound, and not too loud. I'd still be able to hear the skull, Will had assured me. There'd be no mistaking it.

Which both fascinated and troubled me.

To think. A night with a whispering skull!

⤙⚬⤐

There can be distinct layers of unreality in how one thing leads to another. Six nights before, someone had torched a car parked on the southern side of Abelard where our quiet street bordered the playing fields of one of Sydney's most exclusive boys' schools, probably as part of an insurance scam or some last-recourse act of evidence removal. Local residents, myself included, had simply assumed that the white sedan parked across from Number 7 for the past week had belonged either to a neighbour or someone visiting.

But around 2:30 that Tuesday morning, a series of muffled explosions had woken most of the nearby residents, who looked out their windows to see the blazing vehicle, promptly made their separate calls to the fire brigade, then joined other neighbours standing about at safe distances like kids watching a bonfire. The fire engine arrived, a hose was deployed, the fire quickly extinguished. The police were soon there as well, asking their questions. Those not engaged in telling what little they knew continued chatting.

An elderly man on a walking stick moved in next to me, and I recognised him as the widower from 1A at the far end of the street, the "old guy from the big house," as he was often called in front-fence conversations.

"Not something we get very often," he said.

"Not around here," I replied. "I'm Dave. Dave Aspen."

"Good to meet you, Dave. I'm Will. Will Stevens. From 1A down there. You lived here long?"

"Forty-two years. A local boy. Loved your house as a kid, with that tower at the front. Called it the Castle."

"I can imagine."

"I'll never forget there was a skull perched on a cupboard or bookcase in the top tower room. Dark-looking thing, more like a mask. I even borrowed my dad's binoculars for a closer look. Definitely a human skull. Were you there then?"

Will was watching the firemen working at the car. "I was. Not my idea to put it up there, but yeah."

"Well, that bloody skull's been with me ever since. Still dream about it, if you can believe that."

Now he turned to face me. "You do?"

"Once, maybe twice a year at least."

"Well now." Which was the appropriate step-away, leave-it-be point. But old Will kept at it. "What happens in these dreams?"

"Different every time. But when it turns up it talks. Tries to tell me something."

"What does it say?" Will's tone had taken on a distinct edge.

"Can't make it out. It whispers something. But it's important, you know?"

"How do you know that, Dave? That it's important."

"Just how it is. But all these years, I never quite catch what it's saying. Bloody frustrating really. You think we would've reached an understanding."

"Dave, we've been neighbours all this time. Pity we didn't get to talk earlier. That skull you remember. It's still there. Still in the tower, but one floor down now, out of view."

"Hey, I'd love to see it."

"I'd really like you to. Maybe tomorrow, if you have the time. Drop by in the afternoon. You see, it's like you say. It whispers in the night sometimes."

There was the torched car still smoking in the early hours. Police standing about. The fire crew packing up, murmuring to each other in low voices. An unexpected meeting with a neighbour. And now an odd tingling down my spine. And another at Will's next words.

"Who knows? Maybe it's been talking to you all along."

⬥

Late spring in Sydney so often means November afternoons with a riot of sunlit jacaranda blooms above the rooftops, rich mauve against brooding storm-clouds as the ragged end of winter settles into its summer run.

That's how it was when I headed along to 1A at 12:55. I'd spent the morning finishing off the plans for the Quinn-Elliot shopping mall extensions and had sent scans through to Marta and Eric at our architectural office in Brisbane. This would be my reward.

Will answered the front door on my second knock, looking more his seventy-seven years in daylight, more like any other elderly person caught outside their comfort zone but putting their best face on it.

"We'll have a cuppa when we're done upstairs, if that's okay," he said, and turned to the Stairmaster, whose track ran up the wall of the long wooden staircase leading to the upper floor. "You go up first, Dave. Make a U-turn at the top."

I grabbed the banister rail and made my ascent, heard him whirring up behind.

⬥

The skull sat on a thin, dark blue cushion atop a waist-high mahogany stand. True to Will's word about it being "out of view," it was now set in the north-west corner between the tall, all-points windows, facing me as I entered the modest tower room.

"So no impressionable school kids can see," Will said good-naturedly.

I smiled. "It's very discoloured. That honey-amber sheen."

"One of its owners, possibly whoever first found it, lacquered it, coated it with vegetable gums and animal fats, something like that. That's probably what helped preserve it so well. We've been told that it's older than it looks."

"Is that silver on the sides?" For that's what it looked like, added to the zygomatic arches, the nasal bone, and at two places on the mandible.

"Interesting, eh? We keep it polished as best we can, but that's the extent of the maintenance. Makes it seem important, yes? A cherished ancestor or something. Despite trying to keep a low profile, quite a few museums want it. We get letters all the time. But we won't let it out of our sight."

"Is there a backstory? Is it from our colonial past? Brought from overseas?"

"That's the trouble, Dave. Little is known, though maybe you can help us there. It's definitely from a male. Its official name is the Farday Skull, after Lucas Farday, the only owner to record any sort of provenance for it in 1907. As late as that."

"But he wasn't the first owner?" I realised my gaffe. "First post-mortem owner?"

"Two previous owners are mentioned—not counting that original one." He smiled, though in a distracted way, as if considering facts he was leaving out to give the shortest account possible. "But nothing can be verified. Lucas Farday sold it or gave it to my grandfather in 1919. Farday was a bit of a showman, so it came with the usual clutch of rumours you get when skulls are kept as curios, especially those in curiosity cabinets and tent-shows."

"What kind of rumours?"

"That it screams, for instance. Or utters a prophecy every full moon. That it can only be heard by those about to die. Collectors and spruikers encourage such stories."

"You've actually heard it whispering, you said."

"Many times. So has Maggie. So did my late wife. We've just never been able to make out what it's saying. It's always just out of hearing."

"Can it be a sea-shell effect, Will? You know, put one of its openings to your ear, you hear the ocean?"

Will chuckled again. "It's funny how many people never want to put a skull to their ear to find out. But yes, there is the ocean effect, though a skull has surprisingly few openings where you can hear it. But the whisper is much more than white noise, Dave. It can be heard from where we're standing now."

I wanted to ask if there were recordings, or if it had been tested scientifically with appropriate instruments, but I was now being offered the chance to participate in something of a clinical assessment myself. I'd let that be enough on such short acquaintance.

"It's complete, I notice. The lower jaw is wired on?"

"Glued on, actually. So it can't bite."

"Excuse me?"

Will chuckled. "Another urban myth you get all the time when the lower jaw is still attached. Biting skull stories. This was glued on well before Farday parted with it. Perhaps an earlier owner thought it might stop it sounding. You have to love these provenance junkies. They add whatever they like."

"Looks to be from a natural death?"

"Excuse me?"

"No trepanning holes. No autopsy line where the top of the skull's been removed."

"You have a sharp eye. But I guess that's a bit heartening, really. You can pick it up if you want."

"May I?"

"You need to be sure. No faking going on."

"Oh, right. I see."

I crossed to the stand and—with only a moment's hesitation—lifted the ale-coloured orb, rotated it slowly in my hands. I'd never touched, let alone held, a human skull before—this ultimate palace, library, vital stronghold of another being, once a complete entity, someone who had left this "container" behind when he'd vanished in death. It was heavier than I expected, maybe three pounds total, though I allowed that the silver counted for something. Apart from the lacquering and silverwork, it was very clean, divorcing it even more from the organic realities it had once been part of. It was more like a piece of décor or a film prop—an emblem of death rather than an actual artefact from it.

I turned it over and examined the spinal hole in the base. "This opening—?"

"The foramen magnum," Will said. "Where the spinal cord entered the cranial vault. You get the echo chamber effect most there. But, like I said, Dave—it's *not* an ocean effect. The whisper will come to *you* across the room. And you're free to check the skull again whenever you like if you decide to help us. We know you'll be careful."

"So how do we do this? What do you propose?"

"You'll have family commitments, I'm sure. But this is a chance we can't afford to let pass. I was going to suggest you sleep over each Sunday night for as long as you can manage. Till you hear it."

"Or dream about it again."

"Till something happens. Will you do it?"

⤙⤏

At 10:34, I was starting to grow sleepy.

Being this high up certainly made it easier to settle. A basement or a more closed-in space would have added a pressing, claustrophobic feel, but this makeshift tower bedroom had an airy, open quality— made the whole thing bearable somehow.

The only thing I'd done before slipping between the covers was turn the pedestal so the skull was side-on, not facing me with its empty eye sockets. Positioned in left profile, it actually looked like it was keeping watch, just as it had in my boyhood years when it gazed down on the street below.

The inevitable thoughts came, of course, but grew less urgent with familiarity.

*Who were you?*

*Who added the silver and why?*

*What was your death like to cause such embellishment, if the adornment were even remotely part of the death itself?*

No ordinary skull, surely. Then again, there were ultimately no ordinary deaths. No ordinary skulls. Every one was unique.

The long curtains lifted and fell, breathing in the night.

What would it be like when it whispered, I wondered, realizing that I truly did expect it to happen, expected something from those calm inner chambers, trusted that they would draw something in, produce the sighs and murmurs that supported its reputation. The occipital hole was blocked by the cushion now, though from what Will had said that made no difference.

If not tonight then in time. For Will and his daughter Maggie it had just been the whispering. For me it had been a string of dreams over nearly forty years in which a skull—this skull quite likely!—had tried to tell me something. Somehow it meant everything.

-‹o›-

I woke several times, first at 12:02 when Solly jumped off the bed (I hadn't even known he'd paid a visit), then again at 12:55 and at 1:23 for reasons I couldn't quite fathom.

Maybe it was Solly fussing about again, chasing insects in the balmy night, though I'd heard nothing. Each time, I'd check the green numerals of the clock, then lay considering the different sound and spatial signatures of the house, tracking the obvious things—how everything felt larger, higher, older, dustier, redolent of years of waxing and polishing—trying to fathom others far more elusive, far harder to put into words.

Each time I listened for the skull sounding, wondering if it might have done so just now, enough to waken me, but that I had missed what it had to say.

It didn't happen like that. Rather it came on a dream. At 2:18, I was startled awake by the terrifying certainty that the skull was looming over me, poised there with jaws hideously agape and about to bite. It took a while to free myself from that terrible image, but finally I did manage to sleep again.

There was no such image when I woke a short time later, lathered in sweat, heart pounding, just the familiar night sounds through the partly open windows. But there was the chilling sense that it *had* been there, that any breathing, any whispering, that now came would be laden with suppressed screams, thwarted spite, ancient mischief.

The jaws are glued shut, I told myself as the panic ebbed. No possibility of biting. Or screaming. Or whispering, for that matter. It's the mind playing tricks.

But there! Did I imagine it? I kept absolutely still, tried to calm my heart.

Like escaping gas? The hiss of a snake?

A sibilance.

There was. There was. From across the room. I didn't dare switch on the light lest it stop.

A far rush of surf up an impossible shore.

". . . sssssssssssssssssssssssssssssss . . ."

It came and fell away, exactly like the sea.

". . . sssssssshhhhhhhhhhhhhhhhh . . ."

The curtains lifted and settled. Leaves stirred in the night. The sibilance grew stronger.

"Thisssssssssssss . . ."

I had the word, as easily as that. *This.*

". . . chansssssssssss . . ."

*Chance.*

". . . oursssssssssss . . ."

*Ours.*

I'd never forget this moment. Such words. I remembered to grab my notebook and pen from the side-stand, made myself write them down.

". . . adlarssssssssss . . ."

What it sounded like.

But no. No.

*At last!*

*This chance ours at last.*

Then grasped what I'd heard.

Not "Our chance at last" but "This chance ours at last." The odd syntax. The contrived quaintness of it.

It wanted the *s*'s for dramatic effect. No, *needed* them most likely, needed them to slide along, exactly like the sea running up the strand. Economies of delivery. Working with what it had.

"I'm listening." It sounded silly to say it, melodramatic, and part of me resolved to check for wires, a relay or receiver when this was done, some kind of set-up.

Better yet, do it now, I told myself. *While* it's sounding.

I pushed back the covers, swung my feet to the floor, waited for the next word to begin. I'd move on the next word.

It came with the same rush of ocean on sand.

". . . essssss-oarrrr . . ." The ocean slid away.

"What's that?" I said, and moved the short distance to the skull, leant over it. "I don't understand."

". . . essssss-oarrrr . . ." it said again, not even a foot from me, the force of it adding the sense of consonants it could not manage. And this time I was able to lay two fingers atop the cranium before it stopped sounding, felt a deep thrumming as it ebbed, like a real wave sliding back.

And understood.

*Restore.*

Spoke it, fingers still carefully in place. "Restore?"

". . . eeeessssssssssssssss . . ."

Which had to be "Yes." And with the thrumming again, though quickly fading.

"Restore you where?" I asked, but knew the answer. "The room upstairs? Where you once were! Why up there?"

But nothing. Nothing now.

Just the night at the windows. The troubling image of those jaws spread wide, ready to bite.

—◦—

Over breakfast, I asked if I could come back that night, not wait the whole week. Will was equally keen now he knew the skull had spoken.

What surprised him most was my request that we move both bed and skull to the floor above.

"You think that's what 'restore' means?"

"Can't say. But it used to be in the room above the one I'm in. Why was it brought down?"

"No idea. Mum or Dad would have done that, probably when my grandparents passed. This has been the family home for five generations."

"Then your grandparents had it facing out like that. The way I saw it as a kid."

"Can't be sure. Why do you ask?"

"The dream before I woke. The skull was angry, Will. Fiercely angry. It *wanted* to bite."

"You were open to suggestion, Dave. That talk about skull stories—"

"Just saying how it felt. Maybe they had it facing out for a reason. Otherwise why do that?"

"Frighten the local kids."

I had to smile. "But it draws too much attention."

"What do you want to do?"

"Put it back where it was. One floor up, right window facing out. Same angle, same height. I'll carry the bed up now."

"Maggie will be here around ten. You draw a quick sketch of how *you* remember it. We'll do the rest."

-◦-

My darling Marta was good about it on the phone, asking a dozen questions about my new role as ghost-breaker for the neighbours and making me promise to keep her up to date on what developed. She admitted that she was being pressured to stay on as on-site consultant for the Quinn-Elliot mall project anyway.

After dinner, I locked the house and wandered along to 1A, but stood for a moment at the front gate admiring the modest but impressive two-storey Victorian mansion that had always been such a part of my life. In the last golden light of evening, I traced the line of the tower up from the front door to the room at the very top, below the railing and flagpole. There at the uppermost left window the skull sat in its old spot, just as I'd seen it all those years ago.

Right height, right angle now. Fiercely grinning as all complete skulls did. And facing northwest, I realized for the first time, given how Abelard Street was aligned.

Northwest. Such a simple thing to realize. Never watching me at all, really, rather scanning the horizon. The trees would have been smaller then, the view less obstructed.

*It's all about having a better view!*

As I reached to unlatch the gate, I swung my gaze from the top floor down past the windows of the room I'd occupied the night before. There was something in the left-hand pane, I was certain, a smudge pressed to the glass like a thumb-print, indistinct but peering out. There may not have been eyes, but I'd been so taken with the skull that I easily imagined them.

I did an immediate double take, but there was nothing.

Just eye trickery then. Though another thought came. *Ancient mischief.*

After a final glance at the trickster skull looking down—no, *out*, northwest!—I went in to resume my vigil.

◄○►

The uppermost tower room was identical to the one below it, but considerably less by way of a bedroom. My bed was there, the side table and lamp, all my things from the night before, even the chamber pot, but this room was still a storage space. Several cupboards and boxes had been pushed to the side, and the chamber needed a more thorough dusting than time had allowed.

The skull was perched at chest height on the edge of a narrow bookcase in the north-western corner, angled so it peered out the right-hand window just as depicted in my drawing. Maggie had done a great job.

Will and I spent a pleasant two hours at the spacious kitchen table enjoying the delicious casserole Maggie had left for us in the slow cooker and sharing a bottle of his vintage merlot. We talked about everything from his family's extensive property holdings to his collection of limited editions of Poe and Edgar Rice Burroughs, anything but the skull waiting for me upstairs. We agreed that this was best, though it remained the unseen guest in the room.

I went up to bed at ten o'clock, making my way up into the tower wondering what new trials the night would bring, an odd way to think about it—burdens, trials—but that's how it was. I read for a while, but soon fell into sleep so easily that I would later wonder if the skull played any part in that as well.

I was sure that it would wake me when the time was right.

Again it came on a dream—this time of a wild storm at sea, of waves crashing against a reef, great swells lifting and falling over hard stone ridges, beating themselves into vast swathes of whitewater and foam.

Lots of *s*'s to make it easier, I told myself in the dream, self-aware as dreamers sometimes are.

At least there was no skull with jaws agape this time, just these ocean swells being torn into whitewater.

"Trial!" the word came, strikingly clear, known as much as heard.

No *s*'s now, I told myself. The skull uses dreams for the words it cannot say!

"Trial!" it came again, above the wind-lashed breakwater of the reef.

I woke with a start, instantly aware that Solly had paid another visit and now sat perched upon my chest.

No, no, way too light for Solly!

I reached for the side light, pressed the switch, saw with a shock that the skull sat there, eye cavities staring, teeth grinning fiercely, rising and falling with every rapid breath.

I would've leapt up, but terror locked me in place, kept me there long enough for the silver glinting against lacquered bone to make me think: Fragile and Protect!

*Will is doing this!* I immediately thought. *Or Maggie. How else could it move?*

Then the sea came from inside the skull, rushing as it had the previous night.

". . . sssssssssssssssss . . ."

With words carried along, nothing as hard to say as "trial."

". . . see-venssss-eyessss . . . see-venssss-eyessss . . ."

It couldn't say "Will." Like "trial," that name was too much.

*Stevens lies!*

Could it be?

And more.

". . . or-essssss . . . or-esssss . . . or-esssss . . ."

The silver on the cheekbones glinted. The rounded hollows where eyes once sat stared, fully lit. I could see the small holes at the back where the nerves and blood vessels had gone in, was more aware than ever that this was the setting for the jewel of the person it had once carried, someone's only life.

Northwest, of course! I spoke it aloud. "Northwest!"

". . . sssssssssssssssss!"

Such urgent affirmation, harsh with emotion. And more.

". . . essssss-oar! . . . essssss-oar!"

Northwest. Restore.

"Trial. Northwest. Restore."

The inner ocean rushed up the shore one last time.

". . . sssssssssssssssss!"

Such determination, such relief.

I instinctively looked to where the skull had been atop its bookcase facing northwest. There were *two* smudges there now, *two* thumb-print faces, one pressed to the left-hand window pane, one to the right. Not one, *two*!

I had not cried out when I'd found the skull on my chest, but now a frantic yelling filled the house. It truly took moments to realize that I was the one yelling, mine the only skull screaming!

◄◦►

When Will hurried in and learned what the skull had said, he accepted my accusations with "Please, Dave. We'll talk about all this in the morning," and urged me to try and settle again.

I was more surprised than relieved that I could do so. There were no more communications, no further dream messages or nightmares, though I tossed and turned for the rest of the night and came down to breakfast feeling leaden and headachy, as if with a serious hangover.

At least I didn't need to rush home and do a Google search—Will was immediately forthcoming with the real facts about the skull—though I resolved that I would do a net search later, do my best to verify everything away from 1A when this was done.

Will said very little until he'd served us a cooked breakfast and freshly brewed coffee in the kitchen. "I'm so sorry, Dave," he said, taking his place at the table. "There were things we needed you to confirm without prior knowledge before we went any further. You have to understand."

"You said you never knew what the skull was saying."

"We never have. It's the back-story material we misled you about."

"Misled. Much better than lied." I was feeling terrible from lack of sleep, the events of the previous night. "What does 'trial' mean?"

"It's the *Tryal*. Spelt T-R-Y-A-L or T-R-Y-A-L-L, sometimes even the way we spell it now. Australia's first recorded shipwreck. An East Indiaman taking the new Brouwer route to the East Indies. Back in May 1622, she strayed off course on her way to Batavia—Jakarta in Indonesia. Struck what we now call the Tryal Rocks near the Montebello Islands."

"Where are they?"

Will topped up my coffee cup. "Off Barrow Island, close by Exmouth and Dampier on the coast of Western Australia. It's said Captain Brooke abandoned ship prematurely, cast off in a half-full skiff with the silver they were carrying for trade. He reached safety, lived to be absolved of blame and command another ship. But more than half the crew were left to drown. Think of it, Dave. The ship's only surviving longboat was already overcrowded and wallowing. Brooke and the skiff were nowhere to be seen. He reached Jakarta, reported the *Tryal* breaking up four hours after impact.

Accounts from those in the longboat said this didn't happen till the following morning. He lied about what happened."

"You've lied about what happened! And not just about Farday being a dealer and selling it on. Was Lucas Farday the original owner? Is this his skull?"

"We can't know for certain. He may have gone down with the *Tryal*. But he may have clung to wreckage, made it to the Montebello group of islands. They're barren, hardly anything there, and it has to be another thirty miles at least to the coast. But the currents are strong. There's a good chance that his body was washed ashore and found. Identified later from jewelry, remains of clothing. The skull came into our family, however that happened. You have to understand. We *wanted* to believe."

"So what *do* you know about the skull?"

"It's what's called an attract. An object that draws things to it. There's usually one at the site of any haunting: a chair, a book, a hairbrush, the house itself."

"I mean genetically."

"My grandfather called it the Farday Skull. Told us it belonged to our ancestor from the *Tryal*, that he was lost in the wreck on the Tryal Rocks. But, living or dead, he may have reached shore. He may have been the first Englishman to set foot in Australia."

"Will, what did DNA tests show? You must have had it done."

"Negative for a direct link from one. Inconclusive from another. But if it's an attract, it can protect itself. Manage deflection."

"You can't believe that."

Will set down his cup. "Those dreams you've had."

"A way of communicating—"

"But of warning too, yes? Even defending?"

*Biting!* I thought, but kept that to myself. "I still hear wishful thinking."

"You may be right. But, Dave, it *came* to us. *Stayed* with us. In *our* family. Called to you. Why?"

"You think I might be a relation too?"

"Dave, I have to ask. Is there anything?"

"Not much. A great-great-great uncle was a convict on a prison hulk, the *Phoenix*, moored in Lavender Bay in the early 1800s. That's about it. Though at some point there would have been long sea voyages to Australia before it.

Some contact with Brooke's or Farday's descendants may have been possible. We can never know."

"We can't," my elderly neighbour agreed. "So what do we do?"

"Those shadows at the windows. Something's happening, Will. So no more lies."

"No point. It's told you everything *we* were withholding. The Tryal Rocks are northwest of here, on the other side of the continent."

"And it must be furious about that. You've been thwarting it. You cost it years."

"Dave, it never spoke to us. How were *we* to know? What do you say? One more night?"

"One more night."

◄◦►

I knew better than to make any special arrangements. The skull would do whatever it needed, whatever it could manage to do, so I left it atop its bookcase, angled out, watching the night, the far distances, as it once had for so many years.

I still felt wretched from the previous night's events, and so, settling into welcome sleep, I was able to allow that nothing else would happen, that everything had been clarified.

I was wrong, of course, but, feeling headachy and strange, there was resignation rather than panic when I became aware that the skull was in bed with me, clutched in my arms beneath the covers, angled so its sealed teeth were pressed hard against my throat.

I did not scream, did not yell. Not this time. There was even a touch of gallows humour about the whole thing.

"Do your worst," I said, accepting other needs, this other reality, all the while asking myself, what now? What can possibly remain to be done?

◄◦►

I barely remembered the charter flights across the continent to Broome, then down to Dampier. There were the vaguest recollections of a motel room at Cable Beach and another at the Mermaid Hotel, but little else. Finally, on a mild Monday afternoon, after a long-haul helicopter charter out across the Montebello group, we hovered above that roiling point of shipwreck and heartbreak, betrayal and despair, and those deadly rocks broke the surface forty metres below our skids.

It wasn't till then that I came to myself, became aware that I was strapped in and that a charter crewman was reaching over to haul the cabin door back, became aware of Will beside me, first pulling back his headset then mine before handing over the skull and urging me on.

"It's time, Dave. It's time."

I took the thing, hardly knowing what I'd been given at first. But as I prepared to throw it down to the wet rocks that came and went amid the heaving whitewater below, I found I could speak of it at last.

"Brooke's skull, not Farday's. Captain Brooke's, you hear? Farday's ghost borrowed it, possessed it, treasured it, anything so he could come home."

Will had known to lean in close. "You're sure?" he called above the roar of the rotors and the ocean.

"Two ghosts fighting over a single skull."

Then I let it go, felt my twin guests leave me, slip away, saw the skull's jaws snap wide in a scream or a shout, what it looked like, though how could we ever know? But for me it was to bite *something* so they were locked together, fiercely and forever, going to whatever home they could find for themselves in that harsh and unforgiving sea.

# THE WHALERS SONG

## RAY CLULEY

Sebjørn squinted against the pale light of the midnight sun. The sky was cloudless. There was no wind. The sea was still and vacant, except for where it frothed against the hull of the *Höðr*, splitting around them into a wide V of wake. It was so quiet that Sebjørn had become aware of the throbbing noise of the boat's engine, a sound so familiar that he was usually as ignorant of it as he was the pump-thump of his own heartbeat. The regularity of his breathing.

At the bow, Aaron leaned on the barrel of the harpoon cannon. He, too, searched the sea. He wore binoculars around his neck and occasionally he used them, but only briefly.

In the crow's nest, Sigved used his more frequently. He wore his bright orange waterproof, as if he'd seen rain the others had yet to notice. He wore the hood up, cords pulled so tight that it puckered around his face, and he held the binoculars at what little gap remained.

Brage and Nils—one port, one starboard—also looked to the water. Searching, like the others, for a plume of expelled spray. The run-off from an arching back. Maybe birds, sitting on the water, bobbing to eat krill.

There was nothing.

In the wheelhouse, Osvald held them steady. Grim-faced but fierce when others might be sullen. A suitable expression for a captain yet to catch his first whale of the season; of the thirty to forty they were set to catch this year, the crew of the *Höðr* had none.

Minke whales are the smallest of the baleen whales and can remain submerged for twenty minutes at a time. They barely breach when they come up for air, nor do they bring their flukes from the water when they dive. It makes them difficult to spot. For a species so apparently great in number—enough, at least, to be considered sustainable—they were proving to be frustratingly elusive this year.

Sebjørn checked his watch. Another day would soon be over. Another night. He clapped his gloved hands together a couple of times and rubbed them. Not because he was cold but because the gesture felt decisive. *Come on now*, he thought. *Show us something. Give us something to take home.*

Nils, standing close beside him, chose that moment to begin singing. Not a whaling song, but a traditional fishing song. His father, he'd said, had been a fisherman, but then every whaler was a fisherman in the winter.

The men on the *Höðr* knew the song.

Brage turned and smiled at Nils, smiled at Sebjørn, and added his deep voice to the chorus. Sebjørn mouthed the words as well, quietly at first but gaining enthusiasm with the others. Aaron, at the cannon, waved his arms to conduct an imagined orchestra and they sang of the rise and fall of the sea, of the catch and the haul, driven by a rhythm meant to ease hard work, though they had none.

A sudden whistle, brief and shrill, cut the song short. Sigved had the binoculars at his face but was holding them with only one hand; with the other he pointed.

There. A small cloud of spray. The mist of a blowhole, spouting. It settled quickly on such a windless day, drifting just enough to indicate a direction of movement.

Sebjørn offered Sigved a thumbs up. The man nodded, unclipping the radio from his belt and calling through to the captain, but Osvald was already steering the boat around. The men cheered as the vessel turned. This was it. At last, the thrill of the hunt.

There was another eruption of spray ahead and a dark shape emerged from the water before slipping back under.

There were two of them.

Aaron readied himself at the harpoon cannon. Brage took one of the rifles from the nearby rack. He wouldn't need it. The harpoon was grenade-tipped, designed to explode inside the whale's brain, and Aaron was a good shot.

The blast of the cannon shuddered through the deck. The *Höðr* was a small vessel and all of it trembled when the gunner fired. Sebjørn, resting against a rail, felt it thrumming as he watched nylon wire unravel behind the harpoon. Heard it hiss its sizzling echo to the sudden thunder that had launched it.

The whale turned and, with a final wave of fin, it rolled. Raised its side to the sky. Its pale underbelly.

Brage lowered the rifle.

"Eight meters," said Nils beside Sebjørn. Sebjørn nodded. Twenty-six, twenty-seven feet. Half the size of the *Höðr*. About average. But average was good. Small would have been good. Average was *very* good.

Sebjørn looked to the wheelhouse. Osvald, usually so serious, was smiling. Sebjørn was glad to see it.

A metallic whine from the winch signalled the men to their stations. The nylon cord yanked its slack out of the water, flinging seawater skyward as it pulled taut with the weight of their whale, and Sebjørn clapped his hands together.

"Let's get to work!"

◄◦►

The minke laid sprawled across the deck, a ragged pulp of meat and blubber where the harpoon had exploded close to the thorax. A good shot. Sebjørn inspected it briefly, nodded at Aaron, and with the others began to carve the animal into pieces.

They would strip several tonnes from the carcass, reducing it to a head and a tail with only bones in between. The tail had been nearly severed already in coming out of the sea, the winch pulling cord through flesh as the whale's own weight split skin and blubber and muscle down to the bone. The deck was awash with blood. The men were red to their elbows, rubber suits smeared about the chest and waist. Boots sliding in the mess that spread around them.

Sebjørn was in charge of the flensing. He carved blubber into thick strips, handing them to Nils to send below where Brage packed them in ice. Whale blubber was not like animal fat. It was not soft; cutting it demanded strength.

Sebjørn was still strong. He enjoyed the work. It was greasy, stinking work, and he was slick with fat and fluids, but it was men's work and he was happy.

Sigved and Aaron followed Sebjørn's progress. They drew their knives through meat and muscle, laying each thick chunk on the deck ready to go below. They all worked in focussed silence, save for the grunts and exhalations of their exertions. There were plenty of songs they could have used to accompany, even ease, their efforts, but by some unspoken agreement they worked without them. As if a song would make this routine when the catch was far too special: they would honour it with quiet efficiency. There was chorus enough, anyway, from the birds that had appeared from nowhere, circling and diving and crying their impatience, calling at each other in battle over whatever scraps made it to the sea.

The heavy bulk before the men, thick under their hands and firm against their bodies, uncurled piece by piece until the body was an open wet cavity, red and white and steaming in the cold air. The grey-black whale, skin shining like an oil-slick, was swiftly becoming a length of bones. These would be thrown back to the sea; today's whaling was concerned only with the blubber and the meat beneath. The blubber would be rendered down to oil. The meat would be eaten.

Sebjørn cut away one of the fins, let it drop to the deck, and kicked it overboard. The sea had fed the whale, the whale would feed the sea. He cut into the sagging swell of whale belly and reached inside, pushing bones aside to locate the stomach. Cut it loose. He hefted it overboard like a shot-put, startling the birds with its heavy splash. For a moment it rose again, buoyant, but it wouldn't float for long. The birds were already pulling it to pieces, screeching their excitement, fighting. Tossing their heads back to swallow whatever chunks they managed to scavenge while smaller scraps sank for the fishes.

Behind Sebjørn, somebody swore. Somebody yelled. He turned to see Sigved throwing a punch at Nils, who sprawled across the whale carcass. Nils lashed out in return. Sigved turned the blow aside with an open hand but hissed in pain. Sebjørn yelled at both of them. One held the curved blade of a flensing knife, the other a metal hook for dragging slabs of butchered meat, but he stepped between them and shoved them apart. He didn't ask what the fight had been about because it didn't matter. Men would always fight.

Sigved snatched up one of the hoses and washed blood from his palm. A smile gaped there, filling with more blood as he flexed his fingers.

"Get it bandaged," Sebjørn said.

Sigved gestured with a quick jab of his head to where the meat was piling up beside Nils. "He's clumsy," he said. "And he's slow."

Nils was new. He had worked a couple of other boats previously but there was some truth to what Sigved said, Sebjørn had to admit.

"If we don't find another whale for a while you can take it out on each other then."

Sigved twisted a bandage around his hand. He nodded.

Sebjørn looked at Nils. The man was working his jaw, probing his cheek for loose teeth. "Fine by me."

"There's at least one more out there," Aaron said. "I saw it."

"Good," said Sigved, "because I've got more meat hanging between my legs than we'll get off of this one."

Aaron laughed. Sebjørn too, after a moment. Nils slammed his hook into another steak and dragged it away.

The radio at Sebjørn's belt crackle-spat to life and Osvald told him that the next man to strike another would be thrown overboard. Sebjørn acknowledged the statement and showed the men his radio as if the captain's words were still coming from it. The captain of a vessel was its law. Sebjørn looked to the wheelhouse but Osvald had already put them out of mind.

The *Höðr* carried them further north.

—◇—

The men ate together in the cramped galley, bunched around a scarred table, hunched over their meals like hungry convicts. The room was warm and thick with the smell of whale meat fried in garlic and butter. The briny smell of drying clothes. The smell of hard work. And there was beer. They carried very little on board, but there was always something for celebrating the first catch. The men were loud with good humour. Laughing, shoving each other with boisterous banter. Drumming on the table. Around them, on the walls, on cupboard doors, were pages torn from magazines. Centrefolds. Celebrities in varying states of undress. The women had been renamed several times over. They had each been girlfriends, had each been wives. Many of them had been graffitied from boredom. Tattooed in pen, enhanced, made monstrous. Aaron, leaning in his chair, added a geyser gush to one of the ladies, swearing and shaking at the pen dying in his hand, but laughing with Brage's encouragement. Old men being boys. The captain always ate separately from the rest of the crew. It allowed them such freedoms.

Sebjørn shoved his plate aside as soon as his meal was done and grabbed for cigarettes that hadn't been in his shirt pocket for over a year. What he found there instead was the postcard he had replaced them with. He knew all of the words but he read them again anyway, faded though they were. On the other side, a familiar picture. The image cracked, white lines like scars where the card had folded. It was the Snøhuit facility where his son worked, flames spouting hundreds of feet into the air from the gas plant's chimney, higher than any of the mountains behind and casting a fiery glow over the town below. "There she blows!" his son had written across it. A joke, but also a sharp reminder of how times had changed.

"Hammerfest," Nils said, looking over from beside him.

Sebjørn nodded.

"Who do you know there?"

"My son," Sebjørn said, though he didn't really know the boy any more. Didn't know the man. As a father he had always been more elusive than any whale.

"It is a good place," Nils said. He took another mouthful of beer.

It probably was. Anna had always said so, back when she used to try to make Sebjørn feel better. Hammerfest had been a dying town before the gas plant. Now it was not only rejuvenated but expanding. Yet it had been a fishing town once. Sebjørn couldn't help wishing it was still.

"He works there," Sebjørn told Nils, though the man had not asked. "My son."

He had gone away to school, and though he had returned he did not stay long. The young never did. They took work in the cities. Tourist jobs, and the oil industry. They left the island communities behind them. The fishing, the whaling. The winter seas and the challenging summers. When Sebjørn was a boy there were nearly two hundred whaling vessels working the waters off the north of Norway. He worked those same waters now on one of maybe twenty.

"Your son works at Snøhuit?" Nils asked. "Good! That's good!" He slapped at Sebjørn's arm a few times in celebration. "The world's cleanest petroleum project." Nils tried to explain how the company owning the plant separated carbon dioxide from the natural gas. How the carbon dioxide would be injected into the seabed. Some way of helping with global warming. Sebjørn barely listened. He had heard it before.

"Why do you not work in the city?" he asked Nils. "You're young."

"My father."

It was answer enough. Nils's father had been on the *Lofotofangst*, lost last year. Sebjørn had already assumed it must have been something to do with that. Assumed that was why Osvald had hired someone so green. Only last month, the *Bjørn* had gone down with all hands, too. There had been experienced men on both of those vessels but it hadn't made any difference. The sea was like that sometimes.

"We never really got on," Nils said. Sebjørn thought that was probably true of most of the men here. Their own fathers. Their own sons. Nils grinned and said, "I never really liked whaling," and raised his bottle to toast the apology. The challenge.

Yes, he was like other sons.

"It is the same as farming," said Sigved. "They are like cows. It's like slaughtering cows."

Nils nodded. "Like cows, of course. Yes. Except people still eat beef."

"People still eat *whale* meat."

"People *buy* whale meat. It is tradition. They respect the tradition."

"*You* just ate whale meat," Sebjørn noted. In amusement, not to encourage argument. His own view depended on his mood. He was a fisherman, and whales drove the fish closer to shore. Made fishing easier. It was good to have them around. But they also ate the fish, and so he wasn't against culling them either. Sebjørn was a fisherman, but he was also a whaler. It only depended on the time of year. They were all of them hunters. Only the prey changed.

Aaron, who had been blowing a melody over the tops of beer bottles, joined in to say, "Sustainable." It was a word he liked to use.

Brage agreed. "Japan and Iceland do it, too."

"Last year we caught more whales than Japan and Iceland combined," Nils said.

"Didn't feel like it."

"And it's not even legal, not really. There are international treaties and—"

Sigved stood abruptly. He knocked the table hard enough that bottles bounced on their bases. "You don't understand," he said. "You're too young."

He nudged Nils more than was necessary in leaving. Men like Sigved built their arguments on experience. Young men, like Nils, used statistics and what they'd read elsewhere.

Sebjørn looked again at the photo in his calloused hands and relished the day's ache in his arms, his back. His old bones. *There she blows!* He looked at that plume of fire. Looked at the buildings of the Snøhuit and the town around it. He tried to imagine working in such a place and was glad when he could not.

⤙⟡⤏

Sebjørn woke suddenly, thinking of the harpoon cannon. He could still feel its shudder through the boat.

Across from him, Nils stirred in his bunk. He turned to one elbow and rubbed at his face. He started to say something but there was another vibration, a thrumming through the boat from beneath.

Sebjørn leaned out to see Aaron nursing his head in the bunk below. "What was that? We shooting something?"

It wasn't the harpoon cannon. The reverberations were stronger.

Osvald appeared in the doorway. He held both sides of the frame for a moment—"Get up."—and was gone again. Sebjørn called after him but there was no answer to his question. He swung his legs out from the bunk, dropped to the floor, and staggered as the boat suddenly shifted. He fell into Aaron emerging from his own bunk and the two of them grabbed at each other and the bunks to stop from sprawling.

The vessel shifted again. A protracted list to starboard. It righted itself afterwards but was slow doing so.

"Something's wrong."

One of them said it. All of them knew it. Sebjørn pulled himself straight and used the momentum to hurry out to the passageway. The *Höðr* was sitting lower in the water. He could feel it. Could feel the sea pressing in on all sides. They were held in a grip of high water.

Brage was hurrying towards him.

"Where's the captain?"

But Brage pushed past. "We're abandoning ship," he said. Sebjørn grabbed him, caught a bunch of his clothing in his fist as the man pressed between him and the wall, but there was nothing else to say. The clothing in his grip told him everything; Brage was in his waterproofs. He had a life jacket hooked over his head. Sebjørn let him go.

"Come on," Sigved said, suddenly with them. He had his vest in one hand. Then he was gone, hurrying to the deck.

Aaron, pulling on his boots, asked, "What's happening?"

Sebjørn grabbed the handheld, but if Osvald had his radio he wasn't answering.

"All right," Sebjørn said, tossing the radio. He clapped his hands together once, twice. "Let's go."

They fell out of the room as the vessel plunged suddenly under them. The floor dropped away and came up again, pitching them against the wall. They rushed to the deck in a stumble, snatching life vests as they went.

It was bright outside. Calm. Boats could sink in any weather, yet Sebjørn thought there should be winds. High waves. The deck should be getting swamped again and again with crashing water. That was how it happened whenever he dreamed it. Instead, all was still. Brage and Sigved stood prepping the raft between them, taking a final moment to read through the instructions printed on its side. They could have been at the seaside or beside a swimming pool, preparing some novelty inflatable, though they stood to their ankles in seawater. A gentle wave of it washed over Sebjørn's feet.

He glanced at the wheelhouse.

"Where's the captain?"

Nobody answered. Brage or Sigved pulled the appropriate cord and together they threw the raft out to sea to inflate. They climbed over the gunwale and leapt one after the other without a backwards glance. There was no need to consider the necessary actions here. The *Höðr* was already lost.

Sebjørn called to Aaron. The man was patting at his pockets. Looking for something, or performing a mental checklist of all he carried. He looked at Sebjørn long enough to nod then made his way to the raft. Nils was looking around the deck, as amazed as Sebjørn at how it sat almost level with the sea. When it pitched backwards, all of them staggered with it, and then as it leaned to port they ricocheted off each other and fell that way, too. Clutched at the gunwales. Sebjørn hit them just as the boat righted itself again. Flipped over them with the sudden rise of the deck. Span. Grabbed at something, anything, whatever he could. Caught his ankle on something hard that snapped a sharp pain into his brain. Maybe he felt water rushing in over him, but it might have been a moment of unconsciousness. Either way, when he shook the darkness off, he was in the sea. His clothing had ballooned up around him. His vest was high around his neck, too loose on his body and too tight against his throat. He splashed and kicked in a circle to find everyone. A flash of bright pain lit up his ankle again but he saw the raft. Someone, Nils, was being hauled inside.

The *Höðr* was beside him. A protrusion of winch-arm and a wheelhouse roof and that was all. Strangely level, like a floor he could climb up onto, though it wouldn't be long before it sank completely, Sebjørn thought. He wanted to get as far away from it as he could before that happened. He wanted to get into the raft. He twisted in the water to begin a strong, short crawl.

He felt the pull of water. Movement on both sides as the sea tugged him back, pulled against him. He sensed something large behind him, displacing the water he moved in, and imagined the *Höðr* descending. For a moment he thought it moved beneath him, thought he saw its large dark shape in the water, and he grabbed at the air, desperate to pull himself away. His hand came down on the rubber of the raft. Then the others had him around the wrist, the forearm, under the armpit, and they hauled him in from the sea.

◄◦►

Dragging the life-raft ashore is difficult. Awkward. The men are exhausted. They splash through the shallows with their heads down, shoulders hunched against the wind as they stagger towards land. Wavelets froth onto a black shore salted white with ice and snow. Frozen sand cracks and scrunches tight under wet boots as they stumble inland. Raft bumping between them, they make puddles with each footprint they press into the beach. Churn its sand and snow into slush.

Sebjørn has no idea where they are.

Jan Mayen is far west. The Lofoten Islands are east, and closer to land. It is not Svalbard, nor anywhere near it. Osvald has taken the *Höðr* further out than is usual—he had admitted as much in the raft. They are well north of Norway, into the Arctic Circle. Stuck, now, on a barren spit of land they do not know.

The island is a sloping stretch of rock and black sand, lurching into a short chain of black mountains at the northern end. Sebjørn thinks of trolls and Valkyries and wonders where the hell they are. Remembers something his son told him once: in the last three decades, retreating sea ice has freed over a million square miles of ocean. That, he'd explained, was why whales were proving harder to find; global warming allowed them more space in which to disappear. He called this new space "the meltwaters". The Arctic was a ghost. A fading place that haunted the very ocean it created in its passing.

Osvald points, not looking to see which of his men pays attention. Assuming, correctly, that they all do.

White with ice, protruding from the snow-spotted sand, are rows upon rows of wooden racks. Cod-drying racks where loops of twine shine with icicles, some of them so thick and heavy it seems fish still hang there. Translucent. Ethereal. The ghosts of fish.

"Over there."

This time Osvald moves towards where he points. The men follow, dropping the raft, holding their wet bodies tight. Shivering as they make their way towards the leaning shape.

It's a boat. Turned over, propped into a makeshift shelter with poles from the nearby drying racks. Drifts of snow slope up the overturned hull. Curl around the prow and stern. The boat is half buried but still a serviceable windbreak.

Sebjørn runs his hands over the vessel. "Lichen," he says. It's been here for a while. It's wooden. It has been here for a *very* long while.

"We're looking at history," says Sigved. His bandaged hand is on one of the supporting poles. He's looking at where the tip has been forced into the wood of the leaning boat, and Sebjørn sees it isn't part of the drying racks at all. It's a harpoon. A rusting, metal-headed harpoon. The non-explosive kind. No, not a harpoon: a barbed lance. Whales were harpooned from small boats like this one only as a means of attaching the whalers to their catch. They would pull themselves closer, closer, as the animal tired itself fleeing, struggling, and when they were close enough they would stab it into submission with lances like these. Whale hunting has been part of Norwegian culture for centuries, but back in the beginning it had been far bloodier. Sebjørn shakes his head. How difficult it must have been, penetrating all that blubber with a lance. There were no grenade harpoons with their 80 percent IDR back then. No such thing as an instant death rate at all. Only stabbing and hacking until you found the right coil of arteries. Grinding the lance in widening circles as the sea spread red and the beast drowned in its own blood. Sebjørn imagines spouts of that blood gushing in a geyser spray. Falling as hot rain while the whale thrashes with its tail pounding, mouth snapping. Twisting and turning its body until finally—

"Listen."

Osvald has his head turned to a sound he's caught. The men are quiet with him, trying to hear it themselves. Sebjørn hears only the sea, sweeping down the shore. Raking over rocks.

Osvald shakes his head. "It's gone," he says. "The wind," he says.

But to Sebjørn he does not sound certain.

⟶

Not far from the boat, they find the rotten ruins of a building. It rises from amongst the rocks that curve with the cove behind the leaning boat. What is left of its wood is wet and soft. Inside, some collapsed roof, crusted with sand and shells. A shore station. More of the past. A remnant from when whalers would set anchor on an island like this, building a shelter to work from using materials from the ship. There they would wait, looking for whales from shore. Riding the waves out to fetch them, lance them, bring them back. Boil the meat and blubber down to bones. Barrel the oil for soap, paint, varnish. Store the bones for clothing, umbrellas. Ambergris for perfume.

Osvald stands where once there was a door, his head turned and tilted. He has been standing that way for long moments, the men gathered behind him. Eventually, Sebjørn speaks.

"Captain?"

Osvald raises his hand to silence him. The men look at each other. As if another one of them has spoken, Osvald hisses for shush. Says, "Quiet," and winces, as if regretting his own sound. He shakes his head as if to clear it and steps inside what little remains of the shore station. He looks around. He looks at the ground. He scuffs at something with his foot.

"Anything?"

He glances back at Sebjørn and shakes his head again, a silent answer as he listens. Snaps his attention left, then right. Stares at something he sees there instead.

The men wait. Some of them are shivering.

"We should shelter in the raft," Sebjørn says. "We could—"

In two, three strides, Osvald is back outside with them. He seizes Sebjørn by his life vest. Shakes him. "*Quiet.* I will tell you what must be done."

Sebjørn is a large man. He is bulkier, still, in his waterproof clothing and vest. Osvald is greyer with age but he is larger, and he carries the extra weight of his authority. Every man feels it.

He releases Sebjørn. Looks at each of the others. "Bring the raft here."

The men do as they are told and they do it in silence. The only sound between them is the heft of the wind. It comes to shore with more force than the waves, cutting over rock and casting sand at their skin in abrupt gusts. Sebjørn keeps his head down. He tries to hunch deeper into his coat. When he checks on the other men beside him he sees Brage pull hard at his hat, yanking it down to protect his ears. Fumbling at his coat's collar for the hood that is buttoned up inside.

Nils stops walking with them, so Sebjørn stops too and looks at him. He grabs his arm and pulls him forward but the man only stumbles. He points. When Sebjørn looks, he sees the other men have stopped as well. They are looking at the expanse of beach stretched out before them. They are looking at:

"Bones."

The beach is filled with them, scattered like strange seashells. Large lengths of rib protruding from the sand. Lines of broken spine. Scattered vertebrae. Irregular blocks of strewn bone. Giant skulls, half buried, sand spilling in neat slopes from the sockets and open mouths. Long frozen grins. Pale, ice-sheened baleen.

"There are so many," says Brage. He turns his whole body to look at the others, hood pulled down tight over his head with both hands.

"Yes."

So many. As many whales as Sebjørn has ever seen in his lifetime, it seems. Full skeletons, remarkably intact where they have come to rest, washed clean to bleached bone. Collapsed structures holding shape enough to show head, body, tail. A protrusion of fin. Ribs curving up in half-cages, or sitting in arched segments like giant bone-spiders. Too many for drift whales, Sebjørn feels. Surely this many would not simply wash ashore.

And there is so much more shore now. A vast spread of dark sand where moments ago there had been the frothy slush of a cold sea. The raft sits isolated on an open expanse of beach and bones while the tide washes out in retreat, far away. A quiet, passing hu*sh*.

Sebjørn strains to hear it.

*Husshhh.*

A sudden gust of wind flings the sea at him. A fierce spray that stings his skin. Spits salt into his eyes. There has been no crash of wave to explain it, not that he has heard, yet the wind is wet and sharp. He winces into it and sees the blurs of his companions hunker down. Nils crouches. A trick of perspective makes him look like the eye of one of the skulls some way behind him. A foetal man against an elongated dome. A part-swallowed Jonah.

A stuttered shush draws Sebjørn to the life raft scudding across the sand. It comes to rest for a moment against a claw of ribs. At one end, a length of jaw, sharp and beak-like, angles up at the sky. The raft shudders to move again.

"Grab it."

He hurries the men from where they crouch and hunch their bodies. Only Sigved hesitates, his hood pulled down tight in fists that press against his face.

"Sigved!"

The man doesn't seem to hear, but he sees Sebjørn approaching and gets to his feet. He keeps his hands at his ears. The bandage on one of them has begun to unravel. A wet length of rag, dangling.

"Whale brains have a section we don't."

Sebjørn looks at Nils. He is staring into whalebone. "They have a section we can't even understand."

Sebjørn feels like he knew this. Perhaps his son had told him. His unfathomable son.

The raft rests against a skeleton far larger than the others, with a head at one end accounting for almost a third of its length. It does not have the baleen plates of a minke for filtering food. It's a toothed whale. The largest of its kind.

"Sperm whale," says Sigved. He is winding the bandage from his hand around his head instead. Over his ears.

Sperm whales have the largest brain of any animal, even the giant blue whale, but this fleshless head has been opened and emptied of everything. A man could stand inside the case where once there had been a brain and five hundred gallons of thick, precious fluid. The first men to ever see it had thought of sperm. Sebjørn supposes they had been at sea for a while, without women. He wonders, if he put his ear to the skull, what would he hear? The ocean? Would it roar louder than the eerie whisper that currently hushes in with each wave? Or would it merely be the flush of his own blood, pulsing? His own heartbeat, a years-late echo of something dead.

*We're looking at history*, he remembers.

"The raft."

Between them, they prepare to carry it across the sand and snow. Sebjørn looks over the few supplies the others had thrown in with them. Amongst the plastic boxes and foil-wrapped bricks of food lies one of the rifles. Who had paused long enough on a sinking vessel to grab that? Still, he is glad to have it. Its presence reminds him of what they are, these men. That they are not helpless.

"Ssh!"

The men, reaching for handholds around the raft, rummaging at the few supplies within, pause in their actions. Frozen. Looking at Aaron.

"Did you hear that?" he asks.

The men have nothing for a reply, but they listen.

"The captain," Sebjørn says. Not because he thinks he heard him, but because he speaks his thoughts aloud and his thoughts are with Osvald.

Aaron nods. He hefts his side of the raft and says, "Let's go."

They struggle the raft back to the ancient boat amongst the fishing racks. Back to where the shore station rots amongst the rocks. Of Osvald, though, there is no sign.

The captain is gone.

◄o►

The photograph flutters in Sebjørn's hands. There are gaps between the boards of the ancient boat he shelters behind. He has not been reading the postcard, merely holding it while he thinks of Osvald. He is still missing. Tracks they'd found had led only to the sea, nowhere else. They'd followed them to the water's edge, and further still, into the shallows, as if the receding tide may have left some trace of them. But of course there was nothing.

A quick gust snatches at the place Sebjørn has never been, takes it from his hands, and casts it away down the beach. He grabs for it, stands in a hurry to chase it, but leaves it lost when he sees Sigved.

The man has been acting strange since the captain's disappearance. Talking to himself. Looking at places only he seems to see. Now he stands distant at the shoreline, waves lapping at his feet. His head is cocked to one side, bandage askew. Ear turned to the sea that hushes in. Hushes away.

Nils steps close to Sebjørn. "What is he doing?"

They watch as the tide washes out over the long skulls of whales. Each hollowed dome fills and empties with the waves, awash with ocean. Sigved stands amongst them. Head tilted, as if they have something to tell him. Some secret to whisper.

Sebjørn opens his mouth to call Sigved but the sound that comes to him on the wind quietens him. A piping noise, long and low. A melancholy melody sent to him through the bones. Whistling over them and through. One note. Two. Mournful, and haunting, beautiful and—

The raised voices of an argument pull Sebjørn back from his thoughts.

"Let me go!"

Brage is dragging at Aaron's sleeve. Yanking at his jacket. Aaron is pushing back. Shoving at Brage's chest. Kicking at his legs.

"Sebjørn," says Brage. "Help me."

"Help you what?"

But he goes to them. Puts his hands between them, tries to prise them apart. Brage shoves at Sebjørn to get his hands on Aaron again. Grabs the back of his jacket as the man turns away. "Let him go," Sebjørn warns.

Brage pulls so violently that he and Aaron fall. They topple some of the fishing trestles and the rifle that had been leaning against them. Sebjørn stumbles with them but keeps to his feet. He helps Brage to his then puts his body between him and Aaron. "What the hell are you doing?" He pushes him back a few steps.

But it isn't Brage who answers. It's Aaron. He's standing with the rifle cradled in his arms. "Don't you hear it?"

"Aaron . . ."

"Don't any of you hear it?"

Brage lunges at Aaron but Aaron sees it coming and strikes at him with the rifle. He has it turned, stock first, and he hits Brage in the chest. In the face.

Nils stands wide-eyed. Sebjørn glances for help from Sigved but the man has noticed nothing of this. He stands in the receding sea. Further out now, as if the tide has pulled him with each wave.

Brage grabs for Aaron again, this time for the rifle. Manages to get his large hands on the rifle butt. He pulls it to him, hand over hand, gathering it to him like rope, and Sebjørn sees what is about to happen a moment before it does. Too late to warn them. Too late to do anything. Brage pulls at the stock and Aaron pulls at the barrel and his head is flung back with a sudden spray of blood. A following crack of sound.

Sebjørn turns away from the sight of a man sprawled in the sand and watches Sigved wading deeper out to sea, too stunned to say or do anything to stop him.

⤙⤞

"Do you think the captain sent a signal in time?"

Nils is standing, looking down the beach when he asks. There is little to look at. The waves sweep in slowly, barely moving up the shore. Leaving more of it behind.

"Hmm?"

Sebjørn sits in the sand beside Aaron. The wind is making his ears ache. Constantly, now, he hears how it whistles through the bones. How it arcs over the turned boat and cuts between the soft boards of the collapsing shore station. The island is awash with the rise and fall of its music. The keening two-note call that threads through him, low and long.

"A distress signal," Nils says. "Do you think he got one out in time?"

"It's automatic."

The *Höðr*'s beacon would have activated as soon as the vessel took on water, broadcasting their position.

"How long before they find us?"

Sebjørn doesn't answer. After all, the *Lofotofangst* had the same equipment. The *Bjørn*, too.

"Sebjørn?"

"I don't know."

Aaron lies on his back on the beach, staring at the sky. Blood has pooled around his head, a crimson nimbus that refuses to soak into the wet sand.

"Sebjørn? Where's the rifle now?"

"Brage took it."

He can't remember if he knows that or not. Or if he knows where Brage has taken it, either. Can't think much of anything with that constant noise. The peep and elongated squeal. Regular enough it seems like song and frustrating in its patterned resounding. But beautiful, too.

Sebjørn looks back at where the raft sits, nestled between the fishless racks. A red light blinks from it. A white. Mostly they pulse out of time with each other but sometimes, briefly, there is synchronicity. A pattern that stretches out and comes back in and repeats.

"Do you think he'll come back?" Nils asks. Adding, "Brage," because he could have meant somebody else. Anybody else but Aaron.

Sebjørn has no answer for him. He returns to staring out to sea. It has retreated further still, the shore expanding as the waterline recedes, and recedes, and recedes. And everywhere, all he sees is bones. Pale prisons curving from and on the dark sand. Giant skulls, scoured smooth by the sea, grinning their wide lines of baleen. Tails of spine behind pointing to where the sea retreats, retreats. And carried to him from between them, over and through them, comes that watery, drawn-out sound of low notes.

Whale-song.

Sebjørn smiles. Of course it's watery. Water transmits sound far better than air. And then he thinks, we are 80 percent water. Something like that.

He slaps at his ears. Head bowed, he strikes himself a flurry of blows, as if he can knock the noise from his head. Muffle it with the singing sting of pain. Yet it is a smell that distracts him.

Smoke.

Beside the shelter of the overturned boat, a thick column of dark smoke rises from a fire where men warm themselves.

"Hey!"

Sebjørn scrambles in the sand to get up, clumsy with his injured ankle. He lopes towards the men in a limping stagger, dimly aware of Nils moving with him.

"*Hey!*"

The wind tears the smoke ragged, throws it around. Twists the black stink of it into a greasy coil that clings to the skin of the men gathered around the fire. They are not simply warming their hands by the flames. They are working with them.

"What are you doing?"

One of them holds something. He makes downward strokes with a blade.

"Captain? What are you doing?"

The man glances at Sebjørn through the smoke. His face is bloody. His forehead is dark with it. Hair sticks up in oily clumps. His beard is grimcd. It isn't Osvald. It isn't anyone Sebjørn knows. None of them are. Each is filthy with the grime of their work, blood-streaked and soot-stained. They are dressed in simple clothes, all cloth and leather. One wears a coil of rope across his chest like a bandolier. Another carves at a slab of blubber with a rusted blade. He cuts it into sections like pages, each of them an inch or so thick. As Sebjørn watches, he fans them out and drops them into a pot that boils over the black fire. A glut of bubbling blubber, dense and popping, belching the heavy stench of melting meat juices. One of the men reaches into the pot, his gloves thick with grease. He retrieves crisp pieces from the oil, skims them from where they float, and casts them underneath into the flames. Fuel for the fire that renders the rest into something new.

"Sebjørn?"

*We are looking at history.*

Who said that?

As if suddenly aware that Sebjørn watches, each of the men looks up from their work. Together, they open their mouths wide.

Sebjørn slams his hands to his ears and crouches, turning away. He expects that drawn, hollow vowel sound, the two-note chorus of whale-song, to come from the mouths of those who once hunted them, and he turns from it quickly. Strikes the pot suspended over the fire. Nothing spills, though it falls to where there was once a fire and is gone, dispersed into absence like the wind-driven smoke. Like the men, too, gone with the song that retreats, retreats. Summoned away by the sounds of its own diminishing echo as it retreats. Retreats.

And repeats.

Sebjørn scoops up snow and sand with each hand and clutches them to his head. Packs ice coarse with grit into his ears to silence what he can't not hear. Handful after handful of sand, snow, stones. Forcing it in tight. But the song remains inside his head. He fights the pull of it, the rise and fall of its siren call, and shudders. Shivers. Spasms with the cold forever in his bones. And all the while his hands are at his ears, pressing them flat. Forcing a hush of blood that sounds like an empty ocean.

The hand on his shoulder startles him. He makes fists in reflex and so has no choice but to hear:

"What are you doing out here?"

He is crouching at the shoreline, Nils standing beside him. A wave laps over their feet. Sebjørn stands slowly and looks back at the long, long expanse of beach behind. It stretches far away from him . . .

. . . away . . .

. . . away . . .

Right back to where an old boat leans out of the sand like a rotten loose tooth.

Nils reaches for Sebjørn—

"Come on, come with me."

—but Sebjørn steps away. He faces the darkening sea as a wave comes in, bringing with it more of the same music, and when it recedes it takes it away again. Leaves more shore behind. There are prints in the sand, impossible prints that have not been washed away. That lead into the sea and its music.

Nils positions himself in front of Sebjørn, holding his arms out as if to embrace him. Block him. He is speaking, but Sebjørn can't hear more than a muffle of noise because he has covered his ears as he walks with the receding tide. He does not stop walking, treading wet sand into gurgling puddles. A drowned man's splutter. Every step he takes is the sound of a throat closing with water as the sea draws back, and back still, and shows him the *Höðr*. The *Lofotofangst*. The *Bjørn*. Others. All of them beached and leaning vacant.

*We are looking at history.*

Sebjørn limps towards them, hands at his head like a marched prisoner. He thinks of the taut rope that tethers whalers to the whale. The tight line that tows one behind the other across the tops of white waves.

It's not just whales we're chasing, Sebjørn realises. It has never just been whales.

Suddenly the sea retreats from him no more. Where once there had been a growing expanse of shore comes a final surge and swell of surf as the ocean rushes in to meet him. It engulfs his knees, his thighs, climbs high up his vestless chest, and turns him about in its violent tide to show him a beach in illusory movement, the bones of whales rushing back into the swift encroaching sea.

And here are the whales now. Two of them. Three. Four of them. Five. They swim with him amongst them and draw him away, out to sea. Arcing slow curves as they appear, then submerge. Raising tails that make wide Vs in descent. Waves that haunt the minds of men in their beckoning.

On the diminishing shore, Nils struggles to free the raft that will save him, surrounded by whaling men. Sebjørn opens his mouth to call a warning but the water hushes him, rushing in with the roar of a whale exhaling as the island that had been slowly rising to heave itself free of the sea dives once more with a mountainous flip of its tail.

# A SHIP OF THE SOUTH WIND

## BRADLEY DENTON

U ncle JoJim slid his shotgun into its scabbard behind Calico Girl's saddle, then walked into the shin-high tallgrass to retrieve his sixth prairie chicken of the day. Charley, perched atop his chestnut stallion, Bird King, waited alongside Calico Girl. As he did, he looked past Uncle JoJim and saw a narrow plume of smoke a mile to the south. It was too small to be from a grass fire. But it was a definite line of gray against the treeless green hills and cloudless sky. It smudged into the blue as the wind caught it.

"Who would have a fire out here?" Charley asked as Uncle JoJim returned. He pointed at the smoke. "Grandmother says no one lives in these hills except ghosts. Ghosts wouldn't need a fire."

Uncle JoJim paused, looked toward the line of gray, and tilted his head upward. He sniffed, and then he frowned.

"It's no one who will bother us," Uncle JoJim said, stepping up to Calico Girl. He used his teeth to help tie one of the chicken's legs to a rawhide string hanging from the saddle. Charley knew better than to offer to help. Uncle JoJim got along fine without a right arm.

"But who could it be?" Charley asked. "The Kaw are all on the reservation, and the whites are all in Council Grove. Do you think the Cheyenne have come back?"

Uncle JoJim finished tying the prairie chicken to Calico Girl's saddle, then gripped the saddle horn and swung up onto the pinto. "It's not the Cheyenne."

"Who, then?" Charley didn't like not knowing.

"White travelers sometimes pass through the Flint Hills," Uncle JoJim said. "They never stop long. It's of no concern."

But Charley was concerned anyway. "It's too early for travelers to stop and cook supper, isn't it? And they shouldn't make camp out here anyway. The thunderclouds have been coming fast in the evenings. So they should spend the night in Council Grove. We ought to tell them."

Uncle JoJim glanced back at the smoke. "It's rude to tell others their business. Besides, there are those who don't mind wind or water. Or thunder, or lightning." He nodded toward the next hill to the east. "I remember a patch of rock up there. It would be a good place to race to. If anyone wanted to race."

So Charley spun Bird King and urged him up the slope. The July sun was hot on his neck, and he imagined it was Calico Girl's breath.

But when he and Bird King reached the bare patch of limestone and clattered to a stop, Charley looked back and saw that Uncle JoJim was far behind. Calico Girl was moving at a walk. The prairie chickens hanging from her saddle, three on each side, swung lazily.

Charley realized that Uncle JoJim had tricked him. But he didn't know why. Unless it was just to tease him. Uncle JoJim did that, sometimes.

⤙⤗

"You didn't even try," Charley said when Uncle JoJim finally drew alongside.

Uncle JoJim stopped Calico Girl with a click of his tongue, then adjusted his battered brown hat. The wind had bent up one side of its brim. Charley wasn't wearing a hat, and the wind ruffled his straight black hair against his ears.

Uncle JoJim shrugged, and his empty right shirtsleeve flapped. "I didn't say I would race. All I said was that this would be a good place to race to." He patted his mare's dappled red-and-white neck. "Besides, I had not asked Calico Girl if she felt like running."

"I think you were just afraid you would lose," Charley said.

"Of course I would lose," Uncle JoJim said. "I'm a one-armed old man in a loose saddle on a tired mare. You're a boy riding bareback on a young stallion." He paused. "And you've become a good horseman."

Charley was amazed. Uncle JoJim's remark would have been a high compliment from anyone among the Kaw. But coming from Uncle JoJim, it meant even more. Uncle JoJim had given Bird King to Charley and had taught him to ride. And he had offered plenty of criticism in the process. But never, until now, had he offered any praise.

"Thank you, Uncle JoJim," Charley said. "You're very kind. And I don't think you're old."

Uncle JoJim gave a snort. "You've lived eight and a half years. But I was here forty summers before you. And if you think I'm kind, ask your Aunt Margaret. She'll tell you I spend too much of my day in selfishness to have any time left over for kindness." He shifted in his saddle. "No, if I say you're a good horseman, it's because it's true. I ought to know, as I once saw the best horsemen in the world."

Charley was intrigued. "Who do you mean?"

Uncle JoJim squinted toward the northeast. "Twenty years ago, when I had both arms, I was hired to drive cattle to New Mexico to feed soldiers fighting the desert tribes. As I returned to Kansas with some of the soldiers, we were attacked by Comanche warriors. Those Comanches would slip down to the sides of their ponies to fire their bullets and arrows. Then they would slip back up and turn backward so they could keep shooting at us after they had passed. This was all done while riding as fast as their horses would run. One warrior even rode upside-down, shooting arrows between his pony's forelegs. It was as if the horse spat arrows from its chest."

Charley was fascinated.

Uncle JoJim touched his own Adam's apple. "The soldier beside me died with one of those arrows in his throat. But the rest of us were lucky. A solitary white man appeared atop a nearby ridge, and he drew the attention of the Comanches because he was riding—" Uncle JoJim paused. "It was a wagon. He was riding a big . . . wagon."

"A wagon?" Charley asked. "Wasn't he easy for the Comanches to attack?"

Uncle JoJim frowned as he had frowned when he'd sniffed the air. "No. This man told me later that he had come from where the world is nothing but water. As it once was here, long ago." He gestured down at the limestone slab, which was embedded with the fossilized shells of ancient sea creatures. "Coming from the water, this man had never heard of the Comanches. So he wasn't afraid. He also had weapons from his old life, and he killed the first warrior who charged him. Then he killed the horses of the next four. That was worse for the Comanches than being killed themselves, so they fled. Yet even while fleeing, they rode well. Some of them had to ride double, and they were still too fast for the soldiers to chase." Uncle JoJim looked at Charley. "But they were no faster than you and Bird King. And you ride without a bridle. Even the Comanches used ropes around their ponies' jaws." He squinted northeast again. "Of course, I've never seen you ride upside-down. So maybe the Comanches were still a little better."

Charley hesitated before asking his next question. "Were they better than the Cheyenne?"

Uncle JoJim gave another snort. "A month ago, when the Cheyenne came to raid us, we learned that the Kaw are as good as the Cheyenne. And the Comanches were better than the Kaw. But if you tell anyone I said so, I'll call you a liar."

Charley sighed. "I wish Allegawaho had not sent us to Topeka when the Cheyenne came. I wish we could have seen the battle."

Uncle JoJim shook his head. "The Cheyenne numbered more than a hundred, so every full-blood Kaw had to stay and fight. We were the only ones who could go for help. Allegawaho could not have known the Cheyenne would be appeased by sugar and coffee from Council Grove."

"Plus the three horses they had already stolen from the Kaw," Charley said.

"Yes, plus the three horses," Uncle JoJim said. He sounded annoyed. "My point is that fetching the militia was wise, and none of the Kaw could go. It was up to us."

Charley knotted his hands in Bird King's mane. "You might have gone without me. Then I could have watched the Kaw and the Cheyenne ride against each other. The women say it was a marvel."

"I believe they exaggerate. But no matter. Calico Girl and I needed you and Bird King. You helped us ride fast for sixty miles." Uncle JoJim patted Calico Girl's neck again. "I don't think I'll make her run that far or that fast again. She deserves easy rides and hunts from now on."

Charley glanced at the prairie chickens hanging from Uncle JoJim's saddle. "Is today's hunt finished?"

"The sun is starting to slide down, but the moon will rise when it's gone. So we could hunt longer if we wished. But I think six chickens are enough for one day." Uncle JoJim pointed in the direction he had been squinting. "However, there are now two white men and a boy between us and the reservation. The boy is older than you, but not yet old enough to be called a man."

Charley's gaze followed the line from Uncle JoJim's pointing finger. Then he saw them, not quite a half mile away: three sunlit figures on horseback, moving at a trot through the grass, heading for the hilltop where Charley and Uncle JoJim had stopped.

"They might cause us some difficulty," Uncle JoJim said.

-◦-

Charley hadn't noticed the three riders until Uncle JoJim had pointed, and he was embarrassed. True, the wind was blowing from the south. So it was all right that he hadn't heard anything. But he should have seen them.

"Are they from Council Grove?" he asked.

"They're strangers," Uncle JoJim said. "But when they saw us, they changed direction. So they might intend to ask for our help. Or they might intend to rob us. Either way, it will be obvious if we try to avoid them. And they might take offense."

Bird King tossed his head and stamped on the limestone. He had sensed Charley's unease.

"If we just rode away," Charley said, "what could they do?"

Uncle JoJim made a low noise in his throat. "The boy and the man with the red beard have long rifles in scabbards. But those aren't good from horseback. They might also have pistols, but they aren't yet close enough to use them. Although they will be soon."

"We should run, then," Charley said.

"No. The man with the black beard has a Spencer carbine on a strap. He carries it across his chest, so he can aim it quickly. Cavalry soldiers used that gun in the war between the Northern and Southern whites. So if we ran, he could fire at us from his horse if he wished. And he would have seven shots." Uncle JoJim adjusted his hat again. "We should wait. If they want help, we can offer it. And if they want to steal, we can give them our chickens."

Charley's throat tightened. "What if they want your shotgun? And what if they don't like mixed-blood people?"

Uncle JoJim, still looking toward the three riders, gave a slight smile. "A shotgun is good at close range. Even for a man with one arm. And one barrel is still loaded." Now he looked at Charley, and his smile vanished. "If it leaves its scabbard, you must run for home. Tell Bird King *Yici!* And don't stop until you've called the Kaw from their houses. Do you hear?"

Charley struggled to speak through his tight throat. "I hear," he said.

Now Uncle JoJim looked behind them, and Charley's gaze followed his. The plume of gray smoke was still there.

"Maybe we'll be lucky," Uncle JoJim said. He turned back to squint at the approaching riders again. "Maybe these men won't be crazy."

Charley thought that was a strange thing to say, and he was about to ask Uncle JoJim what he meant. But then he too looked back at the riders, and saw that their horses had started to gallop.

"Speak only if they speak to you first," Uncle JoJim said. "And be polite."

Charley tried to take a deep breath and found that his chest was as tight as his throat. "I'll do my best," he said in a small voice.

Uncle JoJim adjusted the brim of his hat yet again.

"Do better than that," he said.

◄∘►

The three riders stopped just short of the flat patch of limestone. Their horses, a sorrel gelding for each of the men and a roan mare for the boy, snorted and stamped. The horses were loaded with bulging saddlebags, bedrolls, and coiled ropes.

The two men were lanky and sun-scorched, and both wore crisp, new, flat-crowned hats. The one on the left had blue eyes and a reddish beard cut short, while the one in the center had dark eyes and a black beard that covered his throat. The man on the left had an expression that Charley guessed indicated amusement. But he couldn't read the expression of the man in the center.

The boy, on the right, had eyes the same color of blue as the man on the left. Straight blond hair poked out from under his straw hat. His complexion was paler than the men's, and his cheeks and nose were freckled. Charley thought he looked about thirteen. His expression suggested both wariness and curiosity.

All three were dressed in a fashion similar to Charley and Uncle JoJim, in sturdy canvas trousers and linen shirts. But the white men's clothes, although dusty, looked almost as brand-new as their hats. And in addition to the long rifles in scabbards and the carbine across Black-beard's chest, each of the men had a Colt pistol jutting from his belt.

Black-beard spoke first.

"I see you are Injuns," he said. "However, since you wear white men's clothing, I assume you speak English." His voice had a deep rasp, as if he had swallowed a fistful of dirt.

"We do," Uncle JoJim said. "I am Joseph James, Junior, and this is my cousin's grandson, Charles Curtis. How may we assist you?"

Black-beard's eyes widened, and he exchanged a glance with Red-beard.

"My goodness," he said. "That was well spoken. And you both have white names, though your skins appear red. What odd sort of Injuns might you be?"

"I am mixed-blood, Osage and Kaw," Uncle JoJim said. His voice was calm, and just loud enough to be heard over the wind. "I also possess French blood, but I don't know those relatives." He nodded toward Charley. "His blood is similar to mine, on his mother's side. He has Potawatomi on that side as well. But his father is white. Mister Curtis went to fight in the Northern and Southern war, and though we've been told he survived, he has not yet returned."

Black-beard gave a low whistle. "Osage, Kaw, Potawatomi, French, and English? That's about as mixed as mixed can be. No wonder you're riding the prairie without other companions. You don't belong anywhere, do you?"

Uncle JoJim was quiet for a moment. Then he said, "We live among the Kaw."

"Yet I don't imagine they consider you to be of their tribe," Black-beard said.

Uncle JoJim was quiet for yet another moment before he said, "That's true."

Charley felt a hot rush behind his eyes. Then he heard himself blurt, "Uncle JoJim and I are both descended from White Plume!"

The bearded men each gave Charley a cold stare.

The freckled boy's nose crinkled. "Who's White Plume?" he asked in a thin, nasal voice.

"Hush, Joshua," Red-beard said. His voice was thin and nasal, too.

Uncle JoJim leaned toward Charley. "You should hush as well."

Charley clenched his jaw. Bird King whickered.

"I know of the Osage," Red-beard said then. "But what the hell is a Kaw?"

"They are also called the Kanza," Uncle JoJim said. "Their reservation is not far, close by the town of Council Grove."

The freckled boy looked across at Red-beard. "Pa, I think the Kanza tribe must be what Kansas is named for."

Red-beard leaned over and spat on the ground. "I reckon," he said. When he looked up again, his upper lip had pulled back from his teeth. "And I told you to hush."

"I've heard of the Kanza," Black-beard said. "Folks in St. Joe say the Kanza fought off a Cheyenne war party a few weeks ago. That so?"

"It is," Uncle JoJim said.

The man looked Uncle JoJim up and down, then turned his gaze toward Charley and did the same. Despite the hot afternoon, Charley had to push down a shiver.

"Hard to believe," Black-beard said.

Uncle JoJim's eyebrows rose. "It was a strange day. But young Charles and I had no part in the fight. The Kaw chief sent us to Topeka to alert the governor, so he could send a militia."

Red-beard gave a high laugh that made Charley think of coyotes. "That must have been a sight! A short, one-armed Injun and a half-breed pipsqueak riding into Topeka and yelling for the governor. I'm surprised nobody shot you."

Uncle JoJim looked at Red-beard. "It was a strange day," he said again. Then he looked back at Black-beard. "How may we assist you?"

"That depends. What's that weapon behind your saddle?"

"It is a shotgun. Two-barrel."

"As I thought," Black-beard said. "Am I correct to assume it's well past its prime? It isn't one of those fancy new breech-loaders, is it?"

"No, it loads the old way," Uncle JoJim said. "And I've used all the powder and shot I brought with me today. But I have a few percussion caps. I could trade for those, if you wish."

Black-beard waved a hand as if brushing away a fly. "No, we need pistol and rifle cartridges. And sugar, flour, and salt pork. Might you have any of those?"

"No. But those things may all be found in Council Grove. Six miles north."

Black-beard gave a snaggletoothed grin. "Sadly, we find that many citizens of Kansas towns harbor resentment against Missouri men who served with Colonel Quantrill. They don't seem to care that our punitive mission against Lawrence took place almost five years ago. Nor, for that matter, that the war has been over for three."

Red-beard spat again. "Kansas people are not reasonable."

"Indeed not," Black-beard said. "So the three of us have decided to move on to New Mexico. But we need provisions."

"New Mexico is a fine destination," Uncle JoJim said. "And the tribes along the way are friendly. I'm sure they will give you what you need."

Black-beard stopped grinning. He placed his right hand on the stock of his Spencer.

"We cannot depend on that," he said. Then he tilted his head upward, using his chin to point over Uncle JoJim's shoulder. "What's that smoke yonder? Might that be someplace we could bargain for goods?"

Uncle JoJim gave Charley a quick glance. Charley wasn't sure what it meant.

"I believe it is the camp of a solitary man," Uncle JoJim said to Black-beard. "But I can't say what goods he might possess. Or what sort of bargain he might make you."

"You can't say?" Black-beard's eyes narrowed. "Why not? You sound as if you know him."

Uncle JoJim's mouth became a thin line.

"A white man has asked you a question, Injun," Red-beard said. "And this particular white man does not appreciate a lack of respect. Some of the denizens of Lawrence might confirm that, were they still alive."

At that, Charley heard Uncle JoJim let out a long breath.

"I have met the man who is making the smoke," Uncle JoJim said then. "But it was many years ago, and I can't say that I know him now. He might not remember me."

"But you remember *him*, I take it," Black-beard said. "Is he white?"

"Yes."

Black-beard shifted the Spencer so that it pointed at Uncle JoJim. "Then you will take us to him. You may say that our names are Jim Barnett and Sam Clark, and that we'll pay him well for any goods he might provide." He gestured with the Spencer. "A brisk walk will be fine. If either your horse or your boy's starts to run, I might be startled."

Uncle JoJim clicked his tongue, and Calico Girl turned toward the smoke. For an instant, Uncle JoJim's eyes met Charley's, and Charley hoped he didn't look as afraid as he felt.

"Remember the Comanches," Uncle JoJim whispered.

But Charley didn't know how he could do that. He hadn't even been alive then.

◄०►

A minute later, Black-beard said, "Get behind me, boy. I don't want you Injuns whispering. It ain't friendly to keep secrets."

Uncle JoJim gave Charley a nod, so Charley tugged on Bird King's mane to stop him. Once Black-beard passed by, Charley let Bird King move again, and they fell in beside the freckled boy's roan. Red-beard rode behind them.

Black-beard took the strap of his Spencer from around his neck, then slid the rifle into a scabbard behind his saddle. But Charley knew Black-beard's pistol was still handy in his belt, as was Red-beard's. Both he and Uncle JoJim could be shot in the back at any moment.

The freckled boy looked at Charley. His gaze was hot on Charley's face, and Charley told himself it was just the sun. But the sun had never made his skin itch before.

"My name is Joshua," the freckled boy said in his nasal voice.

Charley didn't answer right away. Beads of sweat were sliding down from his hair, and they tickled. Between the tickle and the itch, he was going to have to rub his face soon. But he was afraid to raise his hand for fear of how Red-beard might react. He might think Charley was about to reach out and strike the freckled boy.

"I said, my name is Joshua." The boy's voice pitched even higher.

"My son's trying to be sociable," Red-beard said behind Charley. "You should, too."

Charley tried to breathe in enough air to speak, and he just managed. "I am pleased to make your acquaintance, Joshua," he said. "As my uncle said, my name is Charles. I go by Charley. But people in Council Grove call me 'Indian Charley.' I suppose so no one will think they mean some other Charley."

Joshua cocked his head. "That should work. But do you think of yourself as Injun? I mean, you ain't really any one thing, with all those different kinds of blood. I'd think you'd get mighty confused, especially about how to talk to folks."

"I guess I don't think of myself as anything except Charley," Charley said. "And I just change how I talk depending on where I am. When I'm with the Kaw, I speak Kanza. And when I'm with white people, I speak English.

My mother also taught me some French, but I don't remember much of it. No one here speaks French now, anyway."

"Do you speak Kanza well?" Joshua asked.

"Well enough. My grandmother says the first words I ever spoke were in Kanza. Taught to me by my mother, like the French. But I don't remember which words. And I don't remember my mother too much, either. She died when I was three years old."

In the past, whenever Charley had spoken of his mother to others, those others had always said, "I'm sorry she passed on," or something similar. But what Joshua said was, "Tell me some Kanza words."

Charley was puzzled. "What words do you want to know?"

"Well, what's the meaning of 'Kanza,' anyway? Is it just a word the Injuns made up for themselves?"

"My grandmother says it's an old word," Charley said. "Maybe even as old as when these hills were under the sea. It means 'south wind.' So what the Kaw call themselves in English is 'People of the South Wind.'"

As if in response, a gust from the south set the grass undulating in waves. The freckled boy's hat almost blew off, and Charley's sweat-damp hair came unstuck from his forehead. But he still itched, and he was still too afraid to raise his hand to scratch.

Joshua pointed at a red-tailed hawk flying past them to the east. "What's the Kanza word for 'bird'?"

"*Wazhinga*." The word for "hawk" wasn't the same at all. But Joshua had asked for "bird."

"What about 'buffalo'?" Joshua asked.

"*Cedónga*," Charley said.

Joshua looked back at Red-beard. "Hey, Pa. I'm gonna join the Injuns and hunt *cedónga*. What do you think of that?"

When Red-beard answered, his thin voice sounded deeper and thicker than before.

"Ask him the word for 'blood,'" Red-beard said. "And 'scalp.'"

Joshua looked at Charley. "Didja hear?"

Charley's hands, clenching Bird King's mane, began to tremble. Bird King snorted and tossed his head.

"'Blood' is *wabí*," Charley said. Then he realized he didn't know the exact word for "scalp." But he knew the word for "hair." "'Scalp' is . . . *pahú*."

Joshua looked back at Red-beard again. "He says it's *wabí* and *pahú*."

Red-beard grunted.

"Good to know," he said.

Joshua twitched his mare's reins so she moved closer to Bird King.

"Don't worry," Joshua whispered. "They scalped some abolitionists in the war, and then a few Injuns after. But you ain't an abolitionist, and you ain't a full-blood Injun. So they ain't going to kill you."

Charley didn't try to answer. His breath was starting to tremble along with his hands.

"I'm pretty sure, anyway," Joshua said.

⟿

As they came over the last hill, heat lightning began to flash in the darkening sky to the south. And now Charley could see the source of the smoke in the gully below. He could smell it, too. It reeked like river mud that had somehow been set ablaze. The gray plume was spewing from a hole at the apex of a hammered-tin dome set over a circular cast-iron grate that, in turn, was set over a bed of hot coals. The grate was five feet wide, and the dome covered all but the outer few inches. The coals underneath were beginning to glow with a red light as the sun dropped behind a hill to the west.

"Good Lord, that's odiferous," Red-beard said.

But despite the smoke and its stench, Charley's attention was drawn several yards past the bed of coals to an enormous wooden contraption that sat on a patch of flattened dirt. It was built in the style of a curved-bottom overland wagon, but it had no canopy. And it was larger than any wagon Charley had ever seen. At least thirty feet long and ten feet wide, it sat atop four iron-clad wheels that were each a dozen feet in diameter. The wagon and the spokes of the wheels had been painted ochre, but the paint had flaked and faded with age.

Charley glimpsed piles of canvas and a few barrels inside the wagon. But those didn't seem odd. What did seem odd was a fifteen-foot-tall post rising from the wagon's center, fitted with a seven-foot crossbeam near the top . . . and a shorter post-and-crossbeam that rose midway between the center post and the wagon's narrowed front end. Both posts were strung with a baffling network of ropes. Charley couldn't tell whether the posts were meant to be Christian crosses or secular gallows.

As the five riders came down into the gully, a lone figure, stooping, stepped out from the shadow under the high belly of the wagon. When the figure drew near to the glowing coals, Charley saw that he was a tall, broad-shouldered man with long, tangled gray hair and a beard that hung even lower than Black-beard's. He was wearing a dark blue coat with a double row of brass buttons, closed up tight. Charley thought it must be far too warm inside that coat, but the man didn't seem to mind. His trousers were dark and heavy, too. But his feet were bare, and they glowed pink in the light from the coals.

The man held a staff that appeared to be made of ivory affixed to a short length of polished wood capped with brass at its base. Charley thought it must be ivory because it was the same color as the keys of a piano he had seen in Topeka. But this ivory spiraled up around itself like tight coils of rope, tapering tighter and tighter as it rose. It was at least eight feet long, ending in a sharp point.

For a moment, Charley almost forgot that he and Uncle JoJim were in the company of embittered Missouri bushwhackers. Everything he was looking at now was a fascination and a puzzle. But one thing he was sure of was that the tall man with the wild gray hair and the spiraled ivory staff was the same man Uncle JoJim had told him about less than an hour earlier. This was the man who had appeared on the ridge during the Comanche attack, years ago. And the huge wagon behind him might be the same wagon he had ridden then, too.

But Charley didn't see any horses or mules that could be used to pull it. It would have to take ten or twelve. So maybe the man was just using the wagon as his house now, living alone in an isolated gully. With nothing but a bad-smelling fire for company.

Uncle JoJim was still riding in front. And as Calico Girl's front hooves touched the rocky dirt of the gully, thirty feet from the wild-haired man and his glowing coals, Uncle JoJim raised his hand.

"Hallo," he called. "Captain William Thomas! Are you well, sir?"

The tall man scowled, stepped around the fire, then stopped and struck the dirt with the base of his staff.

"That's far enough," he said. His voice was a deep, wet growl.

Uncle JoJim stopped Calico Girl fifteen feet from the man. Black-beard came up until his horse was abreast of Calico Girl, then also raised a hand and stopped. So Charley stopped Bird King, and Joshua stopped his roan.

But Red-beard brought his gelding around the boys and up alongside Black-beard. And Charley saw that Red-beard's hand was on the butt of his pistol.

"Hell if that ain't some kind of Federal coat," Red-beard muttered.

Black-beard glanced at Red-beard. "Stay quiet for now."

"I am sorry to disturb you, Captain Thomas," Uncle JoJim continued. "But my nephew and I encountered these gentlemen, Mister Clark and Mister Barnett, out on the prairie. They wish to confer with you, as they are in need of provisions for their journey."

Captain Thomas remained stock-still and scowling.

"You appear to be a savage," he said. "How is it that you know my name?"

Uncle JoJim removed his hat, hanging it on Calico Girl's saddle horn. His hair, dark and straight like Charley's, was plastered tight against his head.

"We met some twenty years ago," Uncle JoJim said, "in the far southwest of Kansas. Perhaps three hundred miles from this spot. I was with soldiers under attack from Comanches."

Captain Thomas's expression did not change.

"I recall the incident," he said. "It was my first exposure to the fact that the Army is a pack of goddamned fools." ·

Red-beard chuckled. "On that, we are in agreement."

Black-beard glared at him. "What did I say?"

Red-beard glared back. "Wasn't speaking to you."

Beside Charley, Joshua said, "Pa?" in a worried tone. Both Red-beard and Black-beard looked back at him.

At that, Uncle JoJim lowered his hand, and it brushed the shotgun scabbard behind his leg. Charley took a sharp breath.

But Black-beard turned back toward Uncle JoJim. "Careful there, Injun," he said. And Uncle JoJim's hand moved away from the shotgun again.

Captain Thomas did not seem to hear either Black-beard or Red-beard, or to notice what had just transpired. He remained focused on Uncle JoJim, who now spoke again.

"The Army should have paid attention when you demonstrated your ship at Fort Leavenworth," Uncle JoJim said. "Had they allowed you to build your fleet, their war might have been prevented. Or greatly shortened."

Captain Thomas was quiet for a moment. Then he said, "Dismount and come closer."

Uncle JoJim obeyed, leaving his hat on the saddle horn. He murmured to Calico Girl, then stepped forward until he was five or six feet from Captain Thomas.

"You have no right arm," Captain Thomas said.

Uncle JoJim said nothing.

Captain Thomas gave a slow shake of his head, and the slight wind that came down into the gully lifted his long, wild gray hair for an instant.

"I am sorry about that," he said. "I thought you were a Comanche." He scratched his jaw. "But at least I left you the other one."

⟷

Captain Thomas pointed his staff toward the wagon. "Come and sit. I have no chairs, but there are a few kegs. You'll soon be glad of the shelter, as a storm is coming. Oh, and my dinner is just about cooked. There will be enough for all of us, as I was preparing for several days in advance."

He went back into the shadow under the wagon.

Uncle JoJim turned toward Black-beard. "What are your wishes?"

Black-beard dismounted. "We'll do as the man suggests. But we won't stay long, on account of the smell." He gave Red-beard a quick gesture. "Have your boy tie the horses to those ridiculous wheels."

"But Charley's animal ain't got a bridle," Joshua said.

Red-beard dismounted as well. "So take a rope and loop it around the beast's neck." He looked at Charley and grinned. "That will be good practice."

Black-beard and Red-beard stepped up on either side of Uncle JoJim. "You heard the invitation," Black-beard said. "Let's go."

Uncle JoJim did not look back at Charley as he and the two bushwhackers disappeared under the wagon. And for the first time he could remember, Charley felt completely alone.

"Well," Joshua said as the men disappeared into the shadow, "I guess we should get down and tie the horses."

So Charley slid down, rubbed his itching face, and then reached up and grasped a strand of Bird King's mane. He led Bird King to Calico Girl, took the mare's bridle in his free hand, and brought the two horses to the big wheel at what he thought was the front of the wagon. Joshua led the other three horses to the rear wheel and tied their reins to it. Then he tossed Charley a six-foot piece of rope.

"Do a good job," Joshua said, "or Pa might get mad."

Charley looped Calico Girl's reins around a wheel spoke thicker than his leg, tying them with a slipknot. Then he looped the rope around Bird King's neck, knotted it, and tied the loose end next to Calico Girl's reins with another slipknot. Together, the slipknots looked complicated and tight. Or so Charley hoped.

Then he stepped between the two horses. For the moment, he was hidden from the men, and from Joshua as well. But he could hear Black-beard talking.

"I may have heard of you, Mister Thomas," Black-beard said. "This Injun's comments have reminded me. Did you not solicit investors for an 'Overland Navigation Company' in Westport, Missouri, some fifteen years ago? And did you not lose them all when the Federals refused to embrace your fanciful schemes?"

Charley shuddered at the ugliness of Black-beard's voice, then stepped farther back between Bird King and Calico Girl until he stood beside the scabbard that held Uncle JoJim's shotgun.

Captain Thomas's deep voice floated to him from the shadows. "First, sir, I am not 'Mister' Thomas. By virtue of decades in command of both government and private vessels in the Northern Atlantic and other regions, I am 'Captain.' Second, my plans for overland navigation were never fanciful, but wholly practical. All the world was once the sea, you know. And though the waters have partially receded, the same methods employed upon them for generations may also be employed upon the lands that once lay beneath them. Such as this vast prairie."

Black-beard and Red-beard both laughed then, and Charley's reaction to the sound was to reach up and touch the shotgun. If he stretched on tiptoe, he might be able to pull it free.

But then what? The shotgun was long and heavy, and Uncle JoJim had allowed him to fire it only once, at the beginning of today's hunt. It had knocked Charley over, and he had found himself on his back in the grass, staring up at a patch of blue sky. The prairie chicken he had been trying to shoot had flown on through that blue patch, free and clear. Charley was pretty sure the bird had looked down and mocked him.

But maybe now that he had fired the gun once, he could brace himself for its force.

He rose on his toes as he heard a rumble of thunder to the south. And then he heard Joshua's voice.

"Are both barrels loaded?"

Charley jerked back his hand. Joshua had come up beside the wagon wheel and was now standing between the necks of Bird King and Calico Girl, staring at Charley. He had spoken softly, and since they were between the horses, and thunder was rumbling, Charley didn't think the men had heard.

"Just one barrel is loaded," Charley said. "Uncle JoJim used the other on this bird." He touched the third chicken hanging from the left side of the saddle.

Joshua shook his head. "That's no good. You would have to kill both my pa and Mister Barnett, real quick. So you'd need both barrels. Otherwise, whoever was left would cut off your scalp." He tilted his head toward the other horses. "I saw Pa do it once. Both he and Mister Barnett have whole bags of scalps. They're going to use them to trade with the Injuns between here and New Mexico."

Charley's mouth had gone dry, but he forced himself to swallow. "I wasn't going to do anything."

"Yes, you were." Joshua's voice was even softer now. "You're an Injun, and Pa says that's what Injuns do. You think about how to kill white men. But if you try it like you have in mind, you'll die. And that would make me sad. I ain't had much chance to be around other boys, and I like it. I don't even mind too much that you ain't white." He pointed back over his shoulder with his thumb. "Come on, now. Pa will be perturbed at us for being slow."

Joshua backed out the way he had come, and Charley followed. Bird King snuffled Charley's neck as he passed by.

Charley's fingertips tingled. He wished he could have done it. He wished he could have taken the shotgun and used it on Black-beard and Red-beard. But Joshua was right. One barrel would not have been enough. So he supposed he was grateful that Joshua had stopped him.

But he didn't think he would have a chance to be grateful for long.

◄○►

As Charley and Joshua came away from Bird King and Calico Girl, Captain Thomas emerged from underneath the wagon again. He still carried his twisted ivory staff. The boys stopped at the rim of the wheel so as not to cross his path.

"He's sure tall," Joshua whispered to Charley. "And ugly."

Charley stiffened. That had not seemed like a smart thing to say.

But if Captain Thomas had heard, he gave no sign. "You gentlemen may remain seated if you like," he called back into the shadow. "Forgive me for rising again so soon. But I smell rain, and I would prefer to take our dinner from the fire before it arrives."

He strode to the coals, slid the pointed end of his staff through a loop of wire in the hammered-tin dome, and swung the dome away from the grate. A cloud of smoke boiled up into the twilight.

Black-beard and Red-beard came out from under the wagon with Uncle JoJim between them. Charley saw that Red-beard had drawn his pistol and had placed its muzzle against Uncle JoJim's ribs.

On his right side. Where Uncle JoJim had no arm. So he had no chance, not even a tiny one, of knocking the pistol away.

In that instant, Charley found that he was no longer afraid. Now, he was just angry.

Captain Thomas, with his back to the other men, set the tin dome on the dirt. He slid his pointed staff back from the wire loop, then used it to stab at something on the smoking grate.

Black-beard gave Red-beard a glance. He stepped past Charley and Joshua and slipped between Calico Girl and Bird King.

"The Neosho River is a few miles to the east," Captain Thomas said. "And while its offerings cannot match the bounty of the sea, I have found it to be sufficient."

He spiked a long, blackened thing the size of a man's arm, and he turned to face the wagon while holding it high. The coals behind him glowed scarlet.

"I hope you like water moccasin," he said.

Red-beard made a gagging sound, but kept his pistol jammed into Uncle JoJim's ribs.

Captain Thomas's brow furrowed. "Sir," he said to Red-beard. "Why have you drawn your weapon?"

At that moment, Black-beard came out from between the rumps of Calico Girl and Bird King. He was carrying Uncle JoJim's shotgun.

"I have a better question," Black-beard said. "To wit: Just what in hell is that lance of yours? I've never seen the like, even among the Injuns. And I may want to buy it."

Captain Thomas shifted his gaze to Black-beard. And then he smiled, exposing his teeth for the first time.

From where Charley stood, Captain Thomas's teeth looked as if they had all been filed to sharp points. And they glistened.

"I fashioned this harpoon from the tusk of a narwhal," Captain Thomas said. "Not that you will know what that is. And it is not for sale."

Black-beard stepped a few yards closer and raised the shotgun. He pointed it at Captain Thomas's chest.

"That's a shame," he said.

Red-beard spoke then, too. "Joshua, hold the boy."

Charley had taken a step toward Uncle JoJim. But now Joshua grasped both his wrists and pinned his arms behind his back.

"I'm truly sorry," Joshua whispered in Charley's ear. "But I have to do what Pa says."

Captain Thomas was still holding the charred snake aloft on his narwhal tusk. And he was still grinning his sharp-toothed grin at Black-beard.

"Well," Captain Thomas said. "Will you do it, or not?"

Black-beard cocked both hammers of the shotgun.

Now Uncle JoJim spoke. "Before you fire," he said, "I have a request to make of Captain Thomas."

Black-beard kept the shotgun trained on Captain Thomas, but said, "Go right ahead. For all the good it will do you."

Uncle JoJim looked at Captain Thomas. "You owe me a small debt, sir. I'll ask for payment now."

Captain Thomas kept grinning at Black-beard, but he answered Uncle JoJim. "Proceed, Mister James."

Uncle JoJim gestured toward the two geldings and the mare that Joshua had tied to the wagon's rear wheel. "Spare the horses."

One of Captain Thomas's shaggy gray eyebrows rose.

"I cannot promise," he said.

Black-beard gave a growl.

"Enough of your shit," he said. Then he pulled the shotgun's front trigger.

A gout of blue and yellow flame spat from the shotgun's right barrel, and there was a sound like a thunderclap. The shot caught Captain Thomas square in the chest, and he fell backward onto the fire grate. His coat was peppered with black holes over his heart, and two of its brass buttons were gone. The narwhal tusk was still clutched in his right fist.

Charley stared at the dirty, callused soles of Captain Thomas's feet as the man's coat began to smolder and his wild hair began to burn.

Overhead, lightning webbed through the storm clouds rolling in from the south.

⤙⬦⤚

Black-beard lowered the shotgun. "Damn it to hell," he said. "Sam, go drag that son of a bitch from the fire. It's like to burn off his hair, and then that scalp won't be any use."

Red-beard stared at Black-beard. "You think I want to get burned any more than you do?"

"Make the Injun do it, then."

"But you said to kill him once you'd shot the lunatic."

"Well, sweet Jesus, you haven't done it yet, have you?" Black-beard said. "So send him over to pull that goddamned carcass away! He does anything but, and we can both shoot him."

Red-beard took his pistol from Uncle JoJim's ribs and gave him a shove. "Go on. Bring that Yankee out of there before his hair burns, and maybe you'll get to live a little longer."

Uncle JoJim started for the fire. But he gave Charley a sharp look.

"My shotgun has left its scabbard," he said.

Charley knew what that meant. Uncle JoJim wanted him to jump onto Bird King and ride for home. But how was he supposed to do that? Joshua was holding him tight.

"I feel you pulling," Joshua whispered. "Just be still, and you'll be all right. Maybe you can be Pa's slave."

Uncle JoJim approached the hot coals and crouched with his arm stretched out. He turned his face away from the heat, wincing, and grasped Captain Thomas's left ankle.

"Be quick about it," Black-beard said.

Uncle JoJim leaned away from the fire and yanked Captain Thomas from the grate. The force of it made Uncle JoJim fall to the ground, and Captain Thomas's feet came to earth on either side of him.

Captain Thomas pivoted upright, his coat and hair enveloped in a halo of smoke. His eyes blazed like coals. His sharp-toothed grin was a twisted rictus.

Black-beard gave a bellow and raised the shotgun again.

At that moment, a white spike of lightning struck the hilltop to the west, and the thunderclap was like the report of a cannon. As the sudden flash illuminated the gully, Captain Thomas's right arm whipped forward and threw the narwhal-tusk harpoon.

The harpoon stabbed through the air and spiked into Red-beard's groin. Its point emerged from the seat of his trousers, and Red-beard's arms flew up. His pistol shot a small flame toward the sky and then fell away. Red-beard collapsed backward, and the point of the narwhal tusk buried itself in the dirt. Red-beard was pinned to the ground with the blackened water moccasin burning against his crotch. His hat rolled away on its crisp brim.

Red-beard's legs twitched, and his arms flailed. His eyes bulged, and his mouth opened wide. He screamed like a goat being slaughtered.

"Pa!" Joshua cried. He released Charley's wrists and started toward Red-beard.

Black-beard gave a bellow and raised the shotgun, once again aiming at Captain Thomas. He pulled the second trigger, but nothing happened.

Captain Thomas, his coat and hair smoking, stepped over Uncle JoJim toward Black-beard.

Black-beard dropped the shotgun and fumbled in his belt for his pistol.

Uncle JoJim was giving Charley another look.

Charley spun and ran back to where Calico Girl and Bird King were tied. He jerked on Calico Girl's reins to free their slipknot from the wheel spoke, then yanked the end of the rope to free that slipknot as well. Then he jumped up, grasped Bird King's mane, and pulled himself onto the stallion's back.

Bird King jumped backward and wheeled, and the end of the rope whipped into the air. Charley slapped Calico Girl's rump as they passed, and she began to wheel as well.

As Bird King galloped past Black-beard, the rope snapped into the man's wrist, and his pistol whirled away into the fire. Black-beard shouted, then ran for the three tied horses.

Captain Thomas, still smoking and grinning, changed direction and kept walking toward Black-beard.

Charley tugged Bird King's mane to bring him to a halt beside Uncle JoJim, who was getting to his feet.

"Calico Girl is free," Charley said.

Uncle JoJim gave him a fierce glare. "Why have you stopped? Do as I said!"

Charley began to shake his head. He didn't want to be disrespectful, but he had no intention of leaving until Uncle JoJim was on Calico Girl and could leave with him.

But Uncle JoJim slapped Bird King's neck and shouted, "*Yici!*"

Bird King leaped away and charged up the hill to the north. Charley tugged on his mane to stop him, but the horse paid no attention. Uncle JoJim had told Bird King to go home. And Bird King had learned to obey Uncle JoJim in Kanza before Charley had ever spoken a word to him in English.

All Charley could do was look back as Bird King ran across the hilltop and down the other side, watching for Uncle JoJim and Calico Girl to appear behind them. A deep red glow burned at the western horizon as the sun began to vanish, but the sky above Charley had turned purple. Black thunderheads filled the sky to the south and were swallowing the purple as they advanced. Streaks of lightning shot through the thunderheads, and a few jagged spikes zigzagged down to strike the earth. Thunder rumbled and growled, and the wind became a constant hiss through the grass.

Then, as Bird King started up the next slope, the silhouette of a horse and rider appeared at the hilltop behind them. Charley's heart leaped.

But then the rider extended a long arm toward Charley and Bird King, and fire shot from its end.

◄○►

Charley heard the bullet buzz past his ear like an enraged bee. He ducked and urged Bird King to run faster. But Bird King was already running as fast as he could, his hooves pounding even louder than the thunder behind them. And they were heading uphill now. So they were a good target.

Another bullet buzzed past, and Charley was sure that it flew through his hair. So he slid down to Bird King's right side, clamping his legs as tightly as he could against the stallion's body and clinging to his mane. Bird King snorted but didn't slow. He charged on, upward through the hissing grass.

Charley had the sudden thought that he was riding like a Comanche now.

Then Bird King squealed, lurched, and twisted to the right. Charley was flung into the air, and he flew a long way before hitting the ground and tumbling across the slope.

He lay on his back then, trying to breathe. The air had been knocked from his lungs. He couldn't tell whether he had broken an arm or leg, because he couldn't feel anything. Dark blades of grass waved in the wind over his face, framing a patch of purple sky with the black edge of a cloud pushing through. The cloud ate a tiny point of light that might have been a star.

Then the sound of the wind was joined by the sound of a horse's hooves, walking.

Charley was able to suck in a breath. "Bird King?" he said, and sat up.

But Bird King was nowhere to be seen. Instead, Black-beard sat above Charley on his sorrel gelding, pointing down with his Spencer carbine. There was just enough red light from the west for Charley to see his face. It was set in a deep scowl.

"Your elders evaporated like spirits," Black-beard said. "So I reckon you'll have to answer for their insults yourself."

That meant Uncle JoJim and Calico Girl had managed to get away. Charley was glad. But he was worried about Bird King.

"Did you kill my horse?" he asked.

Black-beard gave a shrug. "My shot struck him, but I cannot say whether the wound was mortal. However, he was well enough to run over the hill. Perhaps he fell on the far side and died. Or perhaps I'll retrieve him for myself. Either way, it's no concern of yours."

Another horse stepped up beside Black-beard's gelding then. It was the roan mare, and Joshua was riding it. He had lost his straw hat, and his blond hair danced in the wind. The other gelding walked beside him, riderless, tied to the roan's saddle horn.

"My pa is dead," Joshua said. "I tried to pull out the lance, but I couldn't. It was stuck in the ground. And I begged Pa to move, but he wouldn't. So he's dead. He's dead because of you and yours." Joshua's thin voice quavered, and his face shifted between anger and agony.

Black-beard flipped the Spencer's strap from his shoulders, and he held the butt of the rifle toward Joshua.

"You've lost family," Black-beard said. "So you may do this. It's already cocked. Hold it tight against your shoulder. And don't worry about the horses. They're used to the sound."

Joshua took the Spencer, placed the stock against his shoulder, and pointed the muzzle at Charley.

Charley looked up at him. "I had thought you might feel friendly toward me," he said.

Joshua's hands began to quiver in time with his voice, and the Spencer quivered with them. "You can shut up and be still."

"Steady, boy," Black-beard said.

Joshua hands still quivered. But it seemed to Charley that the Spencer's muzzle was not wavering so much that the shot would miss.

Charley shifted his gaze back to Black-beard.

"Somehow," he said, "you will suffer for hurting Bird King."

Black-beard laughed. It was a snarl terminating in a bark.

"That'll be a good trick," he said.

As he spoke, lightning flashed in the south, and thunder roared. A heavy rush of wind raised the hissing of the grass to a howl.

Both Black-beard and Joshua looked back over their shoulders. And Charley looked, too.

Glowing with red light from the west and flashing with white lightning from above and behind, Captain Thomas's enormous wagon rose over the southern hilltop with a deafening rumble. Huge sheets of canvas billowed from its posts and crossbeams, and it seemed to Charley that they sliced through the storm clouds churning overhead.

With tremendous speed, the wagon plunged down the hillside and then up the next. It drove straight toward Charley, Joshua, and Black-beard, its twelve-foot wheels spinning so fast that the spokes were a blur.

The narwhal-tusk harpoon had been affixed to a bracket at the front of the wagon, and Red-beard dangled from it upside-down and backward. He hung from the point where the tusk had pierced him through his groin and ass, and he swung back and forth. He had slid down to the harpoon's wooden base, and the tail of the scorched water moccasin was visible between his legs. A thick, dark stain spread down his shirt and soaked his hair. His legs flopped at the knees, and his arms waved crazily. His fingertips brushed the tallgrass. And as the wagon surged forward, his face was pounded to a pulp against the ochre boards.

"Pa!" Joshua cried.

Black-beard, staring at the massive wind-wagon speeding toward him, reached toward Joshua. "Give me the rifle!" he cried.

But Joshua turned back toward Charley. His cheeks were wet with tears. He pressed his cheek against the Spencer's stock as he aimed.

"I hate you, Injun Charley," he said.

Then the rumble and roar of the approaching wagon was shot through with a piercing shriek, and the sound startled the gelding tied to Joshua's saddle. It whinnied, stamped, jerked its reins from the saddle horn, and ran. The Spencer's stock slammed into Joshua's eye, and its muzzle swung wide as his mare reared.

Charley dove between the mare's front legs as he heard the sharp crack of the shot. He grabbed the thick cotton strands of the saddle cinch just as the horse came down and bolted. He hung on with both hands, swinging his legs up so they wouldn't be trampled by the rear hooves. He clung there for a few seconds until the horse screamed at a flash of lightning, stopped running, and reared again. Then he let go of the cinch and rolled away, hoping he would make it far enough.

As he came up to his knees, he saw Black-beard a dozen yards away. The man was rising to his knees as well, clutching his left shoulder with his right hand. His fine, flat-crowned hat was gone.

"God damn you, boy!" Black-beard roared. "You shot me with my own gun!"

Then Black-beard got to his feet and turned to face south. He completed the turn just in time for Red-beard's dangling head to collide with his, and it knocked him flat onto the hillside.

The wind-wagon's iron-clad right front wheel rolled over Black-beard's skull, spewing brains and bone through the tallgrass. Then the rear wheel cut across Black-beard's belly and severed his spine, sending his torso rolling and entrails spilling. His legs flew up and thumped against the bottom of the wagon before falling back into the grass.

Charley heard the piercing shriek cut through the rumble again. He looked up and saw Captain Thomas, his coat still smoking, standing atop the wagon at its rear. He was pulling against a heavy beam with his left arm while yanking a bundle of ropes with his right. The ropes rose to the huge sheets of canvas, and the canvas began to twist. The wagon groaned and turned, spinning up chunks of dirt and grass as the gigantic wheels shifted and slid.

"Do you see now?" Captain Thomas shrieked. "Do you see how sweetly she sails?" His long gray hair whipped in the wind like snakes, and his sharpened teeth gleamed with each flash of lightning. His eyes caught the red fire of the sinking sun.

The wind-wagon roared past Charley, its furious wheels spattering him with dark droplets. He tasted copper and salt.

Now the wagon drove to the northeast, aiming for a horse that was spinning, rearing, and bucking. The horse's small rider was clinging to the reins with one hand and a Spencer carbine with the other.

Charley got to his feet. He wanted to call out to Joshua. But he knew the boy wouldn't hear him over the wind, the thunder, and the roar of the wagon.

There was nothing to be said to him now, anyway.

As the wind-wagon bore down, the horse bucked hard and jumped away. Joshua flew into the air, tumbling as the Spencer shot fire, and then the narwhal tusk caught him in the back. The Spencer fell away, and the tusk spiked out through Joshua's chest.

Captain Thomas shrieked again, and the wind-wagon came about, rising onto two wheels. Then it plunged back down the hill, roaring past Charley once more.

Joshua slid back on the tusk and fetched up against his father. He looked down at Charley as they flew by.

Charley could not read Joshua's expression. But he saw that the boy's freckled cheeks were still wet.

The wind-wagon dove down the slope and back up the hill to the south. As it reached the top, it was illuminated by yet another flash of lightning. The sails billowed and warped, and Charley heard Captain Thomas shriek one more time.

Then the rain came in a torrent, and Charley's eyes filled with water as the wind-wagon disappeared.

-◦-

The rain lasted long enough to wash the dark droplets from Charley's skin and to soak his clothes. Then the thunderclouds began to break and slip away even more quickly than they had come. The moon, almost full, rose in the east as the last vestige of the sun slipped away in the west. Its cool light let Charley see where he walked as he began to trudge north.

He whistled for Bird King. But instead, Joshua's roan mare and Blackbeard's sorrel gelding came up to him, whickering.

"I don't want to ride either of you," Charley said. "But you may walk with me, if you like."

They had almost reached the top of the hill when Charley heard another whistle. He looked back down the slope and saw Uncle JoJim approaching on Calico Girl. They were leading the other gelding on a rope, moving at a walk. The shotgun was back in its scabbard. And Uncle JoJim was wearing his hat again.

Charley waited until Uncle JoJim drew near. Then he said, "You might have come sooner."

Uncle JoJim stopped Calico Girl beside Charley. "As I have said, I don't want to make Calico Girl run anymore."

"But I needed you," Charley said.

Uncle JoJim gave him a stern look. "No, you didn't. Besides, if you had done as I instructed, you would have been far away."

Charley knew it was true. "I apologize, Uncle JoJim. I should not have disobeyed."

Uncle JoJim shrugged. "You'll know better next time. Now, take the bags from those horses and leave them. We don't want what's inside. Then tie one of the horses to the one behind Calico Girl. You may ride the other."

Charley frowned. "I will only ride Bird King."

"Disobeying yet again." Uncle JoJim sighed. "All right, tie them both. You may walk."

Charley did as he was told, and then they all started over the hill. As they topped the rise, Charley saw Bird King a little way down the slope, grazing.

"Bird King!" Charley called. "Why didn't you come when I whistled?"

Uncle JoJim chuckled. "He's angry. I can see the wound near his tail. You didn't go home when I said to go home, so Bird King was shot."

"I'm sorry, Uncle JoJim," Charley said.

"Don't tell me. Tell him."

Charley whistled once more, and this time Bird King came. Uncle JoJim dismounted, examined the wound, and said it wasn't deep. And the bullet had not remained in the flesh.

"But it still hurts him," Uncle JoJim said, swinging up onto Calico Girl again. "We'll put a poultice on it when we reach the reservation. For now, it's up to him whether he lets you ride. If he does, I wouldn't ask him to run."

Charley put his hand on Bird King's soft nose. Bird King tossed his head, but then let Charley grasp his mane and pull himself up. Charley untied the rope that was still around Bird King's neck, and he let it fall.

As they started northward again, Uncle JoJim said, "I suppose you may be saddened because of the boy."

Charley brushed water from Bird King's mane. "He was just a boy. Like me. It's hard to know what I should think."

"He was a boy," Uncle JoJim said. "But not like you. And you'll live through many times when it will be hard to know what to think."

They rode in silence for a quarter mile. Then Charley asked, "Is Captain Thomas one of the ghosts Grandmother spoke of?"

"No. Ghosts are easier to understand."

"But the black-bearded man shot him with your shotgun, and he didn't die. Not even after falling onto the fire."

"It was only birdshot," Uncle JoJim said. "And he wore a thick coat. Also, he didn't lie on the fire for very long."

"So he's just a man?"

Uncle JoJim adjusted the brim of his hat. "That would be easier to understand, too. But I'm sure of one thing: He came to pay his debt for my arm. I can't guess how he knew this would be the right time. But it's done. So now he's gone again."

That all made a small bit of sense to Charley. "I'm glad," he said.

Uncle JoJim looked behind them at the tied horses. "Yes. And along with our chickens, we have three ponies to replace those the Cheyenne stole last month. Allegawaho will be pleased. Everyone will be."

Charley pondered. "So now they might consider us to be Kaw?"

Uncle JoJim shook his head. "No. We are what we are." He looked toward the moon. "What we are is good enough."

That made a bit of sense to Charley, too.

"At least we aren't crazy," he said.

Uncle JoJim shrugged yet again, and his empty sleeve flapped. "Not yet."

Bird King began to trot then, of his own will. He and Charley led the way home through the sea of grass.

# WHAT MY MOTHER LEFT ME

## ALYSSA WONG

The sky above Nag's Head is stained an uneasy shade of gray by the time we pull up to my parents' North Carolina beach house. Beyond the dunes and waving field of sea grass, the water is sharp and choppy, the color of slate.

"Shit," says Gina, climbing out of the Range Rover. She shades her eyes, her long, lavender-dyed hair flapping across her face. The wind slaps us both with the salty, thick smell of the ocean. "You brought the keys, right?"

Her eyeliner is perfect, as usual. I can't believe she drew it on in the passenger seat while I was doing ninety on the I-40, eager to put as much distance between us and Duke University as possible.

"Way ahead of you," I say, fishing the house keys out of my pocket. The key fob is a piece of driftwood, carved with the words HOME SWEET HOME and a pair of flip-flops. It's about as tacky as the rest of the house's decor. We trudge up the wooden stairs, wiping our feet on the faded welcome mat printed with migrating birds. There's a thin film of salt on the lock.

I sort through the keys, looking for the right one. I don't realize my hands are shaking until Gina drapes herself over me.

"Emma? Are you okay?"

"Too much coffee," I say. The look on her face tells me she doesn't believe me, but loves me too much to call me on my bullshit. "Just antsy. I gotta pee real bad."

"Then open the damn door." She leans close and blows in my ear. I can hear the sympathy in her voice. "Let's get inside. Whatever's in there . . . we can handle it."

"I'm fine," I say.

"You don't have to be." She squeezes my hand. *It's only been three weeks,* she doesn't say, but I hear anyway. *Your mom is dead. You* shouldn't *be okay.*

"If I don't get inside I'm gonna pee on your foot," I say instead.

Gina bites my ear gently and I push open the door. The air inside the house smells musty, and the ugly, pseudo-rattan wallpaper is warping along the edge of the ceiling. Sure enough, the décor is still stuck in the seventies. The carpet is a matted riot of overbright geometric shapes. There are carved wooden birds sitting on every surface, decoys in the shape of sandpipers, ducks, and other local waterfowl. For a moment, a memory overlaps what I'm looking at, and I can almost see my family arranged in the living room. My dad reading a paperback thriller on the couch, my mom gazing out the window and turning a shell over and over in her hand. I blink, and their phantom bodies evaporate.

A thick layer of dust coats everything, and the first thing I do is flip on all the fans. Gina flips them off immediately.

"Dude, do you want all this stuff in your lungs? We should wipe everything down first." She wrinkles her nose, shouldering her backpack. "Why are there so many dead horseflies? It's like someone held a party and left behind the worst confetti."

"Someone might have left a window open." We trudge upstairs, checking all the rooms. Sure enough, one of the windows in an upstairs bedroom is slightly cracked, and water damage spreads all throughout the room and into the hall. I grimace and shut the window. "Goddammit. At least it's not the master bedroom."

"That's where most of your mom's stuff is, right?" Gina twines her fingers with mine. "We don't have to go in right away. We could get dinner first, or unload the car."

"I need to know if there's water damage there, too," I say, pulling my hand free and wiping my palms on my jeans. The knot of stress and nervousness in my stomach constricts. The beach house had been Mom's haven. She'd always come alive at the beach, bright and vibrant the way she wasn't at home. As far as I knew, she hadn't come up here alone in the ten years since then. "We can unload the car after I check."

Walking the hallway dredges up more old memories. Lying on the carpet by the stairs, playing Pokémon on my Gameboy. My mom singing to herself when she thought she was alone, straightening the pictures on the wall. My dad pulling me aside, nodding at a photo on my phone. *That boy's a keeper. Don't let him go.*

The master bedroom lies at the end of the hall. My hands are cold as I reach for the door. All of the *what-ifs* spin through my head, constricting my thoughts like a lasso. Images of water damage, boxes of ruined possessions beneath the bed, sea-streaked clothing flash through my head. What if someone's carelessness had ruined everything Mom had left behind? What if I couldn't handle what I'd find?

But when I push the door open, I breathe a sigh of relief. Just like the rest of the rooms, everything is faded and covered in dust, but all the windows are locked tight. Mom's ugly rose-pink bedspread is still there, along with the lace-lined pillows and the painting of gulls coasting above the surf. It looks just like she left it.

"Emma?" Gina's voice breaks through my head, and the knot in me eases. I turn and hug her tight, ignoring her surprised noise. Her body is soft against mine.

"It's okay," I whisper. "I'm so glad."

Gina hums and presses a kiss to my forehead. "Me too," she says. "Let's get the beer out of the trunk and sit down for a bit. You look like you could use a drink."

That night, we drink too much and curl up together on the couch. Gina runs her fingers through my hair as I listen to her heartbeat, slow and steady. "I can't believe you wanted to do this alone," she murmurs. "You can rely on me a little more, okay?"

I'm not good at relying on people, but Gina insists. I press my cheek against her chest. "I'll try," I say.

━◇━

The bad weather persists, and we spend most of the next day excavating the house. Gina finds the vacuum cleaner and makes sure we have livable conditions to work in, and I haul giant bag after giant bag of trash out to the dumpster down the cul-de-sac. The worst part, though, is the smell of rotten fish that wafts in halfway through the day.

Gina shuts off the vacuum cleaner and gags, holding her throat. "Em, if you don't open a window, I will actually die."

She's being dramatic, but she's right. Even turning the AC on high doesn't dispel it, and the stench chases us out of the house by afternoon.

The wind kicks sand up around us, and it stings my exposed legs as we walk toward the boardwalk. Gina's got a pair of giant bedazzled sunglasses on, and it's never seemed like a smarter fashion choice. My phone keeps buzzing in my back pocket, and after twenty minutes of notifications, it's starting to make my butt go numb. Gina frowns at it.

"Em, you should've left that back at the house."

"What if we get lost? I need to make sure we can find our way back." My fingers itch toward my phone and she grabs my wrist. Her eyes are clear and serious.

"Don't text him back," Gina says. "You said you were done with him."

I drop my hand and let my thoughts slide away from the barrage of texts from my boyfriend. Clayton hadn't taken the breakup well. He punched a hole in my apartment wall right next to the refrigerator. I'd headed over to Gina's after that, and Clayton's been blowing up my phone since then, trying to apologize. "Sorry," I say. "I'm trying."

She laces her fingers with mine possessively. "Why haven't you deleted his number? He doesn't love you, Em. He wants to own you; that's different."

I wince. Even when we were just friends, Gina never passed up a chance to shit on Clayton. She's usually right, and she only does it because she cares about me. But it still leaves an uneasy taste in my mouth. "I broke up with him yesterday, give me a break."

"I love you, Em," says Gina. Her grip on my hand is tight. "And what you had with him isn't love. Don't let him occupy your head and ruin this trip for us."

That makes me bristle. "It's not a *vacation*, Gina. Jesus. I'm sorry, but is sorting through my dead mom's effects your idea of fun? Because it sure as hell isn't mine."

Her mouth drops open. "I didn't mean—"

My phone buzzes again, and I swear, grabbing it and shutting it off. Clayton's latest text—EM, WHERE ARE YOU? I'M CALLING YOUR DAD—flashes across the screen before it goes dark. When I look back at Gina, the naked hurt on her face is visible even behind her sunglasses. Shit. "Look," I say, guilt gentling my voice. "I just . . . I'm sorry. I didn't mean that. That was really unfair."

"Yeah," she says. "It was."

I rub my face. My eyes sting from the salty air. "Can we just get lunch?"

Her mouth sets in a thin line. "Fine." We walk the rest of the way side by side, not looking at each other.

By the time we make it to the beach, Gina's shoulders have lost some of their tension, and I reach for her hand. She starts to tuck it into the pocket of her jeans shorts, but then she sighs and takes it. "You better be sorry, you bitch."

"Yeah, I am," I say.

"A bitch, or sorry?"

"Both," I say. When I lean in to bump her shoulder with mine, she laughs. "That's for sure."

"You don't have to worry about him," I tell her quietly. "I love you. So don't be insecure, okay?"

Clayton would have dragged the fight out for days, guilt-tripping and giving me the cold shoulder. And maybe it's what I deserve. But Gina nods. She forgives me more than she should, and when I'm around her, I want to do better. I want to be a better person than I am, for her.

I'm leaning in to kiss her when she stops walking abruptly, and I miss her face by a full inch. "What the hell is that?"

A few feet away, a dead fish lies on the damp sand, stranded by the receding tide. Sandflies swirl around it in wild clouds. Its bottom half looks normal, but something has split its top half all the way down its spine. White bones poke out of its back, fanning out like a house centipede's legs.

Then the fish gives a weak twitch, and I realize it's not dead. Its gills flap as it strains for air. As it moves, its flesh catches and bubbles. Its exposed bones dig into the sand.

The tide rushes back in and swirls around it. But instead of bearing the fish back into the ocean, the water tugs gently at its body, and then, in one fluid moment, the fish's skin rips like a soggy piece of toilet paper, parting along the dorsal fin and peeling away in a single ugly, awful curl. Its scales flash and then it's gone, dragged away by the waves, leaving the fish's raw, naked body flopping weakly on the sand.

"What the fuck," breathes Gina. Her hold is so tight that my fingers hurt. The fish's sides flutter frantically, and its eyes roll in its head. The white spines poking out of its flesh shiver delicately. "Em, there are a bunch of them, look!"

She points up the beach. The sand is littered with bodies, half-decomposed fish being dragged in and out by the tide. Some have lost their skin, and others are having theirs torn off in messy segments. All of them have spines peeling out of their bodies.

The rotten smell is so strong that it makes my eyes water. It smells, I realize, like my mother in the weeks before she died. I take a step back from the water, and then another. "We should go," I say.

We run, stumbling through the sand. We don't let go of each other until the beach house is in sight and we're stumbling through the door.

◄◦►

The first thing we do when we get back is Google "silver fish peeling," "ocean fish dissolving," and "coastal fish of nag's head." We learn it's a butterfish, and that no, that isn't something butterfish are supposed to do.

"Please tell me there's a liquor cabinet here," says Gina. When I point it out, she raids it and scours the kitchen for shot glasses.

Even with the AC running while we were out, the salty, rotten smell lingers. This time, it seems to be coming from a specific direction. "Hey, Gina?"

"What?" Gina raises her head, emerging with a hidden bottle of Fireball whiskey.

"I'm gonna go check upstairs," I say. "I wanna know where that smell is coming from." The rotten scent grows stronger the further I go into the house. Sure enough, I find that the window in the water-damaged bedroom has creaked open again. But as I turn toward the master bedroom, the scent becomes suffocating again. When I open the door, a tidal wave of rot-sea-stink hits me in the face. I choke, eyes watering.

The room is completely fucked up. The wallpaper has long rents in it, and Mom's pink duvet lies in a shredded heap at the foot of the bed. The mattress on Dad's side is gutted, from the headboard down. Pieces of foam spill out of its carcass. The pillows are an explosion of feathers. Even the seagull painting is a mess, peeling out of its broken frame. The carpet is soaked in seawater. It squelches underfoot as I tread inside, my heart sinking to my feet.

"No," I whisper. Mom's room. It's ruined. But who could have—

There's a dry skittering noise behind me. I whip around just in time to see a thin, flesh-colored thing launch itself at me. I shriek and stumble back, caught off guard. The creature—not a person, no, some alien *thing*—is light, but when it slams into my chest, it does so with enough force to knock me to the carpet. It raises its humanoid head, its eyeless face swiveling to meet me.

It's a fucking skin. An empty human skin. Its body is floppy and it lurches forward, dragging its empty flaps across me. It's tough, grayed, and scrapes like sandpaper. Almost like there are endless rows of tiny teeth trying to slough off my skin. As it paws at my face, I catch a glimpse of the way its awful, hollow hands are fused partway into fins, each finger tipped with a crumbling acrylic nail.

"Gina!" I scream, beating at it. It wraps its flat legs around me and opens its mouth, its awful empty mouth. I can see all the way down its dry, ragged throat. "Help! Gina!"

The skin bends its face toward mine, and its non-breath ghosts over my mouth. Its curly black hair tumbles around us.

Gina bursts in, bottle of Fireball in hand. She screams when she sees the creature, and immediately smashes the bottle into its head like she's hitting a home run. The bottle doesn't break, but it does send the skin spinning into the wall with a soft *whump*. I stagger upright as Gina seizes the wicker chair parked in front of the vanity and beats the skin until one of the chair's legs splinters.

"It was behind the door," I wheeze.

She pants, red with exertion. The skin lies still, and I don't know if it's stunned or dead, but I'm taking no chances. Together we use the broken chair to prod the skin into the walk-in closet. It scrapes against the chair, but it rolls obediently and lifelessly across the carpet. There are some minor tears here and there from Gina's beating, but it looks mostly intact.

Before I close the door, I poke the skin until it's lying flat on its back. It's the shape of a small woman, with small, sagging breasts. Long, withered gills run down each side of its ribs. Its black curls sprawl on the floor, lit by the flickering closet overhead light. Swallowing, I crouch over it, ignoring Gina's hiss.

There's a familiar birthmark on its right forearm.

"Gina," I say hoarsely. "It's my mom."

The skin twitches as if it's heard me, and I leap back and slam the closet door shut so hard that my ears ring.

◄○►

After Gina pukes—after we both do, if I'm being honest—we regroup in the kitchen and polish off a third of the Fireball. It helps a little, but neither of us can shake what we saw in the bedroom.

"Your dad had her cremated," says Gina. She wipes her mouth, and I smell the sharp scent of vomit on her jacket. "We saw that. We fucking saw it."

"I know!" Back at my parents' house, I'd placed her urn on the mantle myself, and then gone upstairs and cried for hours. "I don't know what that thing is. But it looks exactly like her. It's even got her birthmark."

My earliest memories of my mom involve sitting on the beach house porch, watching her whittle sandpipers out of driftwood. I remember watching that birthmark rise and fall with each deft movement of her knife. I'd recognize it anywhere.

"We need to get the fuck out of here," says Gina. She heads into the living room and throws her clothes and iPhone charger into her duffel bag. "Did you leave anything upstairs?"

My phone pings from where it's charging on the kitchen table. It's a text from my dad that reads: CLAYTON SAYS YOU BROKE UP WITH HIM?

I flip the phone face down. *Not now.* "I'm not leaving," I say. "Not until I know why she's here."

Gina stares at me in disbelief, her hair falling in front of her face. "Are you serious, Em? That thing just tried to kill us!"

"I noticed! But *why* is it here?" I rub my eyes. "Her skin should have been *on* her when she was cremated, not hiding in the beach house like a fucking horror movie monster. How is it even alive?"

"If it's still alive, it's going to come after us. So let's get moving."

My phone vibrates on the tabletop. Another text from Dad: EM, ANSWER ME.

Gina seizes my shoulders. "Emma," she says, low and urgent. "We can figure this out when we're on the road. I'm not staying in the house any longer, not with that thing. I've watched enough horror movies to know that if we sleep here, it's going to murder the fuck out of us."

"Then you go," I say, surprising us both. "I need to stay and find answers." Mom's death is raw, and I know, with utmost certainty, that I *need* to know why she's here. If I back out now and let other people deal with the skin creature, I never will.

"If you're staying, I'll stay too." She glances at my buzzing phone and narrows her eyes. "People who love each other don't leave them behind."

We exhaust Google after a couple hours, and all that comes up are a bunch of Wikipedia articles about various mythologies. None are particularly helpful. I lean across the table and glance around the living room, lingering on the bookshelves against the walls. "Maybe there's something in here that will tell us about . . . whatever that thing is."

"Like what? All I've seen here are birding guides and encyclopedias about different kinds of shells. Your parents don't have a copy of the Necronomicon."

"Gina, my mom's empty skin just tried to take my face off. At this point, anything's possible." I stand up, pushing my chair back. "We should go look. If there's anything, it'll be in their bedroom. They kept all their important shit there."

Gina reluctantly follows me upstairs. The rotting fish smell lingers in the hallway, but when I push the door open, the master bedroom is dark and still. The closet door remains closed.

I remember that the skin has human hands. What if it knows how to work doorknobs?

I flick on the lights and advance slowly. We fan out and check under the bed, behind furniture, and inside drawers. We find nothing but empty cardboard boxes and stacks of old photos of my parents. There are more recent ones too, and Gina pointedly shuffles the ones that include Clayton posing with my family, his arm around my waist, to the back of the pile.

There's one photo that catches my attention. It's of Mom sitting on the wooden steps, gazing wistfully into the distance. The wind sweeps her hair out of her face, and I know she's looking at the ocean. She loved the beach, but Dad never let Mom go swimming. I asked him why, once, and he told me that it was too dangerous. It would damage her skin.

I tuck the photo into my pocket.

"Em, look at this." Gina holds up my dad's old hunting knife. It's the same model as his normal, current hunting knife, from the black blade to the serrated edge by the hilt. But this one is bent out of shape, wildly crooked. It looks like it was dragged hard across asphalt.

There's a faint but steady scraping coming from the closet. I freeze, all the hair on my body standing on end. Gina hisses.

It's the sound of acrylic nails raking against wood.

My eyes meet Gina's. "Let's sleep in the car tonight," I whisper.

She grips the knife tighter. "Sounds like a plan."

The scraping grows more frantic than ever, right before we shut the bedroom door.

◄◦►

That night, I dream that I'm standing on the porch in front of the beach house, and my mom's skin is sitting next to me, carving a wooden bird out of a piece of driftwood. It turns its head, and there's nothing inside it but empty space. I can see the pale flipside of the skin, shining like the moon on the water, through the empty eyeholes of her almost-face.

"Watch," it says, and points its hollow arm at the ocean. I follow the glint of its knife down the long white expanse of sand. Two figures splash in the surf, a tall man with blond hair and a surfer's build, and a woman whose curly black hair swings around her in a long, thick braid. In the distance, dark, sharp-finned creatures glide through the water, each as long as a whale, their massive, long-necked animal heads breaching the surface. I know, somehow, that these are my mom's family. "See what he did to me."

My parents look young, maybe about as old as Gina and I are. My dad's swimming trunks have his fraternity's symbols on them, the same as the ones on all of Clayton's clothes. As I watch, my mom kisses my dad and then turns to face the ocean. Her pod, her family, waits many yards away, just close enough to see. She takes a breath and arcs toward the waves, and her skin ripples, growing gray and rough, her body expanding into a large, powerful shape.

He pulls his hunting knife from the back of his shorts and stabs her between the shoulder blades. He grips the hilt with both hands, and his shoulders flex with effort as he drags the knife down, sawing through her skin. She screams, and her skin ripples again, but he shoves the knife in harder, and as she thrashes it goes in deeper.

Her family howls from the water, surging closer, but Dad drags her onto the sand. Black blood surges from her wounds, fountaining over his hands, but he keeps going. As she struggles, he plants a foot on her back and drags his blade down her spine.

He saws all the way down her spine, tearing away her white bikini, and then he begins to peel her.

I can't look away, and I can't block out the sounds. I watch it all. I see everything.

When he's done, he pulls a pale, wet-skinned thing from her carcass. It's shaped like a human being, like a girl. She looks like the fish that Gina and I saw on the beach earlier, pulled open and exposed. Her naked flesh trembles. Each breath sounds agonizing. Even from this distance, I can see the fine, sharp ridges of her bones against the outline of her body.

He drops her on the sand and bends to pick up the gray, almost-person-shaped skin lying on the beach. It's caught partway between beast and woman, with halfway fins and long, fluttery gills. A few acrylic nails cling stubbornly to each of its partially transformed hands.

He slings the skin over his shoulder. Its flat, sightless face stares at the sky. Once he has it, he lifts her up, too, like she weighs nothing.

Dad walks up the beach house's wooden steps and past me without acknowledging me. My mom sags in his grip, her body dangling in his arms like a deboned fish. Her skin flaps behind him like an empty sock, slapping wetly against his back with each step. Her family wails, and the smell of ocean rot crashes over us like a wave.

I turn back toward the house and find myself looking into my own face. My skin stands empty, sand on its feet, hollow around the phantom shape of my body. It doesn't have eyes, or teeth, or a tongue, but when it speaks I hear its words clearly.

*Run away, Emma.*

I wake in the backseat of the Range Rover, cold sweat pouring down my back. Gina's arms wrap around me as she sleeps nestled against my side.

The texts from Dad keep pinging in, one after the other. The screen glows in the dark, through the pocket of my sweatpants. I swallow. I want to defend him, but I know him too well. My dad loved my mom the way Clayton loves me, which is to say, the way a man loves his favorite sports car. I can see him wanting to keep her with him, even after death. *Just not . . . actually keep her empty skin.*

*But he had her cremated*, whispers a part of me. *Didn't he?*

*But which parts?* asks another.

My skin aches, strangely tender.

I ease out of Gina's grip, and when she blinks up at me sleepily, I tell her to go back to sleep. "I'm just going to pee," I say. She nods and her head droops.

Lightning crackles overhead, and the wind is fiercer than ever. I have to fight my way into the house. The master bedroom is quiet again, and I sit on her side of the mattress, my back to the wall. I look at the carnage on Dad's side of the bed, and I wonder if she did that on purpose. Beside me, the skin creature scrapes at the closed closet door.

"Mom?" I whisper. "I want to talk to you. I need to know—what did Dad do to you?"

Mom's skin moves behind the door, making a whispering sound against the wood. I slide past her ruined favorite bedspread and kneel on the damp carpet, pressing my forehead against the closet door.

"I miss you," I tell her. "I wish I'd known. I wish I could have helped you."

There's a gentle rasp, like she's drawing her nails in circles beside my cheek. It makes me smile, and tears well up in my eyes. When I cried as a kid, my mom used to cradle my face in her hands and trace shapes on my cheeks. Could that have been what she was trying to do when I walked into the bedroom that first time?

"I'm sorry I let Gina hit you with the chair," I tell her. "She didn't know. I didn't know it was you, either."

Thunder rumbles outside the window, and it begins to rain hard. I glance out at the ocean below. The waves are rough, high. I remember the dream, and the image of her family crying and thrashing in the water.

She used to look at the waves with such longing. When I was little, she'd hold me on her lap and sing to me in a language I didn't know. It was a song, she told me, about where she'd come from. The flowers that grew beneath the water, the volcanoes, the canyons she'd grown up exploring. Whenever Dad walked into the room, though, she would stop singing. He told me he didn't want her speaking Korean, which he couldn't understand, around me. It wasn't until I got to college that I realized that her ocean songs hadn't been in Korean at all. I couldn't find a language for them, and when I asked her, she refused to let me record them for my professors to hear.

"I'm going to bring you home," I say, and she stills behind the door. "Just stay still and trust me."

The door handle is cold, and when I open it, a sliver of moonlight falls into the closet. Mom's skin crouches with her knees drawn up against her chest, gazing up at me. Her flat body and eyeless face make me shiver, even though I've braced myself. She smells awful. I hold my hand out, and she places one of hers, delicate, red-tipped, in mine.

There's a sudden banging on the downstairs door, and we both freeze. "Emma!" shouts a man's voice. It's Clayton. "Emma, it's me! Let me in!"

Mom's skin swivels her head toward the sound, and her back arches. Her hands twist into claws. I glance at the window, thinking fast.

There's a back door on the ground floor, but it's a sliding glass door and Clayton might be heading there right now. And—Gina, fuck. Hopefully she's safe, hiding in the car, and he missed her entirely.

"Come on," I say in a low voice and drag Mom to the window. It's not hard because she's so light. I crank it open and crawl out onto the lower segment of the roof, helping her out. The beach stretches out before us, and the wind whips the sea grass violently. No sign of Clayton.

I pull Mom onto my back and ease down the edge of the roof, sliding my legs over the edge and hanging on with my arms. Luckily, the stories aren't too high, and it's not too bad of a drop. Steep, but doable.

"Emma!"

Clayton's voice startles me and I let go too early. The fall knocks the wind out of me, and sand gets in my mouth. Clayton's footsteps hurry close, and I fight to catch my breath, my heart beating so fast that I can feel my pulse hammering in my hands. Where's Mom?

"There you are," he says. He looks just like I remember, but in my dazed state, he's overlaid with the dream image of my young father. "I couldn't get ahold of you, but your dad said I'd find you here. Why aren't you picking up your phone?"

A glint of light in his hand makes me realize he's holding a knife. Dread curls in my stomach. "Clayton," I wheeze. "Put that down."

"Emma," he says, and I recognize the wild look in his eyes. It's the same look he wore when I told him I was breaking up with him before I left. "I love you. I've been talking with your dad, and he said that there was a way to keep you with me forever. A way to make you understand."

I struggle up on my forearms and knees. My ankle's fucked. I don't have a weapon; I scan the area for a rock, or a stick, but there's nothing.

"Your dad told me," he says hoarsely, "that I have to cut you out of your skin. I don't know if I can do it. But I will." He steps toward me, his hands shaking. "For you, Emma. For our future together."

A flesh-colored blur darts past me and tears at his face. He screams, slashing at Mom with the knife. I cry out as he stabs several new holes in Mom's skin.

And then there's an awful crunching sound, and Clayton crumples onto the sand, dark blood spreading beneath his head. Gina stands over him with the tire iron from my Rover, a look of madness on her face.

"Run, Emma!" screams Gina. She swings the tire iron again, bashing Clayton's skull. Down, again and again, her shoulders and chest heaving.

I run, seizing Mom and stumbling down the beach as fast as I can on my messed-up ankle. The rain pelts us, making it hard to see. The water approaches, and as it does, the stench grows. The tide is out, and it's left behind lines of fish bones, running along the beach like veins of quartz. The sand is slippery, sticky with clear, smelly residue. Peeled, deboned fish float to the water's surface in the hundreds, staring up, unseeing, at the stormy sky. Their bodies bump against my legs as I wade into the surf.

The image of Clayton on the ground, blood leaking from his head, flashes through my mind. I struggle through it, biting my lip so hard that it begins to bleed, too.

Clayton—

*Gina*—

I have to stay focused. I wade into the water up to my waist, cradling Mom so she doesn't get swept away. She rests in my arms, like the stingrays I've seen in those big fish hunting shows, gathering their strength before swimming away. Overhead, thunder roars, deafening.

"It's time to go," I say. A lump rises in my throat, and I don't know if it's fear or despair. I don't want her to leave me again. But I know I have to let her go.

Bright pain stabs through my back, and I gasp, lurching forward and dropping Mom. With a quick twist, Mom's skin slithers out of my grip, darting into the water. The ocean floods into my mouth, and I choke.

The pain drags down my spine, sawing an uneven path down my body. It's excruciating, and I want to scream, but I can't breathe. Agony curls my body in half. I claw at the water, fighting for air.

"Stay still," says Gina. I know what's buried in my back; it's my dad's old hunting knife. Gina sounds like she's crying. "Em, please. I had the dream too. I know what we have to do."

She cuts me open, and I can't stop her. The waves batter me and my arms and legs ache, flooded with adrenaline and panic. I can feel everything, and I can't feel anything; my mind's shutting down, pushing me out of my own body.

Then she begins to peel me, and I black out.

*Wake up, Emma,* commands a voice that isn't mine or Gina's, or even my mom's. It's something older than that. Its myriad voices, joined together as one. An image of a pod of strange, animal bodies moving in a single sinuous shape jolts through my mind.

When I open my eyes, Gina's arms are wrapped around my chest from behind, hauling me toward the shore. My body feels raw. I can't feel my legs. Something wet slaps my face; when I look up, I find myself staring into my own eyeless face, the bloody backside of my skin showing through its open mouth.

No, I think frantically, trying to struggle. My skin face looks back at me, empty. No, no, no—

My mom rears up out of the water, lashing out at Gina with a giant, flat tail. It knocks us over, and Gina and I sprawl in different directions. The bottom half of Mom's body is like a giant fish's, half-transformed; the rest of her body is slowly morphing to match it. It still looks flat, wrong, like there's no meat inside of it.

I end up on my stomach, a few yards from Gina. My skin lies at the water's edge and I drag myself on my elbows toward it. As the tide washes in, a skinned fish bumps into my mouth. I spit it out and crawl through the surf, dragging my body over the rows of fine bones. My fingers brush my skin.

*Yes,* says the voice in my head, exultant.

I tug it over my head, and it settles over my face like a mask. The eyeholes are crooked, and I yank with all of my waning strength. Mom's hands, paper-thin and incongruously strong, latch onto my skin's flapping legs. Acrylic nails scrape my raw body as they guide my legs back into the skin.

Once, when I was very young, Mom and I snuck out of the beach house while Dad was asleep. That night, she taught me how to swim. She held me up in the shallows, letting me practice kicking and different ways to pull my body through the waves. Her movements in the ocean felt natural the way they never did on land. And then, when she thought I was ready, she pushed gently on my back, releasing me into the water.

Mom's hollow hand presses on my raw, naked back, and this time, I feel a rush of power. The open flaps of skin fold gently over my spine, sealing me inside.

*Now swim.*

My fingers and legs snap together, and my body explodes into a giant shape, arcing out of the water. My neck arcs in a column of thick muscle, and my face pushes outward, mouth stretching wide. I see my reflection in the surf, all rough gray skin and rows of serrated teeth. I'm monstrous, beautiful.

For the first time in my life, I feel whole.

Gina's staggering to her feet, the hunting knife still clutched in her hand. She looks up as I lunge for her, just in time for me to catch the look of terror and awe on her face. I snap my jaws closed around her, and her body slides under my teeth, small and strangely soft. Blood blossoms on my tongue, and I swallow around her body. She must be screaming, but the roar of the ocean around me, the roar of my own blood in my ears, is so loud I can barely hear.

Maybe she's calling my name. But so is something beneath the waves, that dark and lovely expanse that neither light nor human beings can touch. It thrills me, ringing through my body from teeth to tail. I see visions of a pod of creatures like us, a new family.

Mom's skin flashes bright and swims away from shore, fast and beautiful. I turn and dive into the deep after her, bearing us down into the crushing cold.

# BROKEN RECORD

## STEPHEN GRAHAM JONES

### Day 1

What Jaden remembered of the wreck was screaming and water drops hanging in the air and the thin white mast at a diagonal and then breathing cold water deep into his chest, shrieky regret about too much stuff at once, and now he was here.

A desert island.

It was the kind people in single-panel cartoons are always living on. The only difference for Jaden was that there was no tall coconut tree drooping over him, casting a puddle of shadow for him to move with all day. The rest was the same, though: his vision failing before the flatness over the water did. In every direction.

Jaden sat back into the sand and chuckled. It wasn't that he was amused to be alive. It was that he amused to be alive like *this*, with no cell, no watch, wearing the shorty-short jean shorts he'd packed as a joke, to swim in.

He rubbed his jaw, imagining the epic beard he was going to grow. Except he'd never been able to even get a goatee to come in full. His dad had always told him to wait until he was thirty-five, then he'd miss these babyface days, but, unless some tuna started beaching themselves for him every day or two, he was going to come in nine years short of that mountain man look, he guessed.

Not that this was going to go that long.

Maybe a century ago you could get marooned for months or years or ever, but not in the modern world, right? Not with satellites watching, not with ships crossing back and forth every hour. Not with there not being any more undiscovered islands. Not with Margo looking for him.

Surely she would be.

Jaden had felt guilty for going on the trip without her. Now, having left her there to call in the Coast Guard was going to be what saved him.

"Hello?" Jaden called up into the sky.

It would have been cool if a gull had wheeled around overhead, screeched a response.

There were no birds at all, though.

It was just Jaden.

## Day 2

Jaden woke the same as he had the day before: all at once, gasping on the beach. There was gritty white sand clinging to the right side of his face, and all over his chest.

He was hungry.

He stood, wobbled to what he was calling the down-water side of the little island, and peed into the ocean.

This wasn't so bad, he told himself. He had about the same floorspace as he'd had in his efficiency apartment, the year he'd crapped out of grad school. Nearly four hundred square feet? He walked it off. It was eighteen heel-to-toe steps across one way, seventeen and a half the other. And the plumbing worked about the same as it had in his efficiency. The air conditioner was maybe even better.

He could do this. Maybe some sunburn, sure. But he was going to look rugged when he got rescued, wasn't he? All tan and windblown and scraggly.

Well, tan and windblown and scraggly if a ship pulled up in the next two or three days, he figured.

That was about how long he figured he could go without water. Probably he should have dug a pit or something to pee in. Maybe the sand would filter it into water. Jaden didn't really know how nature worked—he'd never watched the survival shows—but he remembered that from somewhere.

So, in serious lieu of anything else at all to do, he sat at the exact center of the island. It was maybe six inches higher than the rest of the island. He scraped a trench around him, just doing nothing, and then decided this circle he'd traced was the outline of a target. So he dug the bullseye out—the exact center of the island. This was where the coconut tree was supposed to have been.

About half of every scoop of sand sifted back in, but it wasn't like he didn't have time.

What he pictured uncovering was either a coconut or a skull. The skull would be the island's former resident, and would fill him with despair and all that, but the coconut would just mean he'd washed up too early. If in fact a coconut was actually a seed. Jaden wasn't really sure about that.

It didn't matter. He didn't find a skull, and he didn't find a coconut.

He found water.

It was such a surprise that he pushed back, fell away. Looked around.

Still three hundred sixty degrees of unending ocean.

And, at the bottom of the little hole that was a little deeper than his forearm, a few handfuls of cold, mostly clean water.

Jaden licked the side of his finger.

*Fresh* water.

So he wasn't going to have to drink his own urine.

Things were looking up.

# DAY 3

Jaden was writing H-E-L-P not in the sand—there were no branches, no rocks—but on the sunburned skin of his thigh. Over and over. Each time he got to L, the H was fading away.

Passing the hours was turning out to be the hardest part.

His feet were in the water, hanging off into the sharp drop-off all round the edge of the island. His toes were wiggly bait for anything down there.

"Teach a man to fish," he said, and then couldn't find the end of it. It had been going to be funny, though. Killer funny. Something about a mermaid. But, had a mermaid beached herself right then, Jaden would have bitten into her tail, he knew, even eaten the fin.

All the hunger he'd felt before in his life, it had just been mild discomfort. An inconvenience.

What he was feeling now, it was real, and it hurt. He'd already pulled all the frayed strings off his shorts, chewed them to paste, swallowed them. Could you eat your own hair? It was some sort of protein, wasn't it?

Then, like he'd been hoping for, something brushed his shin.

He stabbed his hand down what he considered to be ninja-fast, and what he pulled up was . . . what? It was cold, and solid, and kind of square.

He crawled back from the water, in case he dropped it.

He'd been expecting debris from the wreck to wash up. That always happens in the movies. You get a rope, a trunk of goodies, and, if it was a plane you'd gone down in, maybe some flotation seats or mini-bottles of vodka.

What Jaden got was a double-stick popsicle.

He ceremoniously peeled the waxy wrapper and buried it under the sand near his water hole.

The popsicle was chocolate.

And . . . was it familiar? Had there been any of these on-board?

Probably there had been. Popsicles are great. Especially fudge ones.

Jaden applied his tongue to a top corner delicately, like he was worried the ice cream might have gone past its expiration date.

It was delicious. His first food in three days.

He made himself go slow, to savor it.

Who knew when the next one might come floating in.


# DAY 4

Jaden's tongue was sore. He was still licking the popsicle.

It wouldn't go away. It was more rounded on the corners, but he was pretty sure the rounding was only because he'd moved some of the cold fudge over to the side, with all his licking.

Still? He was full.

He'd gone to sleep with the magic popsicle still in his hand, then woke frantic and panicked. It had been right there in the sand, though. No crabs stealing away with it, no sand bugs crawling all over it. The sun didn't even seem to touch it.

The popsicle couldn't be cold, either, but it was.

Jaden started to dip it into the ocean, but saw himself dropping it, or a shark surging up to steal it. So, even though it clouded up his drinking water, he swirled it around in there, holding each stick with a different hand, and pulled it back up, clean again

He closed his eyes, applied tongue to chocolate.

Just as delicious as before. Just as good as the ones his aunt

*That* was it! The summer he'd spent with Aunt Jolie, when his mom and dad were doing their figuring out their relationship thing, a Schwann's truck or something had lumbered down her street every two weeks, and— "special for her favorite nephew"—she would buy a case of double-barreled Fudgsicles.

It didn't make up for his parents acting like children, but they had been good popsicles.

When Jaden couldn't possibly lick one lick more of *this* one, he dug up the paper, wishing pretty hard he'd unwrapped it more carefully, and rewrapped the popsicle, buried it under more sand than was strictly necessary. If you have a magic popsicle, though, you take good care of it, don't you?

Jaden drank his cloudy chocolate water until his stomach hurt.

For the rest of the afternoon he tried to keep to what he called his fake-n-bake schedule, even though there was nothing fake about it: fifteen minutes lying on his left side, giving his right side up to the hot-hot sun, then fifteen minutes on his back, his front, his other side.

It made the hours go by.

Just before dark he renamed it, too. Not fake-n-bake, but rotisserie. He was the Rotisserie Man.

It was the best reality show ever. It had magic popsicles and everything.

## DAY 5

Rotisserie Man was officially dead. Well, "cooked," Jaden corrected.

He woke with not just his frontside burned, like it had already been, but his whole body.

Nocturnal Man lumbered into being.

Jaden scooped out a sand-angel near shore and snuggled down into it as deep as he could, buried himself as best he could manage. It didn't cover him completely—he'd imagined himself as a head propped up on the sand, which was going to freak somebody out when he smiled—but it was a lot better than nothing.

He'd wanted to dig up in the middle of the island, lie back into that cool fresh water, but he didn't want to mess that situation up.

Near shore, it was white sand for as far down as he dug.

And, of course, as soon as he was dozing off, prepping for his long night of watching for passing ships' lights or beacons or whatever, he had to pee again.

He could go right here in the sand, he figured, in his jean shorts, but just because there's no civilization doesn't mean you can't be civilized. That was something Margo had said once, camping.

She would think this was funny.

Jaden smiled, and then he was crying, and then he was clambering up from the sand, throwing handfuls of it out into the water, kicking it even.

At which point he realized the sand was a limited resource too.

He was living at sea-level, wasn't he? If he threw enough of his island out into the ocean, then the water would seep up over everything he had.

Not that he even halfway understood why or how there was sand in the first place.

Did the rinse-wash-repeat action of a thousand years of waves pulverize cooled lava into sand like this? But wouldn't it be black, then?

But maybe this wasn't volcanic, Jaden figured.

It was igneous. That was a word he remembered from junior high. And another: "Sedimentary!" he screamed out over the water, and then ran to what he considered the other three sides of the island, screamed it out from them as well.

Then, peeing off the down-water side of the island, there was a magazine bobbing on the surface.

It was a *Playboy*.

## DAY 6

Jaden was taking stock. Serious, serious stock: one cistern or aquifer or hand-well or something, one magic popsicle—*Fudg*sicle—one pair of jean shorts, and one gentleman's magazine.

It made him shiver in the hundred-plus heat.

How does a magazine survive the open waters of the ocean long enough to end up way out here in the middle? And, had this one been lost eighteen *years* ago? Either that or the same storm that had wrecked Jaden had dumped somebody's vintage collection overboard.

Porn. Exactly what he needed, yes.

The centerfold's name was Peggy.

Jaden read the issue from cover to cover, twice. There was an interview with Tom Cruise about a Vietnam movie Jaden had never seen, there was an excerpt of a Vietnam novel he couldn't imagine the rest of, there was a Vietnam short story about a river that was in Canada, there was another pictorial of an actress Jaden had never heard of. And there were all the columns. All the stupid, stupid columns.

"Thank you!" Jaden called out to the world anyway.

If you're not grateful, you don't get any more.

This was from Jaden's mom, before she left and got sick and died three states away, not telling Jaden or his father.

But don't think about her.

Start thinking about sad things on a desert island, and there's no one to pull you out of that spiral.

Jaden licked his popsicle until he was full and drank from his hole in the ground and peed in the ocean and buried himself in the sand again.

Soon his hair would grow long enough to shade his face. Until then, he would keep arranging his jean shorts over his head.

Survival was pretty stupid, really.


# DAY 7

Well, night. And maybe it was kind of still day six—Jaden wasn't super sure anymore.

If he was going to turn into a creature of the night in order to preserve his skin, though, then he had to start doing it like this: pinching himself awake all night, burrowing down into the sand during the day.

The sky was a big blue bowl turned over him, it felt like. And he'd been living here for ten thousand years, and had an endless supply of BBs for his rifle, had been pumping it up and taking aim up at that bowl forever, making stars.

"This one's for you, Margo," he said, and aimed his imaginary rifle up, poked another hole in the sky.

He was spelling her name, connecting the dots. He was drawing pictures. Squares and triangles at first, but then he'd leveled up, was on to Dr. Seuss versions of tall, spindly buildings. He couldn't do animals yet, couldn't imagine how the Greeks or Egyptians or Inca or whoever had done all that. Buildings, though, those he could do.

His plan was to get enough going to have a real city up there. Except the stars kept moving. All together, but on their own, too, some of them.

It was only because he'd poked so many holes in the night sky—because he'd let this much light into his upside-down bowl—that he saw the shimmer out in the water. It was different from the white that surged at the top of the waves.

"Don't do it, don't do it," Jaden told himself, but he already was: running out to that shimmer, falling into the water, dog-paddling out to it.

It was flat and hard—another magazine?—but he couldn't look, had to get back to the island.

Out in the ocean, he had the sudden certainty he wasn't going to find shore again in the dark. That some current was going to grab him, swish him around the side of the island, push him out farther than he could swim back. That a whale was going to nibble at his feet, take his whole leg into his mouth to see if he was a big plankton. Even a vine of seaweed brushing him would probably stop his heart.

The island was still there.

Jaden clambered back up, panicking and scrambling when it was more like swinging up onto a roof than walking up a slope—what kind of beach *was* this?—then tried to angle whatever he'd found up to see it.

He had to wait until morning to be sure. Until sunup.

No trumpets played in glory when he could finally make out the picture: a man in a tasteful suit, leaning to his right.

An album, a record.

Vinyl.

MC Hammer, *Don't Hurt 'Em.*

## DAY 9

Jaden was buried in the sand with his popsicle in his mouth.

Just staring. At nothing. He wasn't super sure it was the ninth day, but he was pretty sure he'd skipped the eighth day. Hadn't eaten, hadn't drank. Had just laid there. With Peggy.

Her turn-ons were white roses and children and animals, and her turnoffs were cigarettes and traffic. To be honest, Jaden was confusing her with Margo, some.

His plan was, when he was rescued, to leave the *Playboy* buried in the sand, for the next tenant.

Without meaning to, his tongue worrying over that cold chocolate, he bit into the meat of the popsicle. Into the fudge. The cold hurt his teeth and the popsicle tumbled down into the sand on his chest, but he still had a big chunk of it in his mouth.

He chewed it, swallowed it.

He kind of wanted to look down, see what might or might not be happening with the popsicle, but he also kind of didn't want to watch the goose do its golden egg thing.

But then he remembered: there'd been words on the popsicle sticks that summer with his aunt, hadn't there?

He sat up, sand caking off him, covering the popsicle even more. He dug it up, shook the sand off, rolled over to wash it clean and then bit in again, deeper, faster, more and more, all on one side, enough to free up the stick on what he was calling the right.

He licked it clean, squinted to read the scrolly red font.

*TRY AGAIN.*

And now he just had half a popsicle.

# DAY 10

Night again.

Jaden didn't quite have a city in the night sky yet, but he had picked out three kind-of columns of stars he could build three different-height buildings from, and those stars all stayed together, mostly.

Now he was making up a story for why this light on the seventeenth floor was off, why that one was migrating sideways, or to a lower floor. The stories mostly had to do with candles and a blackout. He called the wandering stars elevators.

Jaden wondered what if he bit off a piece of his calf and ate it.

The popsicle stick he'd denuded—had never got its fudge iciness back. Jaden wore the naked popsicle stick behind his ear now. His first impulse had been to chew it, but that was the kind of indulgence you allowed yourself when there were more than two popsicle sticks in the whole entire world. Or, the world Jaden had access to.

The MC Hammer record was useless. The sleeve was just a sleeve, the record just a record, the tiny print on the label just what Jaden would have expected, had he ever got that record.

And, related: why that record? More to the point, why that *Playboy*? He'd never even owned a single issue, had only ever sneak-looked at his uncle's, that one summer.

He threaded the popsicle stick from behind his ear and set it under his nose like a mustache and pooched his lips up to keep it there.

It was the current contest: how long until his lips cramped, and the coach—it was either a coach or a drill sergeant, Jaden wasn't completely committed yet—how long until that coach or drill sergeant would pull him from the game or the battle, and Jaden would say no, no, he could do it, just give him time.

One of the lights of his buildings in the sky winked out and Jaden blew it a kiss, letting the popsicle stick tumble down his chest.

Game over.

# DAY 11

Bright, bright sun. The only kind anymore.

But there were a lot of kinds of island, evidently.

Until the other night, getting the MC Hammer record, when he'd had to lunge up onto the island instead of just walk, he'd assumed all islands were the crowns of vast majestic never-seen underwater mountains. But mountains have slopes, don't they? Even unmajestic ones? They don't have walls or cliffs leading straight up to the tip-top.

Jaden was no geology major or island-ologist, but this island wasn't quite tracking.

He'd been pondering it all morning, like figuring out the nature of the island might give him, the clue he needed to escape. Finally he planted the popsicle stick straight up and down by the water hole, made sure the *Playboy* and the record were buried together, checked the wrapper on the half a popsicle he had left, and, like a flag he was leaving behind to tell somebody he'd been here, he stripped out of his shorts, laid them out by the upright popsicle stick.

They wouldn't blow away. No clouds, no wind.

And then he walked to the non-urinal side of the island, sat on the edge, and slipped into the . . . not exactly the cold, more like the great empty lukewarm.

Still touching—holding on—he treaded water with his legs, he heavy-breathed, getting his lungs to capacity, and then he ducked under, keeping his hand in constant contact, but going down, and down.

As deep down as he went, and all the way around, the rocky underwater part of the island was the same width as the overwater part of the island, as near as he could tell. Like it was a column thrusting up from the ocean floor, thousands of feet below. Not some conglomeration or stack of rocks, but . . . a lava tube? Craggy but not cracked.

It was stupid. This wasn't a mountain. It was a post. It was a column.

And there was a hand-sized, irregular piece of thin plastic bobbing against the underwater cliff.

Jaden started to put it down the front of his pants, but he wasn't wearing any, so he clamped it in his teeth, let himself float up.

# DAY 12

The plastic he'd found on his brave and useless dive was a blister pack. The cardboard still attached showed what had been in the blister pack: a werewolf action figure.

Jaden had all his items laid out by the water hole: popsicle, popsicle stick, album, magazine, action figure. Well, action figure case.

Counting the popsicle and the popsicle stick as one, that was four things. Four things from what Jaden knew was a list of ten. What Ten Things Would You Have on Your Desert Island?

It had been a contest in a magazine, that summer he spent with Aunt Jolie.

Up in the treehouse his older cousins had built years ago, before they grew up and moved out, Jaden had carefully written down what ten things he would have on his desert island.

He would need food, so why not have the best food ever?

He would definitely want his uncle's magazine.

MC Hammer was amazing.

And he'd always wanted to see a werewolf.

Only, he must have been sleeping when the werewolf bobbed up against shore. So the glue keeping the blister pack to the cardboard had given way, and the action figure had tumbled down to the ocean floor.

Jaden stood, walked over to the edge.

*"What about the record player!"* he screamed out over the water.

It had been the next item on his list. Followed, he was pretty sure, by a power outlet, with power. He'd underlined "with power" three or four times, to be sure.

All so he could sit on his island and listen to MC Hammer. Maybe practice some dance moves.

## DAY 13

Slurping water up from the hole like a sunburned caveman, it hit Jaden that the record player *had* probably been there, but, like the werewolf's blister pack, it had sunk. The popsicle and magazine had floated, because they were wood and paper. The record had floated because it was still in its cellophane, or because it was grooved plastic and cardboard.

But the record player had just gulp-gulped straight down.

Along with the power outlet.

That made seven, then. Seven down.

And, he was pretty sure, in the same order he'd filled them in on the magazine's form, to mail in.

Whoever's list was chosen was supposed to win a year's subscription, plus publication. Not *this*, having to subsist on the actual list you'd written down.

Had that been in the fine print?

Jaden couldn't even remember what the magazine had been. It was just one he'd stole from the convenience store.

What was next on the list, though? That was the real question.

Hopefully not any more records. The one he had was already melted and warped. And, he hadn't asked for a werewolf action figure, he was pretty sure. He'd said what he'd want would be a *werewolf*, the actual monster. Because werewolves are cool.

"Oh yeah," he said then, when he saw the scum of notebook pages floating in on the surface of the water, the blurry words made of large looping letters in purple ink.

*That* was next.

Sandra Peterman from homeroom's secret journal.

Number eight.

## DAY 15

No sleep the night before, or the night before that, or the day between. Just remembering. *Trying* to remember.

That trip to the convenience store *had* to be where this all started, didn't it? When he'd got that stupid magazine? Though "trip" wasn't really the word. More like the power was out for the whole block, and his aunt had hustled him out into the sunshine she said would be good for him.

Walking past the convenience store, Jaden had seen its lights were off as well. He'd wandered in, the door not dinging like usual. No clerk behind the counter. The store was murky grey, like a ghost of itself, and it was cool inside, like the cooler door had been left open to fog the place up.

Jaden hadn't taken the magazine because he wanted it. He'd taken it because he was mad at his aunt, and his mom, and his dad, and the world. He'd taken it because no one was watching. He'd taken it because it was the closest one to the door. Only, somebody'd spilled a coke behind the magazine: when he pulled it, it stuck to the shelf with coke syrup, just, more the color of mucous or saliva. Like the world had heard that he hated it, so was trying to keep him there long enough for the power to come back on, or for the clerk to be walking back from her cigarette. He pulled harder, got away with the torn-out insides, not the cover, then kept the rolled-up magazine pages in the treehouse so he wouldn't have to explain where they'd come from.

Doing the magazine's desert island contest had just been a way to kill another afternoon.

Sneaking that torn-out form into the mail, Jaden had pretended he was rolling up a secret message in a bottle, throwing it out into the water.

Only, it had come back, hadn't it?

Jaden, sitting in the sand of his island with his action-figure blister pack and his *Playboy* and his popsicle that wouldn't melt and his record that would, cringed.

It had come back, hadn't it? Years later, when someone moved their desk, when they cleaned up the mailroom, when that messy postal jeep was retired—when *whatever* happened that got Jaden's contest entry back into the mail, years too late.

Shit.

Jaden stood, paced the perimeter of the island, looking for a coffin bobbing in the water.

# DAY 16

Jaden was still walking around and around the island. No coffin yet. The sand of his path was compacted. He couldn't see it in the dark, but he could feel it under the soles of his bare feet.

He was thinking what if a wave came, pushed too hard on the stalk of rock he was sitting on, crumbled it down into the depths.

He was thinking what about scurvy. He was thinking about chocolate poisoning. He was thinking there was a code hidden in Peggy's turn-ons and turnoffs in the *Playboy*, that maybe each turn-on was a 1, each turn*off* a 0, for some binary message.

He'd broken the record into shards to use as a weapon. He'd tried wearing the record sleeve as a folded-open paper hat but it kept popping off, so he'd used the bare-wood popsicle stick to carve out two eyes.

The ocean looked the same through his mask.

Jaden screamed, whipped the album sleeve out into the darkness then immediately ran to the edge of the island after it.

Maybe it would come back, he told himself.

Please let it come back.

Like the desert island list he'd mailed off.

Running on automatic all those years ago, he'd put his return address down not as his aunt's, where he was mailing from, but his actual home, his usual address.

Three years later, the letter had come back.

It was waiting in the mailbox when Jaden and his dad came back from . . . not his mom's funeral, they hadn't been in time for that. But her grave, anyway. Their own service of standing there with their heads down.

Jaden had loosened his tie and opened the letter, left it on the kitchen table like a joke he wasn't in the mood for.

A week later, he was in the mood.

Waiting for his cereal to get less crunchy before school, he'd scratched out what had been the tenth item, wrote in instead, *Mom*.

Which was why he couldn't sleep.

## DAY 17

The ninth item from his list was a six-pack of toilet paper.

It bobbed up in its plastic, knocked on the side of the island.

Jaden waited half the day before he finally fished it up. What he was waiting to see was if the water would deliver it around the side, let it go on past.

It wouldn't.

"You're for guests," Jaden said to the toilet paper, and nestled it upright into the sand, but it was a lie. He didn't need the toilet paper for what he'd figured he'd need it for—there was the down-water side of the island just a dunk away, and, as it turned out, subsisting on popsicles and water was pretty light on the bowels—but he did need a pillow, as it turned out.

He slept better than he had in two weeks.

## DAY 19

Jaden woke this time to the sand being gently cleared from the side of his face. He didn't know how long he'd been asleep exactly, but he'd peeked out twice in daylight and peed once in the night, he thought.

He opened his eyes to a figure above him.

"Mom," he said.

She smiled.

He closed his eyes and the delicate scraping of her palm on his cheek continued. He was crying now. His throat was full.

She'd woken on the beach, she told him after all the hugging and the rest of the crying.

"Beach?" Jaden said, looking all around.

They smiled.

"I'm glad you're here," he told her.

"This was poking me in the hip," she said. It was a silver straw, sharp on one end. Still in a plastic sleeve.

"Number ten," Jaden said, in wonder, because he thought he'd crossed that one out, to write *Mom* in.

"A straw?" she asked.

"It's for the coconuts," he told her.

His mom looked around for the coconut tree.

"I should have wished better," Jaden explained.

"This is my wish," she said. "Being here with you."

"I only have popsicles," Jaden said.

"I like popsicles," his mom said.

It would have been nice to have a fire to sit by, but there were no matches, and only one popsicle stick for firewood, and one record sleeve, and one straw that was more of telescope, now. Jaden talked his mom through the city he was building in the sky, and, like moms do, she looked where he was pointing, and nodded that she saw it, yes. Right there, and there.

Jaden gave her the pillow, then waited until she was asleep, crept over to where the *Playboy* was buried.

Still crawling—he didn't want to be a menacing silhouette with a handful of porn should she wake—he dropped the magazine over the down-water side of the island.

The glue at the spine, which had already been crackly-dry, gave up altogether, and the pages spread out over the water, bobbed cheerfully right by the island.

Frantic, Jaden scooped precious handfuls of sand onto each of them, until they sunk.

## Day 20

The next day they spent digging.

Jaden's reasoning was two-fold: in one place he'd dug, there'd been water, right? Other holes might have even better treasure. It was videogame thinking, but that didn't mean it was wrong.

And then there was the issue of the coconut straw that his mom had washed up on. It had been there all along, hadn't it? Or, in the right order, anyway. Other items might be buried as well.

The outlet for the record player turned up after an hour or two. The cord snaking down from it plunged down into the island's rock stalk, which he now guessed had to be hollow—even more fragile than he'd thought. More impossible.

It had power, too, just like he'd said with his underlining. Jaden scooped a handful of salty water over to it, dribbled enough in that the twin slits spit sparks back up.

The record player showed up in pieces. An arm under the sand here, a piece of wood laminate there, from the cabinet. The needle, who knew.

It didn't matter.

The record was in shards anyway.

Jaden explained about the down-water side of the island—their self-cleaning latrine—and the water hole, and about burying yourself for the sunlight hours.

His mom didn't care about any of that.

She wanted to know what he'd been doing all those years she'd been gone.

They passed the popsicle back and forth—one rule: no bites—and, with all the buildings in the sky leaning over them, Jaden told her about the girlfriends and the jobs he'd had, about Dad and his hilarious dating life, and when he didn't say anything about Margo, it felt like he was doing that because he would explain her by saying she liked white roses and children, and wasn't into cigarettes. And she deserved better than that.


# DAY 21

The coconut straw turned out to be perfect for the water hole.

"Technology," Jaden said to his mom. He was out of breath from drinking.

She was still cupping her water in her hands to drink.

"And look," he said, blowing into the straw at different depths: it would whistle, too.

"How are we going to cut our hair, do you think?" Jaden's mom asked, threading some out of her face.

"Why did you leave?" Jaden said back, watching her from under his bangs.

The ocean murmured its watery murmur.

"You know," she said, averting her eyes. "I got sick."

"Of Dad?"

"I didn't want to get you sick too."

"And then you died from it."

"I couldn't call at the end. I wanted to. I'm sorry. But it's best you didn't see me. I didn't want you to have to remember me like that."

Jaden stared out at the unbroken blue.

"I stole a magazine," he said. "I think it was a genie magazine, a magic magazine."

She was just watching him.

"I wrote your name on a list," he said. "It was . . . I had to cross the straw out to do it. It was a stupid contest. But I shouldn't have stolen it, I know." Jaden looked out to the open water, called out, "I'm sorry! I'm sorry I'm sorry I'm *sorry*!"

"You crossed the straw out?" his mom asked, looking at it stuck in the sand by the water hole.

"I didn't cross it out enough, I guess," Jaden said. "But you came anyway. I got eleven, not ten."

"Thank you," his mom said. "This has—It's been a gift."

"You're well now, right?" Jaden said.

"I think I am, yes."

"And you're here."

They didn't push it any farther.

"Why that album?" his mom asked, after the appropriate length of time.

"Because I was a stupid kid," Jaden said.

# Day 22

Jaden was playing his game of one of his fingers burying itself and the others going into a minor panic from it when there was a flurry of motion and a hard, fast cough from the other side of the island.

He let his ring finger stay buried and looked over slow and indirectly. In the tight confines of the island, it was polite to give each other privacy on the down-water side, where privacy would be most appreciated.

But this wasn't that.

His mom was lying sideways on the sand. Her back was arched like from being electrocuted, and her fingers were stretched back the wrong way. The tendons in her neck were steel cables, and chocolate foam was coming from her mouth, since she'd had the popsicle last.

"Run," she said, her voice deeper. Dangerous.

Jaden ran *to* her.

"What can I do?" he said, feeling in the sand under her, in case she was somehow on the outlet and getting electrocuted. "What do you need?"

*The popsicle stick*, he thought. He could depress her tongue, keep her from choking. Or—or he could do a field tracheotomy with the coconut straw. He'd seen that on television at least twice, and knew roughly where to stab.

But then his mom's mouth elongated into a canine muzzle, the muscle under the skin bubbling and tearing and creaking.

A werewolf.

He'd asked for a werewolf.

## DAY 23

Or maybe it was still day twenty-two. Was it midnight yet? Jaden couldn't tell.

All his buildings had toppled over.

He was treading water five yards out from the island. It was far enough that his mom couldn't slash out, reach him with her claws, and close enough that he didn't panic that he wasn't going to get back.

Evidently werewolves are afraid of the ocean.

His mom's transformation had been brutal. He'd watched her turn inside out, and inside her had been a snarly wolf-thing.

No, she hadn't been able to call him at the end of her sickness fifteen years ago.

She couldn't physically hold a phone.

She'd barked and screamed and growled at him all night—she could *smell* him—but she'd stayed on the island.

In frustration, she turned on the toilet paper, shredded it into confetti. For a minute or two the island had been a unicorn daydream, all fluff and whiteness.

She didn't eat the popsicle, though. Dogs aren't supposed to have chocolate, Jaden knew. Maybe that went for wolves too?

Jaden wasn't crying anymore. He didn't have the energy.

"Mom," he said for the ten-thousandth time.

His mom's large ears rotated to catch his words. Her whole body stilled, stiffened.

"Mom," he said again, and let himself go under again, told himself this was the last time, that he wasn't coming back up.

## DAY 24

Jaden was hanging onto the island with one hand and throwing up into the water.

It was dawn.

He had stayed in the water for two nights, and the day between. Every part of him was shaking and spent. For a few hours he'd been certain he was being punished for sneaking eleven items from a ten-item list, but then, if his mom was a werewolf—and she was—he figured he'd really only gotten his original ten.

His whole time out in the ocean, no sharks had come. No gulls had drifted down for a closer look. No werewolves had come running across the surface of the ocean, from all his mom's plaintive howling.

She was starving. She was crying with her mouth, with her voice.

She'd finally found the fresh water, slurped and slurped at it, then splashed her pee down onto the sand. An hour or two or three after that, she padded around in a circle, made enough of a bed to curl up in, her tail curling up over her nose. Behind that tail, she shifted back to the mom Jaden knew.

Jaden had waited what felt like an hour after that, being sure, then pulled himself onto the island. He crawled gingerly to the water hole, drank until he threw up again. He threw up as quietly as he could manage.

He sat down in the sand then, staring at his mom. She was lightly snoring.

He flicked grains of sand at her face. Her lips, her eyelids. Nothing.

"Mom," he said, not really that loud. She didn't twitch.

He extended a foot, pushed on her thigh. She rolled with it, stayed there.

He turned away from her and licked the popsicle in what he considered a mournful way.

It tasted the same.

# DAY 25

Jaden hadn't meant to sleep, but he guessed he had.

His mom hadn't eaten him in the night.

Did all werewolves sleep this long when they came back to human?

She'd said it was best he didn't see her at the end, and she'd been right. He couldn't get that image out of his head, now. That pacing, that growling. That hunger.

"I can't do it again, Mom," he said.

No way could he spend another thirty-six hours treading water.

He considered his options. He didn't have any.

The only thing he could do was scratch her name off the list. Either hers, or his own.

And, if she was a good mom, if she really loved him, if she was really her, she wouldn't want it to be him, would she? He wasn't the monster. He wasn't the one who had left. He wasn't the one who was, technically, already dead.

What he'd considered the worst hell before—living with a broken record and a never-ending popsicle—was his dream, now. It was what he had to fight his way back to.

No more werewolves. No more mothers. Nobody eating anybody.

Jaden should have asked for a boat in that contest. A raft. A raft and a compass. No, a shark cage up here on dry land, to keep his mom in.

But there was no shark cage. There was no going back. There was just him, and what he had to do.

He sat down behind his sleeping mom, told her he was sorry, and, pushing hard with both legs, launched her out into the water.

She woke instantly, and fought to get back, but Jaden repelled her, apologizing the whole time, and then he repelled her some more.

She didn't fight so hard, once she understood.

"I'm sorry," she said, treading barely enough water to keep her mouth above the surface.

"I wrote your name," Jaden said.

They were both crying.

"You grew up perfect," she said, butterflying backward into the open sea, and Jaden closed his eyes.

# DAY 26

Night. No city in the sky. Not quite midnight yet, Jaden guessed.

It was quieter now than it had been.

Jaden had been holding his tongue to the popsicle for long enough that it had kind of dried to the chocolate.

The splash to his left turned him around, the popsicle hanging from his mouth.

It was his mom.

She was half her, half not.

Jaden screamed, ran for her, butted her back into the water before she could get steady on the island.

She fought back to the ledge, the shore, and she was panicked—she knew what was water, what wasn't water, and she wasn't going to stay in the water anymore.

Jaden kicked her back, kicked her back again, but he wasn't winning.

She was wolfing out more and more. Because she wanted to stay alive.

Jaden shook his head no, yelled to her to stop, and, when she didn't, he drove the sharp end of the straw down into the hand she'd clawed into the sand.

The straw went through. They both looked down to it. The skin of her hand and the light werewolf fuzz coming in sent tendrils of smoke up.

Silver.

That's what he'd written on the list, right? *Silver straw, for coconuts.* He'd asked for silver because it was antimicrobial, a thing he knew from his aunt explaining her earrings to him when she hadn't been able to answer any questions about where his parents were.

His mom jerked her hand back from the island, from the straw. Her hand—her paw—split down the middle, left the straw standing there in the sand, the werewolf blood on it sizzling away.

"Stop, stop!" Jaden said to her.

She couldn't, though. She couldn't help it.

And, the silver, it was making her go back from wolf.

It was his mom again.

"Jaden, please, just let me come up for a—"

Jaden drove the straw into her right eye, and, when the blunt, hollow end was sticking out, was just blinding her not killing her, when it was just pumping blood and eye juice, he thumped it once, hard, with the heel of his hand, pushing it deep enough that a slow plug of greyish pink came out the straw, drooped down into the water.

His mom stopped fighting.

Jaden leaned forward, held her forearm in his hand, then her hand in his, then her fingers. Then nothing.

## DAY 32

Jaden should have kept the record sleeve. The one with the eyeholes.

And the action figure blisterpack.

He could have fashioned the blisterpack's plastic into lenses for the eyeholes of the record sleeve, improvised . . . not sunglasses exactly—there was no tint—but something to wear when he was buried in the sand, anyway.

It would feel like wearing a mask. Like he was somebody else.

But he was just him.

As of last night and this morning, he'd taken to talking out loud to Peggy.

He was telling her how tonight he was going to have to rebuild a city, window by window. Maybe if he did it right, those stacks of windows would resolve into the portholes of a monster of a cruise ship, right?

It didn't hurt to dream.

Well, it sort of did, but he couldn't help it.

His beard wasn't full yet, he knew. He could tell by rubbing his jawline. His beard was wispy, thin, a joke. But give it a few years. Give it a few years, and he'd be living in his own personal comic strip.

It was going to be hilarious.

# SAUDADE

## STEVE RASNIC TEM

As his taxi raced toward the dock Lee could see the water between buildings and at the ends of streets, filling the space around and beyond distant spits of unfocused land. The ocean smelled like a liquefied cellar. His last time near the ocean was that summer at Myrtle Beach when he was nine. He'd hated the way the sand got between his toes, in his swimsuit, in every private crevice. He'd gone into the water to get rid of the sand, and been alarmed by the volume and the pull of it. Its murky gray was the color of everything dissolved, everything disintegrated, eaten, and disappeared. He never went into the ocean again.

It wasn't too late to turn around. But his girls wouldn't get their money back. And worse, they'd be disappointed in him.

"Dad, it'll be like riding the bus." Jane had tried to be reassuring, but how could she know? Neither she nor her sister had ever been on a cruise. All they knew was from the TV commercials and the colorful brochures. Lee and his late wife had raised their daughters to be skeptical, but it never quite took.

His cell phone began playing that discordant ring-tone Cynthia had programmed to identify her. He fumbled with the buttons and answered. "Hi, honey. I'm almost at the dock."

"Great! I'm sorry we couldn't be there to see you off."

Jane shouted in the background, "Bon voyage!"

"Tell her thanks. How's the internship going?"

"It's going *well*, Dad! We're impressing everybody! You'll be proud."

"I'm already proud. You sure you have enough money? You spent so much on this trip."

"We have *savings*, remember? All that stuff you used to say about the *real world*? We listened."

Lee felt himself tear up. It happened easily these days. "OK then. I'll send postcards." He heard inarticulate yelling, laughter in the background. "Cindy, what's going on?"

Cynthia laughed. "Jane wants you to promise you'll warn us first if you're bringing home a new wife." Lee didn't react, and they said their goodbyes. He wished they hadn't pushed him into this.

Stuck in traffic only blocks from the pier, Lee pulled out the brochure. *Senior Singles Cruise.* The words embarrassed him. But it had been over five years, and he was very much single and feeling older every day.

If the taxi were late it wasn't his fault. The welcome packet stressed that the ship always sailed on time—it was your responsibility to get on board, both at the start and at all stops along the way. The very idea of being marooned in some Caribbean port—he might just stay on board the entire trip.

But the taxi made good time over the remaining blocks. Dilapidated warehouses were the rule on one side of the road. On the ocean side small and mid-size boats were anchored or dry-docked for repair, their hulls chewed with corrosion, the upper parts and edges stained a coffee color.

At the terminal he waited for hours with hundreds of others on brightly colored chairs, an experience not mentioned in the brochure. Eventually he found himself heading for the gangway with a large group. A pretty young photographer offered to take his "Bon Voyage" picture. It was only then he realized the looming white metal wall was his destination. He consented only so he'd have one to give the girls. He smiled as if he were already having the best time of his life.

Once inside the ship a small olive-skinned man with a thick accent offered to take him to his cabin. "My bags?"

"They wait for you," the little man said, "please watch your step," and rapidly led him through various openings and a maze of corridors. After a few minutes he had no sense of location or being on the water at all.

The cabin was like other small rooms he'd stayed in at cheap hotels. An undersized bed and a cramped bathroom, a tiny table and chair beneath twin portholes. He wasn't sure what he'd hoped for—something exotic perhaps. But Lee was used to disappointment.

A printed schedule for "Senior Singles" was on the table. He read it with increasing alarm. Dinner was a "Meet Someone New" event. An equal number of women and men at each table was somehow guaranteed. He'd made a terrible mistake in agreeing to this.

After breakfast there were classes on dance and casino games, Bridge, tennis and other "deck sports," and "Social Skills for Seniors." After a small-group lunch (whatever that was), "cruisers"—oh, *please*—were encouraged to change into sun or swim attire and relax in one of the countless deck chairs. A good quality sun screen was highly recommended. His daughters had bought him enough extremely high SPF products to protect him from anything short of immolation. In the evenings, after the awkward-sounding dinners, live entertainment was offered, and the optional "romantic stroll around the deck." Lee dropped this schedule into the waste bin. He'd brought plenty of books.

He glanced out one of the portholes. The ocean appeared to be in a slow spin around him as the ship headed out to sea. He sat down, struggling not to weep.

-o-

For the first two days Lee asked for people's names and occupations. He listened to their stories and laughed at their jokes, and told a few harmless stories of his own. But "his" stories were stolen from people he knew and had nothing to do with him. He wasn't sure why he lied, except he thought these tales more generally appealing. With each small deceit he felt worse.

Staff were always interrogating him, asking if he was having a good time, offering snacks, providing dozens of fluffy white towels every day. Others ran around with buckets of white paint, coating the barest suggestions of corrosion. Every day there were new brown spots, red streaks of oxidation, holes needing to be plugged before passengers noticed.

"I don't believe I've ever seen you out on the deck," a tablemate named Sylvia said at one night's dinner. "But it's the quiet ones you really have to watch out for." She winked at him and laughed. Lee couldn't remember the last time a woman had winked at him.

"Oh, I've heard that saying," he replied, not knowing what else to say. What in the world was she talking about?

The ever-present waiter interrupted. "Is everything perfect?"

Lee looked up and forced a smile. "It was a very good meal."

"Was there something that did not suit you?"

He had no idea what to say. His tablemates spoke of textures, presentation, and the blend of flavors. Surely they were making it all up as they went along?

When the waiter hustled off, that woman, Sylvia, grabbed his arm. Lee stared at her thin fingers, a large ring on each one. "Don't tell me you've found someone *already*, without giving the rest of us girls a chance!" He looked into her red-rimmed eyes and realized how much wine she'd consumed.

"Sylvie! You're *terrible!*" her companion exclaimed, blushing and glancing his way. Suddenly he was in high school again, not understanding what his classmates were getting at. He was unable to speak the rest of the meal. He embarrassed too easily. Had he ever been able to do this? There had been moments, surely, otherwise he could never have married Ann and raised those two beautiful daughters.

After dinner Lee took an elevator to an upper deck for some air. The motion of the ship was more pronounced at this level, sometimes with a roll that forced him to shift his weight from one leg to the other, or a pitch that almost made him fall, or float off into the air. He knew suicides were sometimes a problem on these voyages, but perhaps some were hapless victims of unintentional flight. He wondered if the onboard shops sold heavier shoes.

At this height the ocean was a boundless expanse of black, borderless width and bottomless depth. There should have been more reflections—the ship was brightly lit. It made a shushing sound cutting through the liquid dark, and the troublesome whispers underneath.

Tonight's moon was low on the horizon, its gleaming reflection painting a path across the water into its very heart. He felt a desire he had no words for.

If he stared into the water long enough he could distinguish blacker areas within the black, moving independently. As the clouds drifted rapidly away and the waves began to rise he saw another cruise ship in the distance, all lit up like an upside-down chandelier. Then an arm of the ocean covered it and it disappeared. He waited for it to reappear, unsure of what he had just seen. Finally he turned away, thinking he had misapprehended.

He heard a broken cackle from the deck below, followed by sobs, reassurances. That woman Sylvia and her friend. Lee took a few steps back in case they looked up. He saw a woman a few feet away in a pale yellow gown leaning on the rail. There was something about the set of her shoulders, a certain absorption. From this angle her face looked wet. It alarmed him enough that he was willing to risk embarrassment. He walked over and stood beside her.

The sky was now remarkably clear—a field of stars extended over hundreds of square miles. "You never see this many stars from land," he said. He should have followed that with something, but he had no idea what. The stars ended in a region near the horizon line where lightning rhythmically fractured the emptiness.

"Lovely, isn't it?" She turned her face slightly and she didn't appear to have been crying. Her eyes were large and outlined in black—make-up or not, he couldn't tell. She smelled of some exotic spice, not perfume, but perhaps something she'd eaten. The rest of her was in shadow. He thought she must be both beautiful and unusual. Still, she seemed untroubled. He had misunderstood everything.

"I'm sorry to have interrupted you."

"You thought, perhaps, I was going to jump."

"Oh no, I was just . . ."

"Attempting to measure my mental state. Do not be embarrassed for a kind urge. People do end their lives on these . . . frenetic vacations. They *insist* that you enjoy yourself. And when you do not respond as programmed, a certain desperation ensues."

"I was thinking that very thing earlier. I didn't want to come, but my daughters gave me this trip."

"And you do not wish to disappoint them. You are part of the seniors group, the 'cruisers' I believe they call themselves."

"Terrible, isn't it?" Then she wasn't part of the group. In this light he couldn't tell how old she was—maybe he was making a fool of himself.

"Loneliness is terrible. Loneliness deadens the spirit. A man who has lost his wife knows much about loneliness, I think."

"How did you . . ."

"A band of discoloration on your ring finger. You might have removed the ring as part of some ruse, but you do not seem the type. So either a divorce, or a passing, and I see no signs of divorce in your face."

Lee looked down at his hand. He couldn't see anything—it was too dark for her to have seen. He had taken his ring off over a year ago. "As I've told my daughters, I'm doing okay. I don't need some . . . intervention."

"We have a word in Brazil. *Saudade. Estou com saudades de você.* I miss you. But it means much more. It is a profound, melancholic longing for an absent something or someone one loves. However much you attempt to think of other things, it lingers. But you may never have even possessed the thing, or the someone, before. The one you yearn for may be a complete fabrication. We Brazilians are passionate, and we are in love with—how do you say?—*tragic* frames of mind. *Saudade* is part of our national character. *Saudade*, I suspect, is why many of these people are here. They hunger for something, someone. What is it that you long for, Lee?"

"How did you—" But she shut off his question with a kiss. Her lips were damp, and unpleasantly cold, but the sensation pleased him. It had been years since he'd kissed anyone on the lips. He pulled her closer into him, seeking more warmth, and found none. Instead, to his alarm, he could taste bile coming up into his throat. He turned away, gagging. "I'm so sorry!" He'd experienced no seasickness since coming on board. He'd been inordinately proud of himself. To have it come now, at the most inopportune time, made him despair.

It took him some time to recover. At some point he was forced to his knees. When he could finally look up she was gone. Who could blame her? He'd embarrassed her as much as himself.

When he regained his feet he searched for her to apologize. The deck glistened where she had been standing. He heard the shush and scrape. He turned—one of those ubiquitous deckhands was cleaning up after him, avoiding his gaze. "Aren't you supposed to put out barriers when you mop? Someone might slip and fall!"

The little man looked terrified. "So sorry, so sorry!"

"I . . . I didn't mean to snap at you," Lee said, and walked away.

He wandered around looking for her, having no idea what he would say if he found her. He didn't want to make her uncomfortable, but she had kissed him, hadn't she?

He took the elevator down and walked up to the bow. Balcony after balcony piled up behind him—when he turned he saw a few people watching from above, one shouting drunkenly. With both feet planted Lee could feel the ship's engines throbbing inside him. He walked around the edge of the deck, paying particular attention to any women standing by the railing, until he'd made his way to the stern. Here he could see the wake of the ship, the furrows of water turned silver by the moon.

An opportune place, if he were so inclined, to leave the cruise and everything else behind. But how horrible to be alone in all this water. After a few hours you would beg to die.

◄◦►

Lee spent the next morning in bed, not quite able to pull himself out of dreams he could not remember. Even with the DO NOT DISTURB sign out there were numerous knocks on his door. Finally he woke himself up enough to yell "Read the sign!" He felt satisfied by the sounds of rapid retreat, but had he missed an opportunity to see the woman from last night? Somehow she had known his name, so it would be no surprise if she could find his door, or had he misunderstood all that?

He needed more sleep to drain any residual sense of unreality, but blasts of the ship's horn made that impossible. Defeated, he stared at his cabin walls. A series of prints conveyed an attitude of eroticism, while still far from explicit so that no one could complain—curves and blurry flesh-colored swatches of color, some lines hinting at a highly abstracted embrace. Highly abstracted embraces seemed the most he could hope for at this stage of his life.

These images recalled a series of Chagall prints Ann chose for their bedroom. He didn't know much about art. Their titles contained words like "lovers," "marriage," and "kiss." With clouds of color that spread across the lines of the forms, it was as if the passion those couples felt extended to everything they touched, everything they saw. It was too much, or at least he had thought so at the time. Now he envied their enthusiasm. The figures were so full of emotion they floated—they'd lost all sense of decorum or gravity.

He remembered those kisses—necks impossibly elongated, their swimming bodies in extremis as they wrapped around each other. Ann had loved them, and he had loved them more than he would say. But they promised so much—had anyone ever felt such passion in a normal marriage?

Yes, yes they had. Feelings he didn't have words for. After Ann passed away he took the prints down and stuck them in the back of a closet so he might forget they were there. When his girls asked what happened to the prints he said he wasn't sure. He had no idea what his life was now, but it wasn't about that anymore.

The kiss last night had been nothing like the kisses in those prints. But it still had been surprising, although not exactly pleasant.

When Lee finally left his cabin he encountered the ship's activities director, her fixed smile more predatory than friendly. From the beginning she'd made him feel bullied. "I'm so *glad* I was able to run into you. You haven't been sick, have you?"

"Out too late," he said, "I suppose having too much fun. You must have hundreds of people, don't you, to be concerned about?"

"All equally important. Tell me, how can I make sure *you* have the time of your life?"

The very phrase *the time of your life* depressed him. "I'm doing fine, easing into things. Relaxing. There's nothing wrong with that, is there?"

"Of course not! But I'm sure we can do better. I know four lovely ladies eager for some male company at lunch."

He began his retreat. "Too much fun to do today, I'm afraid." He turned his back and practically ran.

"You'll leave empty-handed if you don't *make it happen*!" she shouted after him. He felt dizzy and struggled not to fall as the floor appeared, briefly, to melt.

◄◦►

Every afternoon the decks stank of suntan oil. Every lounge chair was full of barely clothed flesh in various stages of destruction. He thought of Jonestown, the bodies darkening in the intense tropical heat.

These were not ugly people. They were just trying to enjoy their vacations. Lee believed there were no ugly people, but he himself didn't have the courage to lie about half-naked, not with his aging carcass. He scanned the faces, looking for his mystery woman, even though she would seem out of place in a lounge chair in the sun.

"Aren't you going to say hello?" He recognized Sylvia's voice, but he couldn't find her in the sea of glistening skin, oversized sunglasses, and floppy sunhats. "Over here, in the red."

He walked over. She wore an old-fashioned-looking red two-piece suit. He thought she looked unusually sober. "You seem relaxed," he said.

"You probably think I look fat in this."

"I think . . . you look fine. Most of us aren't that slim, not at this age. We hold onto that memory of what we used to be too firmly. If you like what you're doing, that's what counts, isn't it?"

"I guess—I didn't expect you to be so enlightened. Most men aren't."

"I'm not enlightened. If I were, I would be dressed in swim trunks."

She laughed. "Will I see you at dinner later?"

"I don't really know. But enjoy the sun."

That hadn't been so difficult. Perhaps he knew what to say to people after all. He continued to look at faces, struggling to remember the features of the woman from the night before. It wasn't a good feeling. No doubt she would be appalled if she knew he was searching. But he was just making himself seen. If she wished to approach him it was up to her.

He strolled through the restaurants and stood at the back of a dance class. He looked for that yellow dress, but wouldn't she have changed by now? He hadn't behaved like this since high school.

He wondered what Ann would have thought of his behavior. Embarrassed for him, possibly, or sad. By sunset most of the chairs were empty. He should eat something, but he didn't think he could. He sat down. He should be writing his daughters, letting them know how he was doing, but what in the world would he say? *I've met someone*, perhaps. Both the truth and a lie.

Both the sea and the sky appeared the rumpled gray of an unmade bed. The horizon line had been almost completely erased. Staring too long into the blurring of borders made him ill.

"You miss her—she is all you can think about." The woman slipped into the next chair. Instead of looking at him she stared into that disorientating gray. Her dress, too, was gray this evening, or some shade of off-white.

"It's more complicated than that."

"You've lost your story, then," she replied. Today he could see that she wasn't a young woman. The skin of her neck was crepey, and there was loose flesh beneath her eyes. Perhaps she was his age after all.

"I just feel I should be doing something, but I don't know what to do." It made him feel unbearably sad to say this.

"You were in a story which worked for you for a very long time. But that story has ended, and yet you find you are still alive, and now you are in a different story you do not yet understand."

"So what am I supposed to do?"

"Live your life. Enjoy your vacation. Life may look quite different when you return."

"But I don't seem to be very good at this."

"Take a walk with me," she said, standing up and grabbing his hand. "You can do that much." It seemed he didn't have a choice. She guided him down the deck until they reached a small door in the hull that said CREW ONLY. She opened it and dragged him inside.

They were at an intersection of corridors. She took him through another door and down some metal stairs. He felt like a child being hand-led like this. The air was steamy. Her gray dress clung like excess skin.

These interior walls lacked the polish of the public areas. No upholstery or shiny white paint—the metal was dirty yellow with brown rust around the seams and rivets and bolts. There were distant echoes of harsh male argument and laughter, the rattle of machinery, metal banging against metal.

Another trip down another set of stairs—the paint completely worn off the grungy treads. They hadn't even bothered to mop up the dirt. Where were all those eager little uniformed men with their mops and smiles you saw on the passenger decks? The filth in the corners and along the edges had congealed into a black scum.

A muscular, shirtless man walked past them without a glance. Pressure was rising in Lee's head, a thrumming against his ear drums. He wondered if they were below water level now.

He wanted to ask her name—it was absurd he didn't know—but it didn't seem like the time. He should have insisted she reveal where they were going but he couldn't make himself speak. Her hand was delicate, yet she gripped his so firmly it hurt. Sweat made her skin appear gelatinous. Sweat was running into his eyes. He struggled with his free hand to wipe his face.

The next level down was packed with equipment. A wall of noise moved through him like a wave. His internal organs shook. Overhead were layer after layer of pipes, cables, gears, gauges, valves. The corridor shrank until it was no more than a catwalk—on either side he could see more machinery and more shirtless men far below, so distant they appeared to be miniatures, or was it possible the cramped working space required dwarves?

The walls of the ship were weeping, rivulets oozing down the seams and gathering in depthless pools below. The air smothered him in the stench of decay.

A narrow ladder dropped into an even darker place—there was no light, no reflection. She made him trade positions and when he hesitated she nipped his cheek with teeth like ice. The blood ran down his face and when he tried to wipe it off she darted forward as if to kiss or bite but licked him instead. Her tongue felt expansive. "You need to go first," she whispered. She let go of his hand as he took the first step down, but when he hesitated—*What am I doing?*—she placed her bare foot on his shoulder—*When did she take off her shoes?*—and forced him down several more rungs. He surrendered and led the way into the jet-black mist.

At the bottom he couldn't see his feet on the floor, if it was a floor. It was something solid, but it felt less than stable. Before he could figure it out she jerked him off his feet. The blackness fragmented into hundreds of glistening bits, resembling butterflies or birds, but which might have been fish. They disappeared as suddenly as they had appeared.

Lee felt the damp on his face but it didn't feel like sweat. Maybe he was crying. Certainly he felt barely controlled, fear and incredible sadness welling up with no words for any of it. He tried to think of his daughters and how sorry he was to leave them but their faces broke down into incoherency. He sobbed, and glistening air bubbles propelled in front of him. He was deep underwater and should have been dead, drowning in excruciatingly slow motion.

She wrapped her arms around him, arms so flexible they might have been boneless. She wrapped those long tubes of skin around his head, her moist whispers ordering him to turn, rocking his head painfully.

A translucent shape came forward out of the nothing: huge eyes and skeletal head, teeth so long and sharp it couldn't close its mouth. Floating around it was an expanse of insubstantial rags, great sheets of peeled flesh unfolding, their bioluminescent edges pulsing slowly. They suddenly darted in Lee's direction. He screamed with no sound. Something caught in his mouth. He reached up and felt his teeth, several inches long and razor sharp. Something blurry went into one of his eyes. He reached up and slowly pulled it out. His eyes were cavernous holes where anything could enter.

He shook his head vigorously. All the loose skin of him, the torn flesh and ragged filaments of him, floated around his face. He looked down at his body and could find neither his arms nor his legs.

He turned to her then, her mouth so wide, her lips so swollen, so dark. *Saudade*, she said, *Saudade*, until she had him completely in her mouth.

⟨◦⟩

Lee was suddenly awake, lying on his bed in the cabin. Water drained off him and onto the sheets, then onto the floor. Everything was wet and everything stank. The housekeepers were always so eager for something to do—he had plenty for them to clean today.

He glanced up at that terrible, banal artwork, and thought of those Chagall prints hidden away in the back of a closet at home. He could send a letter from the ship telling his daughters where the prints were, and that they could have them. Ann would have wanted them to have them. His message would get there before the ship returned to home port.

The intercom came alive and a lovely voice announced that all passengers were welcome to go ashore and identified the day's exit points. Lee hadn't ventured off the ship at any of the ports of call so far, but he needed to, didn't he, if only to buy souvenirs for his girls? When they were little they'd loved souvenirs from his business trips. He'd arrive home and after all the hugs and kisses they'd gather around his giant suitcase on the bed as he opened it to reveal what he'd brought them—usually a little T-shirt or a stuffed animal with the city's name embroidered across the front. It had been this simple ritual that had always made such perfect sense and it had been wondrous.

He climbed out of the wet bed and stripped off his soggy clothing, leaving it on the floor for the staff. Brisk use of a couple of towels left him moderately dry. He found his best shirt and pants in the closet, a pair of dress shoes, clean socks and underwear. Nothing terribly fancy, but still, the best he had brought. Every bit of the carpet was damp and he had no dry place to sit. Water was even dripping off his desk chair. So he stood and balanced himself carefully against the wall, pulling on his clothes and trying not to let them touch the carpet for more than a second or two. It took a while but finally he was dressed. At the last moment he grabbed his good sports jacket off the hanger and left the room.

The water in these Caribbean ports was so clear you could see schools of fish travelling beneath the crystalline surfaces. But so far their perfection had not persuaded him. Lee felt there had to be something terribly wrong behind such movie-magical sets, and he had no interest in discovering exactly what.

But today's excursion was for his daughters. A crewmember swiped his ID card and he walked down the gangway at a brisk clip, eager to get his errands done and then get back on board. His pace fell awkwardly into step with the cacophonous melodies of the ubiquitous steel drums. It was quite the production—the musicians wore non-identical but similar yellow and orange tropical suits. Two dark-skinned dancers performed in complementing colors. The music wasn't exactly unpleasant, but there was too much of it and too much the same. Lee felt as if everyone was looking at him, but doubted that anyone had actually noticed at all.

The beach here was white enough to hurt the eyes. He wondered if the sand was hot to the touch, and remained on the wooden walk just in case. He felt as if he had stepped into a rich oil painting whose colors were almost too intense to bear. What was that style called? He wished he knew more of the proper names for things. Ann certainly had.

But for Lee this was like the worst kind of dreaming, the kind that came when you were running a high fever and you felt as if you were rotting from the inside out, as so many of these islands probably were, what with the fruit, the jungle, their heightened cycle of birth and death. Or had he imagined it all? He knew very little about these places. He didn't even know what island he was on. He hadn't bothered to check.

It didn't take long to find the shop he wanted, one offering native wood carvings—animals mostly, but a few religious icons, and some doll-sized figures with extraordinarily ugly faces, the kind of eccentric gift both his daughters loved. The figures looked more Polynesian than Latin American but that didn't matter. The clerk offered to box them up ready to mail—a shipping center was only a few doors away. Lee mailed them and headed back to the ship.

He chose not to tour the island. Maybe that was a mistake, but what could a casual visitor see anyway? He couldn't imagine an excursion that wouldn't depress him. He'd want to know what was on the other side of the barbed wire or behind the huts. He'd want to know what the tourists weren't allowed to see. He'd want to ask them how you lived on an island in the middle of the ocean. If you wanted to go somewhere, where could you go? And none of this would answer the question of his aching.

He was tempted to find the woman again but knew he shouldn't. Instead he returned to his cabin to write long letters to both his daughters. He wasn't surprised to find his cabin in pristine condition. That was what they did here—they cleaned up all your messes as if they'd never been. They erased your mistakes. It was a complete escape from life. Some people welcomed that.

He wrote his long rambling letters full of memories and feelings and good wishes and everything he could think of to say to the people he cared most about in the world. Exhausted, he signed "Dad" to each and crawled into bed. In the morning he would look the letters over carefully to make sure he hadn't said anything he shouldn't have, and after he was done he would drop them off to be mailed at the next port.

Lee woke up sometime in the middle of the night. He was shaking. He thought at first that the ship's horn had blown, that some disaster had occurred, but he waited there in bed and heard nothing more—no horn, no footsteps outside. He couldn't even hear the ocean, or feel its movement.

He got up and slipped into the same clothes he'd worn that morning. He even put on his sports jacket. It was likely to be cold.

He walked out onto the empty deck. There was no one at the railing, no one in any of the deck chairs. He walked by the closed shops and stared in at the mannequins, willing them to move. The lights in the restaurants and even in the casino were out, which seemed unlikely. The casino was open all the time.

The elevator wasn't working so he took the steps up and down. He encountered no one on any of the decks he tried. He decided he wasn't going to get upset over this, and so he stopped looking. He could have knocked on random cabin doors, but of course he wouldn't do that. Let them sleep—it was the least he could do.

He went back up the stairs to the top deck of the ship. There was a swimming pool, but no one was in it. It was so dark he couldn't even tell if there was water in the pool. He heard nothing.

Someone stood at the forward observation point by the telescopes. He walked up behind her. Of course it was her. She was peering into one of the eyepieces.

He stepped closer. "What do you see?"

She turned around slowly. "I have not been home in a very long time, and I've never seen it from this angle. Sometimes I believe I do not miss it, but actually I miss it very much. *Saudade*, of course. *Saudade*."

He stepped up beside her and looked out at the ocean: boundless, dark, and moving, although he couldn't hear the waves. But he could see no land ahead of them, or anywhere else.

"You should look through the telescope. It might satisfy your yearnings."

He didn't want to do that. But he rested his hand on top of the scope and gazed at her. She seemed different, but he couldn't quite see her face, even though they were very close together. Perhaps his eyes were going bad. Perhaps even if he looked through the telescope he would be unable to see what was right in front of him.

"Perhaps you would like a kiss first," she said, "for encouragement."

He didn't want to, but she came to him anyway. He closed his eyes when their lips met. She tasted of something he did not recognize. He felt his body beginning to lift, to float. Still their lips were locked together, their tongues barely touching. He could feel his neck beginning to stretch, and bend, and soon he was upside down, and floating out over and past the rail, and over the ocean.

But they were still kissing. They were still kissing. Until all his weight returned.

# A MOMENT BEFORE BREAKING

## A. C. WISE

The wave gathers itself, grows, and waits to fall.

Ana stays close to her mother as they crowd onto the boat. Water slaps the pier. Everything smells of salt, fish, and rotting weeds. When they're herded below deck, the smell becomes too many bodies, too much breath. Everyone talks at once. Ana's mother obsessively checks the bag held tight against her body, the one with their paperwork and refugee visas.

Ana wants to go home. She misses her room, and her cousins, but her mama says they're going to a better life. America is the land of opportunity. Her mama will get a new job, and Ana will go to a new school. Ana is afraid she'll have to do the fourth grade over again even though her auntie has been teaching them English.

They're shown to a cabin with two other families. There's a boy, no more than three years old, who cries and clings to his father's hand. Later, there is strange food in a room with long tables. The engines grind, and the ship chugs through the water. Everyone is nervous, excited, afraid.

After the meal, Ana returns with her mother to the cabin and they climb into one of the lower bunks. Her mother lies down with her back pressed against the wall, and Ana tucks herself against her mother. She doesn't expect to sleep, but Ana wakes to the scream of metal. It is the sound of the world being torn apart. The deck shudders, and a klaxon blares, accompanied by a flashing red light. A crackling voice comes over the loudspeaker, but Ana can't hear over the general panic.

Then, for a moment, everything goes still. Underneath the human chaos, there's a noise like a song, a rising chant making her stomach feel like it's dropping to her toes, but it also sounds like a hurricane, a storm.

The deck shudders again. The groan of metal, worse than before, and her mother pulls her toward the door.

"Mama, what is—" But her mother doesn't hear her.

The ship lurches violently, rolls. Ana smashes into a wall that is now a floor, losing her grip on her mother's hand. She tastes blood. Everything is black and red, black and red. The alarm wails, but the chanting threads through it, growing louder. Ana's heart pounds, her fear turning it into a beacon to call the song, then falling to its rhythm. She wills it to slow, to change, but it refuses to obey.

So instead, she curls as small as she can. She doesn't want the singing people to find her. She makes herself into a ball, her face covered in snot and tears, but her traitor heart keeps on screaming *Here! Here! I'm here!*

◄◦►

*Once upon a time . . .*

Ana's eyelids are sticky, crusted closed. She can't open them, and everything hurts.

*Once . . .* The voice falters. Stops.

*Mama?* Her lips shape the words, but no sound emerges. It isn't her mother's voice. It's coming from inside; she hears it in the space between her ribs, and echoing in her head. Her throat is dry, her mouth swollen. Someone is crying, but it isn't her. It's coming from inside, too.

Panic. She tries to thrash away from the sound and waves of pain rip through her body. She chokes on a soundless scream, breath wheezing. Her skin has been peeled away, everything scraped raw. She remembers a sound like bees, buzzing and buzzing. Needles, going in and out of her skin.

*Once upon a time . . .*

The voice again. It comes in fragments, stutters. It is a cold voice, coming from very far away, but also very close, and it isn't human.

Where is her mama? The question comes full of aching need, but Ana already knows the answer. If her mama could come for her, she would. That means she isn't here. Ana is alone, scared, but the voice sounds frightened, too.

*Once upon a time, the King Under the Waves did not sleep as he sleeps now. He ruled at the beginning of time, and he will rule at the end. He is a wave, waiting to fall, and his crown is dead men's bones. He was ancient when the world began.*

Ana doesn't like the story, but it isn't quite as scary as being alone. Knowing someone else is in the dark with her is comforting.

*Now the King Under the Waves sleeps in his court, which is lost, but he will wake in time.*

*Before the King slept, his court magician brought him whispers. She said his people no longer believed in him. They thought him weak, old, tired.*

*The magician was a liar.*

*She challenged him to make something new, something never seen under the waves before to prove his power, baring rows of ghost-pale teeth as she did.*

*So the King rose up in veins of lightning and became a storm. He screamed rain down on a ship, smashed it to splinters and took its wheel. Upon the wheel he hung the bones of drowned men, and the flesh of creatures born in the lightless deep. In his vanity and pride, the King made a creature caught between land and sea. He made a child, a prince, an heir. He made me.*

⤙

Weird purple-blue light seeps beneath her lids, thick like the blood inside a bruise. Her lids are still sticky, but this time, Ana can open her eyes. She's lying on her back, her arms and legs strapped down. She turns her head as much as she can. Everywhere she's able to look there are glass tanks lining the walls, glowing softly in the dark.

She remembers a voice in the dark, telling her stories. Ana blinks. The motion makes her eyes sting. Why isn't her mama here? Where is she?

Her skin still feels raw, worse than the worst sunburn. To distract herself, she focuses on the tank at the foot of her bed, taking up nearly the whole wall. Something sloshes within the cloudy, blue-lit water. She can't make sense of the shape, then it gets worse, a tangled knot of darkness unfolding too many limbs.

A memory, like a blade driven through her skull. Underwater, she lived underwater, and there were things like the thing in the tank, things with needle teeth, hissing at her, hurting her. There are too many people inside her skin. A sob, bigger than a tidal wave, threatens to overwhelm her. Her entire body shakes—a cage, rattled from within.

⤙⚬⤚

Ana wakes for the third time. Calloused fingers press against her wrist. Her first instinct is to jerk away, but the voice, the one inside her head, whispers, *Be still. Hide. Don't let them find you.* Fear tastes like brine at the back of her throat, and she fights not to gag, not to do anything that will let them know she's awake.

"Her pulse is normal."

A man's voice. He runs a finger over her forearm, and her skin crackles like static electricity. The voice inside her flinches, an almost physical shape she can feel moving inside her. The man lowers her arm and replaces the restraint.

"The ritual worked. The prince is contained. Let's dump the others."

Footsteps move around the room, then retreat. When she's certain she's alone, Ana opens her eyes. She turns her head to look at her restraints, and her breath catches. Her skin shines, and it isn't just an echo of the tanks' blue-purple light. Her cousin showed her a video on the internet once of bioluminescent jellyfish, the tide lit up at night with thousands of tendrils. It looks just like that, whorls and swooping lines needle-marked onto her skin. When she tries to make sense of the pattern, her head hurts. There are plants and underwater animals, but it's also a language that tastes like wrong-colored stars and brine and the black depths of the ocean.

A hot, stinging pressure builds behind her eyes. She has to get out. She has to find her mother.

Her wrists are small, and the cuff the man reattached isn't as tight as it should be. She twists her arm. The leather chafes, breaking already raw skin. The tattoos glow brighter, and she swears one of them moves.

Her wrist slips free, smeared in blood. With shaking fingers, she fumbles the other cuffs open. Cloudy water sloshes in the tanks, and she catches a glimpse of something impossibly large pressed against the glass. She scrambles up, ignoring the pain, and runs to the door.

Footsteps from the far end of the hall, the men returning. Ana bolts in the opposite direction. The papery gown covering her newly glowing flesh crinkles and rustles. She ducks through an open door, flattening herself against the wall.

She scans the room, searching for another way out. It's like the one she left, lined with tanks, dimly seen things moving within. And on three cots, three blanket-draped bodies, which makes Ana think of the crying boy on the ship.

The light flicks on. Ana freezes. The men enter the room, heading straight for the cots, and not looking to where she hides.

"You grab that one, I'll take this one, and we'll come back for the third."

The thing inside her coils and uncoils, a pulsing knot of tension. Hatred seethes through her like molasses, thick and dark. The thing inside her hates these men. The men who hurt her. Who held her down. Who marked her skin. Ana hates them, too.

She launches herself forward. Startled, the man closest to her drops the blanket he's carrying and the body slips free. It's not the boy from the cabin, but still. His skin is partially tattooed, angry-looking and red. Whatever they did to her, they tried to do to him, too. Now he's dead.

Ana latches onto the man's arm, biting down.

"Son of a bitch!" He kicks her, and Ana folds.

She tastes blood on her teeth, and licks it clean. The second man speaks a word in a language she doesn't understand. It crawls, twisting through her, making the marks on her skin shudder. Ana gasps. She can't breathe. She's drowning in the air. The word isn't for her, it's for the thing inside of her. They're hurting it, hurting her.

"No," Ana says, but the sound that comes out is something else entirely. It is ships torn asunder and the tide thundering against the shore.

The glass tanks shatter. The things inside surge forth in a rush of foul-smelling water, weak and half dead. As they do, Ana changes. Dark limbs snatch up the men. She is no longer a girl made of skin and bone. She is cartilage and rage and teeth in rows and her body is so much bigger than it should be, filling the room. She tears and tears, not just the men, but the things from the tanks as well.

She bites and swallows and chews. When she is done, chunks of flesh, human and not, and splinters of bone cover the floor. Ana is shaking. She is soaking wet. She is alone. The room stinks of seawater. She looks at her hands and they are hands again. Her stomach roils. What did she bite? What did she swallow? The tattoos pulse. Sated, the thing inside of her rolls over to sleep.

Ana runs.

⤛◦⤜

Rain pounds the overhang, just deep enough to keep her dry. The alleyway smells like garbage. Ana wedges her back against the wall, a stack of jumbled crates hiding her. Yesterday, she stole clothes from a Laundromat. They mostly fit. This morning, she watched the back door of a bakery until a man emerged with a bulging plastic sack of trash, then gorged herself on three-day-old bread and pastries, thick and crusty and sugary sweet.

She has no idea where she is, how far the boat sailed, or where she was taken afterward. She doesn't know how much time has passed. She doesn't know anything.

She's heard people around her speaking English, and other languages, too. She can read some of the signs from what her auntie taught her. The thought that she made it to America, without her mother, makes her heart ache.

She needs a plan. Somewhere to live. She cannot survive on old bread alone. Her mama is gone. Her mama's bag with the papers saying she belongs here is gone. She can't ask anyone for help: she killed two people. Or the thing inside her did, but she wanted them dead, too. She draws her knees up and wraps her arms around them.

"Tell me a story?" Ana's teeth chatter, her stolen clothes inadequate against the cold.

The thing inside her turns over, waking up, unfurling like the things in the tank. Maybe it's a monster, but maybe she is, too. And all they have is each other.

*Once upon a time . . .*

"What are you?" Ana asks softly.

*Once . . .* Something about the voice makes her think of whales singing to each other, a resonating sound she feels in her breastbone. The same cousin who showed her the video of the jellyfish played a clip of whale songs for her once. Tony. He wanted to be a marine biologist. Ana suddenly misses him fiercely.

*Once upon a time, there was a weakling prince.*

There is sorrow in the voice, shame.

*While the King Under the Waves slept, the court magician gathered followers. She called the prince a traitor, a creature half-made for the land and so unable to fully love the sea. Her words passed among her followers, from needle-toothed mouth to needle-toothed mouth.*

The King has abandoned us, *she said.* While he slumbers, we must take matters into our own hands.

*So the King's courtiers, with their strong limbs and rending beaks, bright lures and endless hunger, sought out the prince. They hunted him. They threatened him and beat him, hissed* traitor *at every turn, and drove him from the palace until he couldn't find his way home.*

*The magician rose out of the waves and caught a man fishing alone. She coiled her body around him, and held her dripping face over his. Her words were sibilant, water gurgling through ancient channels cut in stone. With her teeth inches from his flesh, she poured instructions into his ears.*

*She told the man where to find the prince, and taught him secret ways to bind the prince in human flesh. She swore him to be her priest, to pass her word onto the next generation, and the next. When the prince's human body failed, rotting and dying around him, the priest's descendants would find another body, and another. She promised her priest power, a weapon—the immortal prince driven mad by dying over and over again with each fragile human body he inhabited.*

*She promised that when the time came, the priest and his followers would turn the prince against his father and take the kingdom under the waves for their own.*

*She lied.*

*Though the man who would be her priest suspected she would kill those who served her once the kingdom was in her hands, it would be a problem for his children, or his children's children in days to come. By the time the magician's plan came to fruition, he would be long dead, but if he did not agree to serve her now, he would not even live to see another day.*

◄►

"This is less than half what you promised to pay." Ana bristles.

The man is a head taller than her, and almost twice as wide. She isn't a child anymore, but she's a collection of scrawny twig-limbs compared to his solid bulk. He grins, showing glints of gold among the ivory.

"I changed my mind. Take it or leave it. You wanna be stuck with a handful of stolen goods when those new ICE agents come sniffing around?"

"Why would they—" She stops, every bone of her spine going rigid. The man's grin widens.

Underneath her clothing, her tattoos squirm. The prince remembers bared teeth, not glinting gold, but translucent-pale like fish bones. He remembers hisses of *traitor* and being told he doesn't belong. He wants to burst through her skin at the man, and she fights him down.

"I don't want any trouble," Ana mumbles.

It's a lie. She wants to demand the money she's owed. She wants to rip this man apart. A thick finger goes under her chin, tilting it up. The man leans close; his breath stinks of beer and garlic.

"You're nice to me, I'll be nice to you."

There's a knife in her pocket, a small blade she could open with a flick of her wrist. It would be kinder than letting the creature inside her unfold. She imagines driving it into the man's gut, the side of his neck, his eye. Sometimes she remembers the prince's other deaths, the bodies he inhabited before hers. The memory of dying over and over makes it hard to care about the small life in front of her. Ana's hand creeps toward her pocket.

"Hey!" The man grabs her wrist, and she lets out a yelp.

She stomps on his foot as he tries to pin her against the wall. Doesn't he understand she's being kind? She's sparing him? She uses his momentum to pull him off balance, making a run for it when he stumbles. He's surprisingly fast, bouncing off the wall and catching her by the collar, yanking her off her feet.

A shadow falls over her as Ana wheezes, the air driven from her lungs. Her skin burns, the prince pushing at her from inside. *Hungry, hungry, hungry.*

"There you are, cuz. I've been looking all over for you."

A young man grins down at her. He can't be much older than her, but he carries himself like he knows a hundred times more about the ways of the world. He holds out a hand; Ana is so stunned she lets him help her up. The coiled knot inside her calms. The young man turns his attention to the big man with garlic breath.

"This here is my cousin," he says. "I've been looking all over for her. I hope there isn't any trouble."

Ana has never seen the young man before, and he's certainly not her cousin, but she keeps her mouth shut. He wears an easy smile. His stance is loose, but there's a threat implied, only this time, the threat isn't directed at her. A white man with buzz-cut hair and tattoos covering half his face stands behind the man calling himself her cousin. He cracks his knuckles and watches the man with garlic breath.

"No trouble." The man with garlic breath holds his hands up, eyes on the tattooed giant.

"I'm Theo." The young man turns his attention back to Ana. "This is Antonin. You're with us now."

"That man owes me money," Ana says, jerking her chin at the man scuttling away.

Theo and Antonin exchange a look, and Antonin turns to follow the man. Ana feels a moment of guilt, but whatever Antonin has in mind is still kinder than what she would have done. Theo throws an arm around Ana's shoulders, not possessive, not threatening. She can't say why, but something about him feels like family, like home, like they really could be cousins. If Ana squints, she can almost see the resemblance.

"You like pizza?" he asks. "I'm starving."

⋘

*Once upon a time, the King Under the Waves dreamed a box into existence. The box was also a map, and a city, and a palace. A way to find what is lost. A way for the prince to find his way home.*

The alarm beeps and Ana snakes an arm out from beneath the covers. A chalky after-taste coats her tongue, like she's been devouring powdered bones in her sleep. She takes a moment to remind herself she is no longer the child in the room with the tanks. No longer the stick-thin girl on the streets.

She pushes the covers back, listening to the slosh of the water outside and feeling the world bob up and down. Ana sits, stretching her arms until her muscles loosen and her joints pop. Her tattoos glow, luminescent against her brown skin. Sometimes the prince forgets himself and her skin becomes a wave-born undulation of seaweed fronds and coils of limbs, spirals, and nautilus chambers, infinitely unfolding and keeping him caged. It's been happening more frequently lately, the prince suffering nightmares Ana only remembers in fragments on waking.

She wonders if it means the magician's cult is hunting her again. Or if the King Under the Waves is waking. Or both.

Ana pulls on the wetsuit hanging in the miniscule shower. The neoprene smothers the faint light so she can almost forget about her tattoos. At the door to her cabin, she pauses, touching the twenty-year-old framed newspaper page hanging there.

The grainy photograph shows the prow of a ship, jutting from the water, rescue crews surrounding it. The story underneath relates how the ship ran into an unexpected reef, tearing open its hull. How all sixty-seven passengers—mostly refugees—were killed, along with the crew. The story doesn't mention the way the metal sounded, screaming, or the chanting she'd heard that had summoned the reef from the depths. It doesn't mention the children that were stolen. It doesn't say anything about Ana, or her mother.

Ana emerges onto the deck, where the wind picks strands from her hastily gathered ponytail. Theo turns from the rail with a grin.

"What's the word, cuz?"

Ana manages a wave, feeling the weight of her uneasy sleep.

"The word is good, cuz. The wreck is right where you said it would be."

Ana peers over Theo's shoulder at the image on his tablet showing the ocean floor in bright blots of thermal color.

"Private vessel. Probably scuttled for the insurance payout. How did you know? Is it the, you know . . ."

Theo wiggles his fingers and makes a woooo sound.

"Shut up." She snaps the words out harder than she means to, then shakes her head. They've been through so much together, from the streets to this boat, to saving each other's lives more than once. It's been years since she was a stick-thin teenager and Theo threw his arm around her shoulders. They're not family by blood, but they might as well be.

Theo's grin is back a moment later. That's the way it's always been between them—Ana, surly and afraid of herself, Theo smiling, words sliding right off him.

"It'll be a good haul," Ana offers by way of apology, putting up a fist for Theo to bump.

Theo knows more about her than anyone else, other than the prince. More than she wishes he knew, and less than he thinks. She hates keeping secrets, but it's for his own protection. Which is why he doesn't know about the thing waiting in the wreck beneath them. The one useful scrap she's been able to glean from the prince's restless nightmares—a box, dreamed into existence by the King Under the Waves, worked like sand inside an oyster shell to make a pearl.

The man who bought it at auction had no idea what it was. Now that man is dead.

That's another thing Theo doesn't know. How Ana drifted in the waves and let the prince unfurl from inside her. How surprisingly easy it was with the prince's help to convince the man with the yacht to sink his boat for the insurance money. Sink the boat, and himself, and the box, which had been giving him nightmares about things without eyes, without bones, all mouths, crawling dripping out of the sea. Things that flopped and squelched across the deck. Dead and rotted things rising out of the deep.

Overhead, the sky blushes a muddy color between brown, purple, and gray. Ana checks her gear, and Theo hands her the dive computer, which she straps to her wrist.

"I've got it all programmed," Theo says. "Time, depth, everything. You won't even have to think about it."

"Thanks." She manages a smile, pulling up the hood of her dive suit.

"Antonin promised us sixty-forty this time."

Which means Ana will get fifteen to Theo's twenty-five—it's his boat—but she doesn't care. The box is all she cares about.

Theo's expression changes, and it's like watching storm clouds roll in. His eyes, which are normally a color like rich, polished cherry wood, go almost as dark as black coffee. He squeezes her shoulder.

"Be careful down there."

"I always am." She tries to sound reassuring.

He knows what she is, knows she could dive without her suit, if she chose. Maybe that's what worries him. The clouds lift, and Theo flashes brilliant white teeth again.

"Bring back the goods, cuz."

Ana tugs her mask into place, gives Theo a thumbs up, and tips backward into the water. The visibility is low, the world muted greens and browns. She switches on the light clipped to her shoulder, and the ghostly outline of the downed yacht appears below. The designs on her skin shiver with restless hope.

If this works, maybe she can bring the prince home. She can finally be alone inside her skin. The idea thrills and terrifies her.

She's only "seen" the prince once. When she first began dreaming of the box, she started diving before the sun rose, staying down longer and longer each time. Unnerved by the dreams, the prince had been silent, sullen. The time when he would tell her fairy tales had long since passed, so it was Ana who reached for him, screaming inside her own mind while her lungs burned and ached for breath, demanding an explanation and a way to make the dreams stop.

And he'd appeared. A skull, furred with algae and barnacles. It looked something like a goat's skull, and something like an ichthyosaur, rolling loosely atop a body that made no sense. A ribcage, an impossible coil of blue-gray limbs unfurling and unfolding in constant restless motion. A voice like crashed ships, and eyes burning blue flame even underwater. Her prince.

WE ARE ::::

It was the first time she'd heard him speak aloud. She hadn't understood the word, but she'd known it for a name, grinding against her like splintered bone. She didn't understand how he could be inside and outside her body at the same time, but he was.

WE ARE :::: OUR FATHER IS :::: WE ARE LOST.

Ana had wanted to laugh and weep all at once. Part of her still does as she kicks her way to the wreck. If she stops for just a moment to think about her life—the ship, her mother, the thing inside her, the marks on her skin—she will start screaming and never stop.

She pulls herself through the yacht's open hatchway. A startled fish darts away as she enters the main cabin. There's a bed built into the floor, cabinets above it, drawers beneath it, and a desk built into the wall. Ana starts with the desk. The prince is awake, shivering, and his movements make her clumsy. The bottom drawer is the only one that's locked. Ana unsnaps the dive knife from her belt and wedges the point into the gap between drawers. She wiggles the blade as deep as it will go, then smacks the hilt. The lock pops open.

Whorls and twists and coils move across her skin as she lifts the box free. The outside is carved with intricate designs both achingly familiar and utterly strange. *Home.* Ana flips the lid open. Inside the box is a labyrinth, not carved, but grown. It glows faintly, the same sick-bright shade of blue-green as the marks on her skin.

*Home. Home. Home.*

◦

Ana sits cross-legged on her narrow bed. Outside, waves slap the hull. Theo is off with Antonin. She is alone with the prince, and the water, and the box. She traces the raised pattern on the lid, following coiled ways doubling back on themselves. The box is a map. Beneath her skin, the prince twitches a multitude of limbs.

"Do you want to go home?"

A jumble of longing and fear answers her; the words *traitor, weakling*, and *flaw* hammer at her from the inside. Snatches of fairy tales, the story of a prince driven from his home, imprisoned within a human body; the story of a girl, torn from her mother, made into a cage for a monster.

*Unmake me.*

The words echo inside her skull. Whatever the prince wants, it's not this half existence. Ana opens the box. In the dim room, it no longer glows, but draws light into itself. A maze within a maze, haunted by tiny flickers of motion.

The tattoos on her arms and legs lash, uncoiling across her belly and down her spine. Limbs and teeth and a skull and eyes like blue fire. Ana grips the box tight. She feels the suffocating weight of flesh, rotting around her. Around him. The thunder of blood not his own, constantly pounding in his ears.

It's too hot. Sweat prickles beneath her armpits. She has to get out. Clutching the box, Ana staggers onto the deck. She's at the rail without even thinking about it, then up and over, into the water.

The shock of cold slaps her awake. Salt water surges up her nose, she tastes it at the back of her throat. Light from her tattoos seeps into the water. It occurs to her she isn't wearing her dive suit, her mask, her regulator. She shouldn't be able to see so clearly. Her lungs should be screaming for air.

Something tickles the side of her neck. Before she can slap it away, it becomes a burning pain, like a knife slit across her skin. She chokes on a scream, thrashing. She wants to drop the box but she can't; it's seared to her hands. The skin at her neck parts, and she's breathing through gills.

Her pulse jack-rabbits. She is a child in a room filled with tanks. She is a teenager on the streets, and a man with garlic-scented breath is threatening her. There is other skin beneath her own, slick and smoke-colored and drowned; her muscled limbs could tear a man apart, have torn men apart. Her teeth, needle sharp, have tasted blood.

There was a woman named Zarah, once, with burnt-wood skin, who smelled like oranges and dark chocolate and cloves. They drank, and danced, and Zarah called the marks on Ana's skin beautiful. She traced them with the tip of her tongue, and Ana could almost pretend she was human. Until she woke to the sound of Zarah screaming and the bed drenched in seawater. When Ana tried to reach after Zarah as she fled, the arms that reached were slick-black like oil, and she fell in a squirming mass on the floor, seeing the angry, puckered marks on Zarah's legs and back and arms.

What is she? A monster who will hurt those around her if she lets her guard down. Zarah. Theo. Even her mother, the first person the monster took from her. Rage floods her, and when the tide of it recedes, it leaves Ana hollow and cold. She's still clutching the box, and she flips it open under the waves.

A voice booms; the words are thunder and bells tolling on drowned ships and ancient stones cracking under battering waves. They roll through her like lightning, writing directions on her bones. Corridors unwind around her. Massive statues loom at her from niches, larger than the pharaohs and even less human. The walls are stone, emitting light the color of a star, but they are also made of the body of a vast creature long-since decayed. Ribs arching, a nautilus, spiraling endlessly down, the echo chamber of a skull.

At its heart lies her father and a choice, and Ana wants to back away, but she hasn't even moved. She's still hanging motionless, her throat slit with gills, breathing underwater while the prince cowers inside her.

A shadow darts at the corner of her eye. Ana turns and it surges toward her, gray arms unfurling. Squid. Octopus. Shark. None of the words fit. The face is almost human, but the skull slants sharply upward, the eyes are flat back, and when the near-lipless mouth opens, it reveals rows of needled teeth.

*Traitor.*

Ana shoots upward, her head breaking the waves. She hauls in a gasping breath, and for a moment, she chokes on air as the gills fight her and her heart stutters and threatens to stop. She claws for the boat's ladder, expecting webbed hands to close on her ankles at any moment.

Shaking, she collapses on the deck. Her skin seals itself, the flesh smooth as though it never opened. She's no longer holding the box, but the word continues to pound inside her like waves against the shore. *Home. Home. Home.*

She can't help but obey, but if she does . . .

*Traitor.*

Ana hugs her knees to her chest. In the space between her ribs, between her skin and bones, the creature sharing her body curls small as well. Together. Afraid.

◂◦▸

"Once upon a time, a child sailed upon the waves." Ana lies on her side under a pile of blankets.

Theo found her on the deck when he returned. He put her to bed, made her hot tea, fussed over her until she insisted all she needed was sleep. But sleep is the farthest thing from her mind. Her whole body is wired. The prince keens inside her.

When she was alone, when she was afraid as a child, the prince told her stories.

"Once upon a time," she says, "there was also child under the waves who was very ill."

Of course, she wasn't there the first time the prince was placed inside a human body, but she tries to imagine it, and make it into a better story. A happier one. She makes it into a fairy tale, like the ones he used to tell her. Inside, the prince calms, listens.

"And there was a wicked magician who tricked the King Under the Waves into thinking a human body would cure his son."

Ana's muscles relax and un-cramp. She's able to roll onto her back, but she doesn't stop talking.

"The child who sailed upon the waves had always been in love with the ocean. He dreamt of it every night, as though his blood was half seawater and his heart a many-chambered shell. This heart called out to the King Under the Waves, its every beat a siren-song, a beacon.

"So the King became a storm. He found the ship where the child sailed, and fell upon the deck, shattering the mast. He tore the ship in two, ignoring the screams and the prayers of those on board. He found the heartbeat, scooped up the child, and drew him under the waves, but he did not drown."

The story is prettier than the truth, even with the drowned sailors and the ruined ship. There are no needles, no blood, no pain, no terror. But right now, this is the story both she and the prince need to hear. Her tattoos still.

"There was a child under the waves, and a child above them. One loved the sea, and one loved the land. One sank, and the other rose, and after that moment, neither was alone again."

ᐊᐤ

"Here." Ana slides the tablet showing a map and the coordinates for where she needs to go across the small table in the cramped galley. Theo turns it, frowning.

"That's open ocean. There's nothing for miles around."

"Ships wreck in the open ocean all the time." Ana shrugs, looking away.

Of course it's not a ship she's looking for, it's a palace, a lost kingdom, but how can she explain it to Theo? How can she tell him a box in a dream and a voice inside her head are calling her home to a place she's never lived, and she doesn't know what she'll find when she gets there?

"Hey." Theo's voice is soft. She looks up even though she doesn't want to. "Tell me what's going on with you?"

His voice is gentle, and there's that concern in his eyes again. He peers at her to see beneath the hard edges. They've never really talked about it, but Ana knows Theo lost people, too. Why else would he have thrown his arm around her on the street that day? If sometimes she looks at him and sees home, then he must see it when he looks at her, too.

"I . . ." Ana falters. "I need to go there, and I'm not sure I'll be coming back."

It's as close to the truth as she can get. The voice tolling through the waves, calling her home, is not a kind voice. She doesn't know exactly what's waiting for her, but she knows she can't go on like this, afraid of herself, afraid for the prince, afraid of what she might do to someone who gets too close. If she ever hurt Theo . . .

"Then don't go," Theo says.

"It's not up to me anymore." A note of desperation breaks her voice, and Ana hates it, trying to push it back down.

Even now, she can feel it, a tug at the center of her belly, pulling at a part that both is and isn't her. Two lost children, one sailing on the waves and one alone and frightened under them. Maybe they're not all that different. Maybe, by now, they're one and the same.

"If you're in trouble, and I could help, you'd tell me?" It's only half a question.

The way Theo asks it makes him seem like the younger one between them. For the life he's lived, Theo has remarkable faith in the world. He has faith in her, in them together. Ana shakes her head, tears frosting her lashes, but not falling.

"Promise," she says, and it isn't entirely a lie. He can't help her. This time, she's on her own.

Theo watches her for a moment longer, like she's a puzzle he's trying to figure out. Finally, he rises, leaving her alone in the galley. Ana cradles a mug of coffee between her hands. Heat seeps through the ceramic, but her skin remains cold.

◄○►

The wave builds, and holds, waiting a moment before breaking.

◄○►

Ana watches the horizon. The sea and the sky are almost the same color, a pale, washed-out slate. The wind tugs at her hair and her jacket, the nylon making a snapping sound like a sail.

The engine's growl drops to a purr, then a hum as Theo eases back on the throttle. There's a splash as the anchor hits, followed by the long sound of the chain unwinding. Theo cuts the engine altogether.

"This is it," Theo says.

Ana looks at him, really looks at him, as she hasn't in a long time. He squints, deepening the lines at the corners of his eyes. There are a few early strands of gray in his hair, though he isn't even thirty-five.

There's a sudden image in her mind, Theo, older, with his arm around a woman's shoulders; she's nearly a head shorter than him, thick at the waist, hair blowing in the wind as they watch a pair of children run.

"If I don't come back . . ." She looks away. It's easier when she does. "Go somewhere far away from the sea," she says. "Go inland. Find someone to love. Live a good life."

She makes herself look at him then, and smiles, a crooked thing. Her tattoos sway, restless.

"Name one of your children after me, okay, cuz?"

She flashes a grin at his confusion, and before he has time to answer her, she unzips the windbreaker and lets it fall to the deck like shed skin.

"Aren't you—" Theo starts, but the rest is lost as Ana launches herself off the bench and over the rail—no tank, no fins, no dive computer—just the air burning in her lungs.

The water is dark, but she follows instinct. The pain when the skin at her neck slits itself open is barely noticeable this time. She remembers holding her mama's hand as they crowded onto the ship. She carries that pain with her as she goes deeper. She carries the pain of an ill-made child, too, a pawn in a power struggle, despised and afraid. She winds them both around her like armor, and she doesn't feel the cold.

A warning spike of fear makes her jerk to the side. A spear tears her dive suit, just missing her skin. Cold water rushes in, and she whips around, faster than human limbs should allow. The spear is polished bone; the creature that wields it is nothing human. The torso is like a man's, the cheekbones angled hard, eyes flat black, sloping skull giving way to thrashing tendrils like a nest of snakes. Needle teeth part with the familiar hiss, *traitor*.

She grabs the knife from her dive belt, and when the creature lunges again, she slashes its forearm. A shriek of pain, then an elbow driven in her face. Her nose gives with a sickening crunch. Blood clouds the water and pain blooms behind her eyes. Her fingers open, losing the knife. Through the haze, another figure appears. She is snake-long, and there are symbols cut into her blue-gray skin. The magician.

Ana feels the bruises, the cuts her father—the prince's father—never saw. Hears the taunts and the threats and they blend with her own memories of the terrible sound of the ship being torn apart, and the magician's priests chanting, and the needle going in and out of her skin.

No.

Ana becomes inky blackness, unfolding. She opens an infinity of mouths. Ill-made as she is, she's more like her father than anyone knows. She is liquid smoke poured through the water; she is pain, and she is hunger.

Blue-flame eyes meet the magician's. Then a dozen, dozen, dozen more open all over her body, every shape, every color, every size. And they see.

Together, her rage and the prince's fear are stronger than the magician's tattoos and spells. The magician's flat black gaze goes from triumph to fear. She tries to turn away, but Ana is faster. She thinks of the men on the boat, and the man in the alleyway, and even Zarah. She lashes out in every direction at once, catching the magician, and this time, she doesn't hold back. She gives the prince free rein; together, they bite and rip and tear.

Ana is alone. Shreds of her dive suit drift around her, but not even scraps of her attackers remain. She should be cold, but she's not. She should be afraid, but she's not. Ana swims.

Figures pace her, keeping their distance. They've seen what she is, not the frightened, whipped princeling anymore. She is her father's son, come home, and so much more. It is time to wake the King from his slumber.

She passes carved statues whose blind eyes are taller than her body. There are bones, the carcasses of sea creatures from the beginning of time. She feels the beating heart of the kingdom, its sluggish black pulse. Her father. *Home.* She holds the word like a stone on her tongue. She passes through a carved archway so wide she can't see its edges. *Home.*

She opens her mouth. The voice that emerges is and is not hers. It has a thousand tongues, all of them belonging to dead men, save her own. She uses all of them to push out words like drowned coastlines and the shifting of tectonic plates.

WE ARE :::: WE ARE HOME.

Something stirs in the dark. It is not one thing, it is everything. It is every drowned ship since the beginning of time, shattered boards, torn sails, rotting corpses. It is the hungry maw of ocean trenches, every lightless abyss, every dead spot on the map where things disappear. It is lighthouse eyes, and foghorn voice, and the crash of the tide.

CHILD.

A word for her and for the thing inside of her. Eyes open, so many of them, surrounding her. She is seen, utterly and completely, then they blink closed.

Everything leaves her in a rush, a single thread of her pain and the prince's, braided as one. It is pulled from her, and she gives it willingly, every cut, every blow, the needle tattooing her skin, the tanks, her mama, the rage.

And when she's hollow, the King Under the Waves holds her without holding her, considers her with eyes sealed closed, even as he still dreams. In the stillness around her, there is a question.

WHAT DO YOU WANT?

She know the prince's answer—*unmake me.*

But what does *she* want? The magician is destroyed, but her cult is still out there. Even now, they are searching for her, thinking they can control her, make her into the weapon the magician promised long ago. The prince may want unmaking, but Ana wants to live.

And just like that, the thought is plucked from her mind. All around her, the King Under the Waves unfolds. She feels the prince pulled from her, an ache like a lost tooth, part of her ripped away, but in the absence, she is remade.

◄○►

The wave curls, and at its peak, it waits.

Ana is in the wave, and she is under the waves with the King, and she is on a boat, a frightened child, long ago. Time folds and unfolds around her, and she sees what is and what was and what could be.

In a time that isn't now, a field of golden wheat turns bloody under the light of the setting sun. Theo stands on the porch of a house, surrounded by people Ana doesn't recognize, except for one woman she maybe saw once in a dream. The wind howls, flattening stalks, and Theo shelters his eyes. The first drop of rain hits, and the people huddled beneath the edge of the roof look to the horizon, glad they are far from the ocean, and watch the storm rise.

Ana is that storm.

On a beach that isn't now, but sometime soon, the magician's priests and priestesses chant to call her from the sea. The tide hisses over wet stones, pulling back impossibly far. The sound is tumbled bones. The men and women sway. Their voices rise. They don't notice the tide curling into a wave high enough to block the moon.

Ana unfolds and she is limbs and teeth and dead men's bones. She is the wave curled above the beach, full of broken ships, splinter-sharp. She is a monster. She is a little girl clutching her mother's hand. She is the heir to the King Under the Waves. Ana smiles.

Above the beach, the wave finally decides where it will fall. The sky is dark, darker, darkest, drowning the moon. By the time the cultists finally think to scream, it is too late. The wave crashes over, into them, through them. And the wave is full of terrible things.

⤙◦⤚

Once upon a time, a child went under the waves and did not drown. Once upon a time, a child rose, a dripping, monstrous thing, climbing up from the waves again.

# SISTER, DEAREST SISTER, LET ME SHOW TO YOU THE SEA

## SEANAN MCGUIRE

When I went to sleep, it was in my pink princess fantasy of a bedroom, canopied in taffeta and silver sparkles, head cushioned by goose down wrapped in the finest silk. It was all too young for me, and most of my friends assumed that it was somehow ironic, but I loved it. My mother's hand was in every fold and unnecessary spangle. She was never going to hem my prom dress or fuss over my wedding favors; I could at least let her linger in the places where she'd already been.

When I woke, it was because a wave had slapped me hard across the face, sending salt water shooting up my nose and into my eyes. I sputtered and gasped, trying to snap out of this horrible dream.

I did not wake up. Another wave hit me, this time filling my mouth as well as my nose, and for one horrifying moment, I couldn't breathe at all. The world was water, and water was the world, and I was so small in comparison to it. This was where I was going to die, choking on the waves that had replaced my breath.

My body felt like it had been wrapped in cotton, insulated from everything except the cold. I tried to raise my hands—like an open hand has ever done anything to fend off a wave—and realized I couldn't move my arms, or my legs, or *anything*. Something was holding me in place. The world might be water, but I? I was nothing more than a disembodied head, somehow still alive, at least for the moment. Somehow freezing and drowning at the same time.

Even with my eyes open, there was no real light, apart from the silver spangle of the stars overhead. How bright they were, how bright and how beautiful. If I squinted, I could almost pretend they were the stars on my bedroom ceiling, the ones Mom had placed with such precision in the last few good months, before she'd grown too sick to balance on the stepladder.

"If you need me, look for the brightest star, and know that I'll be watching you," she had said, and I'd believed her, seven years old and too naive to understand that when mothers die, they *die*. They don't Cinderella their way into the nearest hazel tree and live on as some intangible but positive influence. They go away, bones and rotting meat under the dirt that covers their grave, and they never come back, and they never come home, and they never help you repaint your bedroom. So it stays the color of roses and rainbow mornings, the color of a dead mother's love, and whenever someone questions it, the answer is quick and clean and easy:

"My mother chose the color. My *dead* mother."

Another wave hit me in the face, knocking my head backward against what felt like stone. *Rough* stone, like the edges of the volcanic tide pools that ringed the local coast. And just like that, I knew where I was, where I had to be:

Olympia Beach. Private. Secluded. Unsafe for the last five years, as the rising sea levels had knocked out the sunbathing and diving areas one by one, leaving only the rocky tide pools and the jagged edges of ancient lava flows. People think Hawaii when they think of lava, not coastal Washington, but we're made of fire as much as anyplace else. Fire, and ashes, and the jagged edges where the water hits the shore.

"Help," I gasped as the wave receded. I was starting to learn their tempo. Every time one of them hit me, I got a four-second gap to breathe. It wasn't enough. I was going to be out of air soon, no matter what I did.

That wasn't going to stop me. I breathed in, holding it as the next wave struck, and then howled, "*Help!*"

"Mmmm," said a thoughtful voice from behind me, outside my limited range of vision. "I'm going to go with 'nah.' Hope that answer's okay with you."

My shock and outrage were enough to make me mistime the next wave. My attempt at a retort was swallowed by a wave of water, turning into so much helpless blubbering. I could feel the wave on the back of my throat, trying to shove its way further inside, further into *me*.

"Aw, wow, I bet that one hurt. If you stay calm, you'll live longer. At least, that's the theory. Maybe even . . . long enough."

My sister's voice moved as she spoke, going from slightly to my left to slightly to my right. Neither direction changed the fact that it was my own damn flesh and blood that had put me in this position. Another wave hit me. This time I managed to hold my breath until it receded.

"Maya, what the *fuck*?"

"Remember last month when I had to go to the dentist, and I had that whole massive panic attack about it, until dear old Daddy agreed to let me see a phobia specialist?" Her voice came closer, malice and self-satisfaction dipped in a hard candy shell of hatred. "Oral conscious sedation, sweetie. Valium and Triazolam and you're off to la-la land while the nice dentist fixes your ouchie tooth. Only I'm not afraid of the dentist. The nitrous was *more* than enough for me. I palmed the pills. Did you enjoy your chocolate milk last night? Was it *delicious*?"

An image flashed through my mind as the next wave struck home: Maya, darling Maya, the sister I'd never been able to figure out or connect with, bringing me a glass of chocolate milk before bed. She'd sworn on our mother's grave that she hadn't spit in it, and foolish little me, I'd taken that to mean she hadn't done *anything* to it. The thought that my own sister might drug me had never crossed my mind.

The wave receded. I gasped for air before moaning, "Why?"

"Why? Gosh, Tracy, I *just don't know*."

I thought I felt her fingers brush the top of my head, a fleeting touch that was gone as quickly as it had come. I thought she was leaning in close. If I had been able to feel my hands, move my hands, I could have grabbed her and pulled her into the water with me.

It was the biggest "if" in the world.

Lips close to my ear, she murmured, "I don't remember what our mother smelled like."

Then she was gone again, retreating to a safe distance as the next wave hit home.

It took longer to catch my breath after that one, longer to come back into the moment. I barely had time to close my eyes before the next wave was hitting me, driving my head into the rock wall once again. This wave felt higher, colder, and my chest grew tight with more than just asphyxia.

The tide was coming in.

"Man, dental drugs are *amazing*," caroled Maya. "Maybe I should rethink my career plans. Now that I'm about to be an only child, I bet darling Daddy would be happy to pay for me to go to dental school. Let me get established in my career, and hey, maybe I can kill people on the side. Wouldn't that be fun? People think dentists are monsters, but they never think of them as *monstrous*."

Another wave hit me. I spat salt water back into the sea and hissed, "You're not going to go through with it. Stop playing around *right now* and get me out of here."

"Aw. Pretty Tracy, always got everything she wanted. Got the perfect looks and the perfect social life and the perfect smile, got to remember our mother as a living, breathing person, not a skeleton strangling in her own skin, got everything, *everything*, and now it's like you can't see the forest for the trees. You're going to die tonight. I'm thirty pounds lighter than you are. I couldn't pull you out of that tide pool if I wanted to. You're *dead weight*, sister mine, and soon you're just going to be dead."

Waves kept hitting me while she spoke, slapping me further down into the water, until it felt like everything she said was being filtered through a screen, distorted by the cutting cold.

"I tried. Never think I didn't try to learn to love you. There's just one problem." For the first time, she moved so I could see her. She was smiling, bright and brilliant as if she'd just won a beauty pageant, and that smile didn't waver as she leaned in and spat her final words at me.

"You're unlovable," she said, and the water closed over my head, and the world I'd known was washed coldly and cleanly away.

⟨○⟩

I am not unlovable. No one is unlovable. Many people say that I'm a good and valuable human being, the sort of person they'd like to have on their team when they need to get something done. I'm not unlovable, I'm *not*.

But Maya was only three years old when Mom died. She was barely more than a toddler, all chubby cheeks and grasping hands, while I was the older sister wrapped in grief, drowning in my own sorrow. The gap between three and seven may not seem like very much when viewed through the jaundiced eye of adulthood. At the time, it was a chasm bigger than the world.

By the time she had been able to find a way to the side where I was standing, the Big Girl side, I was still four years ahead, and more, our father and I had formed an unwanted, inescapable society of two. The Remembering Mom Society. We would have given up our membership cards in a second if it would bring her back to us, but that wasn't going to happen, and more, I had enough resentment for Maya to burn down any bridges she tried to build between us. *She* was the reason Mom hadn't been diagnosed sooner, as pregnancy had masked certain symptoms, making them seem like business as usual. *She* was the reason Mom's time had been divided during the last years of her life, instead of focused entirely on Dad and me.

It hadn't been fair. It could never have been fair. Maya had been a little girl, and it had never been her fault, and I had taken it out on her anyway, and I had told her a hundred times that I was sorry, tried to make it up to her in a thousand little ways, but . . .

But sometimes damage done is damage done, and it can't be repaired. We had been circling each other in a slow détente ever since. I'd assumed that we'd graduate from high school, go to college, and only see each other on family holidays, where we could play nicely for Dad's sake.

I had certainly never thought that she'd *kill* me.

As the waters closed over my head and the weight of the ocean dragged me downward, lungs emptying and bound limbs numb from the cold, it was easy to regret, and to resent, how wrong I'd been.

The water was dark and fathomless around me. I knew the beach was only a few yards away from where I had been deposited; the tide pools came almost up to the breaker wall, missing the parking lot by a stone's throw. Maya wasn't that strong. She would have dragged me to the first tide pool where she was sure I'd be secure, where she was certain that I'd drown.

Drown. God. Was I drowning? Was this what dying felt like? Floating in the endless dark while safety, while *freedom* waited only a few yards away, as unreachable as the moon?

Dying sucked.

Something moved in the water ahead of me, something long and pale as a silver ribbon slicing through the black. I tried to struggle, and once again, I failed. My limbs were as dead as the rest of me was about to become. Drowning suddenly seemed like the better option, when compared to being eaten by a shark.

No. Not a shark. An eel, a silver razor of fins and scales and gaping jaws, which swam closer and closer, finally wrapping itself around my shoulders, its mouth pressed to the tender line of my jaw. I closed my eyes, not wanting to see the moment when the water grew even darker with my blood. At least it would be quick. At least I wouldn't have time to suffer.

*Hello, little mermaid,* whispered a voice in my ear. It was the sound of the undertow rolling through the halls of a sunken ship, the sound of bones rattling in the deep. It was the sound that seashells echoed in their oceanic screams, when held up to the ears of children a hundred miles from the shore. It was the voice of a goddess, of a sea witch, of the cruel and timeless tide.

*You seem to have found yourself in a pickle,* it continued. There was amusement there, yes, and a strange, cold delight, like my predicament was a gift that only came around once in a hundred years. *Would my little mermaid like to live?*

The thought of my own survival seemed ridiculous, unachievable . . . and I had never wanted anything more. I had no breath. I couldn't speak. So I nodded as hard as I could, my chin touching the top of the eel's head, and waited for the moment when it would bite down, or—more likely—when the hallucinations would be too much for my oxygen-starved brain to maintain.

*They always want to live,* purred the voice, as three more eels slithered out of the deep darkness and began to circle me. I couldn't see the source of the voice, the one who was speaking so sweetly, from so far away. I wasn't sure I wanted to. Any voice that could speak to me with such calm unconcern while the water pulled me deeper down probably didn't belong to anything I wanted to look in the eye.

*You will owe me,* it said. *You will be mine forever, but you will live. Do we have an accord?*

I thought of Maya laughing as she drove herself home. Maya slipping into her bed, stretching her legs beneath her sheets, and relaxing into her new, perfect life as the only child she had always wanted to be. She wouldn't be on the outside, not anymore. Dad would grieve, and she would grieve with him, and if her grieving was false, well . . . it wouldn't be like anyone would know.

I nodded harder this time, hard enough that the eel at my throat bit down a little, teeth breaking the skin with a short, sharp pain. Blood billowed up in front of my eyes, somehow still red despite the blackness of the sea.

*Good girl*, whispered the voice, and the eels attacked.

They moved so fast that my eyes couldn't follow them, and my one, disconnected thought was of the squirrels that sometimes came to raid Dad's bird feeders. They always looked fat and furry and slow, but when something surprised them, they could be out of the yard and up a tree in an instant.

The eel at my throat bit down while the other three swirled around me, kicking up a froth born of bubbles and blood. I screamed soundlessly, in shock and pain and terror, and kept screaming as the first eel forced itself into my mouth, squirming wildly. Its sides were slick with mucus, but its fins were sharp as razors, slicing my tongue and the inside of my cheeks. My body still refused to respond to my commands, and so I couldn't even thrash as the eel squirmed down and deeper, leaving my mouth empty and bleeding. I felt its long, alien body moving inside me, coming to rest in one side of my chest, heavy and immutable.

Before I could close my mouth, the next eel was there, forcing itself down, following the first. Then came the third, and finally, the eel at my throat let go and rose to hover, bloody-toothed and terrible, in front of my eyes.

*It is done*, said the voice.

I blacked out before the fourth eel dove into my mouth. Of everything that had happened since I'd woken up in the tide pool, that felt like the first and only mercy.

⟶⟨⟩⟵

I woke when the tide flowed out, leaving me sitting in water to my waist, the remains of the gauze Maya had used to tie my wrists and ankles fluttering around me like a mummy's wrappings. It had been a good choice on her part: since I hadn't been able to struggle, it hadn't left any marks to show that I'd been tied up, and it would have dissolved or been washed away if I had been swept out to sea as she'd been intending.

My body felt like it had been wrapped in a thousand layers of that gauze, rendered heavy and slow and strange by my night in the water. I sat up, working my hands free of their wrappings before raising them to my face, feeling it unsteadily.

There was a cut on my lip. It burned when I touched it, filled with salt, filled with poison.

So: I was in the water, in the tide pools, bound, my body still recovering from the drugs I had never voluntarily taken.

So: there was no possible way I had survived, not with the ocean closing over my head for so many hours. The inside of my mouth burned like my lip, and I knew that if I tried to speak, I would only be able to whisper the language of scar and scab. My tongue was a battlefield, my throat a graveyard, and there were eels curled in the space where my lungs belonged. I was not a dead girl. I was not a drowned girl. But I was of their kin and kind, and whatever had seen me through to morning was unlikely to let me keep their gifts for free.

I leaned forward, picking at the gauze on my ankles until my numb fingers caught its edge and I was able to peel it away layer by layer, involuntary mermaid regaining the use of her legs. Still numb and shaky I stood, bracing my hands on the tide pool wall, not caring when the rocks cut into my skin. I was drenched but I wasn't drowned; my fingers weren't pruney, my skin wasn't loose. Except for the cuts on my lip and the cold that seemed to run all the way to my bones, there was nothing to indicate that I had spent my night submerged. But I knew. Oh, I knew.

Inch by inch, I pulled myself out of the tide pool, water running off my hair, my skin, my ruined nightgown. Inch by inch, I shuffled barefoot toward the parking lot, barely noticing and not caring at all when I stepped on the bits of glass and broken shell that littered the pathway. It was early enough that there were no cars, and so I continued onward, not hurrying. There didn't seem to be anything left in the world that was worth hurrying for.

I made it as far as the freeway, making my slow, waterlogged way along the shoulder, before someone saw me and called the police. Everything started moving very quickly after that, although none of it was my doing. First there were sirens, and then there were ambulances, and men in uniforms, and my father, pushing his way through the crowd, shouting my name over and over again, rushing to take me into his arms and hold me close, my cheek against his shoulder, my eyes searching the faces of the gathered onlookers.

Maya was there. She watched from behind the front rank of the crowd, her eyes burning with hatred and with something stranger, rarer, at least from her. It took me a moment to identify it for what it was: fear. She knew that I could end her with a word, or thought I could. The cuts in my mouth burned and stung, making speech impossible.

Maybe this was the secret at the center of the story, the secret Hans Christian Andersen heard and spun into a fairy tale, sugar and morality and seafoam. There was no mermaid, only a girl afraid of drowning who made a bargain with something deeper and older and wilder than herself. A girl with a ribcage full of eels and a tongue sliced to ribbons, who walked out of the surf and couldn't tell anyone what had happened to her or where she'd gone.

I hoped that girl got to marry her prince and be happy. Watching my sister do her best to blend with the crowd, I didn't think it was very likely.

"Honey, can you look at me?"

I turned obediently toward the sound of my father's voice. He was flanked by police officers, their expressions schooled into calm, non-threatening inquisitiveness. They thought I had been traumatized. They were trying not to frighten me before they knew what had really happened.

They were never going to know what really happened.

My father, familiar face drawn in anxious lines, touched my cheek and asked, "Who did this to you?"

I shook my head.

"Honey, if you don't—"

There was no way around it. I closed my eyes and opened my mouth, refusing to witness the moment when he saw the raw meat of my cheeks and tongue. I heard his sharply indrawn breath. I knew him too well to spare myself completely. Even without seeing the horror I had become reflected back at me, I knew what it would look like, and it burned, like salt on a sliced lip. Oh, how it burned.

"Can we get an EMT over here?" shouted an unfamiliar voice—one of the police officers speaking briskly, quickly, getting me away before I became more of a curiosity than I was already damned to be.

My father kissed me on the forehead before they loaded me into the ambulance. The sound of sirens carried me away from the sea.

◦

Eighty-seven stitches inside my mouth before they let me go; eighty-seven stitches and what felt like almost as many shots, as they fought to lock me up like an abandoned house, slamming all my doors against the possibility of infection. Eighty-seven stitches and whispers behind their hands as they questioned whether I was ever going to speak again, whether my tongue would heal into the shape it had always had or become something new, a lump of dead meat and scar tissue filling my mouth and stopping my voice.

They didn't mean for me to hear, but when you can't speak, it's difficult to stop listening. It was something to distract from the soft sound of slithering within my ribs, as the eels shifted their positions. I didn't know how they were breathing. I didn't know how the hospital, with its gleaming machines and its well-trained doctors, could miss them. I didn't know a lot of things, but I knew something the doctors didn't:

I knew I was never going to speak again, not unless the woman in the water willed it. It was a strange, sad thing to know, but it helped to keep me from flinching away when they looked at the inside of my mouth, when they whispered things they didn't think I'd hear. They were discussing the inevitable. That was easier to live with than a "maybe" would have been. At least I was alive to hear it.

When they let me leave, my father was waiting with warm clothes taken from my room at home, ready to push my insurance-mandated wheelchair to the door and lead me to the car. Maya wasn't with him. That, too, was no real surprise. Maya didn't know how I had survived, or what her carefully hoarded drugs would have allowed me to remember. She would be making plans and setting up contingencies. She would be getting ready for a fight.

The eels in my chest throbbed as I pulled my seatbelt across them. I rubbed my sternum with one hand, trying to quiet them back to sleep, and smiled at my father when he looked at me with concern.

Maya was going to get a fight. It just wasn't the fight that she expected.

We pulled out of the parking lot, my father sneaking anxious glances at me as he drove. Finally, he asked, "You really don't remember anything about what happened?"

I shook my head, putting on my best regretful expression. Let him think I was still lost at sea. Let him think I had no memory of pain. It might be kinder, given what I thought was coming.

When drowned girls come out of the water, they go back. Usually sooner rather than later. It didn't matter that I'd never believed in fairy tales before I found myself bound and drugged and dropped into the lap of one; I had spent enough of my life absorbing them to know that this wasn't the ending. Someone was going to have to pay. Maya was going to have to pay. When she did . . .

The night before, I would have given anything not to die. That's the sort of bargain that shouldn't even be thought aloud. Not unless you want to pay for every breath.

"It's okay, baby." Dad patted my knee, as much to reassure himself as to comfort me. "We'll get through this. Your sister's waiting for us at home."

I nodded, forcing a smile through my stitched and aching lips. We had so much to catch up on, Maya and I. Silent as I was, I thought I still might have a lot to say to her.

Everything I could, before the tide came in.

◄◦►

The house was lit up like Christmas. The day had come and gone while I was at the hospital, and now every window blazed from within, like Maya had decided I was some kind of ghost to be kept at bay with twinkling lights. Dad shook his head as he pulled into the garage, but he didn't say anything. She was supposedly traumatized too, shaken to the core by the news that her beloved big sister had been found wandering and wounded by the highway. Lectures about the electric bill could wait until later.

Then the garage door closed behind us, and we were home. Really home, like I hadn't quite believed I would ever be again. Dad helped me out of the car, into the house, and to the stairs. Maya was nowhere to be seen.

"Do you want dinner?" he asked.

I shook my head, miming folding my hands and tucking them against my pillow. He nodded.

"Sleep makes sense," he said. "Rest well, sweetheart. The police are going to find the person who did this to you. You'll see. Everything's going to be all right."

I forced a smile. He deserved so much more. He deserved decades with his adoring daughters, a family as bright and perfect as the light shining through the windows, as nostalgic as a pink princess fantasy. But he'd lost his wife to illness, and now he was going to lose us both to the sea, and there was nothing I could do to change that. The tide goes out, leaving things like me lying stranded on the beach. It always comes back to collect us.

"I love you," he said, and I mouthed the words back to him, and that was it: that was all there was left for either one of us to say.

I drifted up the stairs as in a dream, feeling the eels in my chest writhe and resettle themselves. They stilled as I walked along the hall to my bedroom and let myself silently inside. The police had been here while I was at the hospital: maybe that explained the long delays while I waited to see another specialist, to receive another round of shots. Out of kindness to the traumatized girl, they had kept me away until my room could be analyzed and recorded, written down on little pieces of paper like they meant anything. They were looking for a culprit, a kidnapper, someone it was safe to accuse of hurting a sweet, innocent girl like me. They weren't looking for someone even sweeter, even more innocent.

They could look forever, and they'd never find Maya. Not unless I accused her, and I wasn't going to do that. This was a fairy tale now. Prison was both more and less than she deserved.

I walked to the bed, the perfect, pink bed, and sat on the edge, looking at the gauzy curtains around it and thinking about my mother, who had been the best of us. Out of everyone in this house, she had been the best of us. I didn't think she would be proud of me now, or of what I felt I had to do . . . but maybe I was wrong. If anyone could have understood what it was to rail against death as their air ran out, it would have been her. We're all mermaids in the end. We all die when we stop breathing.

The eels stirred under my breastbone. I put a hand to my chest, quieting them, calming them. *Soon*, I thought, and that seemed to soothe them a bit. The night was young. All we had to do was wait. So we waited, and I looked at the bedroom that had been mine for as long as I remembered, and I hated my sister for taking it away from me. This was my last night here. No matter how this ended, this was my last night here.

Seconds became minutes; minutes became hours. I heard my father's heavy footsteps in the hall, weary with the weight of everything he'd been through. *Funny*, I thought, *I'm the one who drowned*, and was immediately sorry. Just because he hadn't gone into the water with me didn't mean I wouldn't be taking him with me when I went back to the sea.

All around me, the house settled into sleep as I waited, the eels in my chest slithering in silent anticipation. Finally, just as the tide outside the house was beginning to roll in, my door opened, and Maya slipped into the room. The look she gave me was fear mingled with undisguised hatred.

"How?" she asked.

My tongue was shredded meat and useless tissue, but I had other tongues now, other voices. I opened my mouth as the eels hissed, in ragged harmony, "I found another way."

Maya took a step toward me. *Run, fool*, I thought, and closed my mouth before the eels could echo it. She had given up her right to a warning when she had drugged me and dragged me from my bed.

"This is impossible," she said. "You can't be here. You're not *real*." She stomped her foot. In that moment, that movement, I saw the petulant toddler she had been, the little girl who had wanted nothing more than her mother's arms around her.

"I'll show you," the eels said, with my mouth, and I spread my lips wide, and they boiled forth, all teeth and slick, cartilaginous bodies and slicing fins, and when they struck Maya in the throat, she had no time to scream. One of them bit her nose away. Another pulled off that pretty, pouting mouth, while the last two ripped her throat open like a flower. My pink princess fantasy became red in an instant, painted by the blood jetting from my sister's flesh.

The air turned to ashes in my mouth. I couldn't breathe, I couldn't *breathe*. I dropped to my knees amidst the blood that should have been inside my sister, clutching at my throat and gasping. Something touched my hand. I turned, vision going gray, and beheld one of the eels, wrapping itself loosely around my wrist.

"Please," I wheezed, the word shaped more of silence than of sound.

The eel seemed to nod. This time, when it dove for my mouth, I opened my lips to welcome it inside. This time, there was no pain. There was only the feeling of inevitability; of coming home.

The other three eels were still tearing at Maya's body. She wasn't dead yet; one eye was open, watching me with horror and, oddly, hope. She was hoping I was going to kill her, I realized. She was hoping I would let her go.

"Let's go for a drive, okay?" I said, and smiled.

If she had still possessed a mouth, I think she would have screamed.

◀◦▶

There was no one at the beach when I parked the car and made my way down to the tide pools, eels curled in my lungs and the still-twitching body of my sister cradled in my arms. She should have been dead by now. One more gift, I supposed, from a sea that had proven to be surprisingly full of them.

Gingerly, I walked to the tide pool where she had left me to die and lowered her into the water. She made a soft gurgling sound.

"Don't worry," I said. "It'll all be over soon."

Maya looked at me imploringly. It was good that the eels had left her eyes. She should be able to see the waves rolling in before they carried her away.

*Little mermaid*, whispered a voice. *Little mermaid, come home.*

I turned to look at the rippling black sheet of the sea. It was a far cry from my pink princess fantasy. But it sounded, all the same, like home; like a mother's voice, not prisoned in a hazel tree, but set free to ripple, shore to shore, forever.

The eels in my lungs breathed in salt and surrender as I walked, arms spread, into the waves. Behind me, Maya struggled to scream, and everything was right, everything was true, everything was ever after, and I was going home.

# THE DEEP SEA SWELL

## JOHN LANGAN

"It may be that the gulfs will wash us down"
—Alfred Lord Tennyson, *Ulysses*

If she hadn't argued with the man, Susan thinks, they could have been in a first-class cabin, instead of down here, at the bottom of the bloody ferry. The floor tilts forward. There's a great swooshing sound, the sensation of plunging down a steep slope, the briefest of pauses, and a tremendous BANG rattles the ship's hull. Slowly, the floor levels, then tilts backward. The swooshing returns, accompanied now by the feeling of being on a roller coaster as it climbs a sheer set of tracks. Somewhere near, somewhere inside the ferry, Susan hears the steady drone of a motor. The sweet stink of fuel (diesel?) swirls near the floor, below her bunk. On the bunk above, her husband snores intermittently. The Dramamine they took an hour ago knocked Alan out, the lucky bastard—whereas all it did for Susan was sand the edges off the dizziness and nausea, freeing her mind to run through every disaster-at-sea movie she's seen, from *Titanic* to *The Poseidon Adventure* to a cheesy horror film, what was it called, *Leviathan*? Something like that.

The sail up from Aberdeen wasn't this bad, not nearly. She'd never been on an ocean-going ferry before. The nearest thing had been the ship they'd taken out to Martha's Vineyard on their honeymoon, which was maybe half the size of this one? Less? The Shetland ferry was built to cross the roughly two hundred nautical miles between the northeast of Scotland and the Shetlands, which, as Alan delighted in saying, lay closer to Norway than they did to the UK. There was something romantic about traveling by ship, she'd thought, a notion of taking your time, enjoying the journey as well as the destination. They spent much of their time in bed, trying to work out the mechanics of sex on a surface rising and falling with the sea. She was Sexy Susan, the sailor's friend; he was Able Alan, always up for adventure.

That was in the first-class cabin to which they'd been upgraded after she passed one of the ship's crew a twenty-pound note. She'd been quite pleased with the luxury—which consisted primarily of a room done in seventies-era paneling and set high enough in the ship to have its own window—but less so once they'd been in Lerwick for a day and Alan's university friend, Giorgio, informed her that, as long as there were cabins available, the ferry staff were supposed to upgrade passengers free of charge. "They pocket the money, you know," Giorgio said, letting the air out of her self-satisfaction, and leaving her determined not to be taken advantage of again. In turn, this led to her challenging the crew member who requested twenty quid for a boost to first-class lodgings on the return voyage. (Possibly, it was the same man: several of the staff appeared related, cousins or even brothers, short, broad fellows wearing gray sweater vests under their blue blazers and over their shirt-and-ties, their faces red, their curly hair black yielding to gray.) "You know," Susan said, "one of my friends in Lerwick told me an upgrade to first class is supposed to be no charge."

"Did they?" the man said, raising his bushy eyebrows as if to indicate his surprise at such a statement.

"Yeah," she said, nodding.

"Well . . ." The man smiled, shrugging and spreading his hands.

"My friend said you guys keep the money."

Whatever warmth was in the man's performance chilled. "It's twenty pounds," he said.

Which was how they descended she isn't certain how many flights of stairs to the corridor that brought them here, to a narrow room with bare white walls and a pair of economy-sized bunkbeds in it. "Think of it this way," Alan said, "we're experiencing the full range of travel options."

Those options included a mid-winter storm, whose center lay somewhere to the east, but which had stirred the North Sea to a tumult. They climbed to the dining area, but already, Alan was queasy and opted for a cup of tea and a packet of digestive biscuits, leaving Susan to order a Coke and the fish and chips, which she ate half of before a sudden squall of nausea caused her to set down her knife and fork and not pick them up again. The two of them tried sitting in the large padded chairs positioned in front of the wall of windows looking out over the ferry's stern, but night had fallen hours ago, with the heavy blackness of early January at a northern latitude. All that was visible was an expanse of blackness with a cluster of orange lights twinkling in the far distance, which Alan thought was an oil rig. Although the sea was more sound than sight, the rise and fall of those lights added a visual dimension to the ferry's see-sawing movement. "Next time Giorgio wants to see us," Alan said, "we'll fly." It was an extravagant promise: the tickets from Edinburgh weren't too far shy of what it had cost them to cross the Atlantic from Newark.

"Or he can take the ferry," Susan said.

Not long after, they descended the stairs to their cabin a second time. Gazing out the windows wasn't doing anything for him, Alan said, and Susan agreed. The more she stared at it, the more uneasy the dark outside—its sheer thoroughness—made her, until she could feel panic nipping at the edges of her mind. "It's as if we're already at the bottom of the sea," she said.

"Whoa," Alan said, "touch wood," knocking the chair's armrest. "Although," he added, "it's pretty deep, here. I imagine it's calm, down there."

"You just have to go through the whole drowning thing," Susan said.

"Will you *stop*?" Alan said, rapping the armrest again.

"You and your superstitions."

"The middle of the ocean is not the place to test them."

She supposed he had a point.

In the cabin, they dry-swallowed the Dramamine tablets Susan had in her bag, changed into their pajamas, and climbed into their bunks. Alan sang, "Yo-ho, blow the man down / Yo-ho, blow the man down."

"Now who's tempting fate?" she said.

"It's only a song," he said, his words slurring as the pill tugged him into unconsciousness.

"Remember that when we're saying hi to King Neptune."

"Hey," he began. The rest of his reply disappeared into a mumble.

Despite herself, Susan knocked on the cabin wall. It wasn't wood, but it was the best she had.

The next hour passed with stomach-churning monotony. The ferry rose and fell, rose and fell. Alan snored, snorted, went back to snoring. The distant engine churned steadily. In the corridor outside the cabin, a little girl's voice asked a question Susan couldn't decipher. The ocean rushed along the hull. A woman, likely the girl's mother, said they were just going for a wee lie down. The smell of fuel made Susan's nostrils bristle. Someone laughed as they passed the cabin. The ship slid down into a pause that lasted a second too long, as if the waves were weighing whether to let the vessel continue its descent, all the way down. A woman, the same one from before, said she was just going to the toilet. The sea smacked the ship like a giant's hand, BANG.

In an odd sort of way, Susan has thought, the trip has been all about the ocean, salt water threading its way through her and Alan's winter vacation like a recurring theme in a longer piece of music. The flight across the north Atlantic was only the second time she had traversed the ocean, and she spent the daylit hours of the voyage gazing out the scuffed and scratched window beside her seat at the corrugated gray expanse visible through the gaps in the clouds below. Alan's parents' house in North Queensferry was one of a half-dozen on a cul-de-sac set on a high bluff overlooking the stretch where the Forth River merged with the North Sea. The sea was a constant companion as they drove their tiny rental up Scotland's east coast, stopping for an early lunch at an Indian place outside St. Andrew's, a wander around the ruins at Stonehaven, and then a couple of days in Aberdeen, revisiting Alan's university haunts and a few of his friends who had settled in the city. With one of those friends and his partner, they walked a rocky beach washed by the waves they would ride to Shetland, where Alan's friend Giorgio ran a small chip shop overlooking Lerwick harbor. ("Giorgio?" Susan said. "What kind of Scottish name is that?" "His dad's from Florence," Alan said.)

Once they were ashore on Shetland, however, something about the sea changed—or, to be more accurate, something about her perception of it shifted. The afternoon of their arrival, Giorgio took them for a quick jaunt to a spot where the land on either side of them shrank toward the road, until they were between a pair of narrow beaches onto which water splashed in long foaming rolls. "On that side," Giorgio said, pointing right, "is the North Sea. On this side," pointing left, "is the Atlantic." No matter where they went, it seemed, salt water was visible. When she mentioned this to Giorgio, trying to keep her tone light, care free, he nodded and said, "Aye, someone told me once you're never more than three miles from open water on Shetland." No doubt the landscape of the island, low hills bare of trees, contributed to the sensation, but she began to feel horribly exposed, surrounded by the ocean, which, if you thought about it, could rise and wash over the place without much effort at all.

Nor did the stories Giorgio liked to tell help matters. An amateur historian of the Shetlands and their surrounds, he possessed a seemingly endless supply of narratives about the islands. In the majority of them, the sea figured prominently. They would begin with a bold, almost ridiculous assertion. "You know," he would say over drinks at one of the pubs, "Shetland was part of the actual Atlantis." Then, as she and Alan coughed their beers, he would raise his hands and say, "No, I'm not talking about that Disney rubbish. I mean Doggerland. You've heard of it, yeah? No? Ten, eleven thousand years ago, during the last ice age, all the seas were lower. The water was bound up in the glaciers, right? From Shetland down to Orkney and Scotland, over to Europe, was dry land. You could walk across the North Sea, the English Channel, and folk did. There was a whole civilization spread across the place. As the ice started to melt, though, the sea crept closer. Some of the archeologists think it was a process of years, decades, and the people living there had plenty of time to pack their things and leave. I've heard others say it was more catastrophic, an ice dam broke and sent hundreds of millions of gallons of water rushing through all this low-lying land. That's where your story of Atlantis comes from."

Another afternoon, as they were sitting in Giorgio's car on a local (smaller) ferry from the main island to the neighboring island of Yell, Giorgio said, "When you were coming up, did you notice there was a point the sea went all choppy—I mean, worse than what you'd been used to?" Susan and Alan exchanged glances. Had they? "Maybe," Alan said. "Aye, that was you passing Fair Isle," Giorgio said. "The sea behaves funny there, has to do with currents or some such. You know there was a fellow drowned out there? It was during my granddad's time, a man from down in Edinburgh, a professor—from Edinburgh University, must have been.

He was an anthropologist, studied the prehistoric sites in the north of Scotland, the Orkneys, up in Shetland. The chap took an interest in Fair Isle—in the ocean floor off the island. Something had washed up on one of the island's beaches, and it found its way into the professor's hands. I'm not sure what it was, but it got the man all worked up. He decided he needed to have a look under the water next to the island. This was none of your scuba diving; this was one of those suits with the big round helmet and the hose up to a boat on the surface. Fellow hired a couple of locals out of Aberdeen to man the boat and mind the air pump, and another pair of lads from Fair Isle to help them. The lot of them took the boat to the spot the professor had calculated was the best bet to search for more of whatever it was brought him there in the first place. Over the side he went. The rig was what you'd call low-tech, no diver's telephone. Well. Maybe an hour into the professor's dive, a storm blew in. The sky went dark, the wind rose, and the next anyone knew, the rain was bucketing down, the waves spilling over the sides. It's no fun to be in a big ship when the weather turns against you, and this boat was far from big. At first, the lads thought they could ride out the storm. I gather they gave it their best, but it wasn't long before they realized theirs was not a workable plan. The sea was heaving, and none of them had the experience to maintain the ship's position in these conditions. They tried to contact the professor—there was no telephone, right, but they had this system of bells he'd set up for basic communication. One bell on the boat, and a tiny one in the helmet. I'm not sure exactly how it worked. Morse Code, I'm guessing—had to be. Anyway, as things went from bad to worse topside, the crew were signaling the professor, SOS, COME BACK. If he heard them, he didn't answer. Now the boat was riding waves halfway to vertical. Water was foaming onto the deck from every side. It was all the lads could do to keep from being swept overboard. And still no response from the professor. Funny, the things you'll do in a crisis. One of the crew grabbed a hatchet and, *chop*, cut the diving suit's air hose. It was the end for the professor. You have to hope he found whatever he was looking for." Susan said, "That's terrible. What happened to the crew?" "Oh," Giorgio said, "they made it back safely. Went straight to the police and confessed everything. Only problem was, each man said he was the one had picked up the hatchet, and nothing anyone could threaten or promise would persuade any of them to change his story. In the end, none of them was charged, and the professor's death was ruled an accident. The body was never recovered."

Still a third time, as they were treating Giorgio to dinner at a nice restaurant in a small hotel located on the shore of a slender inlet, he set down his salad fork and said, "There's a ghost in this hotel, you know, right in this very room. A woman dressed in a long dark green dress and a short jacket, with a little hat. Like the style women wore at the beginning of the last century. She sits at one of the tables over there." He pointed to an alcove at the other end of the dining area. "It's always after the last customer has left, and one of the staff is cleaning up. I used to date a lassie had seen her on two separate occasions. The first time, she ran out of the room as if the Devil himself was clutching at her heels with his pointy nails. The second time, Colleen (that was the lassie's name) stayed put. She said the woman stood, turned around, and walked to the door. Her face was in shadow, that was the way Colleen described it. She couldn't manage a good look at her. She said the woman passed through the door, the way you hear ghosts doing. Colleen ran to the door and opened it. Although it was late, this was during the summer, so there was plenty of light for her to watch the woman cross the lawn to the water and keep going, out into it until she was gone, submerged, hat and all. No one knows who she is, or was. Another drowning victim, right? Sometimes I wonder, though: what if we have it backwards? What I'm trying to say is, instead of someone who used to live on land returning to it, maybe it's someone, or something, whose home is the water coming up to have a look and see what all the fuss is about." "Really?" Susan said. "No," Giorgio said, "I'm just speaking out my arse. Still, the ocean is deep and dark and full of secrets, right? Isn't there a saying to the effect that we know more about outer space than we do the bottom of the sea?" "I don't know," Alan said, "sounds good, though." "Aye, so it does," Giorgio said.

Between Giorgio's stories, and the omnipresent water rolling to the horizon, Susan found herself revising her opinions of life beside the ocean. Since she and Alan had met at a mutual friend's house in Bourne, on the mainland side of the Cape Cod Canal, Susan had declared it her fondest wish to return to the area to buy a house overlooking the ocean. It was a favorite fantasy, one she indulged by scrolling through online real-estate listings. If such houses were currently out of their price range (by a factor of several hundred percent), it was of no real concern. Alan was doing well enough at his architecture firm to make the daily commute to Manhattan worthwhile, and the director of Penrose College's art museum was sufficiently pleased with her performance to hire Susan full-time. They saved what they could, and eventually, they would be in a position to afford a place in Bourne, or further out on the actual Cape, in Orleans or even Wellfleet. In the meantime, they had their friend's house to return to. Her dream was in part a declaration of loyalty to the place where she and Alan had so improbably found one another. But she also fancied the Cape an appropriate symbol for the relationship they had discovered, a place of fundamentals, land and sea and sky. Not once had it occurred to her that part of the reason she could appreciate the Bay at Scusset Beach was because the entire continent was behind her, thousands of miles of mountains and hills, cities and plains. Even way out on the end of the Cape, in Provincetown, there was the sense of being connected to something larger, a solid mass of land. Five days on Shetland, and she had learned that being on the margin between sand and water was a different thing from being surrounded by the ocean. Giorgio diagnosed what she described to him as island fever. "It's not for everyone, living up here," he said. "The sea . . ." He shrugged, as if the word was explanation enough.

BANG. As if making Giorgio's point, the water smacks the hull directly outside her bunk, from the sound of it. The metal groans, a loud complaint, which lasts an ominous length of time. Susan stares at the wall next to her. The dread she's been managing since they sailed into the storm surges within her. Her heart breaks into a full gallop. Should she wake Alan, grab their bags, head for the upper decks, closer to the lifeboats? She doesn't know. She can't draw enough air into her lungs. The edges of her vision darken. She's burning up. The panic attack isn't the first she's had, but it's without doubt the worst. She can't keep lying down; she's suffocating. She throws off her blanket, sits up as the ferry begins another slide down down down . . . She grips the edge of her bunk, braces her feet against the floor. BANG. The ship protests, asking how much more of this abuse it's expected to take. Susan has to get out of here. She grabs Alan's bunk, uses it to haul herself to standing. On the other side of the hull, water swooshes as the floor tilts back. She crosses to the door in four lurching steps, opens it, and exits the cabin.

The corridor outside the room is empty, the rest of the cabin doors shut. No sign of the little girl and her mother, the laughing passer-by. Susan isn't so distracted she can't think, *Well, good for them.* One hand on the wall, she turns left, toward the stairs. The ferry levels, tips, lunges. The wool socks she's wearing slide on the floor. She flattens on the wall. BANG. The impact shudders through her. While the ship tilts to climb the next swell, she scuttles along the wall as fast as her feet and hands will move her, which isn't as fast as she'd like, but it occupies her while the ferry slides up and then down. BANG. By the time the ship has summited the following waves, Susan has reached the doorway to the stairs. *Alan*, a distant part of her mind objects, *what about Alan?* She plunges into the stairwell.

It's like trying to play some demented fun-house game, climbing the stairs as they rock this way, then that. Although each stair is covered in studs to aid traction, they benefit her socks little, and she clings to the guard rail with both hands. The acoustics of the space make it sound as if the water streaming past the ship is filling the stairwell, while each BANG shivers all the stairs at once. She manages four flights, two decks, before she has to abandon the stairwell.

As she emerges into a corridor more or less the same as the one she left, the lights dim, then brighten, then go out. "Oh, come on," she says. With a click, emergency lights pop on at either end of the corridor. "Thank you." She backs against the wall to her left and slides down it until she's sitting. Her heart is still racing, but the short excursion she's taken has left her exhausted. Maybe it's the Dramamine having more effect, too. If it weren't for her pulse jackhammering, she'd swear she would pass out right here. She places her hands on the floor to either side of her to help with the ferry's relentless rocking, which feels as if it's grown worse. *We must be close to Fair Isle*, she thinks. *Isn't that the place Giorgio said the sea was especially rough?*

Another BANG and a horrible smell floods her nostrils. She claps her hand over her mouth. For an instant, she wonders if a sewage pipe has broken under the waves' pounding, only to reject the idea. What assaults her nostrils is not the pungent stink of shit. It's the reek of a beach—of a North Atlantic beach at low tide, a medley of decaying flesh and baking plant matter. Tears blur her eyes. At the same time, the temperature in the corridor drops, heat escaping as if out of a hole in the ferry's side. The cold that swirls into its place is thick, gelid. There's something else, a note in the atmosphere that reminds her of nothing so much as the worst arguments she and Alan have had, when hostility foams and froths between them. Malice washes over her. She swallows, shakes her head.

To her left, movement on the floor draws her eye. An eel, long and skinny, slithers away from her. She starts. It isn't an eel: it's a length of hose, dun-colored, the end closest to her ragged, vomiting water as it moves. That's the source of the awful smell, the cracked and peeling hose being dragged towards and through the doorway at the far end of the corridor, making a sound halfway between a hiss and a breath. She can't see what's on the other side of the threshold; the emergency lights cast a veil of brightness her vision cannot pierce.

Even were she not schooled in hundreds of horror films, Susan would know that following the foul-smelling hose to whatever is dragging it would be a bad idea. In fact, she has no intention of hanging around here one second longer than is necessary. She pushes to her feet, and staggers up the corridor to the exit to the stairs.

Up or down? She opts to climb. It's slow going. The stairs are like an enormous metronome. She loses her footing twice, has to clutch the railing to keep from tumbling down. Her heart is still pounding, her skin burning, but she isn't sure if it's from the panic attack continuing or her brush with what was standing beyond the lights at the other end of the corridor. *Or both*, she thinks, one of her favorite rhetorical sayings returning to haunt her: *Why does it have to be either/or? Why can't it be both/and?* When the water smacks the hull, the BANG echoes through the stairwell like thunder. The best Susan can do is two flights of stairs, and then she stumbles out the doorway to the next deck. The motion of the ship combines with her slick footing to send her into the wall opposite; she catches most of the impact with her arms, but the force drops her to one knee.

At least the lights are working properly on this level. The revelation, how-ever, is accompanied by another: the terrible smell permeates the air here, too, and with it are the same cold and the same impression of overwhelming malevolence. A noise equal parts a breath and a hiss jerks her head up, to watch a peeling and cracked hose snaking along the floor. *How . . . ?* The thing drawing the hose toward it halts the thought. Susan has the impression of a figure the approximate size and shape of a man, its hide studded with barnacles, strung with seaweed, a single round eye staring out of its mis-shapen head. Hatred rolls off it in waves. Before her mind can process what she's looking at, she's back in the stairwell, her legs propelled not so much by fear as by some deeper impulse, something preceding and pre-empting rational thought. (*How . . . ?*) The same response sends her down the stairs, flight after flight, until she's back where she started, at the deck where Alan lies slumbering on his bunk in their cabin. *Alan*: for the first time in what feels an eternity, she thinks of her husband as more than a name. What if he woke to find her missing? What if he went in search of her, and encountered whatever is stalking the hallways? Fear for him runs down her spine like ice water. She staggers across the tilting floor into the corridor.

The monster is waiting for her. It swipes at her with oversized hands, and would probably have her if her feet didn't slip and dump her on her ass. The pain registers dimly; she's already scooting backward, her attempted escape hindered by the floor tilting her toward the monster. It leans to grab her legs, spilling a rain of tiny green crabs onto them. Susan jerks her legs toward her, avoiding the thing's grasp, and slaps at the crabs scrambling over her pajamas. She twists onto her stomach, crawls for the stairwell. The ferry levels, and she pushes to her feet. Stiff-legged as Frankenstein's monster, the thing lurches after her. The floor slopes forward. Struggling not to lose control of her balance, she slides on the soles of her socks, as if ice-skating. The monster's feet clatter behind her. She's almost at the stairwell. The sea pounds the ferry, BANG. The monster reaches, catches her left arm, and swings her in a long arc all the way around it into the wall. She tries to get her right arm up to protect her head, but she still sees a brilliant flash of white, feels the impact rattle her teeth. The monster releases her arm, steps in close, catches her by the shoulders. She's spun to face it, pressed against the wall by heavy hands.

This close, the stench brings her to the verge of fainting. Arctic cold envelops her, extinguishing the heat the panic attack kindled in her skin. She twists from side to side, trying to loosen the thing's hold on her, but its grip is unbreakable. Its eye flashes. Malice batters her, its ferocity utter, unrelenting. She turns her head from the thing, closes her eyes—

—*and she is somewhere else, a place mostly dark, here and there dim, an expanse of bare mud ornamented with rocks. Slender, shadowy forms, each the size of a large dog, float languidly in the air, and she sees that they're fish, which means she's underwater, from the look of things, somewhere deep. In front of her and to the right, maybe twenty yards away, a light spreads a yellow cone through the murk. It's a large flashlight, carried in one hand by a figure wearing a diving suit, rounded helmet and all. Its air hose rising behind it, its heavy boots raising clouds of mud, it trudges toward a low heap of rocks. Long, rectangular, the rocks have a consistency of size and shape, which gives them the appearance of having been carved into their present forms. When the flashlight's beam illuminates designs grooved into their surfaces, Susan understands that she's looking at an archeological site, that she's watching the protagonist of Giorgio's Fair Isle diver story as he sees the object of his expedition. (Which means . . .) His flashlight ranges over the stones, picking out symbols she doesn't recognize, concentric circles, a triangle with rounded corners, a crescent like a smile. Other characters are obscured by mud and algae. The arrangement of the stones suggests they've fallen over onto one another. Before one of them, the diver stops, directs the flashlight to a spot immediately in front of him. Something flashes in the mud. Slowly, ponderously, the diver kneels, reaching down with his free hand. He brushes away a layer of mud, and as he does, sends a small white object tumbling up from its resting place. It's a wonder that he's able to catch it, but catch it he does, and holds it up for view. Susan is too far away to see his discovery in much detail. It's circular, the diameter of a saucer, composed of a white material that shines in the flashlight beam. The diver turns it over, examines the other side, then slides it into a bag hung down his chest. He rises and continues toward the piled stones. As he draws closer to them, his flashlight seeks out the gaps between the rectangles. What it reveals quickens his pace. At the pile, he bends forward, bringing his helmet as close as he can manage to one of the larger spaces between them, holding the flashlight beside his helmet. He slides his other hand into the gap. Whatever he's after resists his efforts. He withdraws the flashlight and turns to the side, to extend his reach. He doesn't see the slender white hand shoot out from the space and grab his arm. By the time he's aware of the contact, the hand has pressed his arm further down into the gap, where the space narrows, wedging it there. The diver pulls back, but his arm is stuck fast. The hand retreats amidst the stones. The diver releases his flashlight, which is looped to his wrist, and attempts to use his free hand to pull the other free. It's no use. He pulls; he pushes. He shakes his trapped hand with such fury, Susan can imagine his screams ringing in his helmet. He stops, lets go of his hand and turns as best he can to look behind him. Undulating like a sea serpent, the air hose to his suit descends the water, bubbles venting from its torn end as it falls. Frantically, the diver flails at the back of his suit, where the hose attaches, but he can't maneuver his arm to it. Even if he could grab hold of the hose, it's hard to see what good it would do him. The same thought appears to occur to the diver, who surrenders his attempt. As the hose snakes across the mud, he turns again to the stone heap, sagging against it, his helmet coming to rest above the space that has trapped him. If he isn't dead already, he will be soon. The white hand steals from between the stones and trails its fingers across his faceplate, almost lovingly—*

Susan recoils from the sight, and confronts the monster holding her, which, she sees, is no monster, but the diving suit in which Giorgio's professor met his watery end. The barnacles, the seaweed, the tiny green crabs scuttling across it, are the yield of decades beneath the water, as are the dents that have misshapen the helmet, the cracks spider-webbing the faceplate's glass. It has looped the hose around itself like a bandolier. She can't say if there's anything left of the suit's former inhabitant, though she doubts it. What has remained is his anger, his rage at having made the find of his career, of his life, and then been abandoned to death. Contained in the suit, his fury, burning with the blinding flame of an underwater welder's torch, has sustained it, has maintained its integrity long after time, salt water, and the ministrations of a thousand ocean creatures should have dissolved the garment.

It is terrifying; she has to escape it. She drives the heel of her right palm into the faceplate, hears a chorus of snaps. The helmet draws back, as if surprised. She strikes again, missing the faceplate, hitting the metal beside it with a hollow bong. A surge of hatred blasts her. When she tries a third blow, the thing releases her left shoulder to swat her hand away. It catches her by the throat and squeezes. Never mind that she was years from birth when the professor drowned, that she hasn't the slightest connection to this tragedy. She is here now, the accident of her presence as good a reason for the thing's hostility as any. Fingers thick and cold dig into her neck. She grabs its hand, searching to pry open its grip. It is inhumanly strong. She cannot breathe. Her vision contracts. Somewhere distant, the sea strikes the ferry's hull, BANG. She lets go of the hand, opts for another round of blows, punching the suit's shoulders, chest, striking the hose wound around it, searching for a last-second vulnerability. Her knuckles tear on barnacles, slip on seaweed, rebound from the hose wrapping it. *Oh, Alan*, she thinks. Her arms feel incredibly heavy. She can't have much time left. *Goddamn it*, she thinks, *Goddamn it*, the curse summoning a last surge of strength. Muscles screaming for oxygen, she punches as hard and fast as she can, *one two three four.*

With a crack, her right fist connects with an object that breaks under its impact. There's a burst of something between them, a soundless explosion.

The hands at her neck and shoulder fall away. Gasping for air, Susan collapses into the wall, her fists still out in a trembling attempt at a guard. The diver steps away from her, its hands pushing aside the hose, searching through the seaweed decorating its chest, to a woven bag hung from its neck. Within the bag, the shards of a white disk slide against one another. The damage to the bag's contents confirmed, the diver's hands drop to its sides. The cold is bleeding from the air, taking with it the awful smell. The figure retreats another pace. Its malevolence gutters and puffs out. Susan has the impression of something *behind* the suit, retreating at great speed through the wall, out of the ship, an impossible distance. On slightly unsteady legs, it lumbers to the exit and proceeds into the stairwell. Its heavy boots clank on the metal stairs.

She feels no desire to follow. With a kind of visionary certainty, she knows that the diver is going to continue its climb until it reaches a level that admits to the ferry's exterior. If enough of its animating force remains, it will walk to a bulwark, lean forward, and allow the weight of its helmet to carry it over into the heaving waves. If not, one or the other of the crew members will come across an astonishing discovery, the remains of an old diving suit, apparently washed onto the ferry by the storm. Perhaps they'll examine the contents of the bag around its neck, perhaps the professor will receive his recognition yet. Or perhaps not.

For the moment, all Susan wants to do is to return to the cabin where she hopes she will find her husband fast asleep. There's still a long way to go and the storm has not abated. In the morning, Alan will ask her why she's wearing gloves and a scarf. She'll say that she'll tell him once they're back at his parents', safely removed from the sea, and all its marvels and horrors.

*For Fiona*

# HE SINGS OF SALT
# AND WORMWOOD

## BRIAN HODGE

t was everything about the sea that had always unnerved him, waiting at the bottom in one cold, disintegrating hulk.

Not two minutes earlier, Danny was in another world, the world above the waves, the world of air and land and the hot, dry feel of the summer sun. His wetsuit snug as a second skin, he sat on the cuddy boat's transom long enough to Velcro a lanyard around his ankle, binding him to a safety line with ninety feet of slack. He cinched tight his goggles, round and insectoid, then slipped over the stern. Bobbing in sync with the hull, he sucked wind and huffed it out, cycling a few times before filling from the bottom up: belly, lower chest, upper chest, like trying to cram a stuffed suitcase with more, and a little more on top of that.

In the boat, against the lone cloud in the sky, Kimo held a stopwatch with his thumb on the trigger. "Ready."

Danny squeezed in one last sip of air and plunged headfirst, like a seal, full-body undulations propelling him down, with the safety line trailing after. The swim fins helped. He'd not been blessed with big feet. They never made fun in Hawaii, but guys always made fun here on the mainland. *Hey Danny, with those dainty little Asian paws of yours, how do you manage to even stay up on a surfboard?* Maybe they didn't mean anything by it. Or maybe they did, trying to get inside his head, psyche him out. *Small feet, small . . . yeah.* He converted it to fuel, that much more drive to bring home a trophy, another sponsorship.

But all that was a world away. He was in the blue world now, a gradient of cerulean to indigo yawning beneath him, where the farther down you went, the more the topside laws unraveled.

Until he'd first experienced the shift for himself back in the spring, he had always believed the same as everyone else he brought it up with: that freediving was a nonstop struggle against your own buoyancy, fighting the lift of the air heaved into your lungs.

Another misconception dies hard. It was like that for only the first forty or so feet down.

Make it that far, to what they called the Doorway to the Deep, and there came a transition he had yet to stop regarding with wonder. Buoyancy was neutralized, the weight of the water bearing down nullifying your tendency to rise to the surface. No more struggle, the fight was won. The sea had you then, a downward pull he could feel tugging on his skull and shoulders.

He held his arms along his sides, aquadynamic, and continued to descend, effortlessly now, like a skydiver bulleting in freefall. The trickiest part had been learning how to equalize the pressure on his ears, in his sinuses, and turn back the pain.

The deeper he sank, the more the pressure became like the slow tightening of a fist that would never relax. It had taken some reframing of the changes it made, seeing them as comforting rather than distressing. *This is what happens down here. This is normal, another version of normal.* No big deal, just the mammalian dive reflex: shifts of physiology so distinct, so foreign out of the water, so automatic in it, they could recalibrate a lifetime of thinking after a dive or two. *Maybe we really do belong here.*

Despite the exertion, his heart rate slowed. Even before the threshold forty feet down, his lungs were already compressed to half their normal size. At sixty, they were reduced to a third. If he were acclimated enough to go that far, at three hundred feet his lungs would be no bigger than baseballs.

Here, though, a couple miles out to sea, over a shelf of land jutting from the central Oregon coast, the bottom cut him off at a depth of seventy-six. Almost there, he tucked into a ball and flipped head over tail, to finish dropping flippers first. He touched down with a gentle bounce that stirred the silt, amid a sparse garden of kelp and seaweed that swayed in the current, and all was so very quiet, like awakening to a dream world of slow time and profound tranquility. The need to breathe remained on some far horizon. The pressure was a cocoon, a presence as welcoming as a hug.

All this time he'd been lying to himself. Thinking he knew something about the ocean, and why—because he'd grown up on an island? Because he'd first stepped onto a surfboard when he was seven and had hardly stepped off since? That was how you fooled yourself into believing you truly understood the sea when all you'd ever done on a board was scratch the water's surface.

Above, the day was clear, bright and sunny. Down here, the sun still found him but was filtered to a murky twilight, as if the fog of morning and blue of evening had joined, to wrap around and welcome him home.

It took slow moments to take shape: a mass off to his left, a ragged, edgeless hill rising from the sea floor. Danny moved toward it in fin-encumbered hops, a feeling maybe like walking on the moon. He hadn't gotten close enough to satisfy his curiosity before his tether to the surface ran out of slack.

The dumbest thing in the world would be to strip the lanyard from his ankle. He did it anyway, fearing if he didn't get close enough for a look now, he might never find this spot again. He left the safety line behind, and was truly diving free.

The mass was no longer edgeless, and no hill. A hill wouldn't have two masts, jutting down from one side to dig into the sea floor. A hill wouldn't have rectangular openings, nor broken windows, metal railings, cleats still wrapped with decaying rope. It was somebody's lost sailing yacht, a fifty-footer at minimum, resting on its starboard side. The build was old school, lots of wood where most buyers would've been content with aluminum and fiberglass. Now it was an ecosystem, submerged long enough to have sagged into itself and crusted over with rot and life.

The cold found him through his wetsuit and went for his marrow. Shipwrecks had always bothered him, even from the safety of pictures. Planes lost at sea, too, and sunken cars, and houses and timber groves in valleys flooded to make new lakes.

It was more than the tragedies and calamities they told of. It was their status, things perfectly normal in the topside world, aliens now, lost and alone where they were never meant to be. They were a rebuttal: *You're lying to yourself, you know. It's the hypoxia talking. You think you belong? This isn't your element at all.*

Regardless, the wreck drew him, until he was close enough to touch it.

*Everything down here is so much better suited to belong than you. Here, all you are is a resource.*

Breathing? Soon. The pent-up need, he now understood, wasn't driven by a lack of oxygen. The body had no sensors for that. An amazing oversight. Nobody would ever design an oxygen-powered machine that way on purpose.

*Down here, you're food. All you have to do is wait.*

Instead, the clawing need to breathe came from a build-up of carbon dioxide, and you could hack that to a degree. He let a poof of stale air slip his lips and it bought him a little more time. He squatted and gripped the yacht's tilted gunwale, to shove off it and launch his ascent . . . but to his surprise, it gave way with a muffled crunch and a cloud of debris, crumbs and shards of rotten wood drifting loose.

It was what was inside that really gave him a jolt.

The cross-section of wood appeared tunneled, the burrows full of soft, pale bodies— worms, they looked like, some as short and thin as matches, others the size of a finger, one as plump as a cigar.

Danny vented more CO2, this time not meaning to, a sound of disgust burping loose. And he'd been down too long, his vision starting to close around the edges, with the height of a seven-story building left to swim. He pushed off the bottom and kicked toward the beckoning daylight.

If your vision began turning to a haze they called the pink cloud . . . that was when you really had to worry. What came next was a blackout, and he feared it was moments away— the resetting of the clock to a final countdown. You could drift unconscious for a couple minutes, no harm done, your larynx closed like a valve to keep the water out. Up top, they would know before it opened again, if they were paying attention. You just had to trust your team, they'd realize you were in trouble, haul you up by your safety line . . .

Oh. Right. Shit.

He kicked harder.

Which came first then—the movement out in front of him, or the movement he felt *through* him?

Through, probably. Yeah, go with that. His insides felt stirred, quivering as if he'd hugged a vibrator. Right away he knew what it was, he'd felt the same thing from dolphins— echolocation, a ping of sonar developed over millions of years of evolution, so advanced it made the Navy's best look like a toy.

But this was no dolphin. If a dolphin was a whisper, what he'd felt was a bark.

He lowered his gaze from the beacon of the sun and back to the deep blue haze. Twenty, thirty yards out, it was dimly visible, a darker bulk against the murk, a slick, bulbous head and a body stretching too far back into the gloom to make out. With his vision closing down, Danny could barely see it anyway, and only for a moment before it faded into a wash of pink.

He heard a muffled thump and the sensation enveloped him again.

*If you're lucky and you know it clap your hands* . . . Whatever was out there could've obliterated him without trying. Sperm whales? Loudest animals on earth. Their clicks could be so loud they couldn't even exist in the air as sound. They could blow out your eardrums, maybe kill you as surely as the concussive blast of a bomb.

Lucky. It was only scanning, giving him a sonogram.

Kicking again, with legs starting to feel like tingling rubber, nearly blind now, he rose toward a total eclipse of the sun. A few feet from the surface he spewed a gush of bubbles to empty his aching lungs, then with a titanic whoosh broke through into the glorious air.

"You stupid motherfucker!" Kimo was peering down from the boat as if he were looking at a ghost. Things started going clear again, even the sweat spraying from Kimo's shaved head as he whipped the lanyard at the end of the rope, like shaking a leash at a naughty dog. "What is this? What the fuck is this!"

*My bad* . . . ? Didn't quite cut it under the circumstances, did it?

"What, almost drowning once this year wasn't enough for you, you thought you'd find another way?"

Treading water, Danny peeled off his goggles and flipped his hair back from his face to splat against his shoulders. "Sorry, man. I needed more than ninety feet."

"But you stopped moving." Kimo jabbed a finger toward the sonar screen. "It still makes you dumb as a rock, but if you'd kept moving, you wouldn't have sent me from zero to panic mode, hauling this up and you're not on the end of it anymore." He flung the safety line to the deck. "I was two seconds from going in after you."

"But I started moving again. Obviously. You didn't see that?"

"While giving myself ninety feet of rope burns? No! I don't multitask."

The man had been looking out for him for years, one displaced Hawaiian to another, and his anger was so pure, so righteous, so Kimo, Danny couldn't help but laugh. It was the right thing at the right time—same as below, the body knowing what to do, and doing it.

"I was fine. Really." He took Kimo's hand and clambered over the side into the boat, then tapped the sonar. "How about the whale? Did you see the whale?"

For a moment, Kimo could only blink. Translation: *Good going, asshole. Now you made me miss an entire whale, too.* "You saw a whale?"

"Just for a second or two. My vision was going, so . . ."

"Are you sure you weren't hallucinating?"

"I felt him check me out. I didn't hallucinate that." He turned a clumsy 360 to scan the waves for a breach but saw nothing. "How long was I down?"

"I think you were around two-forty-five, two-fifty when I went for the line. I don't even know where the watch landed."

Danny plopped onto the transom and wriggled out of his fins. "So I had to break three minutes, easy." Nothing impressive by competition standards. Competitive freedivers could rack up depths and times that were off the chain. But those people were all about the numbers, the endurance, not about merging with the sea. "A new personal best and I don't even know what it is."

He tossed his fins aside, then spotted the stopwatch beside their cooler of water bottles. He snatched it up and held it toward Kimo's face, back to normal brown after all that furious brick red.

"Check it," Danny said. "Six-thirty-four and counting."

Kimo rolled his eyes. "That'll look good on your tombstone. '*Still holding my breath, bitches.*'"

-o-

"Shipworms. That's all you saw when the wood came apart," Gail told him that afternoon. "They're called shipworms."

Danny didn't know whether to be fascinated or appalled. A whale, he could wrap his brain around that. Those aquatic grubs were something new.

"Shipworms. That's actually a thing?"

"For someone who's eaten as many waves as you have, your sense of maritime history really is lacking." She gave him a peck on the cheek, as if to say she loved him anyway. "Yeah, they're a thing. In the age of sailing ships, before steel hulls, they were a big, bad, serious thing. Termites of the sea, is the best way to describe them. If they weren't busy eating shipwrecks, they were causing them. Or chewing through wharves, piers, anything like that. Waiting for a nice juicy log to drift by, to turn into a floating condo."

Your home is your food—pretty much the definition of a parasite. Like taking a gander around this cliff-top cottage and thinking, hey, break me off a piece of that wall, I'm feeling peckish. What am I in the mood for? The green room, the blue room? Something in the line of a honey-gold breakfast nook? Yum.

"But they're not actually worms. They're mollusks. Like long, skinny oysters. They've got little shells on the front, that's how they burrow in." She perked up. "If you dive that wreck again, bring up a few. They're supposed to taste like clams."

"That's a bucket of nope, right there." His stomach did barrel rolls at the thought. "How do you know this? You don't even sail."

This was the distinction between them. For all her astonishing symbiosis with the sea, Gail hardly ever got out on it. That was his department. Gail was perfectly happy being its next-door neighbor.

She crossed her arms and, with a cockeyed grin, withered him with a glance. He knew how to translate that look: *Come with me, you fool.*

With a swirl of her skirt, she led him out of the cottage and across the stone path to the outbuilding—her workshop, bright and airy and open to clear out the smell of varnish. Its walls were the color of sea foam, its windows faced a panoramic view of the Pacific, and it was always, always, full of driftwood. Most of the pieces were still raw, just as they had been harvested from the beach. The rest were in various stages of processing and transformation.

Every chunk she brought in was its own starter kit, anything from simple projects like necklace racks to elaborate constructions like lamp stands and chandeliers that she sold through galleries from Portland to Santa Barbara. Last year, she'd taken hundreds of seemingly useless fragments and, where anyone else might have seen only kindling, turned them into a mosaic of a whimsical octopus, with spiral seashells for eyes.

Gail snatched up a sun-bleached branch the length of his arm, peppered with perforations as if someone had used it for target practice.

"After almost twenty years of seeing me do this, you've never wondered where these holes come from?"

"I guess I thought it was weathering." By her skeptical look, she wasn't buying it. "Okay, I guess I never thought about it at all."

She gave him one of those shakes of her head, playful but dismissive, that left him feeling she had so much more wisdom that he did, baked in from birth. "If it doesn't eat the surfboard out from under you, it doesn't exist, right?"

"Pretty much," he conceded.

As a rule, ignorance was no virtue, but if you gave too much thought to the sea, and everything with teeth that called it home, you'd never venture out to meet it.

Maybe that was why she stayed on shore.

⟶⬥⟵

They grilled on the patio that evening, marinated tempeh and vegetables, and as they usually did unless the rain had other ideas, carried their plates out to the wrought iron table on the little redwood deck, so they could eat beneath the sky, facing the sea. The cottage was one of a haphazard nest of six, perched near the edge of a two hundred-foot cliff overlooking the beach and breakers below.

Bellies full, they kicked their feet up on the brick retaining wall around the firepit and passed the evening's joint back and forth.

Danny wanted to say he liked it better living at the condo in Santa Monica and Gail liked it better here, but that wasn't true. Santa Monica was only more convenient. He liked it better here, too. Time passed differently here, the days longer, the seasons more pronounced. On the luckiest nights he might awaken to the faraway squeal of a passing whale—humpback, he supposed, the only kind he was aware of whose songs carried above water. He would roll over to find that Gail was already up, her silhouette framed by the bedroom window, where she sat as still as stone and listened for as long as it would last. They never got that in Santa Monica.

Although she was never farther away from him than she was in those minutes, lost inside a trance, and there was little he could do to get her back but wait.

Anyway. Out with it. He'd been meaning to bring it up for months. Now felt as right as ever.

"I'm going to have to find a business to go into. Or invent." Telling the water but for Gail's ears. "Got any suggestions?"

She looked more concerned with diagnosing causes. "Is it the . . .?"

Fear? That wasn't it, but it made sense she would go there. They'd had to give the topic a couple of airings after his wipeout this spring at Prevelly Park.

The bigger the wave, the more ways a ride could go wrong. Miscalculations, human error, the never predictable hydraulics of any given wave—however it happened, things went wrong. While you went shooting through the tube, the board got sucked up the wall of water curling over behind you. Or the wave rose up while the bottom dropped out, and you got slammed into the impact zone. You were no longer riding the wave. It was riding you, maybe grinding you into the sand and rocks to really teach you a lesson.

He knew of no greater helplessness than that. Being held under by the first wave was terror enough. If you were still down when the next one came crashing in, you felt exponentially worse, battered and exhausted and desperate to breathe. Still hadn't surfaced before a third one came along? That was when it seemed as though the ocean had made up its unfathomable mind: It wasn't letting go.

He'd known a couple guys who hadn't come up alive. But he had. No idea how, but after a three-wave hold-down at Prevelly Park, he had. *The ocean doesn't want me today . . .* It was as good an explanation as any.

But one day, it might. It was the reason he'd taken up freediving. To extend his breath-holding duration. To get comfortable with being under the water a long time, because as a surfer, *under* was the last place anyone wanted to be. And it had helped. He felt recalibrated, more at peace with *under* than ever.

So no. This had nothing to do with fear.

"It's worse," he said. "It's the calendar. And the numbers."

Gail had been holding back a toke, and lost it with a hacking laugh. "I thought it would be at least another twenty years before maybe I'd hear you make a concession there." She fixed him with a hazy leer. "Who are you, foul thing that crawled from the sea, and give me back my Danny."

Which version? He was developing a nostalgic longing for the Danny Yukimura who seemed incapable of thinking about consequences.

Gail rubbed his arm. "It's just another birthday, but with a zero. Don't you know? Forty is the new eighteen, I think is what it's down to."

"That only helps if eighteen is the new as-yet-unborn." He took the joint, made it smolder, handed it back. "It's the rankings. In the top thirty in the world, I've had a good run, but I've never gotten higher than twenty-two, and now I'm right back on that edge. The only place to go is down. That's how this goes. Especially now."

It was the times—thrilling to be around to witness them, but shitty when you were a casualty because you couldn't keep up. People were out there doing amazing things, unthinkable things, feats that had been considered impossible.

"There's something changing in the world . . ."

He traced it back to when Laird Hamilton had caught the Millennium Wave, in Teahup'po. Until then, nobody had ridden a sixty-foot wave. Nobody. It wasn't merely the height; it was the length, the girth, the colossal magnitude. Even Hamilton hadn't been planning on it. He got towed into the wave, then it rose a behemoth. As the tube collapsed behind him, everybody watching thought he was dead, until he came shooting up out of the spray.

A thing like that did something magical. It opened a doorway to unknown realms of potential. Eighty footers? Ninety? Guys were riding them now.

It wasn't only surfers, either. Skateboarders, skiers, snowboarders—superhumans were popping up everywhere. Somebody does something that blows minds around the globe and everyone says, damn, dude, that record's gonna stand for years, then it doesn't even stand a season.

Something in the air, maybe. Something in the water.

He loved seeing it unfold in the world. It was a beautiful time to be alive. But it wasn't his arena anymore. He couldn't compete with that. Go big or go home? He *was* home. He just had no idea what to do next.

"So you launch your own line of boards. Or gear. Or both," Gail said. "Or you open up the Danny Yukimura School of Surfing, and turn into one of those cute old guys with the long white hair and wispy beard, but still a badass, and wait for people to come to you. Because they will."

He wanted to believe. She made it easy to believe.

Even if he still ached for more, and had no idea what it was.

◄◦►

Before the dawn, even before coffee, they made their way along the stairs that zigzagged down a cleft in the land from cliff top to sea level. The wooden steps were perpetually damp, even in summer, crowded over by trees so that the sun never reached them.

They nearly always had the shore to themselves when beach walking this early, sharing it with at most a neighbor from above, out with a dog and a stick.

He knew of no place where dawn was more different from dusk than here, with the sun on the other side of the continent behind a two hundred-foot wall of rock and earth. Here, dawns were gradual and gray, a time of mist and fog. This morning the wind was up, sending ribbons of fine, dry sand skimming over the damp-packed plains of the beach. The surf rolled and pounded behind a veil, as if the sand were of one world and the water of another, and every sunrise it took the proper spell to bring them back together.

They wouldn't be going home empty-handed. They never did. The only variable was what Gail would find, and how long it would take after she shucked his hand and went on the hunt.

He'd never met anyone more suited to spend her life seaside. Not merely to live here, but thrive. She smelled of the sea, tasted of it. Even the ocean knew its own. The sea had recognized this about her as soon as Gail arrived for good, a couple years before they'd met.

She had grown up Midwestern, landlocked in every direction, but the farthest shores had always called her, from as early a time as she could remember. A week after her eighteenth birthday she made the 1500-mile trek west, one-way this time. A week after that, one morning's beach walk set her up for years, when she came upon what appeared to be a peculiar yellowish rock, stonelike yet waxy, embedded in the sand.

Right away, she'd known it for what it really was: ambergris, a solidified lump of secretions from the belly of a sperm whale, nearly three pounds of it. No substance on earth was more prized by the makers of perfume, especially in France. It was illegal to sell in the States, though, so one impromptu trip to Canada later, she returned three pounds lighter, $140,000 heavier, and after making the down payment on the cottage, had hardly left the ocean's side ever since.

Such a find had to be more than dumb luck. Gail had taken it not merely as a welcome, but as a blessing. *You're where you belong now. This is your home. It's always been your home. You just had to find your way back.*

The sea never stopped giving to her. Danny had never seen anything like it, the sheer reliability of it. Some days the swells didn't want to be surfed, and you had to accept that. But Gail and her walks along the shore, harvesting the ocean's castoffs? She always came back with something, and the desire to see what she could make of it. Send her out beachcombing with ten other people, and there was a good chance she'd come back with more treasure than everyone else combined. He imagined salt-encrusted nymphs out in the surf, working on her behalf: *Look alive, mateys, it's her again! Heave to!*

This morning, the farther north they walked, the lighter the dawn became, as ahead of them, Neptune's Throne took shape out of the gray haze.

*Neptune's Throne* was all he'd ever heard anyone call it. It was an observation platform for surfers to watch the incoming, but whoever had built it hadn't made it particularly convenient. It was four solid tree trunk pillars driven deep into the sand, braced with crossbeams and supporting a planked deck just above head height. No steps. If you wanted to clamber onto it, you had to have either the upper body strength to pull yourself up, or friends to push you from below.

It had a back, like a gargantuan chair—a windbreak, he assumed, blocking what the cliffs didn't—two of the trunks joined above the platform with an X, which in turn supported a row of ragged planks that were shortest on the outside and rose to an imperial peak in the middle.

The deck was usually thatched, and at first glance the bristly edges gave it the look of something that belonged somewhere tropical. Kimo recalled more of Hawaii than he did, and said the thing reminded him of rough-hewn structures he'd seen in places tourists didn't get to: burial platforms, and shrines where fishermen laid offerings to the gods of the sea before heading out, or after rowing back in with their catch.

Keep looking at it, though, and the tropical impression faded, darkened. Danny wasn't sure why. Maybe it was the way the two front trunks topped out with the flared stumps of long-gone limbs as thick as the trunks themselves. Neither appeared shaped by hand, only weathered, yet each had the look of a skull that faced the sea, like the bones of a pair of malformed whales.

Who had first built the thing, and when—questions no one could answer. If their neighbor Felicia was to be believed, Neptune's Throne was older than he was, and her as well. Felicia had lived atop the cliff for fifty years, and claimed the structure was there when she and her husband moved in. Claimed, as well, she'd seen a photo dated decades earlier, from the time of the Great Depression, and it was standing then, too. Meaning none of today's throne could have been the original wood—it was too well maintained to have withstood over eighty years of weathering. But in the years he and Gail had been dividing their time between here and Santa Monica, he'd never seen anyone repair it . . . only use it.

When they passed by, Gail patted one of the gray-weathered anchor posts as if it were the leg of a friendly elephant. He lingered, fingertips tracing the little holes along the wood. He knew what they were now, but wasn't pleased about that, as if there were a chance he could probe far enough inside to find a tangle of worms that had learned how to live outside the sea.

In their present direction, north, they were nearing their terminus, where a point of land fit for a lighthouse curved around from the right and speared out into the waves. At the base of the wall ran a stream fed by tributaries that trickled down the hillsides, then joined and cut ever-changing channels in the sand before emptying into the sea.

It was here she found it, a still-wet chunk of driftwood the size of a truncated log, mired in the sand of a delta that might not be there tomorrow morning, erased by the tide and recut somewhere else.

Gail knelt. She scraped off sand and picked away rags of seaweed. "You want to do the honors, my strong guy?"

Danny wrestled it free of the beach's hold and stood it on end. It was lighter than it looked, would be lighter still after it dried. Regardless, he didn't relish the thought of lugging it two hundred feet up slick wooden stairs.

"Wow," she said after she'd had a longer look. "If I didn't know better, and maybe I don't, I'd say this was something that had already been carved."

They traded places, Gail holding it up while he stepped back for a view. She was right. It had a suggestion of form—human, or maybe he was biased that way. Still, working with the contours and curves of what remained, he could discern legs, pressed together and thickening into hips. A waist and sloping shoulders. A head. It would be unrecognizable without a head.

"The figurehead off a ship's prow, maybe?" He recalled yesterday's yacht, being gnawed to slivers on the ocean floor. Maybe not that boat in particular; a stray chunk of someone else's bad luck. The ocean was forever digesting the remains of bad luck and coughing up the pieces.

"A lot of figureheads were big-breasted women. Traditionally speaking." Beside it, Gail went ramrod-straight and perked up her chest, comparing. "If I squint just right, I can make out a couple of boobs." She looked him in the eye, squinty. "And if you say, 'But what about the wood,' I will murder you in your sleep."

She had him call heads or tails, then they took their places at either end and began to shuffle the thing home.

⟶

Two days later she found another one washed up half a mile to the south, longer by a few inches, but shaped almost identically. Two half-rotted figureheads on the same beach at the same time? Not likely. By now he was leaning toward dismissing it as a case of pareidolia, the tendency to see ships in clouds, the man in the moon, and Jesus on a burnt tortilla. Or making a face out of two holes, a bump, and a line.

Even so, lugging them home felt like carrying corpses, complete with grave worms. The sodden outer wood sloughed and squished in his uncertain grip. Halfway up the cliff with the second one, his fingers broke through as if piercing a crust, and pulped an embedded shipworm as thick as a sausage. He nearly dropped the log and went down with it. The stairs were damp underfoot and slick with wet flora—treacherous for carrying this kind of load.

When Gail found the third one a few days later, he had no idea what to make of it. If pareidolia was simple pattern recognition, okay then, what sort of pattern was this? On the surface it seemed the same old relationship Gail had always had with the sea and the generosity of its tides. But it had never given her the same exact thing time after time. If it was going to do that, why not be *really* generous, and keep lobbing more lumps of ambergris at her.

She first left her finds outside on heavy racks to dry in the July sun, turning them every few hours like hot dogs on a grill. Then she moved them into her workshop, lined against one wall, standing in a row.

They'd turned pale now that they were dry, bleached by the elements and time. With the muck wiped off and the water-bloat gone, finer details emerged. The pieces all tapered and thickened the same way, with dual concavities that suggested eyes, and a nub that suggested a nose, and a crack against the grain for a mouth. They were just humanoid enough that Danny didn't like turning his back on them, as if they were shells that would break open and release some worse form gestating inside.

"Gotta be a simple explanation," Kimo told him on the boat while out on another freediving trip. "Maybe they're something that fell off a cargo ship, some shipment of carvings that weren't very good to begin with. Or there's some asshole out here who lives on a boat, thinks he's an artist, and dumps his mistakes overboard when nothing turns out the way he wants. Whatever they were, now that they're washing up, they look that much worse."

"Incompetent artists," Danny said. "Really. That's your explanation."

"If you had a better one, you wouldn't have asked me what I thought."

Point taken. But the wobble in this theory was that nothing about any of these pieces appeared to have been carved. Danny had looked, and closely. No evidence of chisels, rasps, scrapers, drawknives. They showed no obvious signs of hand-tooling at all. Even the ends looked broken, not sawed. What was the likelihood that someone who couldn't turn out a carving that looked more than vaguely human was, nevertheless, skilled enough to keep everything smooth, free of facets?

"Erosion. Wear," Kimo said. "You ever see a jagged stone in a riverbed? Not me. Pick any rock, you don't know how it looked when it went in. You're just getting what's left."

And when Gail found another—number four, but who was counting? —Danny wasn't even surprised. Well, yes, he was. Not by the find, but by the irritation he felt at the news. How many of these things did she need, anyway? Just because they washed up, did that obligate her to accept every single one, bring them *all* home?

It wasn't like him to be resentful. But analyze it anyway. Things hadn't merely come easily for Gail. They came effortlessly. The ocean gave and never ran out. All she had to do was show up and take possession.

He'd been lucky to be able to make a decent living doing something he loved. But it had never come easily. It had taken thousands of hours of wave time to hone his skills. It had taken near-drownings, lacerations from coral, jellyfish stings, reef rash, a staph infection, various sprains, two separate concussions when the board smacked him in the head . . . and that was before factoring in every competitor on the tours breathing down his neck, eager to take his ranking and sponsorships for themselves.

Worst of all, it was life with an expiration date. He couldn't keep doing it forever, and he was nearly there. He could feel the downward pull as surely as he felt it during a dive, after entering the Doorway to the Deep.

Gail, though, went on as ever, bringing up trinkets as though she were being wooed by the sea. The same sea that she claimed to love, but wouldn't go out on, not even with him.

As she began to spend more hours in her workshop than ever, he wondered if it was karmic payback. If this was what it had been like for her over two decades, forced to share him with a passion that consumed him, sent him around the world to wherever the waves were at their biggest and baddest: from Mavericks to Waimea Bay, from Tavarua to Padang Padang. Maybe that was the part that hadn't come easily for her.

But by the time the fifth one turned up, even Gail seemed past taking any joy in it. Something about this was not right. It had never been quite right.

"This feels like a cat sometimes, bringing you its kills," she confessed in the workshop one evening. At the bank of windows, the sun dropped boiling red into the cauldron of the sea. "It loves you. But it's love on a whole different wavelength."

He had no idea what to say to that. Along the north wall, the carvings seemed to be daring him to try. He was beginning to hate them. Whatever secret they knew, they weren't telling.

At the center of the shop, a rectangular worktable, as stout and sturdy as a stage, held half a dozen pieces of driftwood in various stages of transformation—sculptures and a bonsai planter—none of which had progressed in three days. All Gail did now was come out and sit with them, seemingly stymied by the new arrivals that were piling up. As if they'd come to tell her that her work was at an end.

Her methods hadn't changed in all the time he'd loved her, across nineteen years of being together, seventeen of marriage. Each piece of driftwood she harvested merited its own staring context, a still, silent interrogation during which she divined what it wanted to be, needed to be, in its new and resurrected life.

But these? These unblinking humanoids? Gail was treating them as if they were complete already, in no need of refinement. They didn't seem to be going anywhere. Like her, they were home.

"You know, we've done the seaside thing for more than half our lives," he said. "If I'll be retiring soon anyway, maybe we should give mountains a try."

She almost laughed. "Lie awake at night listening for elk? I don't know if that would work or not."

She turned at the window and faced the rolling waters. He followed her gaze in case there was something to see, but if there was, only Gail could see it.

"Did you ever hear about the 52-Hertz Whale?" she said.

He hadn't.

"It's the saddest thing ever. Researchers have been picking it up on hydrophones for years. It's only ever been heard, never seen." She was still facing the window, as if telling the ocean, and he was just around to eavesdrop. "This whale, this one single whale, that sings at a higher frequency than all the others. Fifty-two Hertz. All the usual suspects—blue whales, fin whales, like that—they're down around fifteen or twenty or thirty. So nobody even knows what kind of whale this is. All they know is that it just keeps roaming the Pacific, calling out, singing its song, and nothing else is answering."

She turned her back to the window, facing him again.

"Better keep your mountains. I don't think I could handle that with an elk. They'll come right up in your front yard."

He left her to it—all of it, the worm-eaten pieces of wood and the stalled magic she wielded over them—and traded the workshop for twilight. Out here on the grass, the fifth refugee carving remained wedged in its drying rack. Horizontal, it looked helpless. As he stepped closer, Danny wondered how she would react if he dragged it toward the setting sun and threw it off the cliff.

He hadn't given this one a second look since it was cleaned off, and mostly dry. What would've been the point? They were all the same, more or less.

Except this one . . . wasn't.

He dared to touch it, to run his hand over what had been obscured before, and was still barely visible: a faint impression scored around it, near the bottom end, like the groove on a finger after taking off a wedding ring, tattooed with a trace of rust.

*No way*, he thought. This whole time, assuming these had started out as ordinary logs, when they were nothing of the sort. *No way*.

◄◦►

The great thing about Kimo was that there was almost nothing he wouldn't drop at a moment's notice to take his boat out. He'd saved the GPS coordinates of the sunken yacht, so even after three weeks it was easy to find again. Once Danny was in the water, Kimo waved the coil of rope before tossing it over the side.

"I'm giving you a longer leash, so leave it on. If you touch the lanyard this time I'm going to break your arm."

"Yes, Mom." Danny huffed wind to saturate himself, filled up, locked it in, then ducked and plunged.

By now he'd traded his frogman flippers for a monofin. Kimo called it his mermaid ass. It fit over both feet and forced his legs to move together, scything the water like a whale's flukes to turbocharge each kick. It made the hardest part of the dive easier, if no faster; he could equalize the pressure in his head only so quickly. But it took less energy to power downward, dolphin-kicking, and to maneuver around once he got below neutral buoyancy, and that was what mattered.

Seventy-six feet down, the wreck waited in the hushed indigo haze, still tipped onto its starboard side with its mast jutting down into the ooze. And if the boat still unnerved him, helpless, disintegrating in a grave of silt and mud, it was at least familiar now. He knew it was pointless to check the prow for a figurehead but felt compelled to do it anyway, and of course there was no evidence of one ever having been there.

He turned onto his side and swam parallel to the sea floor, really mermaiding it now, cruising the length of the deck from bow to stern, inspecting the damage and the rot. He was gliding back the opposite way when it struck him: He'd been so focused on the small details that he had missed the big obvious one right in front of him.

He'd been looking for a hole ripped in the deck, or a broken stump, evidence of a missing mast. He'd been looking over what remained for signs of mast hoops, iron reinforcements especially, that might have chafed a groove of rust and wear around the bottom of its mast in the push and pull of the currents.

And they were there.

It was only when he took in the big picture that he realized: Three weeks ago the wreck had *two* masts, angled down toward the sediment. Now there was only one, the foremast.

There appeared to have been three, total. Masts detached from wrecked ships, sure, it happened. *But where were they now?* No telling how long the rearward mizzen had been gone. But within the past twenty-two days, the main mast shouldn't have gotten far.

Shouldn't. But had.

He feared he could guess where thirty-plus feet of them might have ended up. Where, but not how. There was no how he could imagine. There was no how he *wanted* to imagine. There was only his quickening heart and the hunger to breathe and the air above the waves.

He surfaced and plunged, surfaced and plunged again, like a pearl diver looking for a prize too big to be misplaced. He widened his search to the limits of his safety line, and still it wasn't enough. Looking out toward deeper waters, beyond the spot where he'd caught that glimpse of the whale emerging through the dim blue, he saw how the sea floor sloped away, and that down the incline, some indistinct patch of shadow waited. A trick of light would waver. This didn't waver.

"We need to move," he told Kimo the next time he surfaced. "Forty or fifty yards that way."

Never thought he'd see Kimo balk at piloting the boat. "Dude. You've had a month of downtime since the Corona Open. Is this really how you want to spend your final days of it, instead of getting your mind on the Billabong Pro?"

Treading water, spitting salt: "Yeah. It is. It helps. Everything helps."

"What's so special about fifty yards that way?"

"Because I'm ready for it."

Kimo made the move, grumbling, but insisted on doing a sonar reading of the bottom. Ninety-four feet—Danny had never dived that far. Not a huge leap from last week's new personal best of eighty-three, but still, it meant more pressure and another twenty-two feet of round-trip. This was not insignificant.

He went anyway. Deeper, bluer, colder, darker. He relaxed into the squeeze, welcoming it like an embrace.

From above and to the side, he couldn't yet tell what was waiting below. Submerged another eighteen feet lower than the yacht, even less light reached his target zone. But it was more than that. The water looked cloudier here, too. As his vision acclimated to the gloom, he could make out what appeared to be a slab on the sea floor, three times the width of a car, furred with growth and set in the midst of a forest of bull kelp. Their stalks swayed with the currents, their fronds wavering like pennants in a breeze.

The further he sank and the closer he drifted, the less natural the slab looked, like a mound of sand and mud and stones scraped into a heap and packed together with intent. For no reason he wanted to explore, its flatness and order—its look of *purpose*—reminded him of the worktable in Gail's shop. Again he was overcome with the uneasy sense of facing something out of place, lost from above and drowned without pity.

Because rising from the mound was a grove of logs, eight of them, seemingly jammed into the muck to hold them in place. Their tops were ragged, splintered, a sight that nearly locked his mind. He could imagine no force in the sea that could take a ship's mast and break it up this orderly way, or would even want to.

Around each piece, a thrashing cloud of motion churned and blurred the water. By now he knew a shipworm on sight. Even at their most normal they still filled him with loathing, but he didn't think they were supposed to behave like this, hundreds of them visible, like hagfish burrowed into the side of a decomposing whale. They streamed over the wood with the furious energy of a feeding frenzy.

The dread crept in cold, from the outer dark. This was something no one was meant to see. Ever. A hiker would feel this way, stumbling across the half-eaten carcass of a mule deer, then smelling the musk and carrion scent of the returning grizzly.

Danny flicked his fin to drift close enough to see the hard little shells on the worms' heads, scouring the wood, shaping it as surely as rasps and chisels and lathes.

He recognized the human form gnawed free from the lengths of mast. Anyone would.

He knew their contours. He'd lugged their predecessors up from the beach five times already.

And among the three that appeared farthest along, he recognized the face taking shape out of the grain. He had loved it for the past nineteen years.

Danny tried to will the sight away as an illusion born of low light and a brain hungry for oxygen. But it wouldn't resolve into anything else. He pinched off a half-dozen of the worms, fat and lashing, and flung them to the silt so he could caress his hand along the fresh-carved visage. Even blind, in the dark of an infinite abyss, he would know that cheekbone, that nose, that jawline, that hollow at the throat.

Already, the worms he'd dropped were wriggling back up to her face, to dig back in and resume their task. Mindless, they seemed to obey a directive he couldn't begin to fathom. But if something out here was capable of snapping a ship's mast into pieces like a pencil, then maybe it followed that it had workers, drones subjugated by the kind of group mind that turned a school of fish in perfect unison.

There was no *why* he wanted to imagine, either.

Five above, eight down here, and who knew how many more might be drifting unfinished somewhere between. In revulsion, in the grip of something he felt but couldn't name, he gave the foremost effigy a shove to send it toppling back, pulling free of the muck and thunking into another behind it, then a third gave way, a slow chain reaction that disturbed the silt, but the worms not at all.

Abruptly, his legs were yanked from beneath him and he was upside-down again, moving up and away, something reeling him in like a fish. He nearly panicked and lost the breath locked inside, until the tug on his ankle made sense. Kimo being Kimo again. He couldn't right himself under the tension, never enough slack to turn around. Rather than flail at the end of the rope, he relaxed and let it happen, until he broke the surface spewing bubbles and foam, and breathed with a violent gasp, once more a creature of land and air.

Kimo peered down from the boat as if expecting to see him floating motionless. Huh. Must have set another personal best without even realizing.

"How long?" Danny said. Normal. He had to act normal.

"Seven minutes."

Seven? Whoa. He would never have guessed.

"I had to pull the plug. And yet . . . you're fine."

"You sound disappointed about that."

"No. That part's good." Kimo shook his head—never again, never again. "You need to find somebody else to take you out for this. All you do is scare the shit out of me."

Poor Kimo. Danny felt genuinely bad for him. Bad for them both. Because it wouldn't have helped one bit to tell Kimo that, no, he wasn't fine. He hadn't come up fine at all.

—◦—

Worse, he couldn't tell Gail, either. How was he supposed to convey a thing like this? *They're you. They're supposed to be you.* He couldn't even be sure how she would react—if she'd find it flattering, the best thing since ambergris, or if the balance would tip and this weird synergy between her and the sea would finally leave her spooked.

Once she picked up on the obvious, that something was wrong, his only option was to lie. Had a bad dive. Burst a blood vessel in my nose. It happens.

All he could do was look ahead. Try to get her away for two weeks, inject some time and distance to break this encroaching spell, and leave whatever carvings might wash up next for someone else to find.

"Why don't you come with me to Tahiti, for the Billabong? It's been years."

"I know. But I should stay. I don't have the kind of work I can take with me."

She was hardly doing the work now. "It'll still be here when you get back. You might even get some new ideas there to bring home."

"Like tiki carvings? I went through my tiki phase years ago."

Oh. Right. She had.

He packed and planned and tried his best to make it sound enticing: Seeing the Pacific from another side would do them good. This could be the last time he went there as a competitor. None of it seemed to quite get through.

"I know. I just like it here. There's something about here. Some people go their whole lives looking for the place they should be. I found my *here* a long time ago."

Even before she'd found him—Gail was too kind to say so, but it had to have crossed her mind. He was one more thing the sea had given her, the one thing it was most capable of taking back. That worried her. It had all along.

*I love you. You've always been my anchor*, she would tell him. *But it scares me what could happen if the anchor chain ever broke.*

—◦—

In that way of sounds, unusual enough to penetrate, familiar enough to not alarm, it worked its way into his dreams before teasing him awake. The dream dissolved at once, so he lay in the dark with the only thing left: the far, reverberant squeal of a whale rolling in across the water and floating up through the open window.

"Listen," he whispered, and reached over to give Gail a gentle shake. But her side of the bed was empty, a sure sign she was listening already.

She wasn't at the window, wasn't in the kitchen, wasn't in the bathroom or front room. He knew the feel of a house emptied of any other heartbeat than his own. Danny yanked on enough clothing to call himself decent, a T-shirt and shorts that felt backwards, then stumbled outside, but she wasn't on the deck, either.

The night was as bright as nights got . . . all moon and no clouds, and the sea a glittering expanse of silver-white and blue-black. It was the world. It was their entire world.

Braced against the redwood deck, he peered down at the beach. After a moment, his fingers gripped the rail with the same steadying ferocity as his toes gripped a surfboard. He felt every bit as much in motion, shooting through a rolling barrel that collapsed behind him.

From up here, he was so accustomed to the sight of Neptune's Throne that the high-backed platform was as familiar a fixture of the landscape as the ridge on which they lived. But now . . . now its shape was different, wrong. He couldn't see what, exactly, only that some hulking form occupied it, bulbous and enormous, wet enough and slick enough to catch the moonlight with an iridescent gleam.

To his left, a form no bigger than a person traversed toward it, small and dark against the pale sands.

He heard it again, rebounding from the cliffs—the same high, rolling squall that had brought him awake, the forlorn cry he'd always taken for a passing whale, roaming the endless waters and calling out for what or who might answer.

Danny sprinted for the beach stairs, the zigzag flights up which he'd helped lug a lifetime's worth of the sea's gifts, clueless, never imagining what it might have wanted, or expected in return.

Pounding down the steps he was as good as blind, the moonlight trapped above the canopy of leaves that crowded up and over. Although he held the rail, heedless of the splinters he picked up along the way, he went tumbling before he knew what happened, something damp and slick skidding beneath his bare foot.

His leg torqued one way while the rest of him torqued another. If pain glowed, his knee could have lit the night. No wave had ever flung him more violently than this, than gravity and his own momentum. He juddered down the stairs, sometimes on his hip, sometimes on his rump, every hardwood step another bruise. When he thudded to a stop he had two flights left to go, and scooted the rest of the way on his ass.

Down on the beach he tried to stand but his knee wasn't having it. He tumbled to the sand, still warm from the day's sun. He crawled, striving to see through the pink haze of pain, first making out the moon-etched lines of the cliffs ahead, then below them, the suggestion of some lesser mountain that rose up and slouched back toward the sea.

Danny crawled until he found a line of dimples in the sand, footprints, unbroken and resolute. He followed them, dragging his useless leg behind him, hearing nothing but the wheeze of his breath and the crash and retreat of the waves.

He crawled until the pillars and planks of Neptune's Throne loomed above him, empty now, but darkened with water and draped with robes of seaweed, the air around it rich with a heavy musk of brine. The sand before it was churned to wet clumps and crooked furrows, as if between here and the water's edge the beach had been plowed by some dragging thing, bristling with appendages, that had tried to walk but was never meant to move on land.

Alongside the disturbance, the line of her steps turned, veering toward the water. He followed these too, scrambling on both elbows and one good knee, until they were no longer dimples but true footprints pressed into the wet sand, heel and arch and five small toes. He scurried ahead, frantic now, as step by step the prints began to change, the impression left by each toe deepening, as though dug by a hooked and spiny claw, with a growth of webbing in between. He followed them to the foaming lip of the sea, where he lost them, her last footprints erased as the water washed across and smoothed the sand blank again.

Still, he floundered onward as the waves battered him head-on, stopping only when he was slapped across the face and shoulder by something solid, heavy as a wet blanket, that clung like a caul. Sputtering, he peeled it away, and when after the longest moments of his life he accepted what the tattered thing was, he had no idea what to do with it. He couldn't bring himself to pitch it away, couldn't think of any reason to keep holding on.

If Gail didn't need her skin anymore, then where on land or sea was it supposed to go?

Out past the breakers, beneath the moon, a gleaming bulbous dome submerged with an elephantine skronk that he felt ripple through the waves and shudder through the sand.

Then he was alone.

He knew the feel of a shore emptied of any other heartbeat than his own.

He retreated far enough to keep from choking, then rolled onto his back to face the stars, exhausted and sweating from the pain. The water surged in and out for a thousand cycles, and a thousand more.

In time he wondered which of the ligaments in his knee were in shreds. ACL, PCL, LCL, MCL . . . any and all. He surely had a motherfucker of a hamstring tear, as well. Whatever the damage, his career was done even sooner than expected.

By the time he was ready to move again, the sky had lightened to a formless gray. Fog had crept in across the waters, and with it a stinging drizzle of rain. His knee was swollen double and he couldn't bend his leg, but nothing much hurt by default anymore.

There was dawn enough for him to spy a familiar shape stranded in the channels where the sea met the freshwater stream from the cliffs. He made for it, mocking thing that it was . . . as complete a carving as he'd seen, even farther along than the ones sunk amid the kelp beds. Or maybe this was one of them, finished along the way.

He knew its shape, knew the face, the hands folded as if in prayer. But he knew nothing of the changes wrought upon the rest of her: the thin, frilled slits at either side of her throat; the fins along each forearm and lower leg. But he did know, and had all along, that she'd smelled of the sea, and tasted of it, too, and that the ocean and its gods knew their own.

She must have known, as well, somewhere inside. Must have cherished the sea even while living in fear that if she ever went out on it, she might not come back. It would never stop wanting her.

He had to admit that this carving—all of them—appeared to have been made with love. But love, as Gail had said, on a whole different wavelength.

He rolled the effigy back out into the surf, fighting the wishes of the waves, the most grueling thing he'd ever done. But it was still a log at heart. It floated. The first twenty yards from shore were the hardest, the next hundred a little easier. He clung to this new Gail until he could no longer push off the sandy bottom, then threw his good leg over and across, straddling it like a surfboard and paddling out to sea.

In time, the roar of the breakers faded behind him, until he was left with the quieter slop and splash of a calm sea, as the dim sun rose over his shoulders and began to burn the fog away.

He paddled as far as he could, until he thought he might have just five more good, strong minutes left inside. The ocean yawned deep and dark beneath. He could still breathe, but with one leg, could he kick hard enough to overcome the air in his lungs? Could he reach that threshold that changed everything? He had to believe he could. Forty feet. He only had to make it another forty feet.

Two days ago, he'd spent seven minutes under, and it went like nothing. There had to be meaning in that. Superhumans were popping up everywhere, remember. Something in the air, something in the water. A beautiful time to be alive.

He rolled off the log and made the plunge.

He would find Gail again, or he wouldn't.

He, too, was ready for another way of life, or he wasn't.

The ocean would accept him. Or it wouldn't.

He could still be a part of it either way.

# SHIT HAPPENS

## MICHAEL MARSHALL SMITH

was pretty drunk or maybe I'd've figured out what was happening a lot sooner. It'd been a hell of a day getting to Long Beach from the east coast, though, kicking off with a bleary-eyed hour in an Uber driven by a guy who ranted about politics the entire way, then two flights separated by a hefty layover, because Shannon, my PA, is obsessed with saving every penny on travel despite—or because of   the fact she's not going to be the one spending hours wandering an anonymous concourse in the middle of the country, trying and ultimately failing to resist the temptation to kill the time in a bar. Once I'd had a couple/three there it seemed only sensible to keep the buzz going with complementary liquor on the second flight, and so by the time the cab from LAX finally deposited me on the quay beside the boat I was already sailing more than a few sheets close to the wind.

When I say "boat" I mean "ship." The company conference this year was on the *Queen Mary*, historic Art Deco gem of British ocean liners and once host to everyone from Winston Churchill to Liberace, now several decades tethered to the dock in Long Beach and refitted as a hotel. I stood staring up at the epic size of the thing while I snatched a cigarette, and then figured out where the stairs were to get up to the metal walkway that took you aboard. I hadn't even finished check-in before a guy I know a little from the London office strode up and said everyone was in the bar and it was happy hour for God's sake so what the hell was I waiting for?

I hurried my bag to my room and brushed my teeth and changed my shirt, taking a second to remind myself of the name of the British guy (Peter something-or-other, I evidently hadn't noted his surname) so I could hail him when I rocked up in the bar. See? Totally professional.

The bar turned out to be at the pointy end of the ship, and—wonder of wonders—featured an outside area which not only had a great view over the bay but you were allowed to smoke there *while drinking*, which meant there was basically no good reason for me to leave it, ever, or at least for the duration of the conference. The bar wasn't even super-crowded, because the conference didn't start in earnest until the next day: I'd only arrived Thursday because Shannon had been able to shave a few bucks off the flights that way. Of course it meant paying for an extra night on the boat but she assured me that was actually a good thing because of some unfeasibly complex points system she's got me locked into—and began explaining it in detail and cross-referencing it with her own plans for the weekend—but after a while I stopped listening.

Most of the guys and girls present were from outposts in Europe, arrived early to make a head-start on recovering from jetlag, which many seemed to believe involved the consumption of alcohol at a rate some might consider injudiciously brisk. I knew most of them only by sight but when you work for the same multinational tech giant and have access to strong, relaxing beverages—and are all a little hyper as a result of being away from home and out of the normal grind—it's not hard to get along. Peter-from-London insisted on taking me on a tour of the boat to point out the curved metal and worn wooden paneling and general faded grandeur of the whole deal (out of Brit pride, I suspect, and also to temporarily remove himself from the sight line of a freakishly tall woman from the Helsinki office whom he'd evidently slept with at the previous year's event, and who was drinking hard and fast with her colleagues and staring at Peter like she either wanted to bash his head in or else renew their acquaintance right away).

Aside from that I stuck to the bar—itself no slouch when it came to looking like the set from some glamorous black-and-white movie where people spoke in bon mots and drank cocktails and broke into dance every ten minutes. I was all too aware I had to give a gnarly and unpopular presentation explaining why the update to our flagship virtual networking module had been delayed *yet again*, but that wasn't until Saturday and hey, it isn't every evening you got to drink heavily on a damned great boat.

I drank. I chatted. I went out front to smoke and watch the sky darken and the lights from the city across the bay come on—and then gradually start to dwindle and fade, as a fog came in. I stuck to beer in the hope this might help the hangover remain dreadful rather than crushing, and after a while this started to catch up with my bladder. Luckily my earlier exploration of the boat with Peter (the Finnish woman was now hanging with our group, and it was becoming clear that the only vigorous acts on her mind were the kind that would have a bedstead banging against a cabin wall into the small hours) had included locating the nearest john. It was down a narrow and windowless corridor that led down the middle of the boat and seemed to have escaped the attention of most of the guys, who instead marched off down one of the much wider walkways on the outer edges, to the main restroom mid-ship that—while significantly larger and nicer—was much further away. The closer one looked like it had been converted out of a far more lavish single toilet (there was still a lock on the outer door to the corridor, and the sink, two urinals, and stall retrofitted into the space were seriously cramped) but never let it be said that I can't make do with what's available, especially when I really do need to take a piss.

Coming from the sophisticated Old World as some of these people did, the proportion of tobacco users was higher than with an all-American crowd, and by nine o'clock over half of us were in permanent position out on the smokers' deck. Peter and the Finnish chick were nowhere to be seen, suggesting that a two-person tour of some low-lit and discrete corner of the boat might be under way. A few of the others had staggered away toward other regions of the boat, looking a little green around the gills, though promising to come back once they'd had some air. The view had also disappeared, blotted out by a thick, chewy fog that was getting thicker and thicker and smelled very strongly of the ocean.

I headed indoors—accepting in passing the offer of yet another pint of the strong local IPA from some suave dude from the Madrid office—and wobbled off down the corridor. Two collisions with the wall en route made me realize I ought to slow the drinking down a little, and I promised my tomorrow-morning self to at least consider the idea.

When I got inside the gents' I saw the stall door was closed and felt the customary beat of gratitude for the fact that my digestive system, decided long ago that one comprehensive defecation per day (early morning, in the comfort of my own home, right after my first coffee and cigarette) is all it needs. As I stood swaying in front of the urinal furthest from the stall (still almost within arm's reach) I glimpsed a pair of shoes planted on the floor within, dark slacks pooled on top, a couple inches of pale, hairy calves. I coughed as I began meeting my own needs, as is my practice, to let the guy in there know he was temporarily not alone.

Nonetheless, a moment later, there was a quiet but clear straining sound. I winced—it's bad enough knowing there's some dude nearby voiding ex-food out of his ass, without getting auditory updates—and tried to hurry my business.

A moment later I heard another noise from the stall. This was more of a grunt. It was followed rapidly by another, broken in the middle by several panting intakes of breath. And then one more. Long, low, and painful-sounding.

"Shit," the guy said, in a low voice. "Ah, fuck."

"You okay in there, pal?"

The words came out without conscious thought. There was silence from the stall, and I realized the guy maybe hadn't heard my warning cough earlier. Awkward.

But then he made a groaning noise again. It was five seconds before it tailed off this time.

"I'm sorry," he said, sounding wretched. "I'm sorry."

I was well-oiled enough to be breezy about the situation, and it was something of a relief to be talking to a fellow American after a couple hours parsing foreign accents. "I'm just glad I didn't have whatever you did. What was it? An entire bowl of jalapeños?"

"No."

"Hot sauce? Stick to the brands you know, is my advice. Some of those local-brand bad boys will put you in a world of sphincter pain if you're not used to them. I've been there, trust me. Avoid anything with Ghost Chili in it, for sure."

"Nothing like that. Just . . ."

There was a sudden and very loud growling sound, evidently from the guy's guts. Then a sploshing noise.

And then—wow.

I mean, *holy cow*. One of the worse stenches I'd ever experienced. Maybe *the* worst. There's that saying about how your own farts never smell as bad as other people's, but seriously. This was *bad*.

I abruptly realized I'd finished pissing and there was no reason for me to be there anymore. I hooked myself back into my pants and muttered a "Good luck with that, buddy," farewell while I took the single step from the urinal to the washbasin—again realizing just how drunk I was when I managed to bang my shoulder into the clearly visible corner wall. The smell had blossomed further and was so very bad that I considered going rogue and leaving without a hand-wash, but (though I won't spend the ten frickin' minutes some guys will, like they're about to perform heart surgery and have spent the last hour with their hand up a cow) the habit's too deeply ingrained.

I held my breath, did a water-only rinse and grabbed a paper towel. The guy groaned again as I was making a hash of drying my too-wet hands, the paper tearing into damp shreds. There was another growling sound and I flapped off the last remnants, knowing a similar noise had prefigured the smell last time and having no desire to experience the second wave.

Too late. This time the sploshing noise was shorter and louder and far more explosive. I had my hand on the handle to the outside door when I heard something else, however. It was quiet, a sound he'd tried his hardest to keep inside—a kind of focused, tearful gasp.

"Shit, dude," I said, stepping back from the door. "You don't sound good at all."

"Sorry," he said, quietly.

"Look, is there someone out there that I should tell . . . like, a friend, or something? I could let them know you're having a moment, and will be back out in a while?"

"No," he said, quickly. He sniffed, hard. "I'm fine. I'm just . . . It feels *really* bad."

"Definitely not a chili-related malfunction?"

"Haven't eaten any in days. And it's not . . . Look, it's not my actual asshole that hurts, okay? It's . . ."

He broke off, and groaned again.

The second wave of the smell had hit me now, and it was a struggle to speak in a non-strangulated tone. "Is it the Norovirus?" I'd endured that back when it was new and fashionable a decade ago, and it's not a lot of fun.

"I don't think so. I had that a few years ago. It's fast and liquid. And it sucks but it doesn't actually *hurt*."

"This hurts?"

"*Hell* yeah."

I couldn't believe I was having this conversation when there was a beer and convivial company waiting for me, but it would have felt rude to simply walk out. "Though not at the point where stuff, uh, exits?"

"No. Inside. Like there's a fist squeezing your fucking guts. And lets go, but then squeezes again, even harder."

"That doesn't sound good."

"It's really not. And it came on super-fast. I was hanging out in the bar, having a blast, and suddenly there's this searing pain. I got here just in time. Look, I'm Carl, by the way. Carl Hammick. From the Madison office."

"Rick Millerson," I said. "Boston."

"Oh, hey. Any update on the RX350i?"

"Still delayed."

"I figured."

"Keep that to yourself until Saturday, though. I'm doing an announcement thing on it."

"Sure. Rather you than me, pal."

"Tell me about it."

I was about to wish him well and get the hell out but it occurred to me that the guy could have touched a bunch of stuff on his way in. I'm never sure how communicable stomach bugs are, but—especially with the presentation to make—this guy's problem was one I really didn't want to have.

I stepped back to the sink and washed my hands properly, using plenty of soap. From now on I'd be making the longer trek to the other bathroom, too. While I did this there was a grunting sound from the stall, and a sharp intake of breath. I rolled my eyes. I'd had enough of this scene now, especially the smell.

"Another wave coming in?"

"I think so," he said between gritted teeth. "Holy crap, this feels even fucking worse."

He made a non-verbal sound. This time it was an actual sob, hard, fast. Followed by another.

I was trying to work out what I could possibly say that would be reassuring but not too weird when I realized my phone was buzzing. I pulled it out and saw Shannon's ID on the screen. I was torn between not wanteing to answer—especially in these circumstances—and knowing I probably should. One of the reasons I tolerate Shannon's tight-fisted travel bookings and pay her significantly more than I have to (and in fact stole her from another office, somewhat controversially) is she's the best PA I've ever had, or even heard of. That includes knowing how to deal when I'm out of the office. Reminders pre-set on my phone, remotely updated. Digest email of where I need to be and when, and with whom, and why, delivered to my inbox at 6:30 every morning. If necessary she'll send a brief text to alert me to late-breaking changes, but she won't call unless it's something I'd look dumb for not being right on top of—like some fresh disappointment in the slow-rolling train-wreck that is the fucking RX350i.

The guy in the stall grunted again, harsh and loud. There was a sudden bang on the door to the corridor. I flipped the lock before anybody could come in.

"Busy," I said, loudly.

Whoever was outside rattled the handle and banged on the door once more, but then seemed to go away. Shannon went away too, so I guess it hadn't been that important after all.

"Thanks, man," Carl said. "Bad enough having you in here. No offense. But I'm not selling fucking tickers."

"I hear you. And look, I'm going to leave you in peace, okay? When I'm gone . . . maybe you could bunny hop out of there and lock the outer door? Give you some privacy, right?"

"Sure, if I ever get a chance to get my ass off this . . ."

He stopped talking suddenly, making a sound as if he'd been punched in the gut, and a moment later I heard that bad stomach-growling noise again. Shorter, but really loud.

"Christ," I said, reaching once more for the outer door—but my phone started ringing again. It was Shannon, again. If she was pinging me multiple times then I really had to engage. "Look, uh, Carl—I'm actually going to have to take this call, okay?"

"Sure. Whatever."

"Just try to . . ."

"Try to what?"

"I dunno. The smell, dude."

"I can't help it."

"I get that. But if you can hold it back for a couple minutes that'd be super-cool."

"I'll try." The last word was strangulated, and ended in a gasp.

I hit ANSWER. "Rick?" Shannon said immediately.

"Well, yeah, Shann, of course it is. This is my phone. Kind of caught up in something right now, though."

"Are you drunk?"

I'd hoped I'd hidden it better. "Shannon, Christ's sake, of course not. Well, a little, yes, obviously. Okay, I'm drunk. What's your point? And why are you calling me?"

"You need to leave."

"I need to what?"

"Didn't you *see my email?*"

"Email? No—when?"

"*Over an hour ago.*"

"Shannon, I'm *at the conference.* I'm talking to people. From all over the place. London, Helsinki, uh, Wisconsin. I can't be checking my phone every ten minutes."

"Haven't you seen the TV?"

"The bar doesn't have a TV."

"*There's no TV?*"

"It's not that kind of bar."

"Rick—you need to get on land."

"I'm *on* land, Shannon—seriously, what the heck?"

"No, you're on a boat."

"But it's *attached* to the land. By . . . walkway things."

"It's in the actual ocean, still, though, right?"

"I guess, *technically*, but . . ."

"On TV they said to stay away from the ocean. Any part of it. That everybody should *stay away from the ocean.*"

"What are you *talking about?*"

Carl grunted again suddenly, far louder than before. This time the growling was coming up out of his mouth, like a long, rasping belch.

"Oh shit," he groaned when it abated. "Oh Jesus fuck." He sounded confused and desperate.

"Shannon," I said, "can you give me a simple, declarative sentence to respond to? Imagine you're texting me. Try that."

She said something but I couldn't hear it because of another sudden barrage of blows on the outer door. It wasn't the kind of sound you get from a person requesting entry. It sounded more like someone trying to break in.

"Busy in here," I shouted. There was a momentary pause, and then the banging sounds started up again, even harder.

"Tell them there's another restroom down the boat," Carl said. He sounded very tired. "My head really hurts. I can't take the banging noise."

I opened my mouth to do that but the banging suddenly stopped. There was silence.

Then what sounded like a scream.

I stared at the door.

"What . . . was that?" I'd forgotten I still had the phone pressed to my ear, and Shannon's voice startled me. It sounded as though she was right there, as if our heads were on pillows alongside each other. Which they never have been, though since my divorce she's the one woman who's seemed to give a damn, my mother being down in Florida and also the most foul-tempered and least maternal person I've ever met.

"I don't . . . know," I said.

"Was it a *scream*?"

"Kind of, yeah." She sounded panicky and I spoke as calmly as I could. 'Look. *Who* is saying *what* on TV?'

"It's on all the stations," she said. "And the Internet. Twitter's gone insane with it. A few hours ago people posting about odd things happening. Kind of, well, nobody really seems to know. Things going weird, near the coast. And not just in one place—everywhere. Not the lakes. Just the ocean. Something's wrong with the ocean."

"But *what*?"

"I don't *know*," she said. "A fog coming in."

"A fog," I said, remembering how it had been on the smokers' deck when I left it . . . What? Ten minutes ago? A dense sea fog. Getting thicker and thicker.

"Right. But then it started to snowball and now they're saying it's not the fog after all, or maybe that's part of it but not the main thing. But nobody *knows*."

"Stay on the line," I told her.

"Hell's going on?" Carl said. His voice sounded weak and strained.

"I have no idea," I said, flipping over to Twitter on my phone. All my follows and followers are business related—tech rivals and bloggers and a bunch of "influencers" and "growth hackers" who are super-annoying but I nonetheless track in case they start trash-talking the company and in particular the fucking RX350i and why it's *still* not on the market. As a result my feed is usually crushingly dull.

One flick with my thumb showed this wasn't the case now. Nothing tech at all. A mass of retweets from news organizations and randomers, blurry footage of people running, others asking if the country was under terrorist attack—and yes, a consistent message urging people to get away from the coast.

"What are you *doing*?" Shannon asked.

"Looking at Twitter. It's a dumpster fire. What the fuck?"

I heard another scream from out in the corridor. This one approached like a siren and went past like one too, as though someone was sprinting down the corridor outside.

The sound suddenly cut off.

The silence afterward seemed so loud that I barely noticed the growling noise from the stall, followed by another explosive release of air and something splashing into the toilet bowl.

"Oh no," Carl said, very quietly. "That's . . . oh no."

"Who's that?" Shannon asked, sounding freaked. "I heard a voice your end."

"I'm . . . in the restroom. It's a guy from the Boston office."

"Carl Hammick?"

"You *know* him?"

"Not in person. But it's my job to know who—"

"Whatever. Shann, what *I* need to know is . . ."

I tailed off. I didn't know what I needed to know. My Twitter feed was still spooling down the screen, absurdly fast, showing more of the same. I flicked sideways to trending stories and saw identical retweets, the same information—or lack of it—being rotated very quickly.

Then one popped up that said: *Santa Monica to be evacuated?*

My heart was thumping in my chest now. It was impossible to believe this was real. But then there was a retweet of something that looked like a genuine news source. The problem with social media is it'll recycle bullshit without anybody stopping to check it has any basis in reality, but then—there it was: a different source saying the same thing.

This source was CNN.

And regardless of the forty-fifth president's views on the matter, I consider CNN to be real fucking news.

There was a thudding sound above me, then a heavy crash. I didn't know the boat well enough to know what would be on the next floor, but it sounded like some large piece of furniture had been overturned. I hoped it was that, anyway—because if the noise had been caused by the collision of a body with something, the person could not have survived.

"Shannon," I said, "where are you right now?"

"In the car," she said. "You're on speaker."

"Going where?"

"Wait . . ." She stopped talking, and I caught the faint sound of other voices in the background.

"Are you with someone?"

"No—it's the radio. There's some guy from the army saying they think *definitely* it's the water now."

"Not a terrorist thing? I saw—"

"No. They bailed on that idea half an hour ago. This isn't terrorists. It's *something in the water.*"

"But what *kind* of thing?"

"They don't *know*. Just *get onto land*, Rick."

I heard another person run past in the corridor, this time shouting—a deep, tearing, guttural noise. It sounded like a man's voice, and he stopped to hammer on the door of the restroom with a truly terrifying degree of force, before running on. "That may not be a straightforward undertaking. Sounds like things are pretty fucked up out there."

"Rick—*get off the boat.*"

The smell was truly appalling now. I'd stopped noticing the warning sound of growling from the stall and further splashing sounds. The last couple of pints I'd drunk had come home to roost, too, and I felt muddle-headed, off-kilter, unprepared. *Really* drunk. So much that it took me a couple of seconds to get my head around the fact my phone was vibrating, again, and work out what that meant.

Another incoming call.

The screen said: PETER???—LONDON

"Hang on, Shann. Don't go away."

"What are you—"

I muted her and accepted the call. "Pete?"

"Where are you?" Pete said. He sounded terse and clipped and pretty drunk but a lot more together than I felt.

"The john."

"Which one?"

"The small one you showed me. Near the bar."

"Is the door locked?"

"Oh yes."

"Good. Keep it that way."

"What the hell's going on? Where are you?"

"Up on top. Of the boat. Came up here with Inka to . . . doesn't matter."

"Is she there with you?"

"Not anymore. I pushed her down the stairs."

"You . . . *what?*"

"We left the bar because she was feeling queasy. I assumed it was just jetlag combined with a truly astonishing amount of vodka, and also perhaps she had something else in mind—but no, she genuinely wasn't feeling well. So I escorted her to the restroom. When she came back out she said she felt better and so we came up on the top deck for some air but then she started behaving *extremely* strangely and . . ."

"Pete, wait one second. My PA's on the other line."

I flipped over and said: "Have you heard anything new?"

"No," Shannon said. "They're recycling the same clip."

"Are you still driving?"

"Yes. And Rick—"

I cut her off and flipped back to Pete. He'd evidently missed what I'd said and just kept talking in the meantime. ". . . blood dripping down my fucking cheek. I had no choice—*she was trying to bite my face off.*"

"Christ," I said. "Is anybody else up there?"

"No. Hang on, shit. I can smell burning."

"What kind of burning?"

"The *burning* kind of burning, Rick. I . . . oh. In the fog . . . there's a glow. I think the burning smell's coming from the shore."

"Where the walkways are?"

"No. The other shore. Where *the city is*."

I abruptly remembered there was one thing at least that I could do to improve the situation. I pulled out my cigarettes and lit one.

"You can't smoke in here," Carl said from the stall. His voice sounded weak.

"Seriously? Have you even been *listening*?"

"It's no-smoking in here."

"This room smells like I am literally *inside a turd*, Carl. That's on you. So deal with the fucking smoke."

"Who's that?" Peter said in my ear.

"Carl. From Boston."

"I know Carl. But what was that about a smell?"

"He's . . . Carl's experiencing intestinal difficulties."

"Oh fucking hell. Get out of there," Peter said, very seriously. "Get the fuck out. Now."

"You told me to stay *in* here."

"Yes, but that's what happened with Inka. Weren't you *listening*?"

"I missed that part—I flipped across to my PA to check she was okay.'

"Inka's stomach . . . It gave out. When we were up here. It growled and then there was a flood of—it was truly disgusting. But then she said, "Oh, I feel a lot better now," and *that's* when she came at me and tried to bite my—"

"Carl," I said. "How're your guts feeling now?"

The answer came in the shape of a sound in the stall. Not a growl, but an explosive impact of something in water.

"Oh no," he said. "There's more blood in it."

"*More blood*?"

"It's everywhere."

I took a cautious step back from the cabin door. From this angle I could see a patch of the floor within the stall. It was liberally splattered with red. I looked up and saw there were splashes of blood all the way to the ceiling too.

"But . . . I feel better," Carl said. "A lot better."

I heard running feet again outside the cabin. More than one set. A distant shout, and broken, high-pitched laughter.

"I think it's over," Carl said. There was a strange, dreamy quality to his voice. "Yes. I feel fine."

I'd lowered the phone but I could hear Pete's voice from the speaker, still shouting at me to get out. "Uh, maybe you should stay where you are," I told Carl. "And I'll go find a doctor or something."

"I'm good."

"There's *blood all over the place.*"

"That's okay. Honestly, Rick—it's all fine." His voice sounded normal. Strong, confident. "And thanks for being a pal. Is that Peter Stringer you're talking to? From London?"

Stringer, *that* was it. "Yes."

"He's a solid guy. We should go find him—and work out what the hell's going on out there."

I heard Carl sliding the latch on the stall door, and mainly I was thinking: Yeah, that's an actual plan. Three of us, three guys together—that had to give us a decent chance against . . . whatever the hell was going on out there. Right?

But then I saw that while Carl was approaching the door inside the stall, his pants were still down around his ankles. That seemed weird to me.

When he opened the door I semi-recognized him. We'd met before at some event or other. Though not like this. His lower half was naked and awash with red and brown liquids, and his eyes were bleeding down his face.

"I'm hungry," he said, looking at my throat.

I kicked the stall door back at him as hard as I could.

He was knocked back into the stall, banging his head hard against the tiled wall. He stayed on his feet, however—slip-sliding in the confined space because of all the stuff on the floor, but remaining upright.

I heard Pete's voice shouting at me to tell him what was going on, and put the phone back to my ear.

"Carl's . . . I don't think he's okay anymore," I said.

"Knock him out," Pete said. "Do whatever it takes. Keep doing it until you're sure it's done. I had to kick Inka down the stairs three fucking times before she stayed down."

I realized Carl was coming at me again and I slammed my foot into the stall door even harder this time. He crashed back down into the narrow space between the toilet and the wall. Started to move again, but sluggishly. As he turned his head I saw that the back of it wasn't the normal shape. Impact with the wall had broken his skull.

He was still trying to get up, though, reaching out with hands that were trembling and shaking.

"Pete—what the hell are we going to do?"

"We've got to get off this boat," he said.

"*How?*"

"Come find me up top."

"Can't you come down here instead?"

"Look, mate, this ship is full of people trying to kill people. I'm up for working together on this but I'd be out of my fucking mind coming back down to where you are."

"Nice. Seems last year's team-building weekend was a waste of money, hey."

"There's no 'i' in team, you twat, and *I* do not want to get *fucking killed.*"

"Wait a second."

Still watching Carl—he'd managed to lever himself up halfway to his feet again, but was still trapped behind the cistern, one eye open, the other closed—I flipped to the other line on my phone. "Shannon?"

"I'm still here," she said. "What's going on?"

"Carl Hammick is trying to kill me."

"Because of the delay on the RX350i?"

"*No*, Shann. Because *he's lost his fucking mind.*"

"Get out of there. I'll be as fast as I can."

"What are you talking about?"

"I'm coming to get you."

"You're . . . Shannon, it will take *days* to drive here from Boston."

"You don't listen to a single word I say, do you?"

"I do, but . . ."

"If you *had*, you'd have heard me saying earlier in the week that because you were going to be out of town, I'd decided to visit my mother in Las Vegas."

"You're in *Vegas?*"

"Not anymore. I'm . . . oh, gosh."

"What?"

"Another accident. It's . . . God, that's horrible. There's dead . . . and people are . . . Eurgh. Everyone's driving like maniacs. Mainly going the other way."

"But you're . . ."

"Coming as fast as I can."

"But why would you even *do* that?"

"Because I'm your PA, you dick. It's my job."

"It's really *not*, Shannon. And Las Vegas is a very long way from Long Beach. I mean, like, hours and hours."

"Unless it gets much worse than this I think I can do it in five, and I've been on the road nearly two hours already and I'm driving as fast as I can. I'm going to hang up now so I can focus on the road, okay? I'll call back in a while."

"But what about your mom? Will she be safe?"

"Nobody's affected in Vegas. It's a long way from the ocean. As a precaution they've made everyone stay indoors wherever they were when the news broke. My mom's locked inside the Flamingo Casino with a hundred bucks in change and a long line of margaritas and literally could not be happier. Just get off the boat, Rick."

And then she was gone.

I turned just in time to see Carl had managed to haul himself to his feet again and was shambling in my direction, grasping hands outstretched toward me.

I braced myself against the wall and kicked him in the chest as hard as I could. I didn't land my foot squarely, though, and so he spun lop-sidedly away, crashing into the urinal I'd used, slipping and smacking his face really hard into the metal fixture at the top.

The sound this made was bad and the way he crashed onto the ground looked extremely final, and I realized with incredulous bafflement both that he'd looked exactly the way they made these things look on television and also that I'd just killed Carl Hammick from the Wisconsin office.

Except I hadn't. After maybe three seconds of stillness, his fingers started to twitch, and his shoulders bunched as some impulse deep inside pushed him toward movement again.

I remembered I'd left Peter hanging. I kept a close eye on Carl and flipped to the other line. "You still there?"

"Look, I'll meet you halfway," Pete said. "You're right. I can't expect you to come all the way up here, and anyway that's not how we're going to get off the boat."

"Deal."

"I'll meet you at reception. Where I saw you when you first arrived. That's where the main walkway is. Be as quick as you can, Rick. I'm not going to wait forever."

"Understood."

I ended the call, stowed my phone in my pocket. Carl was pushing himself up from the floor, slowly but irrevocably. I tried to think of something to say but couldn't imagine what it would be, and doubted he'd even understand it any more.

So I put my ear against the cabin door and listened. I could hear noises out there, but they seemed distant and I couldn't tell what they were. The one lesson I learned from years of video games as a teenager is when you reach a new level you don't screw around. You get going immediately, before the situation has a chance to get worse.

I opened the door and stuck my head out.

The first thing I noticed was a long splash of blood on the opposite wall of the hallway. It was still dripping. There was another splash of something much darker and brown below it. It smelled bad and was still dripping too.

I glanced left, back toward the bar. Some of the sounds were coming from there. They weren't good sounds, and some of them were to do with the fact the place looked like it was on fire. An orange glow, crackling noises, the smell of smoke.

Nonetheless I started cautiously in that direction, as I recalled there was a lateral sub-corridor that would take me to the outer and much wider walkway, which I figured would be a faster and safer way to the stairs that'd take me down the single flight to the reception level.

I'd barely gone three yards before someone came lurching out of the sub-corridor. A waiter. One I'd been dealing with earlier, in fact—who'd put my personal Amex by the register so I could run a room tab. The card was still in there but I decided it was going to stay that way. The left side of the barman's face was raw and burned and he was missing an eye and most of one check and I could see his teeth through the hole. He was dragging one leg behind as he stumbled toward me, too, and leaving an unpleasant brown trail, but nonetheless closing in fast.

I swept my foot to hook out his good leg, and as he crashed to the ground I turned and ran back the other way.

The door to the toilets flew open as I got level, smacking me into the wall. Carl came staggering out, still with his pants around his ankles, still intent on getting his hands around my neck.

He managed it, too, but some instinctive memory triggered me to use the single piece of useful advice my mother ever gave me. I grabbed him by both ears and head-butted him on the bridge of the nose. It's because of the implications of nuggets of maternal wisdom like this that I've never blamed my father for leaving home when I was nine.

Carl collapsed to the ground and I ran.

It was plain sailing down to the open area where the expensive little wine and cosmetics concessions were. As I hurtled toward the grand staircase, however, jumping over the prone body of someone I'd been drinking with earlier, I saw a woman coming up to my level. She was completely naked and liberally splattered with blood and it was clear both that none of it was hers and that she was keen to add to her collection.

She saw me and came running, and I didn't know for sure what language she was screaming in but I thought it was probably German, which would imply the Dusseldorf office. She was fast, and gleeful, and next thing I knew I was smashing backward into a curved glass cabinet that was probably eighty years old and quite valuable. Thankfully I hit it at an angle and the shattered glass didn't sever anything important, but then the woman was straddling me and trying to stuff a thumb deep into each of my eyes.

Her breath smelt awful, the kind of stench Carl had been producing in the toilet, but coming up the other way, out of her mouth. My eyes started to sparkle and meanwhile she was feverishly trying to knee me in the balls, so I gathered all the strength I could muster and planted both feet firmly on the ground and thrust upward, trying to buck her off.

It didn't work but for a moment she was off-balance at least, and so I twisted sideways instead, managing to roll on top of her. I banged her head down onto the parquet flooring—very hard—and scrabbled to my feet. She was snarling and I could barely see anything because of the stars in my eyes, but as she started to get up I sent a swinging kick at her head and managed to catch her in the jaw.

I didn't wait to see her land but sprinted the remaining yards to the stairs, leaping down most of the first flight in one jump. This meant I nearly went sprawling and bounced painfully into the wall on the next return, but thankfully I kept my feet and half-ran and half-fell down the next flight.

As I landed chaotically in the reception area I saw a group of people attacking each other. It was impossible to tell who was trying to kill whom. It's possible everybody was trying at once. I also saw Peter, at the reception desk, repeatedly smacking someone's forehead down onto its polished walnut surface, lifting it up and bringing it down again.

He saw me coming, whacked the person's head down one final time—there was enough of their face left for me to recognize him as the clerk who'd checked me in when I arrived—and turned to me, panting. His face and shirt were smeared with something brown. "You took your fucking time, mate."

I sniffed. "Are you covered in shit?"

"Yes."

"Why?"

"I thought it might help."

"Again—*why?*"

"When I came down the steps from the top deck I found out Inka was still alive even though both her legs were broken. She grabbed my ankle and I fell down. We ended up rolling around in her, well, her *shit*, until I could get away from her again. I thought about wiping it off but then I wondered if maybe it'd help, if the smell would make these fucking loonies think I was one of them or something."

"Does it work?"

"Not even slightly. It was a bad idea."

"Hell yes."

As we ran to the walkway Pete dodged over to the souvenir store, undoing his shirt and throwing it to the ground. Grabbed a *Queen Mary* sweatshirt and pulled it on.

As he turned back he also picked up a souvenir coffee mug, shaped like one of the ship's funnels.

"Why the hell are you—"

I ducked just in time and the mug reached the target he'd intended—the head of the naked woman from upstairs, who'd come running up behind me. The mug smashed to pieces on her face and she fell like a sack of bricks.

"Dusseldorf?" I asked as we looked down at her.

"No," he said. "Warsaw."

"Oh. Well, thanks anyway."

"You're welcome. Now let's get the hell off this boat."

We ran through the doors and out into the fresh air, along the metal walkway toward the staircase that'd get us down to the parking lot. "Why are *we* okay, though? Why isn't this happening to us too?"

"Don't know, don't care," Pete said. "That is a problem for another time, if ever."

"Jesus—look at it back in there."

There were now forty people or more in the reception area—all tearing at each other—with others joining them from above and below. It was hard to tell who were victims and which were attackers, though I did spot the guy from Madrid who'd bought me a pint I never got to drink, and it seemed like he was trying to escape, rather than kill. "Do you think we should try to . . ."

"Fuck that," I said. "I'm not going in there."

"I'm of like mind," Peter admitted. "But what the hell *are* we going to do?"

"Get off the boat. Properly. Onto dry land."

"Obviously," he said, "but look." He pointed down toward the dock area. Figures were running back and forth, screaming. Some had weapons. Others were attacking people with their bare hands. "It's no better down there."

"So we find somewhere to hole up."

"For how long? And *then* what?"

"My PA is coming."

"Shannon?"

"How the hell do you know who my PA is?"

"Seriously? Everybody knows you stole her from the Chicago office by doubling her salary. All the other PAs are seriously pissed off about it."

"Okay, well, maybe that wasn't such a bad decision, okay? She's on her way from Vegas right now to pick me up."

"That's an impressive level of dedication."

"This is my point."

"She may not make it here, you know that."

"I do. But I owe it to her to be ready and waiting if she does."

"Definitely." He reached into his jacket pocket, pulled out two small bottles, and handed one to me. "Here."

"Hell is it?"

"Jack Daniel's," he said. "Nicked them off the plane."

"You do good work, Pete."

"Cheers." We knocked the drinks back in one, threw the bottles away and ran together to the stairwell and pattered down the three flights to ground level, pausing only to simultaneously kick a fat man who tried to throw himself down on us from the flight above, but thankfully missed us and instead landed with a bad-sounding crunch on the concrete landing.

At the bottom we stepped cautiously out into the parking lot. A car was on fire in the corner. In fact, every car I could see was in flames. The air was full of smoke and choked with the smell of burning tires and the sound of distant sirens. A helicopter flew fast and low over our heads but with no intention of stopping—instead heading out over the bay. When it was clear of land a soldier stuck a huge machine gun out of the side door and started firing down into the water.

"That doesn't seem like a positive development," Peter said.

"No. You figure something even worse is fixing to come out of the ocean?"

"Looks that way. Christ."

"We've got to get farther from the ocean—and fast. Over the causeway and onto the mainland."

"But how's Shannon going to know where to come?"

"She knows where the conference was. She'll have established the ways in and out. Knowing Shannon, she'll text me a map with estimated walking/ running/fleeing times under post-apocalyptic conditions, and knowing her, it'll be right."

We headed across the parking lot toward the access road to the bridge back to the mainland. We both ran in a relaxed mode, keeping it loose, not knowing how far we were going to have to go. Pete clocked my style and nodded approvingly. "You run?"

"Of course," I said. "Though only a 5k or so, couple,-three times a week."

"Me too. I hope that'll be enough."

"You'll be fine. Your form's pretty good. You still stink of shit, though."

"*Everybody* does, Rick. I never realized the end times would smell this bad."

"Me neither. And it's only going to get worse."

As we ran onto the bridge we watched a group of four women in the middle, as they took each other's hands, stepped up onto the ledge, and threw themselves silently into the bay.

"I fear you're right. But there's one thing at least."

"What's that?" I heard shouting behind and glanced back to see that a group of men were staggering out of the parking lot. Arms outstretched. Coming for us.

Peter saw them too, and picked up the pace. "Nobody's going to give a damn about the RX350i being late."

Then both of us were laughing as we ran faster and faster, over the bridge and toward a city on fire.

# HAUNT

## SIOBHAN CARROLL

May 31, 1799
INDIAN OCEAN
17°10'N, BY RECKONING 9°W OFF CAPE NEGRAIS

Swift did not think about the *Zong*. The *Minerva* was a different kind of ship, plagued by different kinds of misery. Her hull, for one. Swift did not like the feel of the boards beneath the waterline. Leaning over the jollyboat's gunnel, he plunged his arm deeper into the ocean, seeking further damage.

"How's she fare?"

Swift shook the water off his arm. "A stern leak between wind-and-water," he said. "'Tis an ill wound for an old ship to bear." He glanced at the sun, a yellow smear in a haze of gray. A storm was brewing.

"And her hull wants copper-plating," Decurrs stated. An able seaman, he heard what Swift did not say. "We must move quickly. Pass him the oakum, boy."

There were three of them in the jollyboat: Decurrs to manage the oars, Swift to patch, and the watch-boy to assist and learn. But, like her mistress, the *Minerva*'s jollyboat was ill-provided for the sea, and the boy had been bailing since they'd launched her. Swift reached for the oakum himself.

"Mind how the patch goes," Decurrs said to the boy, as Swift stuffed the sticky fibers between the boards and laid over the tarred canvas. "When the waves surge high, the oakum will swell. The leak will suck the canvas inwards, stopping her mouth." Decurrs raised the oar to fend off the hull. The jollyboat knocked against the ship anyway, a jolt that shuddered into their bones.

"Aye," the boy said. He'd left off bailing and was staring intently at the horizon. "Look," he said suddenly. "To starboard. '*A something in the sky!*'

Swift wiped algae scum onto his trousers. "Hand me the sheet-lead," he said.

"*A haunt!*" The boy said. "It follows us!"

"The sheet-lead," Swift snapped, "and quick about it."

But it was Decurrs who handed Swift the gray sheet of metal and who helped him nail it to the *Minerva*'s hull. Like Swift, Decurrs did not scan the horizon for phantoms. He kept his eyes trained on his hands, on the work that could save or kill them.

"The Nightmare Life-in-Death," the boy breathed. "Just as the ballad said."

"The Devil take your ghosts."

Swift ran his hand over the edge of the sheet-lead, making sure the patch lay flush. There was something in the corner of his eye. A flicker of white.

Back aboard ship, Swift was taken aside by Captain Maxwell. "How's she fare?"

Swift rubbed his chin thoughtfully. His hands were still gummy with the oakum pine-tar that gave sailors their name. It smelled like a distant forest, like a place he'd never see.

"The patch will hold," Swift said. "But if the seas run high again . . ."

Maxwell stroked his beard. Swift could see the man considering his charge. The *Minerva* was a three-masted ship with eleven passengers aboard, forty-eight crew, and a cargo of teak bound for Madras. To turn back to Rangoon would delay the shipment by weeks, and the Company must have its profits.

*I should not have shipped on the* Minerva, Swift thought. *I should have waited for a better berth.*

"The coast is a lee shore," the Captain said, "and her waters are shallow. We will make for Madras." He coughed, wetly, against his arm. Then he said, awkwardly: "The *serang* says one of the Lascars saw . . . something in the swells. Did you happen to spy anything? In the waves?"

Near the windlass, Decurrs was scolding the boy. The boy protested vigorously, pointing toward the horizon.

"No, sir," Swift said. "We saw nothing. Nothing at all."

◄◦►

The gale blew into their teeth on the first of June, a choking whirl of greenish mist. "She's taking on water," came the cry from below. Swift clung close to the windward rigging of the mainmast as he climbed, flattening his body against the damp ropes. Far below him, the deck heaved with the rising swells.

On the yard he pressed his belly against the hard beam and stepped sideways onto the shivering footrope. It was his stomach, now, that bore his weight as his hands clawed in the heavy canvas of the mainsail. Beside him, two other able seamen did the same, rushing to tie up the ship's largest sail before the winds rose.

A cry rang down the yard. One of the Chinese sailors had straightened up, pointing at something behind the curtain of rain. Swift hastily turned back to his reef knot, even as the Chinese sailor straightened further, pressing his weight back on the footrope at the very moment the ship rolled. A flurry of motion, and the man fell out of Swift's vision.

A crash below told Swift the sailor had slammed into the deck. "*A kinder death than drowning,*" the old salts said. In the rising wind the Chinese sailor's loose canvas flapped like the wing of an angry bird.

"Belay that sail!"

A Lascar slid sideways on the yard to take his shipmate's place. The Indian sailor worked quickly, his eyes intent on the task. His own reef knots tied, Swift pulled himself back to the standing rigging and slid back to the frenzy of the deck. The Chinese sailor's body rested amidships. His fellow seamen stepped around him, their eyes on their assigned lines.

Swift leaned over the man—a young fellow, his eyes wide, staring at the sky. A red stain spread beneath his body, mingling with the wash on the deck.

"He saw a ghost," said the second belay, eyes on his line. "That's what he screamed. A *sei-gweilo* in the waves."

"Belay that nonsense." Swift ran his palm over the Chinese sailor's eyes, doing what he could to close them. When he raised his hand a half-moon of white showed through, as though the man's spirit studied Swift from the other side. Swift felt a chill that had nothing to do with his sodden clothing, or the rising gale.

"Pumps in full labor," said a voice. It was Manbacchus, one of the Lascars. "She takes water."

Swift felt the heaviness in his gut, what the old dogs called the "sinking feeling." He hoped it would not come to that.

⬥

Crouched in the forecastle, the starboard watch discussed the rumors. The sails were close-reefed and the leak patched, but still the *Minerva* took on water. They said the bilge smelled almost sweet. A bad sign.

"The Lascars say there is a haunt that follows our wake," Holdfast Muhammad said. Though he hailed from London, Holdfast had the tongue, and often he passed the whisper from the other Mussulmen aboard. "They say it pressed A-kou."

"There *is* a haunt," their mess-boy said proudly. "I saw it, when we were in the jollyboat."

"You saw a cloud," Swift said sourly. "For I too was in that jollyboat and I saw no such thing."

But the tide of conversation was already moving past him.

"I saw a haunt off Ireland once," said Glosse, the third mate. "I'm no Frenchman to turn tail and run, but I tell you boys, I was damnably scarified."

"You saw a haunt and lived to speak of it? You're a lucky man, Glosse," Decurrs said.

"That I am, boys." Glosse laughed. "A jack tar with the devil's own luck."

"It could be the Dutchman that follows us," mused the fresh-faced sailor they called Pretty Pol. "Him that cursed the name of God. He cannot put into port now, but must sail the seas endlessly, eating only red iron and gall. He seeks out all the old sinners of the sea, to press them for his crew."

"It could be the *Mystery*," the boy said. "The slave ship where the Negroes bound the captain to the mast, and forced him to sail 'til the end of time."

"That's the *Wake*," said Pol. "The *Mystery* was the slave ship turned into a rock, to stand to this day as a warning. One of its crew was a magician. He killed the Negroes first, and then the sailors, and last he bound the captain to the foremast, and forced him to stand watch 'til the Devil came to claim him."

The forecastle had grown quieter at the mention of slave ships. Decurrs watched the boards, Holdfast Muhammad, and Glosse. Swift knew then that they'd all worked the Trade.

"Warning of what?" The boy was deaf to the silence swelling around him. "And why would a tar kill all aboard?"

"Perhaps it was a Negro that was meant," Cobb said, thinking aloud. "For plantation men sometimes call Negroes *blacke*, on account of their complexion."

Pol, whose own deep tan had been put down as *blacke* in the ship's log, scoffed. "'Twas one of us, a tar, who told me that tale," he said. "And 'twas one of us, a tar, that sunk that ship. But he was a Yorkshireman."

"Ah," Cobb said. Everyone knew it was unlucky to sail with Yorkshiremen.

The boy's brow remained furrowed. "But why would a tar kill all aboard? On a slave ship? If—"

"You've not sailed under many captains," Glosse said. The crew laughed the way men do when they're eager to change the subject.

"What do you think, Swift?" said Holdfast Muhammad. "Does your patch still hold?" It was telling, Swift thought, that the man would now rather talk of leaks than haunt-ships.

"She holds," Swift said. "The *Minerva* has life in her yet."

The men settled under the forecastle, listening to the drum of rain above. Swift rubbed his scarred hands together for warmth. He did not think about the *Zong*.

⟨◦⟩

For three days, they labored constantly at pumping. Even the Gunner, who'd normally be excused from such work, turned his blackened hands to the pump. Sailors like Swift, who could handle carpenters' tools, did their best to repair the pumps as they choked with the sand-ballast drifting free in the water-logged hold.

"Is there else you can do to stop the water?" Captain Maxwell was regretting his decision to sail without a carpenter, Swift could tell, but it was too late now.

"Not in this sea," Swift said. "We must get to port, if we're to save her."

The captain nodded, and looked over the rain-misted deck to where passengers huddled—a small group of women, merchants, and servants, European, Indian, and Malay, seeking relief from cramped quarters.

"So be it," he said. "We'll set what sail we can and make for the coast." Suddenly the captain's eyes widened. "What's that?"

Alarmed, Swift squinted his eyes against the rain. At the rear of the ship a small light wandered erratically up the mizzen mast. For a moment Swift thought it was a man carrying a candle, and he was filled with anger at whatever fool would bring an open flame into the rigging. Then he saw how the flame moved. Lithely. As though it were alive.

"St. Elme's fire," one of the tars murmured. "Quick, mark where she lands."

"Best get below decks now," Captain Maxwell advised his passengers, his voice betraying a hint of strain. "The wind is picking up."

The flame flew suddenly to the middle of the ship, and soared to the top of the main mast. It hovered there, about a foot above the spar.

"The *Supero Santo*. It guides the haunt to us!"

"It predicts how many will drown," a tar corrected.

"If atop, and only one, it means a storm will soon be over. We should all bid it goodspeed."

The flame broke into three pieces and sank toward the deck. Sailors recoiled, scrambling to get out of the way of the spirit-fire. The corpusants hovered over the *Minerva*'s dark boards, still and silent.

"Three a-deck," the captain muttered, almost under his breath. "That's no good omen."

Swift's mess-boy edged forward, studying the triangle of flames with a cat's intensity. Decurrs yanked the boy back and cuffed him on the ear.

"Oh look," one of the European passengers said. "There's more."

Horrified, Swift followed the passengers' gaze over the side of the vessel, to where a hundred or so of the tiny flames reeled and spun. Beneath the corpusants, the ocean burned like witch's oil, green and blue.

"*Allahumma rahmataka arju*," prayed one of the Mussulmen, "*fala takilni ila nafsi tarfata 'ain . . .*"

"Wish them goodspeed," the captain ordered, his voice thick. "And see to your lines."

"Have you ever seen that?" The boy asked as his messmates hurried to their stations. "Saint Elme's fire? And so many of them? What does it mean?"

Swift had no answer. Around him, he could feel the wind rising.

‹o›

"I've drowned no cat and killed no albatross," Glosse said in the mess. Above the starboard watch's heads the second day of the gale howled and roared. "I have whistled down no wind. Yet death-fires reel about our rigging, and the damned follow our wake, sending good tars to their deaths."

"It's not the haunt-ship that made A-kou lose his footing," said Holdfast. "The Lascars say he had hungry eyes."

"It was the haunt-ship that killed him," Glosse said firmly. "And it'll kill us all until we give it what it wants."

Swift's throat was dry. He wanted no part in this.

"And what does it want?" Decurrs said sharply. "Have you hailed that vessel, Glosse? Have you taken a message from the dead?"

"I am no fool, Decurrs, to hail a haunt. No," Glosse said. "In dreams I heard it so. My lost brother came to me last night, his mouth full of seaweed and his shoes full of sand. In his hands he held a copy of our crew's list, burning and smoldering. As I looked closer I saw one of those names afire, and knew then it was the Jonah who'd cursed us."

"Whose name was it?" The boy sounded a bit too eager.

"If I had my letters I could tell you," Glosse said. "But I'm no reading man. We have a Jonah aboard, and the haunt-ship wants him. That's all I need to know."

The rain drummed above their heads. The mess-table, suspended from the ceiling, creaked on its chains.

"And what do you wish us to do, Glosse?" Decurrs's words jabbed the air. "Hunt down a Lascar to hang? For so they did on your last berth, or so I'm told." There was a glitter in Decurrs's eye. He was one of those who thought the captain had made a poor choice in Glosse, that the position of third mate should have gone to a more senior seaman.

The old fear thrilled through Swift. He shook his head warningly at Decurrs. Glosse was a mate now, after all, and had the power of the lash.

Holdfast Muhammad looked up from the swinging mess-table, his face grave. "Is that true, Glosse? I'll pass no whisper for you if it's so."

Glosse waved his hand. "That was a different matter," he said. "A theft."

"The captain would not look kindly on you if you stir mutiny among the Lascars," Decurrs said. His eyes met Swift's, and Swift knew Decurrs expected him to speak up, to draw on his authority as the other old hand in the mess. Swift dropped his gaze.

Glosse forced a smile on his face. "Now, now, fellows," he said. "What's this talk of mutiny? I ask only that you keep your ears and eyes open, that's all. "'Tis no more than good tars should do."

Tension loomed around them, and then the boy spoke up. "Perhaps the haunt is a mutiny ship," he said helpfully. "Like the *Eagle*."

"Perhaps it's your arse," Cobb said. The men laughed. But Glosse gave Decurrs a sidelong glance and Swift knew it was not over between them.

◀◦▶

Three days later, the gale winds still blew, and the ship pitched low and heavy. The waves ran mountains high. Swift, his arms numb with fatigue, slipped across the wet deck to his station. They would keep the *Minerva* before the wind, with bare poles.

At three bells, a sailor rushed up from below to shout in the captain's ear. Someone else took up the cry, the words straining over the roar of the wind. "Water's reached the lower deck."

Captain Maxwell kept his eyes on the yards. "Keep to your stations," he shouted, but his words were muffled by the gale.

The *Minerva* veered. Lashed though he was, Swift had to hook his hand around a wooden cleat to steady his footing. Looking toward the main mast, he saw to his horror that the reefed sail had come loose. One of the knots had been poorly tied—perhaps the dead sailor's, perhaps Swift's own—and now they might die for it.

The *Minerva* lurched as the loose sail caught the wind. Captain Maxwell, to his credit, did not hesitate. "Stand by to cut away the main mast!"

The sailor closest to the axe stood stupefied, his gaze transfixed by the terrible swell of the sail. Holdfast Muhammad undid his rope-anchor and slid his way over to the axe. Balancing like a man on a tightrope, he carried it over the tilting deck to the tallest mast on the ship. Some of the landsmen moved to join him, machetes in hand. The sharp crashes of their blows were muted by the deafening wind.

Swift could not help but turn to watch the mainmast shudder. After an age the mast sagged sideways, and with agonizing slowness tilted into the ocean. Such was the wind-sound that he could not hear it fall, but he saw the mast drop, and saw also the terrifying snarl of rope and timbers that moved with it.

"No," Swift said. They had not cut away the rigging properly. He ducked as the stays tore loose. Wood splintered. Heavy wooden blocks careened across the deck.

The captain shouted orders into the wind, but no one could hear him. Horrified, Swift watched the ocean rise up behind the larboard gunwale. Distracted, the helmsman had let the ship broach to. Now, broadside to the wind, the *Minerva*'s deck tilted into a wall of water.

The wave smashed across the deck. Swift grabbed hold of a cleat, struggling to keep his footing as warm seawater drenched him. The ship's bell clanged faintly, desperately. *Abandon ship.*

A Malay woman staggered out of a hatchway. Swift stretched a hand to her, grabbing her by the wrist.

"Help me," he shouted to his fellow sailors. He could not hear his own words above the wind-roar, but Decurrs, clinging to the gunwale, nodded. Together they managed to pull the confused woman, her heavy skirts darkening with water, back to the quarterdeck. Swift looked for a stray sheet with which to lash her to the standing rigging, but the water on the deck seemed to be washing ever higher.

Swift pulled the woman to the windward side of the mizzen shrouds and showed her how to grasp the thick black ropes from the sides. "Keep a vertical rope between your legs," he yelled in her ear, and stepped onto the horizontal ratlines.

Together, he, the woman and Decurrs climbed up, away from the ocean. He could hear faint screams from below. The lower decks were almost fully submerged —one or two of the passengers must be searching for air against the ceiling. It would not last long.

Captain Maxwell clung to the standing rigging above their heads. He nodded upwards, gesturing that the woman should enter the crow's nest. They passed her silently through the lubber's hole, then followed themselves. A collection of passengers clung to each other on the firmer footing of the crow's nest, limbs slipping and flailing as the ship rolled. Swift kept his arm locked around a shroud, as did Decurrs.

After a time, the wind died. Cries and prayers drifted up from the rigging, calls to God and to Allah. The relentless wash of waves surrounded them.

"How many do you think are clinging to this mast?" Decurrs said in his ear. "Look down." Swift did and saw a muddle of bodies. Thirty, maybe forty souls clung to the mizzen, dangling above the seethe. If the mast collapsed, they would all perish.

Swift followed Decurrs down, climbing recklessly, hand over hand. Pulling out his belt-knife, he sawed at the sling-ropes that bound the mizzen yard to the mast. Beside him Decurrs did the same. The yard arm sagged, then dropped away, releasing its weight with a flurry of sail. Below them, someone screamed.

They rested in the rigging, swaying back and forth in the glowering night. It seemed the *Minerva* would not sink; this sometimes happened when water had covered the initial leak, and the ship carried a wood cargo. But she could not sail, either. The *Minerva* was not a ship anymore, and not yet a wreck. Something in-between.

⤖

Dawn cracked the sky, but brought no hope with it. The sea ran mountains high, raising and plummeting the remains of the *Minerva* into the troughs of its waves. Men and women clung to wet rigging, while the spray of wind-driven foam whirled about them. Most held to the mizzen mast rigging; a few sailors near the front of the ship had managed to scramble up the foremast. The stump of the main mast had offered no purchase to anyone. Somehow, through all this, the ship stayed afloat, though its upper deck was going to pieces, a strew of boards and ropes. The *Minerva* seemed to have found her level. She might float like this for many days, Swift realized.

Swift climbed up to the crow's nest to check on the passengers. A European woman on the mizzen-top was shivering; she was clad only in a shift and straw petticoat. Swift offered her his jacket.

"Thank you, sir," she said. "My name is Mrs. Newman. I am much obliged."

Captain Maxwell, his collar turned up, stared at the waves. Looking down at the swamped ship, Swift racked his brains, searching for something that could save them. The jollyboat was gone, dragged beneath the waves. Perhaps they could fashion a raft? The quarterdeck beneath the mizzen was bare when the waves receded, but the violence of the sea was such that nobody dared climb down to her, for fear of being carried away.

"Someone will find us, surely," said Mrs. Newman.

"Oh aye," Captain Maxwell said. "They surely will." He did not sound convinced. The man kept staring at the ocean, his face set. Swift did not like his look.

"I will go below," Swift said, "and see if there is anything useful in the wash." He said it as much to the passengers as to the captain; they should know that things were being done. But as he climbed down the rigging he felt despair roll over him. They were clinging to the remains of two masts above the remains of a ship that could no longer sail. They were at the mercy of wind and current now, in the Bay of Bengal, in monsoon season.

He climbed around the shivering sailors and landsmen until the rigging grew too crowded to pass. Embracing the shrouds, he watched the flotsam that swept to and fro across the quarterdeck, hoping to spy something useful, knowing that even if he did, the waves were too high to fetch it.

Resigned, Swift climbed back to the upper rigging. He rested beside the Gunner, who had taken up position below the crow's nest.

"Do you think it a sin to eat a man?" the Gunner said.

The question made Swift's scalp crawl. Swift had had little to do with the officer during the voyage. It was pirates and Indian Ocean slavers the Gunner watched for. And mutiny, of course.

"By God, sir," Swift said. "It will not come to that."

"I've been wrecked before," the Gunner replied. "It will come." He rested his chin on a ratline and closed his eyes.

◄◦►

The wind died. The sun stood overhead, vertical and bloody. Still the *Minerva* did not sink.

Swift's throat was beginning to ache with thirst. He fumbled for a still-damp corner of his shirt. Tilting it to his mouth, he succeeded in squeezing free a drop or two.

"This is how it starts," the Gunner said, watching him. His eyes were sunken and bloodshot, a sure sign of thirst. "When we are driven to drink salt water, that's when destruction comes."

"You should not talk so much," Swift said. He realized as soon as he spoke that he'd left off the obligatory "sir." But the man did not deserve it, and he could not whip Swift now. "You'll scare the women."

The Gunner shrugged to show it did not matter, and lay back against the shrouds.

"We could dip our coats," said a voice from below. Glancing down, Swift recognized his mess-boy huddled between two Lascars. He was surprised at his own surge of relief: he was glad the boy had lived.

The boy said again, in a small voice: "Captain Inglefield, in his Narrative, said he dipped his coat in the water and lay against it, so the water seeped into his flesh and left the salt on his skin."

"Is such a thing possible?" A tar, dug into a lower ratline, sounded doubtful.

"Let us try," Swift said. He did not say, "It will at least keep us busy." Anything was better than lying endlessly against this swaying grid of ropes, thinking on death. He was a sailor: when Death came calling, he wanted it to catch him doing something useful.

A sailor donated his jacket. They fastened a rope belt to it and passed it down the ladder, so the lowest man could dip it into the ocean before passing it back up. It was a laborious, careful task on a swaying mast—exactly the thing to occupy a man and keep his thoughts from dreadful tales.

The women, however, had no such action to take. When Swift clambered up to the crow's nest, he saw Mrs. Newman weeping, the other women staring straight ahead. Their skin had begun to blister in the heat. Swift passed the wet coat to the women first, and showed them how to daub their arms with it. Mrs. Newman moved slowly, as if in a dream. "Take your time," Swift said, as kindly as he could.

"How bad is it?" she asked. "Truly."

"We're still afloat," Swift said. "Perhaps a passing ship will spy us. Indeed," he lied, "I thought I heard a gun last night. We are not the only ship in this sea."

"Aye," muttered a sailor below, "but I'd rather we were alone than with that ghost ship alongside."

Mrs. Newman's nostrils flared. She looked for all the world like a small animal trembling inside a Rangoon market cage. "What is he speaking of? What does he mean?"

"It is nothing," Swift said. "Just tar's talk." He could have kicked the man.

"Don't you worry about her," the Gunner said as Swift retook his position on the standing rigging. "She'll outlast us all. Her type always does."

❧

Night descended on them like a cloud. Though the weather was warm, Swift found himself shivering. Now that the wind had died, the groans and cries of terrified people surrounded him. *The* Zong, he thought, but he was not there; this was a different ship.

Swift woke with a start. Something—a feather? A wing?—had brushed his cheek. He thrust the bird away before it could peck out his eyes.

"Forgive me, Mr. Swift," a woman's voice said. Looking up, he saw the faint outline of Mrs. Newman's face peering at him. A strip of fabric—the coat?—dangled in front of her. "I only thought—Is that a sail?"

Hope surged through Swift as he adjusted himself on the ropes, trying to get a better look at the ocean behind him. Something stirred in the haze of darkness, something pale and large.

"A sail!" came an exultant voice from the forecastle. "A sail to starboard."

The shape turned. For one wonderful moment Swift saw it clearly, a square-rigger full to the wind.

"Does anyone have a pistol? A gunshot's what we need."

Another sailor hallooed into the wind.

Decurrs started forward in his ropes. "Do not hail that ship!"

"What?" Now Swift was fully awake. He glanced back at the vessel. This time he saw what Decurrs saw: the way the clouds slitted their gaze through the ship's sails, the way her edges blurred with light.

"Do not hail that ship!" Decurrs shouted. From the foresail he heard a shout in Malay; angry voices rose from below. Others were realizing the danger.

And yet the hallooing man would not stop. Perhaps he was a landsman; perhaps he was desperate enough to not care about the consequences.

"Ahoy!" the man yelled. Bare-chested, he leaned out from the mizzen, his shirt fluttering in his hand as an improvised flag. "We are here!"

The man's body flew away from the rigging. His arms and legs bewildered themselves in the air as he fell into darkness. The sailor who'd pushed him leaned back in, to the congratulations of his fellows.

"Too late," Decurrs whispered.

Swift raised his gaze. The ghost ship was turning their way, her cobweb sails filling with impossible wind. Her whiteness was a loathsome thing: the white of a bone pushed through the skin; the white of a shark's tooth as it eats a man alive.

"What *is* that?" Mrs. Newman said in wonder. Her words called Swift back to himself.

"Look away, madam," he said. "Do not gaze upon that ship. Your soul depends on it." He turned his face to the shrouds. The moaning, heaving noise of the wreck faded into a new kind of silence, in which Swift could hear only the breathing of the wind and the waves.

Light moved over the rigging. He squeezed his eyes shut.

In the distance someone wailed. The rigging trembled, then stilled.

After a long quiet the Malay maid spoke, her voice traveling far in the stillness. "Ship gone," she said, and added, "It took."

◄○►

In the afternoon, a group of men from the lower rigging tried to swim over to the foremast, seeking a less-crowded position. The waves crashed over them. Four of them struggled through the spray to the mast and clambered up to the foretop. One of them looked like his messmate, Holdfast. A shout drew Swift's attention to one of the less lucky ones, a man whose head now bobbed far outside the ship, drifting further and further away. Soon Swift lost sight of him altogether.

◄○►

The tars had no shoes to eat. They'd worked the *Minerva* barefoot, in the Lascar style. Some tried gnawing the leather on the rigging but soon laid off, declaring it too bitter to be endured. Instead they made do with scraps of canvas and pieces of lead, which they passed up and down the line.

"You should not eat that," Mrs. Newman croaked as Swift took up a piece of lead the size of a coin. "It's poisonous."

Swift put the lead into his mouth. It tasted like nothing; like the air itself. He sucked on it, enjoying the temporary sensation of moisture on his tongue.

"The haunt," someone said wearily. "It's here."

The sun was still in the sky, and yet there the ghost ship was, a miasma against the waves. It approached silently, the way Swift had seen sharks approach a woman struggling in the water. He turned his head away.

But this time he saw.

White tendrils slashed out from the haunt, ropes that were not ropes. Some twisted around limp bodies—dead passengers, Swift thought, or the tars who'd drowned earlier—but one arced past him, right past him, and snatched a man from the mizzentop. Swift's last glimpse of Captain Maxwell was of the man staring straight in front of him, too terrified to scream.

Below them someone did scream, loud and long. The ropes under Swift's hands pulled taut. For a dreadful moment he thought the entire rigging might go, ripped free by this man fighting for his life, but then ropes sagged back in place. Behind him, the man's scream faded into a strange and awful distance.

"That is no ship," Mrs. Newman said in a small voice.

Swift chewed his piece of lead to powder, and swallowed it down.

-◦-

"Did you smell it?" Decurrs asked.

Swift was caught off guard. "The haunt?" The old salts said that ghosts had a smell, a stench by which a lore-steeped sailor would know them. "I did not catch it."

"I did," Decurrs said. "It smelled like sick and pus swept together on a hot deck. It smelled like a hold full of shit and fear. I know that smell. So do you."

Swift felt ill. "I smelled nothing," he said.

"I think I saw her netting, when she came about," Decurrs said.

Swift pressed his forehead against the ratline. He could feel the rough fibers of the rope cutting into his skin.

"You think she's a slaver?" The words surprised him; Swift had not thought to speak, not out loud.

"Aren't most ghost ships slavers? They are in the tales." Decurrs leaned forward to eye the snoring Gunner, then lowered his voice.

"I knew you'd been in the Trade by the Guinea scars on your legs," he said. "Aye, and by the scars on your back. You sailed under a hard man?"

"They're all hard men," Swift said.

"Aye, but some are harder than the Devil himself." Decurrs leaned into his shroud, his face in shadow. "Were you articled? I was. Woke up on the tavern floor with a crimp holding a paper in front of me. He said I'd signed, so what could I do?"

There was a sour taste at the back of Swift's throat. "I was in debtors' prison," he said. "I took the Guinea door."

"A hard choice," Decurrs said.

"Not for me," Swift said. "Not then." He remembered how Bessie's hands had twisted as the captain described the offer—Swift's debt paid, if only he'd agree to sail aboard a slaver. And he remembered watching Emily clutching the bent twig she called a doll, thinking how tired he was of watching his child play in a prison cell.

Swift was no fool. He'd expected to die on that voyage, as most slave-ship sailors did—from disease or from the captain's beatings. But with his debt paid, his family would be free. He had not known then, how his debt would accumulate onboard; that it would be not one voyage, but two, then three, that he would owe. Bessie and Emily were long dead now, but Swift's debt was still alive, out there somewhere, looking for him.

"*Beware, beware, the Bight of Benin*," Decurrs said. "*There's one comes out for forty goes in.* Well, we're the ones who came out. Now here we are. And here's the haunt-ship come to collect."

The Gunner laughed. The sound jolted them both; they had not realized the man was awake. "You think the haunt comes for you? How fine you are, in all your sins. Me, I have drawn lots to eat men. I have cracked a boy's leg open and sucked the marrow from it. I have heard this talk before, of curses and Providence, aye, and eaten the flesh of those who talked so."

Decurrs shifted away from the man. He climbed downwards, not caring that he had to contort himself around the other bodies on the rigging. Swift followed, but he could still hear the Gunner talking after them.

"Here's your truth," the Gunner called. "The haunt comes like the wind comes. You fools think it comes for your sins because you want to believe there's justice in the world. There isn't any."

"He is mad," Decurrs said when they reached the lower rigging. "We will all go mad here."

They hung on the ropes and watched the deck below. The sea was calmer now. A few sailors had left the rigging and were trying the quarterdeck, staggering about on the wet boards.

*We should get the passengers below, to stretch their legs while they can*, Swift thought. *We should build a raft.*

"Glosse was right," Decurrs said after a time. "We must have a reckoning."

⟡

The sailors had come, finally, to speaking of the Trade.

"The *Nancy*'s captain stood the other Negroes on deck so they could watch. He had lines tied under the arms of the ringleaders. He ordered them lowered over the side," said Cobb.

"Go on," said Glosse.

The remnants of the starboard watch had gathered on the abandoned crow's nest for their consultation. Far below, passengers and sailors tested out the limits of the quarterdeck. As third mate, Glosse stood as judge on the *Minerva*. As far as they knew, he was the only officer left on the wreck, save the Gunner, whose strange calm they all suspected.

Cobb looked away, as though scanning the horizon. Swift knew his gaze had gone somewhere else.

"When the water turned red, he gave the order to hoist them up. The sharks had taken No. 3's legs off at the knees. I thought she was already dead. But when we lowered her again, she started screaming. So I suppose she had only fainted."

"How long did it take?" Glosse was precise. It was important to focus on the facts, in such matters.

"I think an hour before all three were dead. The captain cut the ropes on the last one; it took too long."

Glosse nodded, satisfied.

"Did you not protest the order?" the boy exclaimed. How he had maintained his capacity for horror, Swift did not know.

Cobb shrugged, his sunken eyes flat and hard, like sea-washed stones.

"Who else?" said Glosse, ignoring the boy's question. "Not the *usual things*. We all know them." He paused. Swift wondered if the boy could hear everything that lurked in those words, but he stared bewildered; Pretty Pol's face was closed. This was a current that flowed past them, the sailors who had not worked the Trade.

"And what have you done, Glosse?" Decurrs's voice sliced knife-sharp. Glosse scratched his chin. Like the rest of them, his blistered skin had begun to tear, hanging off in dead strips.

"I've lashed and pickled," Glosse said. "Aye, I've done the *usual things*. But not to the children. Not like some." Decurrs blinked and looked away.

"Did you not pass the whisper?" The boy was still incensed at Cobb's story. "Mr. Clarkson and his 'bolitionists are forever combing the docks, asking tars to testify. You could have passed the whisper at least."

"Aye," Cobb said sourly. "And didn't some Bristol boys club Mr. Clarkson and try to feed him to the sea? When the owners pay good coin to kill Cambridge gentlemen, what do you think the chances are for a common tar like me?"

"That Negro seaman, Equiano, him what wrote the narrative," the boy said stubbornly. "He passes whispers for tars. He passed the whisper on the *Zong*, even—"

Swift's blood drummed in his ears.

"—and they haven't killed him yet."

"I had a shipmate who passed the whisper once," Decurrs said. His voice had gone low and strange. "Listen," he said, fixing them with his gaze. "There was a ship. She sailed under a hard man. A Negro caused trouble in the hold. No. 37. So this Captain Bremmer—" Decurrs's face contorted for a moment, as though he would like to spit, but thought better of it. "This Bremmer, he ordered the man whipped and pickled with salt water. You know," he said to Glosse, "the *usual things*. But this captain, he went further.

"He hung the man up on deck, and tortured him with thirst. He would give the Negro no water, he said—though that number was strong and would have fetched a good price in Antigua—he'd give him no water but urine, and no food but shit to eat. The captain's own shit."

Decurrs gave a strangled laugh. "The captain sent his cabin boy to fetch it, but when he made the boy go—a boy younger than you, mind," he said to their mess-boy, "eleven years old he was, and new to the Trade. He didn't know how it is," he added to Swift.

Swift nodded, hoping Decurrs would fall silent, knowing he wouldn't. There was a kind of madness that came upon slave-ship sailors sometimes, a fever in their blood. Some blamed the disease on the African air, but it was more than that, and Decurrs, blasted raw by sun and wind, had it now. It was this fever and not courage that sent tars into the courts to testify, knowing they'd be killed in the alley afterwards, knowing their wife and mother would be brutalized on the streets. It was this rage, Swift knew, that sent a tar to point his hand in court, which made him into a monstrous revenant that was not a man at all, but some dead-alive thing returned from the sea. A witness.

"He didn't know," Decurrs repeated. "And he refused the order." He wiped his face with his skinny hand, considering. "The captain had him flogged and brined, of course. Sixty lashes, but it wasn't enough. He dragged the boy up the deck and put a plank over him. He ordered us to walk on it," he said dispassionately. "He stamped on his breast so we could hear his bones splinter. The boy's shit came out of him, and the captain forced it down his throat. Then he hung the boy up on the mainmast. He gave him and the Negro the urine to drink, and forbade us all to bring water or food to them.

"For three days they hung there, while we worked. I don't think anyone dared try to give them water. I know I didn't. The captain gave the boy eighteen lashes each day, even as he died. When I sewed him into his sail, his flesh felt like jelly to the touch. His body was purple and swollen huge. You could not tell it was a child anymore. The sharks took them both."

Decurrs glared at them. "I did not pass the whisper, but my shipmate did. Fourteen years old, he was. They found his body floating by the docks. I said nothing. I said nothing for all my days sailing the Triangle. I said nothing after. Only the cabin boy spoke up. And my shipmate. Children. Only them." Decurrs rubbed his chin again. "I think you know what must be done," he said to Glosse.

Glosse shifted uncomfortably. Decurrs's story seemed to have taken the wind out of his sails. "Is there anyone else?"

*There was a ship*, Swift thought. He could feel the words in his mouth. *She was called the* Zong.

"There's no one else," Decurrs said, cutting off anything Swift might say. He stood up abruptly, wobbling on his weakened legs. Swift reached out to steady him.

"No," Decurrs said, and patted Swift's hand. Swift released his grip.

"Shipmates," Decurrs said sternly. "I leave you in a sorry state. But if I've accursed you I do remove it now. If any of you live, carry word to my sister. Do not tell her about the ship."

Then, before anyone could intervene, Decurrs tipped himself backwards. Sky bloomed through the space where he had been. Swift leaned forward, searching the ocean with his eyes, but Decurrs had already vanished under the waves. He did not come up again.

After a while, Glosse shifted his weight. He did not look at them.

"We must get off this wreck," he said. "We must get off today."

◄◦►

The sea was hot and smooth, like a silver plate left in the sun.

"This is our chance," Glosse said. He'd been signaling the men on the foremast with a handkerchief. They, in turn, had employed themselves in making a raft from the fore yard and sprit sail yard, lashed together with ropes and spars rescued from the flotsam.

In the afternoon they launched her, paddling with pieces of plank they had whittled with their belt knives. The survivors from the mizzen mast waited to greet them.

"Avast," said a sailor on the raft, baring the blade on his belt knife. "The raft cannot support you all."

"Only the strongest can come," said another. "All hands must paddle if we're to make the shore."

"None of the women," the knife man said in a kindly tone. He gestured with the point of his blade to the Malay maid. She guessed the meaning of his words and stepped back a few paces, dropping to her knees on the few planks that remained of the quarterdeck.

Cobb stepped forward. "I've got life in me yet," he said. "I'll sail with you."

"And I," said one of Lascars.

Glosse stepped forward. "You'll need my help to find the land," he said. "I can reckon the stars." They motioned him forward. As Glosse stepped forward, the mess-boy caught at his shirt sleeve. "This is wrong," he said. "You cannot leave the passengers here to die."

Glosse snatched his shirt away. "Where and when they die is up to God, not me." He stepped forward onto the bobbing raft, sinking his weight low to keep his footing.

"What about you, Swift?" Holdfast Muhammad looked up from his corner of the raft. "You've got a good hand with the carpentry. We could use you."

"Aye," Swift said reluctantly. He looked at their raft, a shaky net of spars and canvas, lashed together with rope. "But I'll stay here." He did not know what decision he'd make until the words were out of his mouth, but there they were.

"You know how it'll go if you stay," Holdfast Muhammad said in a low voice. Swift appreciated that he did not speak of dying in front of the passengers.

"I know," Swift said. "I'll stay."

Glosse looked at the boy. "You should come with us," he said.

"No," the boy said, trembling with self-righteousness. Had Swift ever been that young? "I'll stay here."

Glosse shrugged and took the paddle handed to him.

The raft took on three more sailors and two of the merchants. Then they set off, paddling determinedly away from the *Minerva*.

Swift sank to his haunches and watched them go. They were trying, he knew, to be well clear of the *Minerva* before the haunt returned.

"Do you think they'll make it?" the boy asked. His voice had lost its ring of certainty now that the raft grew smaller in the distance, now that the moaning from the rigging was rising around them again.

"I do not know," Swift said. He put his hands to the shrouds and climbed back up the rigging.

Mrs. Newman had resumed her place in the crow's nest. "Those men on the raft," she said through cracked lips. "Have they gone to seek help?"

"They have," Swift said.

The Gunner was slumped in the ropes. Ugly red ulcers dotted his skin, and it was only by his breathing that Swift knew he was alive. Swift took up his old position by the man's side. Staring straight ahead, he could almost believe that Decurrs was still beside him, perhaps a step or two down on the ratlines.

He waited for the haunt to return.

⟶

On the third night they heard screaming over the water. Not a lot of scream-ing—two, maybe three voices. One went on for some time.

"That was the raft," the Gunner said. "I cannot abide a raft anymore. Not after what I've seen."

Swift opened his eyes. The Gunner had died two days ago, and his corpse slowly rotted in the flotsam below. On a slave ship, the sharks would have found his body already, but this was the *Minerva*, and the dead man studied Swift with desiccated eyes.

"You will drink the salt," the dead man said. "It will help for a while, and then it will drive you mad."

Then it was not the Gunner beside him on the ropes, but the governor, large as life. He had his pistol on his hand, same as he'd had on the *Zong*. Swift felt like laughing at the man, just as he had all those years ago. You did not threaten a slave-ship sailor with a quick death. They'd lost all fear of such things. It was the slow death and the slow pain they feared. The thirst, the pickling, the sharks.

"Water," someone croaked above him. It was the Malay maid. She dangled the coat to him. Swift took it from her and wrapped it around his shoulders, for his hands were losing their grip. He descended the ratlines slowly, step by step, stepping carefully around the living and the dead.

The sea was calm. The boy lay stretched out on the quarterdeck. Swift shook him, and he stirred.

"You should climb," Swift said. "The waves will wash you away in the next gale."

"I'm terribly sorry, Mr. Swift," the boy said. "I do not think I have the strength for it."

Swift looked up at the rigging. The numbness in his muscles told him he did not have the strength to pull the boy up. But he grabbed the boy under his arms, and, leaning his weight back, managed to pull him to the rail. The stars overhead made fantastic patchworks of light. They reminded Swift of the Saint Elme's fire that had danced on board, warning the sailors of their deaths. *Such a beautiful thing*, he thought in wonder. *So beautiful.*

He eased out his rope belt and lashed the boy to the quarterdeck rail. Then he lowered the coat into the sea. He dribbled some drops of salt water into the boy's mouth. Lowering his own head to the deck, Swift lapped at the waves like an animal. The wetness in his mouth shocked him with a relief that surged through his body.

Then he saw the haunt.

It lay two points abaft the port beam, an eerie shine on the ocean. Its tendrils were out again, touching the water so delicately it resembled one of those strange underwater flowers that bloom and curl in foreign tide pools. It was feeding off the men on the raft, he supposed. Or was that something the Gunner had told him?

Swift soaked the coat in salt water and placed it on his back. The precious water cut icy pathways across his shoulders as he climbed, finding every groove in his shrinking body and pinching him with cold. Still he climbed, and at the crow's nest he handed the three women who'd taken refuge there the sodden coat. They sucked at it eagerly.

"Will we die soon, do you think?" Mrs. Newman's eyes had sunken so far it was almost a peeling skull Swift looked into, and not a face.

"Don't worry," he told them. "It will all be over soon."

But it wasn't.

⟶

The living and the dead lay side by side on the ropes. The thick, sweet smell of death lay over everything.

Swift climbed up and down the rigging, wetting the coat and passing it to those too weak to move. The boy was still alive. He could tell by the way his limbs quivered when the waves washed over them, though Swift could no longer detect the sound of breath when he dribbled water into the corner of the boy's mouth.

In the evening, when the air began to cool, Swift went in search of survivors. He grabbed the bodies he passed on the shrouds. He patted their bloated arms, their naked, festering legs. No one moved. They were as still as if painted, upon a painted ship, upon a painted ocean.

Mrs. Newman's swollen body sat upright, looking expectantly ahead. From time to time Swift followed her gaze, trying to make out what she saw.

⟶

"Well," the governor said. "What will it be, men? To die of thirst's a cruel death." He gestured again with that foolish pistol of his. The *Zong's* crew stared back at him. They'd been working on less than a quart of water since entering the Torrid Zone. The rainwater casks that loomed so lovely behind the governor's pistol were never for the likes of them, and they knew it.

"A vote," the first mate said. "A vote on this." The first mate despised them all, Swift could tell.

"What's the captain say?"

"Captain Collingwood's sick abed," the governor said. "And Kelsall's been taken out of the chain of command. The situation is clear. The cargo must be jettisoned. Not all—only the sick and the dying. Collingwood has given me his list."

"For your insurance monies, you want the cargo jettisoned. That's murder, sir," said the first mate. "I'll have no part in it."

"A vote," the boatswain said. "We must have a vote."

Silence on the *Zong*. A parched boat on a parched ocean.

"Who votes yea?" the governor asked. He raised his own hand and looked meaningfully around. A few of the officers hesitantly raised their arms in the air.

"If you vote yea," the governor said, "I'll see to it that every tar here gets a cup of water in his ration."

Swift raised his hand.

❧

Listen: there was a ship. She was called the *Zong*. She was low on water, or so they said. Part of her cargo needed to be jettisoned, or so they said. Her cargo was a collection of humans in chains.

They pushed the women and children out one by one, through the cabin portholes. The first ones went quietly enough, but the others struggled. The slaves could hear the screaming as it drifted through the hold. They understood they were going to die. You have no idea how much even a sick child can fight you when she knows you are dragging her to her death.

The governor kept pointing. *This one*, he said. *That one*. They took the healthy along with the sick. The governor couldn't read, Kelsall said, so what was the point of a list?

Some of the tars joined in. *This one*. A woman scratched Swift's arm as he reached for her chain-mate, so he grabbed her by the hair. *This one*.

It is no great thing to drown a slave or two, when they are sick, when they have caused trouble. It is a usual thing.

They jettisoned fifty-four the first day. The governor said the number should be noted down, for the insurance claim. *54.*

The next day they marched the men up to the quarterdeck, this time with the chains and shackles still on. They'd fight less that way, the governor said. And the chains would drag them down quicker. *42.*

They had to stop for a time, to see to the sails. One of the Negroes had some English; he said all in the hold were begging to live, promising to survive on no meat and no water until port. *38.* Ten women committed suicide, leaping from the deck to join those in the waves below. *48.* One man managed to climb back aboard. They kicked him from the netting, into the screaming ocean. *144* in all. Or maybe more? Despite the governor's efforts, they'd lost count halfway through.

A usual thing. The descent into the stinking hold, the lash with the cat, the feel of a man's arm resisting as you haul him forward, the shouts, the crying, the pleas. Usual things. Save that first day, when Swift rushed above, because the stench of the hold was getting to him, that was all, and he rested his burning arms on the gunwale, and saw. A pregnant woman, giving birth in the waves.

◄◦►

"I did not pass the whisper," Swift told the boy. "Someone else did. I don't know who. Before the second trial, one of the Gregson men found me on a dock, told me, 'we know you're a fine man, we know you'll remember what's good for you.' But they never called me to testify. Not one of the seventeen crew were called. I never did get to find out what kind of man I was." He raised his hand to scratch one of the scabs beneath his eyes, and noticed, idly, that his fingernail had fallen off. He did not remember losing it.

The boy's corpse was swollen. Its swollen limbs still floated every time a wave washed in. In and out.

"There was a ship," Swift said to himself, trying out the words.

The sun stared down.

◄◦►

Swift waited patiently as the haunt approached. On inspection, he agreed with Mrs. Newman that it might not be a ship at all. The haunt had the general look of a ship—the hull, the masts, the sails—but its cobweb gauziness confused his gaze. He could not figure how such a thing could sail. He supposed he'd soon learn.

The haunt was selective in the corpses it chose. It paused over one body, then took the one beside it, lifting it into the air in a slow arc. One of the corpses it pulled from the rigging fell to pieces, a torn limb splashing into the darkness. The haunt continued its delicate search, serene.

When one of its glowing tendrils passed near him Swift stiffened—some part of him still wanted to live—but then he forced himself to relax. He no longer had the strength to fight it, if he ever had.

The tendril brushed over his shoulder, a prickle of heat and light. It had a dry, horrid smell, like burning bone. The tendril drifted over to the boy, wrapped itself around his torso, lifted him up. Swift's knots held—he was proud of that—but another tendril arced out of the sky, ripping the rope away. The boy was carried aloft.

The haunt's light faded, its too-white glare dimming to the muted color of the moon. Its graceful tendrils curled back to the ship like the closing petals of a flower. Slowly, relentlessly, it turned away from the *Minerva*.

"No," Swift said. This last outrage was too much. "You don't get to leave me here. I'm the last one living, aren't I? The Jonah?" He expected the ship would turn back at the sound of his voice, but the haunt sailed on. It retreated with surprising speed into the darkness.

Cold flooded Swift's body. They could not leave him here.

"Come back!" The words were hard to force through his parched mouth. He threw himself on his belly, scrabbled forward to the water's edge, palmed in water to wet his tongue.

"Come back!" His voice was louder now. They'd surely hear him.

Darkness wrapped itself around him. He could not see the haunt at all.

◄o►

Swift lay alone on the rotting deck, alone in the silent sea. He sometimes thought he heard the dead conversing above him, but he could not make out their words.

He expected them to return, the dead. Surely they'd come back. Decurrs and Glosse, the boy, the women, Bessie, Emily, his little girl as he'd seen her last with the blood cough dribbling down her dress. Or the slaves. No. 23, at least. Or the woman from the waves. Surely they had something to say to him. Some last accusation to make.

But they did not come.

The sun pressed down. The clouds hid the moon.

There passed a weary time.

Something edged into the corner of his vision. A triangle of white. A sail?

Swift lifted his head. A wave of relief filled him. It was the haunt, come to put things right.

But the sail was too solid. He could not see through it. It was, he realized wearily, a living ship.

He watched it pass. There was no reason now to summon it. No one to save.

But the silence pressed down on him, heavy and terrible. An agony of silence.

Swift tried to speak, but his tongue had withered with thirst. No noise came out. It was too far now, to reach the waves that washed the quarterdeck. So he raised his arm to his lips. Bit down. The warm taste of blood freed his tongue. He croaked. Shouted. Wordlessly. A cry from the deep.

The angle of the ship's sails changed. They'd heard something.

Swift let his head sink down again. He floated on the deck, suspended between life and death, between one possibility and the other.

But he did not think he could die, not yet, not yet. There was a name on his cracked lips. A word like the blood in his mouth. A thing he had to tell.

◄◦►

Author's Note:

"Years ago, while working at the National Maritime Museum in Greenwich, I came across a sailor's account of his visit aboard a slave ship. I was struck by the effort he'd made to mobilize his fellow sailors against the slave trade. A few months later I read Marcus Rediker's magisterial *The Slave Ship*, which helped put this document into context. In writing "Haunt," I relied heavily on Rediker's searing description of the daily operations of slave ships. Readers interested in learning more about sailors' relationship to the abolition movement should consult this book.

The murders I describe in "Haunt" are all based on real incidents. Of these, the most notorious is the *Zong* massacre. As James Walvin points out, the mass murder that took place in 1781 became notorious not because the drowning of sick slaves was unusual (it wasn't), but because British abolitionists made it their first cause célèbre. As with so many slave trade atrocities, we will never know the names of the Africans murdered on the *Zong*. Given the owners' destruction of the ship's logs, we will also never know the names of the ordinary sailors who executed the murders or (according to the first mate's testimony) of the few who protested the massacre. Nor is it likely we will learn the name of the person who first passed the *Zong*'s story on to Olaudah Equiano, the black 'able seaman' and anti-slavery activist responsible for turning the massacre into a historical milestone. The victims of the *Zong* never received justice in a court of law. However, thanks to the efforts of Equiano and other abolitionists, their deaths helped galvanize the popular movement that, decades later, would abolish the transatlantic slave trade. This is not the same as justice. But it has its own meaning."

# ACKNOWLEDGMENT OF COPYRIGHT

# ABOUT THE AUTHORS

**Simon Bestwick** is the author of four story collections, a chapbook, *Angels of the Silences*, and five novels, most recently *Devil's Highway* and *The Feast of All Souls*. His work has been published In *Black Static* and *Great Jones Street*, podcast on *Pseudopod* and *Tales to Terrify*, and reprinted in *Best Horror of the Year*.

A new collection and a new novel, *Wolf's Hill*, are both in the works, and his novelette *Breakwater* is forthcoming from Tor.com. Until recently, his hobbies included avoiding gainful employment, but this ended in failure and he now has a job again. Any and all assistance in escaping this dreadful fate would be most welcome. He lives on the Wirral with his long-suffering wife, the author Cate Gardner, and uses far too many semicolons.

**Siobhan Carroll** is an Associate Professor of English at the University of Delaware, where she specializes in nineteenth-century literature and the history of exploration. She trained as a tall ship sailor on board the *Kalmar Nyckel* and qualified as a rigging-climber in 2012. All errors in nautical jargon and judgment are to be laid at her door rather than that of the *Kalmar Nyckel* crew. For more fiction by Siobhan Carroll, visit voncarr-siobhan-carroll. blogspot.com.

**Ray Cluley**'s work has appeared in various magazines and anthologies. It has been reprinted in Ellen Datlow's *Best Horror of the Year* series, Steve Berman's *Wilde Stories 2013: The Year's Best Gay Speculative Fiction*, and in Benoît Domis's *Ténèbres* series. He has won the British Fantasy Award for

Best Short Story and was nominated for Best Novella and Best Collection. His short fiction has been collected in the mini-collection *Within the Wind, Beneath the Snow* and *Probably Monsters*.

**Bradley Denton** was born in Kansas in 1958, and his first professional story appeared in *The Magazine of Fantasy & Science Fiction* in 1984. Since then, he's published a few dozen more stories and five novels, including *Buddy Holly Is Alive and Well on Ganymede, Blackburn, Lunatics*, and *Laughin' Boy*. His work has been nominated for the Hugo, Nebula, Bram Stoker, International Horror Guild, and Edgar Allan Poe awards—and it has won the John W. Campbell Memorial Award, the Theodore Sturgeon Memorial Award, and the World Fantasy Award. Brad currently lives on the outskirts of Austin, Texas, with his wife, Barbara, and their dogs, Sugar and Tater. His most recent story collection is *Sergeant Chip and Other Novellas*.

**Terry Dowling** is one of Australia's most respected and internationally acclaimed writers of science fiction, dark fantasy, and horror. Dowling's horror is collected in *Basic Black: Tales of Appropriate Fear* (International Horror Guild Award), Aurealis Award-winning *An Intimate Knowledge of the Night*, and the World Fantasy Award-nominated *Blackwater Days*. His most recent books are *Amberjack: Tales of Fear & Wonder* and his debut novel, *Clowns at Midnight*.

His newest collection, *The Night Shop: Tales for the Lonely Hours*, was recently published by Cemetery Dance Publications. His homepage is at terrydowling.com.

**Christopher Golden** is the *New York Times* bestselling author of *Snowblind, Ararat, Tin Men*, and many other novels. With Mike Mignola, he co-created the cult favorite comic book series *Baltimore* and *Joe Golem: Occult Detective*. Many of his short stories are collected in *Tell My Sorrows to the Stones*. As editor, his anthologies include *Seize the Night, The New Dead*, and *Dark Cities*, among others. Golden has also written screenplays, radio plays, non-fiction, graphic novels, video games, and (with Amber Benson) the online animated series *Ghosts of Albion*. He is one-third of the pop culture podcast Three Guys with Beards.

**Brian Hodge** is one of those people who always have to be making something. So far, he's made twelve novels, over 125 shorter works, and five full-length collections.

Recent and upcoming works include *I'll Bring You the Birds From Out of the Sky*, a novella of cosmic horror with folk art illustrations; his next novel, *The Immaculate Void*, coming in early 2018; and a new collection, coming later in the year. Two recent Lovecraftian novelettes have been optioned for feature film and a TV series.

He lives in Colorado, where he also likes to make music and photographs; loves everything about organic gardening except the thieving squirrels; and trains in Krav Maga and kickboxing, which are of no use at all against the squirrels.

Connect through his website (brianhodge.net), Twitter (@BHodgeAuthor), or Facebook (facebook.com/brianhodgewriter).

**Stephen Graham Jones** is the author of sixteen novels and six story collections. Most recent are *Mapping the Interior*, from Tor.com, and the comic book *My Hero*, from Hex Publisher. Stephen lives and teaches in Boulder, Colorado.

**John Langan** is the author of two novels, *The Fisherman* and *House of Windows*, and two collections, *The Wide, Carnivorous Sky and Other Monstrous Geographies* and *Mr. Gaunt and Other Uneasy Encounters*.

With Paul Tremblay, he co-edited *Creatures: Thirty Years of Monsters*. One of the founders of the Shirley Jackson Awards, he serves on its Advisory Board. Currently, he reviews horror and dark fantasy for *Locus* magazine. Forthcoming is a new collection, *Sefira and Other Betrayals*. He lives in New York's Hudson Valley with his wife and younger son.

**Seanan McGuire** lives, works, and watches way too many horror movies in the Pacific Northwest, where she shares her home with her two enormous blue cats, a ridiculous number of books, and a large collection of creepy dolls.

McGuire does not sleep much, publishing an average of four books a year under both her own name and the pen name Mira Grant. Her first book, *Rosemary and Rue*, was released in September 2009, and she hasn't stopped running since. When not writing, she enjoys Disney Parks, horror movies, and looking winsomely at Marvel editorial as she tries to convince them to let her write for the X-Men. Keep up with McGuire at seananmcguire.com, on Twitter as @seananmcguire, or by walking into a cornfield at night and calling the secret, hidden name of the Great Pumpkin to the moon. When you turn, she will be there. She will always have been there.

**Michael Marshall Smith** is a novelist and screenwriter. He has published over eighty short stories and four novels: *Only Forward, Spares, One of Us,* and *The Servants*—winning the Philip K. Dick, International Horror Guild, and August Derleth awards, along with the Prix Bob Morane in France. He has won the British Fantasy Award for Best Short Fiction four times, more than any other author. A new novel—*Hannah Green and her Unfeasibly Mundane Existence*—was published in July 2017.

Writing as Michael Marshall he has also published seven internationally bestselling thrillers, including *The Straw Men* series (currently in TV development), *The Intruders*—a BBCAmerica series in 2014 starring John Simm and Mira Sorvino—and *Killer Move*. His most recent novel is *We Are Here*.

He lives in Santa Cruz, California, with his wife, son, and two cats.

**Steve Rasnic Tem**'s last novel, *Blood Kin*, won the Bram Stoker Award. His new novel, *UBO*, is a dark science fictional tale about violence and its origins, featuring such historical viewpoint characters as Jack the Ripper, Stalin, and Heinrich Himmler. He is also a past winner of the World Fantasy and British Fantasy Awards. Recently, a collection of the best of his uncollected horror—*Out of the Dark: A Storybook of Horrors*—was published by Centipede Press. A handbook on writing, *Yours To Tell: Dialogues on the Art & Practice of Writing*, written with his late wife, Melanie, is also out from Apex Books. In the Fall of 2018 Hex Publishers will bring out his middle-grade Halloween novel, *The Mask Shop of Doctor Blaack*.

Visit the Tem home on the web at: m-s-tem.com.

**Lee Thomas** is the two-time Lambda Literary Award- and Bram Stoker Award-winning author of *Stained, The Dust of Wonderland, The German, Torn, Like Light for Flies*, and *Down on Your Knees*, among others. His work has been translated into multiple languages and has been optioned for film. Lee lives in Austin, Texas, with his husband, John.

**A. C. Wise**'s fiction has appeared in publications such as *Clarkesworld, Tor. com, The Best Horror of the Year*, and *The Year's Best Dark Fantasy and Horror*, among other places. She has two collections published by Lethe Press, *The Ultra Fabulous Glitter Squadron Saves the World Again*, and *The Kissing Booth Girl and Other Stories*, which was a Lambda Literary Award Finalist. In addition to her fiction, she contributes a monthly review column to *Apex Magazine*. Visit her online at acwise.net.

**Alyssa Wong** lives in Chapel Hill, North Carolina, and really, really likes crows. Her story "Hungry Daughters of Starving Mothers" won the 2015 Nebula Award for Best Short Story and the 2016 World Fantasy Award for Short Fiction, and she was a finalist for the 2016 John W. Campbell Award for Best New Writer. Her fiction has been shortlisted for the Hugo Award, the Bram Stoker Award, the Locus Award, and the Shirley Jackson Award.

Her work has been published in *The Magazine of Fantasy & Science Fiction*, *Strange Horizons, Nightmare Magazine, Black Static*, and *Tor.com*, among others. Alyssa can be found on Twitter as @crashwong.

# ABOUT THE EDITOR

Ellen Datlow has been editing science fiction, fantasy, and horror short fiction for almost forty years. She currently acquires short fiction for Tor.com. In addition, she has edited about ninety science fiction, fantasy, and horror anthologies, including the series *The Best Horror of the Year*, *Fearful Symmetries*, *The Doll Collection*, *The Monstrous*, *Children of Lovecraft*, *Black Feathers*, and *Mad Hatters and March Hares*.

Forthcoming is *The Saga Anthology of Ghost Stories*.

She's won multiple World Fantasy Awards, Locus Awards, Hugo Awards, Stoker Awards, International Horror Guild Awards, Shirley Jackson Awards, and the 2012 Il Posto Nero Black Spot Award for Excellence as Best Foreign Editor. Datlow was named recipient of the 2007 Karl Edward Wagner Award, given at the British Fantasy Convention for "outstanding contribution to the genre," was honored with the Life Achievement Award given by the Horror Writers Association, in acknowledgment of superior achievement over an entire career, and the Life Achievement Award by the World Fantasy Convention.

She lives in New York and co-hosts the monthly Fantastic Fiction Reading Series at KGB Bar. More information can be found at datlow.com, on Facebook, and on Twitter as @EllenDatlow.